Praise for *Lies of the Heart*

"*Lies of the Heart* is a rare find: a beautifully rendered portrait of a marriage ended by violence, a deeply moving account of one woman's journey through grief, and an utterly gripping page-turner. Michelle Boyajian has penned a remarkable debut—deep, gorgeously written, and true."
—Lisa Unger, *New York Times* bestselling author of *Die for You*

"Michelle Boyajian deftly intertwines a suspenseful murder trial and a soulful examination of modern marriage, breaking open the heart of love's exhilaration and angst. Her characters' stories are drawn with a nuanced realism that pulls us fully into their lives, their souls, and the tides of secret strife that make both the family we come from and the family we create such a complicated dance."
—Carol Cassella, author of *Oxygen*

"Oh so rarely do we get a suspenseful thriller, a psychological study, and a warmhearted narrative of distinctive literary quality all in the same book. You're not going to want to get up until, wide-eyed, you read the last page."
—Clyde Edgerton, author of *The Bible Salesman* and *The Floatplane Notebooks*

"Seductive and riveting debut." —*The Denver Post*

"Nuanced murder mystery . . . compelling and suspenseful."
—*Wilmington StarNews*

"*Lies of the Heart* is a remarkable debut. We can only hope to hear much more from Michelle Boyajian." —*BookPage*

"With its riveting courtroom scenes and nuanced presentation of the characters' psyches, this genre-bending first novel combines insightful domestic fiction with the page-turning suspense of a legal thriller." —*Booklist*

PENGUIN BOOKS

LIES OF THE HEART

Michelle Boyajian is a graduate of New York University, Miami University, and the University of North Carolina Wilmington, where she received her MFA and the Austin Robert Hartsook Fellowship in Creative Writing. Her most recent short stories appeared in *Third Coast* and *Timber Creek Review* and were nominated for a Pushcart Prize.

To access Penguin Readers Guides online, visit our Web sites at www.penguin.com or www.vpbookclub.com.

Michelle Boyajian

Penguin Books

LIES OF
THE HEART

For Mom and Dad

PENGUIN BOOKS
Published by the Penguin Group
Penguin Group (USA) Inc., 375 Hudson Street, New York, New York 10014, U. S. A
Penguin Group (Canada), 90 Eglinton Avenue East, Suite 700, Toronto, Ontario Canada M4P 2Y3
(a division of Pearson Penguin Canada Inc.)
Penguin Books Ltd., 80 Strand, London WC2R 0RL, England
Penguin Ireland, 25 St. Stephen's Green, Dublin 2, Ireland
(a division of Penguin Books Ltd)
Penguin Group Australia Ltd, 250 Camberwell Road, Camberwell, Victoria 3124, Australia
(a division of Pearson Australia Group Pty. Ltd)
Penguin Books India Pvt Ltd, 11 Community Centre, Panchsheel Park,
New Delhi - 110 017, India
Penguin Group (NZ), 67 Apollo Drive, Rosedale, North Shore 0632, New Zealand
(a division of Pearson New Zealand Ltd)
Penguin Books (South Africa) (Pty) Ltd, 24 Sturdee Avenue,
Rosebank, Johannesburg 2196, South Africa

Penguin Books Ltd, Registered Offices: 80 Strand, London WC2R 0RL, England

First published in the United States of America by Viking Penguin,
a member of Penguin Group (USA) Inc. 2010
Published in Penguin Books 2011

1   3   5   7   9   10   8   6   4   2

PUBLISHER'S NOTE: This is a work of fiction. Names, characters, places, and incidents either are the
product of the author's imagination or are used fictitiously, and any resemblance to actual persons,
living or dead, business establishments, events, or locales is entirely coincidental.

THE LIBRARY OF CONGRESS HAS CATALOGED THE HARDCOVER EDITION AS FOLLOWS:
Boyajian, Michelle.
Lies of the heart : a novel / Michelle Boyajian.
p. cm.
ISBN 978-0-670-02131-4 (hc.)
ISBN 978-0-14-311854-1 (pbk.)
1. Trials (Murder)—Fiction. 2. Widows—Fiction. 3. Grief—Fiction. 4 Married people—Fiction.
5. Marriage—Fiction. 6. Speech therapist and patient—Fiction. 7. Psychological fiction. I. Title.
PS3602.O924L54   2010
813'.6—dc22   2009044783

Printed in the United States of America

Prologue

It's one of those surreal moments in life, sitting there in the courtroom and staring into the eyes of her husband's killer. Katie wasn't at the recreation center the day Jerry LaPlante shot Nick, but looking into Jerry's light blue eyes she actually sees Nick's face jerk with confusion and pain as the bullet tears into his brain by way of the soft skin between his right eye and the bridge of his nose. She sinks into the blueness of Jerry's eyes and follows the bullet's path as it rips through Nick's frontal lobe, instantly severing memories of their boating trips to Cape Cod, their wedding day, and late nights curled up together in bed, whispering. She sees the bullet career off the back of his skull, exploding and fragmenting, the shards of graphite destroying his sense of taste and smell, his ability to blink and smile, his capacity to match images and feelings with words. She watches the bulk of the tiny bullet puncture Nick's hypothalamus—what the regional pathologist has called the center of all human emotion—where it finally comes to rest. In her mind she imagines that this fragment explodes every happy feeling Nick has ever experienced, that in the seconds before death claims him his shattered brain has one last gray-matter extravaganza, and that she is in there somewhere, smiling and touching his arm with love. One last cerebral orgasm before he leaves her world and she ends up here, in court, staring into the eyes of her husband's killer.

ONE

1

It would only take about twenty seconds—twenty-five, tops. But Katie times it in her head again anyway, because Richard is really on a roll now, he's pacing back and forth in front of the jurors and unbuttoning the jacket of his dark suit. Katie knows exactly what this means, knows that now he's presented her husband to the jurors—Nick's faithful service to the speech-pathology community, his selfless behavior with his clients, his devotion to the mentally handicapped population—it's time to tell them about that day, it's time for Richard to take Nick away again. So she closes her eyes and carefully counts it out again:

Five seconds to rise and make her way to the end of the front row. She will be polite, of course, she will say *Excuse me, excuse me* the whole way, but she has to be quick so she won't hesitate if she accidentally tramples a foot or two. Another five to push open the little gate, to step through, and then walk around to the right and face the defense table. At least a full ten seconds to throw herself directly across the table and onto Jerry, to dig her right index finger into one of his eye sockets, hooked and pulling, or to slam the heel of her palm up on the underside of his nose, hard. Yes, about twenty seconds. But possibly another ten if the bailiffs are quick, if they beat her to where Jerry is sitting there, hunched over a yellow writing tablet with a pen.

A pen.

Add a few more seconds to wrestle it out of his hand, to raise it high and then plunge it—

"And then that defendant walked into the Warwick Center gymnasium on May fifth of this year, at approximately two-thirty in the afternoon, where Nicholas Burrelli was playing a game of pickup basketball with two of his clients," Richard says in his confident, sonorous voice.

Katie opens her eyes, because she knows what will happen if she keeps them closed, how the words will begin to form and take shape, how she will see it all over again: her husband sidestepping with the ball, his face flushed with happiness, the beads of sweat forming. And then, always too soon, the blind rush of film moving forward—her husband flat on his back, face ghostly, fading. Dark blood pooling underneath his head, the fingers of thick liquid slowly escaping from underneath.

Richard stands in front of the jurors, his arm outstretched and pointing at Jerry. Jerry's lawyer, Donna Treadmont, places her hand lightly on Jerry's back, but Jerry stays bent over the pad.

"And Jerry LaPlante reached into the pocket of his windbreaker"— Richard mimes this, puts his hand into his pocket and then pulls it out with his index finger pointing, thumb up in the air—"and he pulled out a gun. He raised the gun to eye level and walked across the basketball court toward Nick, who had his back to him."

Richard holds his finger-gun in front of him and slowly walks to the defense table. Donna's hand makes wide, swirling motions on Jerry's broad back, but he's still focused on the pad, the pen moving carefully across the page.

"And he didn't stop until he got to within three feet of Nick."

Richard stops, gun trained on Jerry's lowered head, and there is complete silence. But it's too late for Katie, because his words have already taken form—she sees Nick's face, his dark eyes squinted and filled with laughter, and she hears the sound of the bouncing basketball echoing off the walls, the squeaky shuffling of sneakers on the court. And then the inevitable happens, in the precious seconds before the bullet takes Nick to the floor: he is suddenly in the room with her, she feels Nick's hand in hers, his warm breath against her neck. Her entire body full of him, of who he *still is,* until Richard's dramatic sigh intrudes.

She checks on the jurors, turns quickly to follow their intent stares: Richard has become a statue in front of the defense table, body frozen in place, gun still pointing. Katie stares, too, and then a sudden anger zippers through her body, a hot scraping on the inside of her skin—Richard's pose so theatrical, so deliberately staged that she has to turn away. She flicks her eyes over to the jury box, focuses on an elderly male in the middle of the back row—his hand flat over his heart, mouth slightly open. *Better,* she thinks. *We should all have our hands over our hearts.*

"And Nick turned around," Richard finally says, glaring briefly at Jerry's lowered head, dropping his finger-gun and walking back to the jurors, "and he sees the defendant standing there, aiming the gun right at his face. And Nick says, 'Hey, buddy.'"

There is a sharp intake of breath from a juror in the front row, a heavy, middle-aged woman with thick mascara and penciled eyebrows. Richard nods at her: *I know.*

"And do you know what that man said, ladies and gentlemen?" A weary arm rises in Jerry's direction, palm facing upward. Richard's voice is soft with disbelief as he shakes his head. "Do you know what that defendant said right before he pulled the trigger and shot Nicholas Burrelli in the face? He said, 'Time to go, Nick.'"

Richard grips the banister with both hands, lowers his head, offers the courtroom another exaggerated sigh. Again there is silence, and the anger returns—pinballing inside Katie's head now, ricocheting with short, fierce thumps against her skull. *This is real!* she wants to shout as she watches Richard's pretense of composing himself. She wants to stand, walk through the little gate, step up behind Richard. Poke him on the shoulder with one finger. Say quietly, but firmly, *That's enough, Richard. Really.* It would only take about fifteen seconds.

Richard tips his head up at the jurors. "'Time to go, Nick,'" he finally says, softly, almost wistfully.

The laden quiet that follows expands inside Katie's body, clogging her throat like a thick yellow wax.

"Then do you know what he did next?"

Katie can barely hear him now. Even Judge Hwang is straining forward.

"The defendant, Mr. LaPlante, smiled."

Richard stands straight, rubs his face with both hands. There is a fierce buzzing in Katie's ears, in her chest, as she watches the affected, incredulous look form on Richard's face. *It isn't just a story,* she thinks, *It isn't* your *story.* But then she sees the court reporter, stationed between the jurors and the witness stand. How her fingers are poised over the keys, waiting for Richard to continue.

"He *smiled.*"

It's a whisper this time, then Richard raises his right hand and slams it down on the banister. "And BAM!" He rushes to the defense table again, suit jacket flapping, finger-gun pointing. Donna grips Jerry's shoulder now, her knuckles white from squeezing, but Jerry's attention never leaves the page before him.

"*This defendant* pulled the trigger and shot Nicholas Burrelli directly in the face from a distance of three feet. He *smiles* and shoots Nicholas Burrelli right in the face!"

Richard shakes his head in disbelief again, turns and walks back to the jurors.

"You're going to hear a lot of words repeated when the defense's experts take the stand. Words like 'awareness' and 'diminished capacity' and 'moral culpability.' And a lot of people are going to sit in that witness chair and talk about the defendant's childhood, about the difficulties he's had to face in this life. But most of all," Richard says, his voice an octave lower, eyes narrowed, "they're going to tell you that because the defendant is a mentally retarded man, he shouldn't be held responsible for his actions. Because he's mentally retarded, he doesn't know the difference between right and wrong. Because he's mentally retarded, he didn't know what he was doing the day he murdered Nicholas Burrelli, and that he shouldn't be sitting in a court of law today. You're going to hear a lot of things that make you doubt that moment when Mr. LaPlante executed Nick, but will you all promise me one thing?"

Two female jurors in the back row are nodding in sync.

"Will you remember that moment? Will you remember that moment when he walked straight up to Nick, *smiled,* and then shot him in the face? Not for me, but for all the people Nick tried to help, day after day? Not for me, but for Nicky's wife, Katie, who is sitting right there in the front row, a widow at only thirty-two years old—"

She knows that Richard is pointing at her, that his face is filling with practiced sympathy, but Katie has closed her eyes, is counting seconds again now that the words about that day have stopped. But there are two targets for her rage now, and all she can think of is the kind of permanent damage that can be inflicted with fingernails, teeth.

And then, like it has so many times in the past six months, the simmering rage begins its inevitable mutation, it transforms from a fierce red pounding into something else, something heavy and colorless— a melting that spreads inside her like the slow, cold flooding of a basement.

Dead. She's here because Nick is *dead.*

And then all she can do is cover her face with both hands, and let the tears rise.

•

"*Kay-tee.*"

They're trying to handcuff Jerry, but he's waving a piece of yellow paper high into the air; he darts his head past the bailiffs and court officer, past Donna, who attempts to snatch the paper away. Jerry's blue eyes are searching for Katie's.

"Okay, Jerry, okay," Donna says.

"It is for *her,*" Jerry says, hand still high and waving. Before Katie can blink it away, she thinks how proud Nick would be if he were here: even under pressure, Jerry remembers to enunciate carefully.

"I'll give it to her, okay? Jerry?"

Jerry's supporters from the Warwick Center, packed into the rows behind the defense table, watch in mute shock until Donna sends an urgent look over her shoulder; immediately there is movement forward, soft encouraging words, hands reaching out. Katie reacts physically to these sounds and motions, to these people who were once her friends—the impossible weight of betrayal settling inside her stomach and chest until she feels the tears gathering again, just from the simple, familiar sight of Judith Moore, a volunteer from the cafeteria, impatiently swiping at her bangs. Or Veronica Holden, the work program's receptionist and probably her closest friend at the center, lifting her arm to pat Jerry—her wooden bracelets slipping down her arm, making that clunky noise Katie knows so well. *Just last spring,* she thinks, *I borrowed them for a wedding.*

But she indulges only briefly in this heaviness that cements her to her seat, in feeling sorry for herself, because then she locates it again: the sharp, exacting comfort of anger. It's become a constant in her life now, this back-and-forth, the sadness and then the sizzling antagonism. The newness of reaching out to this anger is unsettling at times, so unlike the way she's dealt with conflict before, but also utterly effective: the tears are gone now. She sits back on the bench, crosses her arms.

The bailiffs finally get Jerry cuffed, reddened faces betraying their frustration, and Katie allows herself a longer look. His chest is wider than both bailiffs put together, it looks like he's going to burst right out of the dark blue suit she and Nick bought him for his forty-second birthday last year. His thinning brown hair has been neatly combed and parted to the left side, and there are red bumps on his cheeks and chin from a quick, careless shave. Jerry's eyes, lost in the roundness of his face, are pinned onto hers.

The people and the sounds in the room recede instantly. All she can do is stare back.

"*Kay-tee,*" he whispers, low and urgent, "it is *me.*"

He's been medicated. Katie recognizes the droopiness in the eyelids, the way his fleshy lower lip hangs, the paleness in his plump face. Like that time she gave him Dramamine out on the boat, right before the air show started above Narragansett Bay—the gentle rocking causing havoc deep inside Jerry's belly. She remembers how he scanned the sky with troubled eyes that day, the way he pointed. "God up there," he said, his other hand on his stomach, and both Katie and Nick knew what he meant: every pain he felt was an indictment, a punishment for things he couldn't understand. He took the Dramamine from Katie without question, fell asleep in the cuddy long before the fighter jets roared overhead. But she remembers how hard he fought it, how that sleepy face searched out hers and Nick's and the pale sky with drowsy excitement—the terror of sin and punishment temporarily forgotten once again.

And now those sleepy eyes are penetrating hers, asking a hundred questions, and it happens in a flash: she sees the bullet enter and move through Nick's brain, she watches Nick forget her and everything they shared together, the furious path of the bullet erasing both of them, inch by inch.

"*Jer-ry.*"

Confusion in every blink of his eyes, in every movement of Jerry's head as he turns right and left, guided by both bailiffs to the side exit.

She remembers holding him when that look came during the nights, his sloppy sobbing and sniffling, the way his long arms wrapped around her and hugged her so tight, so tight. *God come tonight, Kay-tee? He come and get me tonight?* She knows all about the concentrated pain that settles inside Jerry's head sometimes, the chaos and panic that comes back to him in the darkness. She knows exactly how small and afraid this enormous man feels when his eyes look just like that.

She pulls her eyes from his, turns away.

•

Later, in the courthouse bathroom, Katie is patting her face with a brown paper towel in front of the mirror when Donna Treadmont walks in.

"Mrs. Burrelli?"

Katie watches Donna's approach in the mirror. She knows that the director of the Warwick Center has handpicked Donna from the Protection and Advocacy office because Donna looks like someone's mother, like she'd look more comfortable with an apron around her thick middle and holding a pan of warm cookies. Donna's purse is probably full of Band-Aids and safety pins and hard, stale peppermints, Katie thinks, and then she sees the yellow piece of paper in Donna's hand.

"I'm sorry to bother you," Donna says. Her lipstick is pale pink, the color of cotton candy.

"I don't want him talking to me," Katie says.

"Of course—"

"I mean it. He shouldn't talk to me. Ever."

"Okay."

"You're his lawyer, and it's up to you to make him understand that."

"Yes."

They watch each other in the mirror for a moment. Donna looks away first, pats the back of her graying permed hair, and presses her pink lips together.

"Anyway, he made this for you," Donna finally says, trying to smile. Her eyes skip to the door and back.

Katie turns from the mirror to face her, automatically takes the extended piece of paper.

"I know this is unusual," Donna says, but Katie's eyes are already scanning the picture in her hand.

She follows the lines of Jerry's boxy, crooked house—the loopy smoke curling out of the chimney, the rectangle door with a big circle in the middle for a doorknob, the two squares for windows above the door. The house lists to one side like it's about to topple over, and there, in the front yard, is a snowman with a long triangle nose, button eyes, a top hat. Standing beside it are three stick figures holding stick hands: a medium-size one on the left, a small one on the right, a big, towering one in the middle. They all have U-shaped smiles that extend out of the circle of their faces.

Katie and Nick used to have dozens of these pictures taped all over their house, pictures of boats and seagulls, and snowmen, and big turkeys made out of the tracings of a big hand—all different except for the stick figures in each, the three people who are always holding hands, always smiling so widely it reaches past their faces. She stares at the picture, blinks hard a few times.

Donna places her hand on Katie's arm. "He's so confused," she says, and Katie nods quickly, keeps her eyes on the picture. "I try to comfort him, but . . . but he keeps asking me if God is going to come and get him."

Katie's left shoulder jerks forward involuntarily—even now it's organic, this sudden, corporeal impulse to race to Jerry's side. But then Katie focuses on the medium stick figure, on the stick fingers that reach out—on the wide, curving smile.

Nick.

And then she feels him again, the weight of his arm slung casually across her stomach in the night, the heat of his thigh as it brushes against hers.

It's like getting punched in the stomach, every time. Every time she thinks about Nick, and hears his name inside her head, and pictures his dark eyes looking into hers. It happens a dozen times a day, a *hundred,* and every single time it's the same—it's just like getting punched.

She looks Donna in the eye. "Why?" she says, just above a whisper.

"You know his history, his fears at night—"

"No," Katie says, shaking the paper at her. *"Why?"*

It's a relief to say it out loud, this one word that runs in a constant loop inside her head—especially to this woman, who might actually *know* the real reason Jerry did it. But the relief drains quickly, because Donna is stepping back, shaking her head.

"You know I can't discuss the particulars of Jerry's case with you."

"Then what do you want?" Katie almost spits at her.

Donna takes another step back. "He just—Jerry just wanted you to have the picture. I promised him."

Katie's eyes move back to the paper.

Nick. Still inside the frame, still smiling, even after Jerry has taken him away.

"Could you tell him something for me?" Katie says quietly.

"Yes, of course."

"Please tell him that I did this," she says. Katie raises the paper to eye level, rips it in half.

Even after Donna has walked out, Katie is still ripping the pieces in half, and in half again, until they are too thick to tear.

•

They're in conference room number six at Katie's request, away from the cameras and microphones and hungry men and women who push from all sides.

"It's a technique, Katie, that's all," Richard tells her, leaning on the table with steepled fingers.

"But you didn't even know my husband."

"Look, it's my job to make the jurors—"

"But why would you call him Nicky if you never even met him?"

She's latched onto this name, because it's all she has—she can't point fingers and accuse, because she understands, if nothing else, that Nick belongs to Richard now, he belongs to the state. It doesn't matter how disconcerting it feels to have a virtual stranger in charge of Nick's life now, or that Nick has become a *job*, a *case*. Her feelings aren't pertinent to the trial, she has no say about posturing and posing, but she can at least remind him of this: Nick was hers first, and he was *real*.

Richard walks over to his open briefcase, starts to straighten the already straightened papers inside. "Sometimes we use names to make the jurors sympathize with the victim," he says. "That's why I referred to Jerry as Mr. LaPlante today. So that they see him as a man."

"Jerry *is* a man."

"Well, of course."

"My husband didn't like to be called Nicky."

"I didn't know."

"He let his mother call him that, but only her."

"Okay," Richard says, nodding, "Good enough." He keeps his eyes on his briefcase as he snaps it shut.

"Nicholas or just plain Nick," Katie says. "That's who he was."

"Right."

She turns on her heel, reaches for the door.

"We're going to get him," Richard says. And when she keeps her back to him, "Look, I know what you're thinking."

Katie turns her body halfway, keeps a vise grip on the doorknob. *Do you?*

"But you have to stop worrying. Remember, this isn't the first murder case with a mentally retarded defendant," he says. "There've been countless cases like this one tried in court. Countless convictions, too. The only concession, really, is that as of 2002 we can't pursue the death penalty."

He gives an artificial, rueful shake of the head, like they're still in the courtroom, like the jurors are still tracking his every move.

"I can't imagine—" Katie begins quickly, then stops herself when she hears the next words inside her head: *that you have* any *idea what I'm thinking right now.*

"I know, but you can't second-guess this, Katie. We've gone over it already—Jerry's low IQ isn't the only determining factor here. There are crucial issues involved in cases like this. Intellectual development regardless of IQ, a defendant's adaptive life skills, the capacity to make choices and operate successfully in his environment. The fact that the defendant clearly knows right from wrong. We have to prove Jerry's culpability, and we can. We *will.* It's been done dozens of times in courts all over this country—in Texas, North Carolina, Virginia. Jerry's case is no different."

A sudden smile spreads over his face as he regards Katie with an expression of gratitude.

"Well," Richard says, tilting his head at her, "with one difference. It'll probably be easier to prove with this one, thanks to all the great information you've provided."

She softens just a little under this look.

Richard flicks his eyes to the clock above the door—the charming expression slips off his face, then returns automatically. "We have motive—"

"We don't know anything for sure."

"But we have enough, Katie, and we have premeditation, a deliberate act. It's going to happen," he says. "Life in prison."

"It's all I want," Katie says with sudden conviction.

"I know."

"He has to go—you have to make sure."

"I will," Richard says.

Katie nods, takes a deep breath, turns back to the door.

•

Driving home, she thinks about Richard in the weeks following the shooting, when her head was so cloudy with grief, so full of questions and unknowns—how the people and days and formal procedures all ran together: the arraignment, the indictment, endless preliminary hearings, the competency hearing, all the meetings and consultations in between with him and his staff, and even a psychologist at one point. A million times during those first blurry weeks, she would crawl into bed at night, exhausted and ready for sleep, only to close her eyes and see the scene inside the gym once more. And always, after she saw Nick lying on the floor, the same question: *why?*

But she doesn't remember anything specific about Richard's behavior back then, only the tense certainty on his face a few days after the shooting when he told Katie and her family that he believed in this case, he would fight every step of the way to make sure Jerry was convicted. And then every day, every night, and every second in between, Katie imagined what could have happened in the month leading up to the shooting, when she barely saw Jerry. Wondering, with a sick, churning feeling in her stomach, if she was somehow responsible—if she could have played a part, however small, in Nick's death.

—You couldn't know what Jerry was planning, Richard said.

—You weren't there when Jerry was incited, and you couldn't have stopped it, Richard's staff told her.

And Katie would nod, but it didn't make the fear or the nebulous, guilty feelings disappear, because the truth was, no one knew these two men better than she did, and no one knew exactly why Jerry did it— and Jerry wasn't supplying any answers. Or if he was, his defense lawyers weren't sharing—not back then, not now. There were theories, there were decided moments leading up to the shooting, but that's all they were, and if Katie thought she would learn something in all these meetings, she was mistaken, because so many times the questions were baffling, seemingly unrelated to Jerry's walking into the gym that day, leveling the gun at Nick's face.

—Did Jerry have a big appetite? Richard's staff asked Katie. (Yes, and he loved her mother's cooking most of all.)

—What were Jerry's favorite shows on TV? (Cartoons, especially Bugs Bunny.)

—Was Jerry kind to animals? (Yes, as far as she could remember, but they didn't have any pets because Nick was allergic.)

There were other questions, too, but they didn't have anything to do with Jerry, or why he would kill a man he loved so much.

—On a scale of one to ten, ten being completely open and one being distant, how would you rate your interactions with your family? (Ten, Katie supplied automatically.)

—On a scale of one to ten, ten being supportive and nurturing and one being completely unhelpful in times of stress, how would you rate your family? (Ten, she said again, thinking of her sister, Dana.)

Later she understood—they wanted to make sure she wouldn't fall apart during the trial, during her testimony. Or, if she did, that someone would be there to pick up the pieces.

They told her that they wanted to interview her parents and her sister, too, because they also had a relationship with Jerry. That these questions would focus exclusively on Jerry's behavior.

—But I knew Jerry the best, Katie protested.

—Yes, but when you're close to someone, the staff psychologist explained, It's difficult to recall specific moments that could be telling.

During those first weeks, when Katie walked around her house like a stranger, her family tried to lighten the mood at dinner. Her sister Dana, raising her forkful of pasta:

—On a scale of one to ten, ten being delicious and perfectly seasoned and one being oversalted and/or bland, how would you rate Mom's carbonara tonight?

Her father laughing, checking on Katie's reaction, as their mother shook her head at all of them.

Back then Katie tried to imagine other questions they might ask her family without her knowledge, how her parents and sister would respond.

—What was Katie like as a child?

—Difficult to know, she imagined her mother saying immediately, that disapproving look on her face. —Katie was the opposite of her sister.

—A quiet kid, just independent, Katie imagined her father saying, still trying to gloss over her mother's criticisms.

—Did she have many friends as a child?

—Some, her mother would say, but not like Dana, who always made friends easily.

—Can Katie rely on your family during the stress of the trial?

—Yes, Dana might say. —But sometimes it's hard for Katie to express herself, to really open up to people.

—Even with you?

—No, not really. (And then Dana's thoughtful expression, her sigh, not meant to be unkind.) —But—well, *yes,* sometimes even with me Katie holds back.

And they would be right, Katie thinks now, admonishing herself quietly as she makes her way home through the darkened streets.

•

There are rooms she can't go into yet. There are spaces she won't let her eyes linger on too long, walls she still won't lean against. Like in the kitchen, between the counter and the sliding glass door that leads out onto the deck, because that's where Nick used to stand and chew on the inside of his cheek when he talked to his mother on the phone. She won't use the half bathroom on the first floor either, because every time she does, she hears his voice—*It's convenient because sometimes we only HALF to pee*—so she always bounds up to the second floor, where there are no images of Nick slapping the wall and laughing at his own stupid jokes. There are lights that must stay off at certain hours in the night because of the spaces they illuminate, spaces that are no longer filled with anything but air, lamps that must be turned on at dusk so that they swallow the shadows where he used to lie on the soft gray rug to watch the sun dip behind the oak trees in the backyard.

The only safe place, really, is in the basement, where she keeps her equipment—her cameras, projector, reels of film, editing table and board—but tonight she doesn't want the walls pressing into her, so she grabs the tripod and projector and hauls them upstairs, then returns to lug up the small, heavy sound box.

Before she steps outside, Katie turns off the phone; she's already called her friend Jill, and her parents and sister have checked in, so she doesn't have to worry about any of them rushing over, their faces pinched with worry. Since the end of the competency hearing and the announcement of the quick trial date, the calls have become a constant again, an endless ringing inside her house, her head, and she is weary of the automatic answers she must supply to everyone: Yes, she's eating, sleeping. No, she doesn't want any company. No, she doesn't need anything. Yes, she's keeping herself busy and she's fine, she's really *just fine*. She gathers her equipment, shoulders the sliding glass door open, steps outside.

Katie sets up the projector on the deck and aims it toward the side of the white shed in the backyard. She pushes a few buttons, adjusts the size of the block of light that takes up most of the wall of the shed, and waits for the hum of film moving inside so she can cue up the sound. There's a brisk autumn wind blowing, so she pulls the blue plaid blanket off the chaise lounge and wraps it around her shoulders as she settles into the chair.

An image finally appears on the side of the shed, but it's too big, too fuzzy. She hops up to adjust the image size, tweak the focus.

And then there they are, Arthur and Sarah Cohen in her backyard, on the wall of her shed: small, brittle bodies almost swallowed by the brown couch they sit on, their faces deeply lined and spotted, but what a sight—*beautiful*. Sometimes Katie forgets they're really gone, that she can't just run into the house to call them and say for the tenth time that she's making progress, that their documentary is finally beginning to take shape in her mind. She sits back down, adjusts the volume.

"I ask you, a little pastry should cost that much?" Arthur asks, shaking his head, his voice blaring out from the sound box by Katie's side. It's eerily disconnected from the image of Arthur on the shed, yet the sound is a comfort just the same: a proud, rumbly voice, with hints of laughter grazing the edges of every word. Arthur's big, black-rimmed glasses make his eyes enormous, owl-like, but they are opened even wider in disbelief. His wife, Sarah, *tccchhhes* with a smile, slaps playfully at his hands; she pushes a strand of her long gray hair behind her ear, rolls her eyes at the camera.

A breeze blows Katie's hair into her eyes as the dry leaves move and shake into one another in the tall oak trees that line the backyard. She knows that New England weather can turn in an instant—from spring into blazing-hot summer, autumn into deep winter overnight—and she wonders how much longer the winter will hold back, how much longer she'll be able to see Arthur and Sarah like this: bigger than life, *alive*. She reaches out from underneath the blanket, tucks her hair behind her ear, and watches a leaf dance across the lawn. Inhales the brown, loamy smells of fall and snuggles deeper into the chair.

"So I say to her father—you see, I was brave back in those days, and I saw her, beautiful girl, peeking out from the kitchen—and I say to him, this man, 'So this pastry, it's filled with gold for that price?'"

Arthur leans forward and laughs, slaps his knee with a gnarled hand, then uses his index finger to push his glasses back into place. Sarah fiddles with the hem of her shirt, her eyes cast modestly down, but there is a small smile tugging at the corners of her lips.

"This is a bold thing, you understand," Arthur says, "nothing good could come of it, I knew. But what does it matter when a man sees the girl he's going to marry for the first time? The head, it's not on straight."

"He was a serious man, my father. A respected man," Sarah says, looking up. "This was not the best way to begin."

She tilts her head toward Arthur, who nods and places his spotted hand on her knee.

"But this love, it is a serious thing, too, no?" he says. "How do you convince a boy not to be bold after he looks into this beautiful girl's eyes?"

And then Sarah is giggling like a teenager, her cloudy eyes are squinting up at his with love, and their bodies are leaning into each other from across the years, meeting again for the first time.

•

Watching Sarah and Arthur smile and touch and travel through the years together tonight requires a drink that will burn on the way down, something that will help her relax, so Katie's on her knees in front of the liquor cabinet, pushing aside bottles. Of course this plan to work during the trial seems ridiculous at times, even absurd—returning home each night after court, keeping her emotions in check and her head clear enough to make this project come together. But her mother has given her countless looks of uncertainty, and perhaps this is what has finally compelled Katie to persist: a stubborn compulsion to prove her mother wrong, to show her and everyone else just how strong she still is. So while she does have her own suspicions about her explanation—that her nights will be easier if she can make some headway on this film rather than coming home to relive every word, every emotion from the trial—Katie does see the glimmer of reason behind it, too. Shifting her attention onto the Cohens could be just the relief she needs to get through the long days ahead of her.

When Katie articulates it like this inside her head, she feels a trace of that relief, but there's still the same snag; she has watched Arthur and Sarah Cohen speak to her for so long, and she *still* has no idea what she needs to keep, what needs to be edited out. What the real story is.

She spots the tall bottle of Dewar's at the very back of the cabinet, ducks her head in and reaches for it.

Katie wonders how Richard will handle the questioning of witnesses tomorrow, how many times his words will summon Nick into the room, how many times Nick's presence will whisper into the air around her as she sits there in the front row, alone. She's asked her family and her friends to stay away, has explained to them that reliving the details of Nick's death will be transforming, healing even, if she's left alone to process the facts by herself one last time. They've all agreed for now—the majority of them much too easily, and some, like her sister and parents, with reluctance and more than one look of misgiving—but she has convinced most of them that in some ways it will actually be *good* for her. Of course she doesn't believe this for a moment—she wants to indulge her anger, to soak and simmer in it every time Nick's name is mentioned, every time another detail is brought to light, and she doesn't want any witnesses.

Katie feels a quick jolt of anger now at the picture of Richard in the courtroom today, his theatrics with the jurors. And yet she understands what he's doing up there, how he creates an entire world with his words, with the way he moves his body, with his silence. When he speaks to the jurors—when he lifts his hand and offers them his palm—another part of Nick's life is somehow instantly reborn in their minds. When Richard stops speaking, when he lowers his head to knead the back of his neck with his fingertips, she knows that another image of Nick is suddenly

hand—the space between her friends closing, their bodies moving back together again.

.

Later, Katie sits in the dark, staring at the side of the shed where her friends were only moments ago. She's thinking of possibilities, of what life pretends to offer—of what it bestows instead. How she was sitting in this very chair that afternoon, though it was pushed to the edge of the deck to catch the last rays of the late spring afternoon on her bare legs. She remembers that she was strangely happy that day, for no particular reason except that Nick *might* call—he *might* be thinking of her at that very moment, too. And then the phone rang, and she smiled, suddenly filled with hope; she jumped up, hurried into the house. Answered the phone, almost breathless, still smiling.

Less than an hour later, she waited on the other side of the window, willing herself to stand—to keep standing.

—*Just a few seconds,* the woman beside her had said, *to confirm the identity.*

In just a few seconds Nick would grant another part of his life to Katie, irrevocable: an image that would permanently inscribe itself into her brain, fusing with every memory they ever created together. Every time she recalled something specific between them—a casual conversation over dinner, an early spring morning in bed and inside each other's arms, a fiery argument about his mother—this new picture of him would forge its way to the surface, superimposing itself over the passionate, the ordinary. Katie couldn't shake the almost cinematic feeling of the moment, the blurred, dreamlike quality of what was about to happen; she imagined the blinds opening, her breath compromised, her eyes roaming over Nick's ashen face as the blood drained from her own. This last picture of him carving deep spaces inside her, pushing aside everything that existed before. She saw the curt nod she would give the woman who insisted on standing too close, like she was waiting to catch Katie's inevitable crumble to the floor.

Around her, sounds were filtered through cotton: a door opening, the approach of clicking footsteps—muffled and distanced, but somehow still so loud they felt like sharp fingernails jabbing into Katie's ribs. And then a voice, right behind her, icy and clear:

—I'm here to identify the body.

Candice. Nick's mother.

Katie looked straight ahead. Placed her hands on the ledge of the window. The woman beside her uttered some confused words—Katie heard only "wife" and "kin," and then Candice's reply.

—My son left her a month ago. *I'm* his next of kin.

Katie sensed the woman looking at her, but she kept her eyes trained on the window. As if on cue, the blinds opened and a man in a white coat nodded at her, walked around the metal gurney. Gently pulled down the sheet from Nick's face. Waited patiently for Katie's affirmation, because she was staring at him, at this attendant, instead of at her dead husband. Trying to assemble a response for Candice before she saw Nick for the last time. *I asked him to leave. Temporarily. He was still mine.* But before the words would come, Candice's cold voice again:

—That's my son. That's my Nicky.

Finally Katie turned her eyes to the table, to the sheet rising over Nick's face. She saw his thick eyebrows, a patch of dark hair, before the sheet was pulled over him completely. Fought the urge to bang on the glass with the palm of her hand, to yell, *Wait, wait—I didn't see!*

She sensed Candice staring at her, refused to turn around. Katie had nothing to be ashamed of—she didn't do anything wrong. Nick would have come back to her.

—He was a brilliant man, Candice finally said to Katie's back. Proud and accusatory at the same time.

Katie listened to her mother-in-law's footsteps clicking away (her ex-mother-in-law now?) and wished she could shout at the woman— just hurl those last revelations Nick had shared with her before he left, the kind of husband-wife secrets that would ravage Candice on lonely nights.

And then she wished, despite herself, for that last tormenting image of Nick to crowd into her memories, to obliterate everything else that came before this moment. Instead of this, instead of finally turning around to watch his mother walk away, her head held high, strangely triumphant.

2

Yes, Nick comes back to her in the nights now—in the shadowed recesses of their bedroom, in her dark, wandering dreams. And he is there in the day, too, when she prepares her solitary meals, when she makes the bed and smooths her hand over the comforter on his side, when she aimlessly flips through channels and catches herself stopping on the Discovery Channel, his favorite. Even when she stumbles into the bathroom in the morning, Nick is there and not there: the absence of the coffee ring he used to leave on the sink each morning before work, no matter how many times she asked him to clean it up. The surprise, the catch in her throat even now when she sees the gleaming porcelain.

Always this fixed, shapeless weight—he is still gone, he is still with her.

He is never far away, even when this heaviness lifts temporarily, and the moment is hers alone: in the shower, when she bends her head under the stream, the delicious feel of heat on her neck; in the car, an old song on the radio, the music recalling family vacations and her sister dancing into the ocean. Glorious, forgetting moments, like brief pockets of extra-oxygenated air—but then it is worse, because seconds after, there is the quick pulse of remembering, and Nick steals back into the frame completely. And another face, too, peering at Katie from the background. Jerry. Teasing his way into their story.

Today, before court begins, the moment comes with the dark brown smell of coffee sputtering into the pot downstairs as she runs a brush through her hair; as she inhales deeply, Nick slips away, and Katie feels the visceral joy of anticipation, the deep-roasted heat on her tongue. And then, before she can stretch inside the moment, she is propelled back once again: Nick in their kitchen on Sunday mornings, the clink of their mugs as he takes them out of the cupboard, his soft, happy whistling drifting up the stairs to her. And Jerry, he is there, too, bundled under the covers in the spare bedroom upstairs, asking her to tell it again to start his day with them. *It May,* he'd always begin, and Katie would settle at the edge of the bed, her hand resting on the rise of Jerry's arm underneath the blanket. Wanting to go to Nick instead, to accept the mug of coffee and the first lazy kiss of the day, but not before this—not before giving her story with Nick to Jerry all over again, like a gift.

—We met on Patience Island, just after sunset, she'd always begin, but Jerry wouldn't be fooled.

—No, Kay-tee. It *May.* His voice dreamy, a child waiting for a favorite fairy tale from beginning to end. Knowing each word by rote, ready to point out inconsistencies.

—It was May, she'd start again, and watch him grip the covers up to his chin, his eyes round with excitement. —The afternoon of Dana's engagement party.

—It too hot, Jerry would say, and she'd nod.

It *was* too hot for May, and a deep, repressive heat had settled in her parents' crowded backyard, wilting the streamers and the potato salad, the big YOU'RE ENGAGED! sign that one of her aunts had tacked over the back door. Katie sat away from the crowd in a scratchy lawn chair positioned under a canopy of leaves, fanning her face with a paper plate and waiting for the couple to arrive. At her mother's insistence, she had spent twenty minutes mingling, taking part in mundane conversations with her extended family, until an uncle she hadn't seen in years cornered her by the grill to comment on how much she'd grown, how much she looked like her older sister now. *Twenty-one now, are you?* he said. *Twenty-two,* Katie corrected, and he nodded, squinted hard at her. *The spitting image of Dana five years ago,* he declared, then nodded briskly as if he were trying to convince himself. Katie managed a smile at this well-intentioned compliment, then escaped to her private block of shade to wait it out.

From across the lawn, Katie suddenly heard someone's happy catch of breath, and then her sister, Dana, stunning in a sky blue sundress, was stepping out the kitchen door and onto the lawn. The backyard exploded with spontaneous clapping and cheers, with earsplitting whistles. Katie rose and clapped along, watched Dana's modest smile grow. Her sister turned back to the door, pulled Michael out beside her, covered his hand with both of hers. Their relatives took this as their cue and instantly vultured around the beaming couple, offering their congratulations, touching and fussing and demanding equal attention. *I hope Michael shaves before the wedding,* Katie thought idly. *Otherwise we'll never hear the end of it from Mom.*

—He not shave, Jerry would interrupt here, giggling.

—No, he never did.

But even if Michael's thick beard and curly brown hair were a little too scruffy for their mother's taste, it was clear that he made Dana happy, that he adored her. As Katie looked around now, it was clear that *everyone* adored Dana, something Katie was used to by this point—it didn't surprise her one bit that just seeing Dana could make the applause erupt, could make the family jostle each other out of the way to get closer to her. Katie wiped the sweat from her forehead, tried to ignore the jealousy that had come, unbidden, and then the sharp stab of guilt—always the guilt. Because if anyone in the world deserved to be loved and cherished like this, it was her sister, Dana—her kind and beautiful sister, the best person Katie knew. (Though these feelings of jealousy and guilt, along with many other things, she always remembered to keep from Jerry.)

The late-afternoon sun made a perfect spotlight for her sister, highlighting the thick auburn hair that framed her delicate face, turning her light brown eyes almost green as she stared up at Michael. Katie watched as Michael turned Dana's hand around, leaned down and pressed his lips into her palm, half serious, half for effect; her relatives murmured their approval anyway, their faces bright and knowing.

—Dana pretty, Jerry would always say here, the sigh in his voice suspiciously familiar, like the sighs of the boys who had paraded in and out of their house from the time Dana was thirteen until she went away to college.

—Yes, Katie would say simply. —Dana has always been beautiful.

That afternoon Katie waited patiently until the crowd dispersed a little, and then she walked over, gave Dana a sticky hug.

Lucky, Katie accused in her sister's ear.

You, too, Dana whispered with feeling, and Katie instantly knew what her older sister meant: Someday you'll be lucky, too. You'll meet him even if it doesn't feel like it now.

Where's Mom? Katie asked, pulling away, and Dana smiled, pointed to the back door: inside the kitchen still, micromanaging food and drinks and her own sisters, bossing around their aunts and everyone else and then doing it all herself anyway.

After the burgers and antipasto and endless platters of food, after the toasts and gifts and thank-you speeches, Katie retreated under the tree again, thinking of ways to stay out of her mother's direct path until she headed back to school that night—leaving behind the unspoken but always present accusation that she was wasting her time, because a degree in filmmaking was useless in the real world. It didn't help any either that Katie was already twenty-two and taking extra time to finish because of a disastrous semester of mono and dropped classes: ever since the announcement a few months ago that she wouldn't be graduating in June, that she had to take a summer class and then return in the fall, her mother had hinted endlessly at Dana's tireless work ethic—finishing her master's in social work at twenty-three, a year early! And now four straight years with the same agency, and not a single personal day! Her father had only smiled patiently at Katie, winked at her. Said later, when their mother left the room, *It's okay, sweetie, you know how your mother gets.*

Dana's exaggerated coughing interrupted Katie's cloudy plans of avoidance; she looked up, saw her sister pointing, her eyes wide with warning: their mother was barreling out of the house, had finally given up her oven mitts and spoons and directives and was pushing her way through the crowd. Small and compact, her dark hair rolled up on top of her head, she charged forward, searching the yard. Her mother had held back long enough.

Has anyone seen Katie? she demanded from no one in particular.

The people stationed around the grill with Katie's father were shrugging, watching her determined progress through the backyard. Her mother ignored them all, eagle eyes roaming.

Katie knew that look—she rose quickly, caught Dana's eye again. Gave her sister the customary grimace and eye roll, and then they held each other's glance for a moment. Dana waved her away—*Go, go, it's almost over anyhow*—and then Katie was moving fast, ducking around the side of the house and heading for her car. There was a party on Patience Island tonight—her friends Jill and Amy had called and told her about it this morning—and while she hadn't had the slightest desire to go then, it sounded like the perfect plan now. Maybe she could still catch up with them before they left the marina.

She jumped into her car, cast one look back. Imagined her mother's indignant voice over the phone tomorrow or the next day, the miles between them collapsing: *You went where? I can't believe you just left without saying good-bye, for God's sake! Your father almost had a conniption!*

—Chance? Jerry would ask here, and Katie would smile.

—Yes, she'd say, and she shivered just a little, each time. —Nick and I met completely by chance.

She told Jerry this story so often that it became his, too. Meeting Nick again and again with Katie, their story merging effortlessly with Jerry's over time.

And maybe this is why Nick won't leave her, why he comes back to her even in the smallest moments she should be able to claim for herself: she had offered the discovery of Nick, and of Nick's love, to Jerry without question. She stands in her kitchen, sipping her coffee, and hears Jerry's excited voice:

—More, Katie. You tell more.

Yes, she thinks now, placing the mug on the counter. She had given Nick to him right from the start.

3

Katie and her friends flew across the bay, the bow of the boat slapping up and down as they crashed through the gray, choppy water on their way to Patience Island.

—Your mother is going to *freak*! Jill shouted over the engine and churning water, her long hair flying around her face.

Behind the wheel, Amy shook her head, grinning. —No shit, Katie, are you crazy?

Katie grinned back at her friends, shrugged. Two beers and skidding across the ocean made her brave, but she wasn't stupid: there would be a withering phone call tomorrow or the next day, a punishingly long Memorial Day weekend at her parents' coming up. But for now she just laughed and opened another button on her shirt so the still-cold ocean could spray against her skin. Feeling powerful and free and reveling in the commiserating laughter of friends who had spent their teenage years terrified of her mother, even when they weren't doing anything wrong.

It was about an hour before sunset when they beached the boat beside four others on the pebbly shore of Patience Island. They hopped out with their beer and ice, joined the crowd milling near a long row of coolers set up on a small dune. Two guys started stacking wood on the sand, and Katie and her friends helped gather the tall grass beyond the dune to ignite a fire.

—Look at that one, Jill said, elbowing Katie.

He was tall and blond and tan, and when he looked at them, he tilted his head to the side with a "these are my teeth" smile. Before Katie and her friends went off to set up their blanket on the narrow beach, he caught Katie's eye, nodded at her in a way that said he appreciated more than her pulling up dead grass. She caught the surprised looks between Jill and Amy, pretended not to notice or care about this unexpected switch in the natural pecking order: Jill chosen first, *always* first, because of the cascading strawberry-blond hair and big blue eyes, the easy, quick laughter. And then Amy next, with her athletic body, her bold teasing. As early as junior high, this order was established—Katie last, and sometimes not even that, which gave the other two a chance to be benevolent, to happily sympathize with her the next day. *Guys are such idiots anyway. You didn't miss a thing.* Katie always laughed it off, told them she didn't mind a bit, because back then it really *was* okay at times just to have two friends sitting close, declaring their loyalty. *It would have been way more fun if we stayed in and watched a movie with you*, they'd tell her, and Katie accepted the lie for what it was—a compliment nonetheless.

The smiling guy wandered over to their blanket later, just before sunset, and introduced himself: Dave, a native southerner staying with cousins for the summer and waitering at the Coast Guard House in Narragansett Beach.

—Y'all should come in sometime, he said to them, then looked meaningfully at Katie, his eyes skipping to her open shirt. She nodded, tugging her shirt closed, and thought of the dozens of girls in bikinis and barely-there skirts he'd be waiting on all summer, girls who would giggle and sigh at his accent and then write their phone numbers on checks and cocktail napkins and his tanned arms. Dave stayed by her side for about twenty minutes, just enough time for Katie to hope, to make hazy plans inside her head to come home for the weekends, enough time for Jill and Amy to wander away for more beer even though their bottles were still half full. Just enough time for a stumbling, blushing girl in tight shorts to trip over their blanket.

Within minutes Dave was disappearing into the tall brush to help the girl look for her earring, and Katie understood immediately: he wasn't coming back.

She sat on the blanket alone, facing the channel that separated Patience and Prudence islands, and watched the sun turn the sky a rusty haze before sinking below the horizon. Her legs and arms bumped up whenever a warm breeze whistled gently between the islands, and she listened to the sounds of the emerging night: frogs burping into the descending darkness, the buzzing of nighttime bugs just waking, the distant, colorful carnival music from the Rocky Point Amusement Park that traveled to her on the wind. There, in the dusky light on the far eastern shore of the mainland, the red and blue and yellow lights of the Ferris wheel blinked on and off as it circled into the sky. Sitting there with her arms around her knees, Katie suddenly remembered what it was like to be ten again, sitting in one of the rectangular rocking chairs with Dana's protective arm around her, slurping something sticky and pink. Thinking she could see the whole world from up there—the whole big, hopeful world that was just waiting for Katie to grow up and be a part of it like her popular teenage sister.

She pictured Dana then, and her family clapping, saw again the admiration and love in their eyes. Dana deserved it all, she really did, but it was hard being Dana's little sister sometimes, now and growing up—Dana just enough older to be a protector, a role model instead of a playmate. The beautiful, accomplished older sister who would hit the milestones first—the A's in school, making the cheerleading squad, dating boys who called nonstop and showed up with yearning faces. These five years too much for any true companionship or secret-sharing, and then not enough when it seemed to count: the memory of Dana's accomplishments overshadowing the little sister who was a whiz at writing essays in her English and history classes, who was asked twice to tutor her classmates; the little sister who was smart and pretty, too, but not *quite* as pretty as Dana at that age, who didn't make friends quite so easily and who wasn't as friendly or *something* Katie could never name.

—Such a smart, thoughtful girl, her aunt Ginny said once, cupping Katie's chin in her hand, and Katie turned to her mother, saw her benign smile. A look that said, *Of course my Katie is smart,* but revealed little else.

Katie had spent years watching her family admire Dana, listening to their whispers (*Keep your eye on this one, Such a special girl*), and even if she agreed with them, she hated the jealousy—and then the shame—their words and looks could summon. Maybe, Katie thought now, it was this devotion that gave Dana her poise, her confidence and ease with the world, because Katie never felt that ease—not at school, even when she was singled out, or with her family, and especially not with her mother, whose critical eye would find Katie wandering away by herself, on the outskirts of their family still; the perennial outsider lurking on the fringes, looking in. —You need to make more of an effort, her mother said often back then and even now, and Katie would nod, knowing that her mother was right—wanting so badly to be different, to be *better*. Still, as much as she wished for this, as much as she loved Dana, she also wished her older sister didn't shine so brightly, didn't pull everything and everyone into her orbit so completely.

Katie turned away from the colored lights of Rocky Point, looked down the beach. About a hundred feet away, the fire snapped and popped into the sky, smoke and wispy ashes wavering in and out of the flames. Farther along, on the other side of the fire, the boats tipped back and forth on the shore, slowly losing ground. Katie couldn't see Jill or Amy in the mass of moving, swaying bodies, couldn't hear their voices in the shouting and laughter and clinking of bottles. Probably hooking up already, she thought, and tilted her head back to scan the dark sky. Just as in childhood, and later as a teenager, Katie would cast her eyes upward like this, wondering if God could see her. Wondering now if He noticed her sitting there, thinking too much again, tired of waiting for love to come—hoping He might finally show her how to make her life feel important anyway, to make it begin.

But even God was a million miles away tonight, His eyes skipping over Katie, missing her there in the dark with her feet plunged into the cold sand, wishing for *more*. She listened to the small waves curling onto the shore, the plink of restless fish cresting the water, and then the loneliness flooded back to her, too fast, like it always did: alone again, always alone, it seemed, even when she was in a crowd. She wanted so much, so little, it made her body hurt.

But she wouldn't cry.

She wouldn't be one of *those* girls, the kind who drunkenly sobbed at parties, splotchy-faced and leaking mascara, stumbling into their friends' arms. In high school and even during the past four years of college, there was always one at every party, and Katie wasn't sure what bothered her more: the crying girl and her need to be publicly petted and consoled, or the friends who ushered this girl away with too-serious faces, with hooded looks thrown over their shoulders to see who was interested in the unfolding drama. Katie prided herself on never being that girl, on never needing Jill and Amy or anyone to console her, drunk or otherwise, and she knew, even long ago in the eighth grade when she first met her friends, that this was part of her allure: Katie accepted life with barely a complaint, was easy to be around because she demanded so little most of the time. Even when they were in high school, and Amy and Jill had one of their epic fights and went to Katie to bitch about the other one, Katie simply listened and soothed and kept most of her own sadness and frustrations about life to herself. Always accepting, later, how her friends seemed to make up magically—Amy pulling in to the driveway with Jill already in the passenger seat, even though Katie lived closer, right around the corner from Amy.

—Pretty girls, her mother said once when they pulled up. But not great beauties. Katie knowing what left unsaid (*not stunning like Dana*) watching the same unhappiness cloud her mother's face ever since Dana had left for college. Seeing this made Katie grateful once again for meeting Jill and Amy so soon after Dana had left, when so much was missing in their house, when her mother would walk through rooms, sighing. And while Katie had always recognized that her friends were just very pretty girls and not gorgeous like her sister, when she saw Jill there in the front seat, she knew: it didn't matter what they looked like, or how much the guys preferred them because of their boldness, their spunky self-assurance, because even in their intimate circle of three, Katie was sometimes the third wheel.

Stop it, she thought now. *Stop feeling so damned sorry for yourself!*

She heard the rumble of the engine first, saw the quahogging skiff slicing through the dark water at the last minute; the engine cut off, and it slid onto the shore alongside the other boats beyond the fire. It was too dark to see much, but when the wind shifted and the embers and smoke from the fire cleared momentarily, she saw the guy on the boat—tall, dark-haired, shirtless. He was wearing jeans, and when he hopped up onto the bow, she saw that he was barefoot. Heads turned, a few hands went up in greeting as he hopped off the skiff. He grabbed a roped anchor off the bow, walked up the beach a ways, dug the prongs deep into the sand. When the crowd shifted, blocking her view, Katie sat up on her knees, straining to catch another glimpse.

She watched this man, crouched down now, his cupped hands pulling sand up against the anchor; she watched the muscles in his back, the way they moved in the light and shadows of the fire; she watched the dark curls slip up and down the nape of his neck; she watched him. Something slow and liquid and warm formed inside her stomach, expanded gradually throughout her body.

—Nick! someone yelled.

He walked toward the crowd slowly, restlessly, as if he were already forming a plan to escape. If he kept walking in this direction, Katie thought, if he ignored the crowd and walked straight through the fire and kept going, he'd walk right up to her.

She watched him. Waited.

.

The bonfire had burned down to a small pile of crackling embers, the laughter quiet and conspiratorial now. Couples wandered to the other side of the island or sat in the sand, hands exploring. Jill and Amy had disappeared long ago, too, but Katie had to get back to school.

—Will you hold these? Nick asked her, and Katie nodded, took the keys to his skiff and squeezed them hard. Her heart was beating out of control, and she tried to laugh at herself—stupid, it was just a ride back to the marina.

In the two hours they had sat beside each other, watching the crowd and listening to the drunken banter, they'd exchanged only the basics. Yes, she was a student in filmmaking, and she was going back tonight because she was taking a summer class; he, too, was a student, just finishing his master's degree in speech pathology. She was twenty-two, he twenty-five. And then, after a prolonged silence, Katie had turned to him, surprised herself. Said, without censoring herself for once, how she wished she were somewhere else tonight but couldn't really say where; how it always seemed this way, but one day she hoped she'd know exactly where she wanted to be. Her heart beat painfully inside her chest as she spoke. But Nick had only nodded pensively at these words, kept his dark eyes on hers longer than before. Like he understood exactly how this felt.

And now he was taking her back to the marina, where she had parked her car, and in a few minutes they would be completely alone.

Yes, she had been alone with men before, had twice allowed clumsy gestures to lead to sex, but both times it was the same; instead of feeling closer to them, instead of discovering her own body through their touch, she felt as if every move, every whisper and kiss, had been studied and practiced before, and that she was simply there as a part of their ongoing training.

And now Nick.

Standing above her there on the bow, coiling the anchor rope around his arm. She could feel him—she could feel *herself*—in every inch of her body, in every nerve ending, in her pulsing blood and skin and teeth and even in her hair and fingernails. Just watching him made her body feel like it was becoming her own, and her mind quickly took inventory of places she'd barely considered before: the dip in the small of her back, the tender skin around her ankles, the soft indents behind her ears. She imagined Nick discovering them with her, his fingers tracing those places, how his touch would help her finally own them. *Is this what love does to you?* she wondered, shaking her head. She wanted to laugh it off as childish, to remember that she had met him only two hours before, but there was the wind blowing against the backs of her knees and in an instant she pictured Nick kneeling down, caressing her slowly there, his eyes studying those small spaces on her body. A shiver at the base of her spine grew and traveled upward. Katie wanted to bolt into the tall brush and hide, she wanted to jump up and down and call out to her friends, she wanted to race headlong into the dark water and disappear into the perfect circle of moonlight that wrinkled in the water between the two islands.

Nick pushed his quahogging skiff back into the water, head bent forward, arms straining; he didn't ask for Katie's help, she didn't offer it. When he was knee-deep in water, he put a foot on the ladder, pulled himself up, and hopped on board. He turned back without smiling, held out his hand to her.

She waded into the water, the cold, liquid circles climbing her legs, and placed an unsteady foot on the ladder. She reached for him, and he pulled her up and inside, held her elbow steady as she stepped beside him.

—Careful of the quahog rake, he said, motioning with his chin at the seaweed-covered claws.

He took the keys from her, moved to the dash, started the boat. The engine hummed to life, the low bubble of the engine vibrating in her heels and up into her ankles.

—Hold on, he said, flicking his eyes to the water, so she moved beside him and held on to the metal bar right above the dash. Nick pointed the boat toward the lights of Rocky Point, and then the bow was lifting and they were gliding over the water in silence. Only then did she remember Jill and Amy, how she hadn't tried to get word to them that she was leaving.

As they cruised through the darkened water, Katie reviewed her night. Spent mostly like this, quiet and alone and lost inside her own thoughts—but she wasn't alone right now, was she?

—At least . . . at least there was the night, Katie said almost to herself. —I like listening to its sounds.

Nick turned to look at her then, closely, like he knew her from somewhere but couldn't place her.

They slid through the bay without speaking for a few minutes, the cold water spraying their faces, the sound of the engine humming along with the water as the boat crashed through the crosscurrent that led back to the marina.

—There's this stretch of beach at Point Judith where that's all you can hear, Nick said, finally breaking the silence. He kept his eyes on the water, and she shook her head in confusion. He turned to her again, not bothering to hide his impatience. —The night, he said. —That's all there is.

She only nodded, trying to match his cool demeanor, and he shrugged and turned his attention back to the water. Katie was afraid she had failed some sort of crucial test, even if she didn't know what the test was; she scrambled for a recovery.

She moved closer to Nick, her mind clamoring, and then she saw: his hands tensing on the wheel, a muscle twitching in his jaw.

It made her feel suddenly courageous, so she turned all the way around and closed the space between them. Allowed herself to openly admire him in the moonlight. The deeply tanned smoothness of his back; the broad, slightly freckled shoulders; the thick black hair full of salt and sand that curled up at the ends. Nick didn't move, didn't shift an inch, but his face said that he was aware of her attention—that he liked her eyes on his body.

—I'd love to see it, she said. —That stretch of beach.

He kept his eyes on the water, nodded slightly. Spun the wheel. The bright lights of the Jamestown Bridge winked at them in the distance; beyond them lay Narragansett Bay, and the jutting cliffs and dark beaches of Point Judith.

•

He beached the skiff on a small block of sand enclosed between two towering cliffs. Nick's dark eyes shifted shyly to the moonlit beach, an invitation, and Katie finally understood, for the first time in her life, the possibility of not always feeling alone in the world.

4

The hallway outside the courtroom is quiet today, now that Judge Hwang has ordered the television crews out of the building. Katie pretends to listen to Richard, she doesn't turn away from him, but most of her attention is focused on the large group of people from the Warwick Center huddled about twenty-five feet from where she and Richard consult, just outside the courtroom doors. Every time Richard pauses or stops to shuffle through papers, she strains to catch a word or two of the group's discussion.

"It's definitely a risk," Richard says to her, "but Carly's really the only viable witness."

Katie nods, tries to assemble the last clear memory she has of Carly and Nick together. —Has anyone seen my baseball glove? Nick had asked after the yearly picnic ended and everyone was engaged in the chaos of gathering things up. —I've lost it and— Oh! maybe it's in here, he said, and then his hands were plunged deep into the mass of curls on Carly's head, searching. —Okay, I think we've got someone's keys in here, he called out, and Carly had laughed for five seconds, a miracle, before she punched Nick squarely in the gut.

"If it backfires with this girl," Richard says now, "we'll have plenty of time to make up for it."

"Right."

Katie's eyes skip back to the Warwick Center employees. She can easily imagine the words that are being shared in that group, the certainty in the speaker's eyes. *We are a team, we are a family, we are strong.*

Nothing and no one can change that. And she can see the nodding heads, too, the faces full of pride and confidence from these people who stand so close to her, who so diligently ignore her.

"Katie?"

"Sorry, what was that?"

"I said, at the very least the jurors will see the emotion and horror of that day firsthand through this girl's eyes. We have that going for us, even if she is technically for their side— Hey, you okay?"

Richard's eyes have a dull, plastic look of concern in them as he reaches out to touch her arm, and Katie flinches before she can catch herself. She is rewarded by the quick pulse of recognition in Richard's face, the brief flicker of understanding that he's aware of her opinion of him. He doesn't miss a beat, though, just reaches down to retrieve his black briefcase from the floor between them. When he raises his head, his face is neutral, calm.

He points the briefcase toward the courtroom door. "Ready to go in?" he says, pushing the door open for her.

She heads inside, knowing that the Warwick Center group is ready to move into the courtroom as well, now that they don't have to pass by her and make small, contrived signals of surprise and greeting.

• • •

She can't believe she's forgotten to warn Richard about Carly, knows she should motion to him right now, whisper it in his ear. But as she leans forward, struggling to catch his eye, she sees Richard bowing his head at the defense table, suddenly trying his best to look concerned and grim as Carly makes her way up the aisle. So Katie leans back in the middle of the front row, folds her hands neatly in her lap. Feels the anticipation starting to build slowly, despite herself.

Her attempt to keep her eyes trained on the front of the room falters for only a moment. A quick glance at the defense table confirms that Jerry has the same yellow tablet in front of him, the same confused, sleepy look in his blue eyes. It's unnerving, the blank stare he gives Katie before she turns back to watch the bailiff swear Carly in—as if overnight Jerry has forgotten what Katie looks like. And then a second later, she understands: Donna must have instructed him to take out his contacts, but Katie's not sure what Donna hopes to keep from his field of vision. Her? Carly? Everything?

Judge Hwang, who has looked perpetually hungover and sullen since jury selection—dark purple circles under her eyes, a permanent scowl on her face—is actually smiling for once. She adjusts her wire-rimmed glasses, softens her normally raspy voice.

"You understand what's expected of you, miss?" she asks Carly, whose pudgy, four-foot-ten stature makes her look like a doll next to the bailiff.

"Course I do," Carly says in a nasally, clipped voice that sounds like she's hearing-impaired—a speech pattern common with Down syndrome.

Carly hikes up her long pink dress into both fists and settles into the chair. Her small, pinched face is full of determination, her normally wild curly brown hair pulled into some order by a large clip on the top of her head.

"I'm ready, let's go," Carly announces, crossing her arms over her chest.

There are nervous chuckles in the courtroom, especially in the rows behind the defense table.

"Your witness," Judge Hwang says to Richard.

"Thank you," Richard says. He rises, buttons his suit coat. "My name is Richard Bellamy, Carly," he says, offering her an avuncular, "I'm sorry I have to do this" smile. "Do you know who I am?"

"Yah, I know," she says with a little toss of her head.

"Okay, good," he says. "So then you know that I have to ask you some questions today, right? And that some of them might be really hard?"

"Bring it on, buster, I don't care," Carly says, lifting her chin.

Richard turns to the jury, eyes wide, as the laughter bubbles up around the courtroom. Judge Hwang glares, her gaze shifting left and right, and the laughter stops instantly. She squints at the back of the room, and Katie hears the whoosh of the door closing; most of the courtroom turns to see Dana sheepishly make her way down the aisle.

"Sorry," Dana whispers to no one in particular.

Even though Katie has asked her not to come, she is suddenly relieved that her sister has ignored this request. There clearly isn't any room for Dana in the front row, but she glides through anyway, squeezing in between Katie and Richard's assistant, Kristen—a stylish young woman with a blanket of blond hair draped over one shoulder—who lets out an indignant huff, then a louder one when Dana ignores her. Dana leans into Katie's shoulder with her own, keeps her eyes glued to the front. The air around Katie fills with the comforting smell of fruity perfume and cigarette smoke.

"Hey," Dana says out of the side of her mouth.

"Hey."

They both watch Richard wink conspiratorially at Carly, his smile widening.

"Okay, Carly, I can see that you're a smart cookie," he says, walking toward the witness stand.

"Uh-oh, did you tell him not to—" Dana whispers, pulling her arms out of her coat, but Katie shakes her head quickly, pretends she doesn't see her sister's questioning look.

"I know better than to try to fool you," Richard says. "So I'll just ask my questions, and then we'll be all done, okay?" He pauses for a moment, doesn't even blink at the suspicious look on Carly's face. "Can you tell me how you know Jerry LaPlante?"

Katie feels her sister's hand move on top of her folded ones and squeeze twice. Their signal since Nick's death: *I'm right here.*

"Jerry is my good friend," Carly says, forehead rippling.

"Is he *just* your friend?"

"No, 'cuz of we work together, too."

"Do you know him from anywhere else?" Richard's voice is mischievous; he raises his eyebrows and smiles like he knows a secret.

Carly's face suddenly lights with curiosity, as if they're playing a game. "Oh, dumb!" she bursts out, slapping her forehead, "I almost forgot. And he's my roommate. Yup."

"So Jerry lives in the same house as you?"

"Yah, in the same group home. He . . . he . . ." There is a fleeting look of confusion, a small shake of the head. "He did, I mean. *Before.*"

"Before what, Carly?"

Carly stares blankly at him.

"Before what?" Richard repeats softly.

"Before . . . before that day."

Carly lowers her chin, and her lips begin to move almost imperceptibly—counting her fingers, over and over, a relaxation technique Nick taught her shortly after her mother was killed in a car accident.

"Carly?" Richard's voice is soft, apologetic. "I'm so sorry, but I need you to tell me what you saw that day when you were playing basketball with your friend Nick."

Carly raises her head, and Katie sees that same look on her face, the one she used to see years ago, right after Carly moved into the small house on Dixon Street in Cranston, where Jerry already lived with two other clients. Katie and Nick would drop Jerry off on a Sunday night, and they would see Carly, her face filled with that same strange mixture of ferocious anger and helplessness as she sat on the wooden stool by the phone. Waiting for her sister Jennifer to call from Tacoma, even though, week after week, she never did. Vivian and Eric, the weekend house staff, would nod and whisper, *Since ten this morning,* or *Eight hours and counting,* and Katie would have to keep herself in check and remember that she couldn't just reach out and hug this small, vulnerable girl with the fierce eyes. That she had to somehow earn her trust first.

Richard sees this look, sees Carly's eyes searching and then fastening in on the defense table, so he shifts slightly, blocking her view of Jerry before he speaks.

"I want you to just take your time now, okay?" Richard says, but his voice has assumed a slow, encouraging tone, as if Carly were a small child, or worse, an idiot. It's his first mistake, and Katie is actually glad for it, glad when she sees Carly lean forward and glare at him, her hands coming up to rest on the banister like she's trying to gain leverage to jump over.

Richard instantly sees his mistake—he lowers his head apologetically, scratches at the back of his head in discomfort. He shifts his weight from his left foot to his right, shakes his lowered head. *I'm such a jerk,* his whole body says, and Katie has to admit it's perfect. When he lifts his head and sighs, Carly squints suspiciously at him, but the tension begins to leave her body.

"Whenever you're ready," Richard says in the respectful tone he usually reserves for Judge Hwang. He walks over to the banister, and before Judge Hwang can object—he hasn't asked to approach—he reaches over to Carly as if he will give her a hand an apologetic pat.

But it's mistake number two.

Katie leans forward, holds her breath, watches his hand snake over to the banister—it happens in slow motion for Katie, who stays perfectly still and watches the distance disappear between the two hands, the anticipation rising. Richard's hand finds its mark, lands confidently on top of Carly's little one.

"Oh, *shit,*" Katie hears Dana say beside her, just before Carly jumps up and thrusts her finger at Richard.

"False touch, false *touch!*" Carly screams, and there is a sudden, almost inaudible popping sound, and the hair clip is flying up and over, and Carly's curls are bouncing into life, springing out in every direction. Richard falters, both hands come up, and he takes a shocked step back.

"False touch!" Carly screams again, pointing, her face flushing a deep red. She struggles for a moment—it looks like she's trying to rip off the top half of her dress—but then she yanks a long string necklace out from underneath the top and inserts the end of it into her mouth.

The courtroom fills with the piercing sound of Carly blowing her emergency whistle, and then there is complete chaos. The bailiffs rush forward, the court reporter half rises out of her chair, and the entire courtroom erupts, Judge Hwang pounding her gavel and saying, "Miss, *miss!*" The court officer, a heavy, balding man, rushes back and forth, his hands bouncing up and down to signal quiet.

Jerry is standing, too, his fleshy lower lip hanging in confusion, his body slanted forward over the defense table. Donna grabs at his arm, pulling, and other arms extend forward from the front row of the courtroom audience to rest on Jerry's large shoulders. They are trying to get him to sit.

Carly points at Richard with both hands now, arms straight out in front of her and bouncing up and down as she jumps, still blowing her whistle. Richard looks at Judge Hwang and then at Carly, then back at Judge Hwang. The Warwick Center employees, and people with alarmed, serious faces—probably from the several advocacy groups that are monitoring this case—rise and move forward, offering advice.

"Why don't we try to stay calm—"

"Maybe if we could just give her—"

"If everyone could please—"

Judge Hwang bangs the gavel even louder, but for once no one is looking at her.

For the first time since forever, Katie feels the laughter building inside, feels it starting deep in her belly and moving upward. She covers her face with both hands, pretends to go into a spasm of coughing.

"Oh, Katie," she hears Dana say beside her in a sad voice, but Katie doesn't care, just lets the luxurious bubbling of laughter rise up within her.

And then, just like that, as the laughter gains momentum in her body, she remembers that she has forgotten, and Nick returns.

Katie's eyes slide around the room now: all of it, all this chaos, because of Nick. Because Nick is gone. She turns to Jerry, who is squinting in her direction, and then he is back, too, inside Katie and Nick's story again, even before they met him.

But there is this one satisfaction, something small to hold on to in the midst of all the confused voices and the relentless banging of the gavel: *I didn't give you all of us, Jerry. I kept most of this part of the story all for myself.*

5

Katie's class that summer was an elective, a boring survey course of films from the sixties, taught by a short, stocky man who spoke in monotone, his sentences drifting off at the ends. His voice lulled Katie back to her weekends with Nick, and when her professor shut off the lights and turned on the projector, the effect was complete. In the darkness she felt Nick's fingers on her again, pulling at her skin, caressing her neck, his tongue trailing slowly from her breasts to her pelvis. Sitting there in the back row, the hum of the projector in her ear, Katie could actually feel his elbows gently urging her legs apart, the heat of his breath on the inside of her thigh. Sometimes she hid her face in her arms, sure that even in the dim light another student would turn and see the telling glow on her cheeks; other times she had to squeeze her hands between her knees to keep them still, to keep her fingers from gingerly touching places where Nick's hands or lips had traveled.

When the lights came up and the professor resumed his droning lecture, Katie would focus on a spot on the wall, and in only a few seconds Nick would reemerge: straining above her, eyes closed tightly as he moved inside her, his hands gripping her hips. *Katie,* he would say in a dissonant whisper, and each time Katie's body seemed to expand, to fill up with the sound of Nick speaking her name.

Other times, when her professor scribbled on the board or sorted through his dusty collection of videotapes, other scenes pushed their way to the forefront, intruding into Katie's blurry happiness: Nick, examining a callus on his hand, fingers splayed, and Katie's own hand finding his—then waiting for his reaction, which always formed gradually, as if he needed time to remember how to assemble the smile that would eventually come. Or that humid Sunday afternoon when they were in the water at Potter's Cove, Katie's arms wrapped around Nick's neck, ankles crossed around his middle. Blissful, the sun warming the tops of their heads, their limbs slippery and sliding while they looked into each other's eyes. But then that diver surfaced a few yards away, pulling off his mask, walking to the beach: an old man, his white beard dripping into the water, a canvas sack roped around his torso and a heavy air tank in one hand. —Do you know him? Katie asked, but then instantly let go of Nick. The haunted look on his face scared her, made her turn back to the old man in an attempt to see what Nick saw in his grizzled, sun-worn features. She didn't repeat her question or ask what he was thinking, afraid that she would be one of those girls who requested too much, who pushed away her lover with too many questions. But she collected those times, too, when Nick turned away from her, when he became quiet and distant, sequestering them to a corner of her mind for later inspection. And she watched him.

She watched Nick all the time, how his body moved when he was close to her, how he looked at her, and away from her and at the world, and then the need would come to Katie in heavy, rolling waves. Because she wanted all of him, wanted to crawl inside him and know every single piece of him, to hold those pieces in her hand and examine them, inch by inch—wanted the confirmation that he understood her, that he knew about loneliness, too. She needed to know that somewhere in those prolonged silences between them, when his eyes would wander away from her to places she felt uninvited, his love for her was growing, was real. That she was the only girl for him, the only and exactly right girl, and this was just Nick's way. So like Katie's, but unnecessary now, *finally,* because they had found each other.

One Thursday afternoon in class, Katie was dreaming of her escape to Rhode Island in just a few hours when her professor announced that they would review several short documentaries. Minutes later Katie was again startled out of her reverie by her professor, who spoke in an uncharacteristically animated voice.

—Here, he said to the class, slapping the screen. —What do you see here?

A black-and-white picture of a young soldier filled the screen, his face muddy and tired, the strap of his helmet hanging. Beside him, a man who could have been sleeping if the scene were different, if there weren't the constant sounds of explosions and gunfire in the background. If he weren't lying in a ditch, his gun sunk into the mud next to his body.

—War, the students said. —Death.

—But what does the camera capture? the professor asked impatiently.

The camera zoomed in on the soldier's face—a disturbing look because of the combination of vacancy and concentrated sadness, a young-old face, its deep lines embedded with blood and grime.

Hands rose, hypotheses voiced.

—The meaningless of life? someone said.

—The acknowledgment of impending death?

Each time the professor shook his head, sighed, and waited.

The soldier patted his coat, and then an explosion only a few yards away rocked his body; he ducked down, sticks and clods of earth raining onto him and into the trench. He stood and scanned the scene before him, patted his coat again. A clump of dirt rested on the dead man's chin, unnoticed.

Katie, suddenly interested, said in a voice louder than the rest:

—He's thinking about love.

Heads turned to the back of the room where she sat. Her professor quickly closed the distance between them, pointing.

—Your name? he demanded.

—Katie, she whispered.

—Who?

—Katie, she said in a louder voice to the professor, who stood too close now.

—Love? the professor said. —But why, with a man dead or dying beside him?

It was only what Katie wanted the soldier to think about, what she *hoped* he was thinking about, despite everything around him. And now too many eyes were on her, so she turned back to the screen, watched the soldier pull out a small piece of rumpled cloth from inside his coat.

He lifted it to his nose briefly but didn't inhale; instead he swiped it angrily across his cheek and then looked at it, eyes flashing at the patch of dirt left across the bottom. In the corner of the cloth, partially hidden by the dirt: the top half of a looping, monogrammed letter, a *B* or a *P.* The soldier stuffed the cloth back into his coat.

—You forget the camera is there, don't you? the professor asked Katie quietly, and she nodded, realizing that there *was* a camera, that the young soldier didn't seem to notice it hovering over his shoulder. Didn't have time to hide the way he felt.

The professor addressed the class.

—Imagine, now, if this soldier turned to the camera, talked to us. Imagine what he would say with his eyes, with his body and limbs. He might talk about impending death, the meaningless of life, the professor said, shaking away the students' words with his hand. —But we would know better, wouldn't we? He turned back to Katie. —Yes?

A voice-over in the film reported how this soldier died a week later, how this same piece of cloth had to be pried from his hand.

—A little melodramatic, the professor said dryly. —But you get the point.

And then to Katie, before he popped the tape out for a new one: —You have an eye for reading people, Katie. Keep both of them open.

On the way home that afternoon, she held the excitement of her professor's words close to her. Finally she had an eye for *something,* and her heart raced along with the car as she barreled toward Rhode Island, toward Nick. Just one simple sentence, and at last she understood: first Nick and now this, a hidden talent, a purpose—her life had begun in earnest. Not even the congested traffic on I-95 could take away her joy; she couldn't wait to share her news with Nick and with her mother, to watch the cynical lines of doubt smooth away on her mother's face. *I'm going to make documentaries,* she imagined telling her mother, *because I have an eye for it.*

In Warwick she pulled in to the sandy parking lot at Sealark Marina, where Nick slipped his skiff. Before she reached the ramp to the dock, she saw him standing on the bow, hosing off the salt water. Three burlap bags overflowing with quahogs sat on the flaking wooden dock, and Katie giggled with happiness; Nick had waited for her before trading them in, knowing that she loved the sunburned old man at the shack, his gruff, bantering ways and how he tried to slip his hand underneath the scale to shortchange Nick. A simple, repetitive game just for Katie's benefit. Nick waved, and she sprinted down the ramp, across the rickety dock.

—I have an eye! Katie shouted to him. Nick laughed at her, shaking his head.

He stuck his thumb over the spout of the hose, pointed it in her direction, and she ran straight into the mist, twirled underneath it on the dock until her clothes were drenched.

—Get up here, Nick said in a deep voice she understood, and pointed to the bow in front of his feet. Katie scrambled over the side of the skiff, clothes dripping, and fell into him.

—My professor said— she began, but Nick's strong arms were crushing her, his mouth stopping her words.

His fingers teased up under her wet T-shirt, exploring, his tongue licking at the back of her teeth. And then everything else melted away, became distant and unimportant. Inside Nick's arms it was always the same for Katie, dizzying, like flying in circles when she was standing still.

A prayer rose up on its own accord, selfish and urgent. *Please, God, please let it always be like this.*

—Now, what did this professor say about your eyes? Nick said in mock jealousy.

But in his arms there was room for only this. Only Nick.

In bed that night, Nick worked on her with tongue and teeth and nails, until her hair matted against the sweat on her face, until her neck and back muscles started a slow, raw hum. And she watched him above her, behind her, all around her, straining to see his love.

—*Katie.*

Her whispered name like a plea—and Katie's body rose to meet his. She turned on her back, put her hands on each side of his face to hold him steady above—needing to see it, needing to see herself in him. *You have the eye,* she told herself. *Keep looking.*

Nick, moving inside her, his eyes tracking her face so intently. She felt the lonely spaces within her leaving—finally, gloriously. Not a prayer any longer, not a fervent wish cast at the sky to God, but this: what could be, the hope of coming together in this world.

6

She's waiting for Dana outside the women's bathroom, across the hall from the courtroom. Dana's probably perched at the edge of the toilet at this very moment, Katie thinks, taking two or three furtive puffs from a Merit 100; Katie can picture her sister perfectly, cigarette dangling out of her mouth, one hand waving away smoke while the other one mists the air around her with the slender tube of peach- or melon-burst spray she always keeps in her purse.

After Carly was finally calmed and order restored, Judge Hwang had called for a fifteen-minute recess; she dismissed the jurors, barely waiting for the door to shut behind them before leveling her gavel at Richard, then Donna. She tossed it onto the bench, gathered up her robes, and stormed through the door at the back of the courtroom to her chambers.

"Meet me on the second floor, conference room three," Richard said to Katie, his face impossible to read. He snapped his briefcase shut, followed Donna to chambers. Across the room Jerry sat hunched over the defense table as Daniel Quinlin, the Warwick Center's recreation assistant, sat beside him talking quietly. The bailiffs stood close by, trading glances and eyeing Jerry.

"C'mon, Dana," Katie whispers under her breath now, seeing exactly what she hoped to avoid: the Warwick Center people emerging from the courtroom, one after the other. *Oh, great,* Katie thinks, but is relieved to see them almost instinctively walk in the opposite direction from her, toward a long bench by the elevators. Sure enough, there's Patricia Kuhlman, the acting director of the Warwick Center, a tall, older woman who has always intimidated Katie by her stern and officious manner. She converses with Veronica, the receptionist, their heads bent close together. And there is Daniel Quinlin again, this time with his arm around little Carly, and Jan Evers and Billy Zahn, and a few others Katie knows from both the work and recreation programs. Trailing behind them is Judith, the heavyset woman from the cafeteria, her bangs flapping on her forehead as she lets out short puffs of air.

The last time Katie saw so many of them together was at Nick's funeral in May. Watching them now, she replays their stubborn solidarity that day, the way they determinedly went through the receiving line as a group—some touching the top of her hand or arm briefly, some going in for quick, boxy hugs—all murmuring how sorry they were for her loss. That entire day Katie had waited vainly for one of them to pull her aside, to acknowledge the obvious complexity of her grief. Nick packing up and leaving their home, and then, before he could come back to resume their life together, leaving the world forever. Their entire future decided in a split second by Jerry. Did any of them even *try* to imagine how unfinished it all felt to Katie? All the unanswered questions and fears and every complicated little moment and gesture between Nick and her in the month they were separated adding up to exactly nothing now that he was gone for good? She had wanted someone, *anyone,* to ask her what it was like to stand in that receiving line, beside Nick's impossibly polite mother: Nick's wife, yet not his wife precisely for the past month—never his wife again. The anger and confusion that came with feeling like an impostor at her own husband's funeral as she accepted their condolences next to a woman who acknowledged her presence with only a stiff smile.

A couple of them did make an effort afterward—a card from Dottie Halverson, the cheerful and motherly nurse who lived only a few streets away from Katie; an apologetic, stilted phone call from Eddie Rodriguez, the athletic director at the recreation center. But now, as they slowly gather around the bench near the elevators, they transform from her friends once again, become that same dark, amorphous mass from the funeral, and Katie's glad. It's easier this way, easier not to want them near—easier to think of them instead as "those people."

Dana is just emerging from the bathroom when Carly's insistent voice rings out in the hallway.

"I can *too* if I want," she says.

"Uh-oh," Dana says, stepping beside Katie.

They watch Carly disentangle herself from underneath Daniel's arm and push past the group, face unyielding. She stamps toward them, her pink dress hiked up high.

"Remember, she doesn't know any better," Dana whispers in Katie's ear.

Carly stops in front of Katie, lets the folds of her dress go. Plants both hands on her hips.

"Katie," Carly says in a huff, a statement. She stands in front of Katie, breathing hard, her small face fixed in an irritated glare, her hair sticking out at a dozen curling angles.

"Hi, Carly," Dana says, shifting into Carly's line of sight. "Remember me?"

Carly doesn't even acknowledge her.

"Hey there, Car," Katie says softly, but that's all Carly is really waiting for, all she needs. With a small whimper, the girl throws herself at Katie, her chubby arms circling Katie's waist.

"It's okay," Katie says, holding her close.

Carly rubs her face into Katie's shirt, and then the sobs come out, choking and long. Katie feels the wet tears through her shirt, strokes Carly's hair and plants noisy kisses on top of her head.

"Missing you, lady," Carly manages some minutes later.

"Me, too, honey."

"And . . . and that dumb . . . *Nick*."

"I know."

"Missing both of you *tons* now," Carly says, squeezing her hard. "Too much, lady."

Daniel is by their side after a couple of minutes, looking sheepish and awkward.

"Hey, Katie."

"Hi."

"We should go, sweetheart," Daniel says, his hand on Carly's back. She loosens her grip on Katie and turns to Daniel, glowering.

"Hold on one minute, buster," she says, wiping her nose across her sleeve. She sniffles loudly and tugs at Katie's hand, pulling her a few feet away.

Carly reaches down her dress and yanks out her string necklace with the metal whistle attached. She pulls it over her head.

"Yup, I got tons of them at home, you bet," she says, all business once again, so Katie leans down and lets Carly put the whistle around her neck. "Just in case, lady," she says with serious eyes. "You never know round here." Carly turns to Daniel.

"Okay, let's go, I'm hungry," she commands, gathering up her dress. She marches off to the group by the elevator without looking back, Daniel trailing behind her.

•

The conference room smells like the yellow, moldering pages of an old book, Katie thinks as she looks again at the clock above the door. Almost eleven-fifteen and still no Richard; there's probably no chance they'll resume before the lunch break now. She fingers the whistle around her neck, considers blowing it just to get Dana to say something to her.

The floor-to-ceiling windows on the east side of the room let in big blocks of sand-speckled light that sparkle and illuminate the dark table in the center of the room, where Katie sits. Dana stands near the windows in the shadows, arms crossed, one knee bent with her foot pressed against the wall.

"I thought you had clients all day," Katie finally says. "I thought social workers didn't have time for the extras."

"You're not an extra, Kate."

Kate. Her sister and mother are the only ones who call her that, and only when they're upset, or about to say something "important." A long moment draws out between them, and then her sister finally breaks the silence.

"You knew Richard might touch her," Dana says. "You knew."

"I forgot to tell him," Katie says. "But how could I know he'd do that?"

"Because for some reason you always know," Dana says. "You always know about people, the things they'll do. Especially after you've spent some time with them."

She slides out the cushioned brown chair beside Katie and sits down, eyeing her. The red highlights in Dana's hair bring out the amber-green flecks in her eyes, and for a moment Katie is suddenly amazed, once again, by her sister's confident beauty.

"Please don't pull the therapy stuff with me, Dana," she says, recovering quickly. "C'mon. I need some air, and you can have a cigarette."

Katie is halfway out of her chair when the door opens and Richard walks in. She sits back down, shoulders tense. Richard's eyes fasten on the whistle around Katie's neck. He carefully places his briefcase on the table, fingertips resting on top.

"Look, I really don't care at all what you think of me and what I do," he says quietly. "I really don't."

The trembling in his voice is unsettling, but Katie reminds herself that this emotion has nothing to do with Nick—with her losing Nick.

"I thought we were in this together and that you actually wanted to *help* me prosecute the man who killed your husband. But if you're going to withhold pertinent information"—his voice rises a little with each word—"then I really don't see the point of meeting with you, because it's just a huge waste—"

"Excuse *me,*" Dana says, rising, but Richard lifts his palm at her, a stop sign. He turns his head slightly in her direction, his eyes addressing the table.

"No, look, I'm going to say this," he announces, then turns back to Katie. "I see it, you know, the contempt in your eyes. And that's okay, that's fine. But don't meet with me and my staff and then act like we're a team, Katie, don't pretend you're going to give me the inside scoop on these people so I can keep this very dangerous guy in jail, because it's pretty clear to me that I'm in this *alone.*"

Katie is the first to look away.

"So if we have that clear—"

Dana steps around the table toward him, her voice calm and soothing. "Mr. Bellamy," she says, "I think it might help if we all took a few minutes to relax."

He finally looks directly at Dana. "Well, that's a great idea, actually, because we have all the time we need to relax. We're done for the day."

Katie sucks her breath in surprise, and he turns back to her.

"That's right. After an hour of arguing about procedure and viable witnesses, Judge Hwang said she had to call it a day because she felt ill. But she made one thing very clear—another scene like that and she'll call a mistrial, which means this starts all over again."

"I'm sorry, I didn't know—" Katie doesn't trust her voice to say more.

"The judge, jury selection, the whole nine yards, all over again. Only this time we get jurors who've read about the circus back there, about the asshole assistant DA who bullied the little retarded girl—"

"Of course you didn't bully her," Katie says, instinctively reaching out to him, but now it's Richard's turn to flinch.

"If these jurors are dismissed and talk to the press? That's how it's going to translate, Katie. The truth won't matter." He runs a hand through his hair. "Jesus, I didn't know what to do in there."

For once this gesture seems sincere, and Katie wants to tell him that, wants to explain that if only he could act like this in the courtroom, it would be better—it would feel *right*. But he turns away from her, grabs his briefcase.

He stops at the door, doesn't look back. "There's a mob of reporters down there," he says. "You might want to wait it out here a little longer."

● ● ●

Right after Nick and Katie separated, she realized that just sitting down inside their home was going to be a problem. Sitting down to eat, sitting down to watch TV or to write out a grocery list, because every place in the house looked like someone else should be there already, waiting for her. Now that there's no chance of Nick's return, the hardest thing is to stop moving, to find herself suddenly sitting someplace where Nick should already be, waiting for her, or where he will eventually come, with a smile and a funny story about one of his clients who has a combination stuttering/saliva problem. Instead Katie finds herself at the table with a cold plate of spaghetti or under the blankets in bed with her sketch pad resting against her knees, pillows propped behind her back, and she catches herself turning to where he used to be, where he *should* be. Sometimes she even pauses and tilts her head, because she's sure that sound is his car pulling in to their rocky driveway, the stray stones rattling against the side of the house, or she's positive that she's heard the refrigerator door just close, because of course Nick would be on his way back to the table with more grated cheese—he couldn't get enough. But he's never there, he never comes, and she's not sure how to stop sitting and waiting, to stop sitting and listening for him or hoping that at some point he actually *will* walk into the room, a big apologetic smile on his handsome face. *Sorry, I didn't mean to take so long.*

So Katie finds new places to eat dinner, to read the paper, or to sketch the storyboards for Arthur and Sarah's documentary, hoping that this will help her find her own spaces in their house—to reclaim it slowly, piece by piece, until she can finally cuddle up on the soft blue sofa again with a book, look around, and think, *Yes, this feels like mine now, too.*

Tonight she's sitting on the washing machine in the small closet space Nick built in to the wall near the stove, an uneaten chicken salad sandwich forgotten on a plate next to her on the dryer. The white louvered doors are opened, and she dangles her legs, letting her heels bang the front of the machine. Stretched across her knees is Nick's old ratty gray sweatshirt, the one she was always trying to turn into rags. In the winter he wore it at least once a week, always managing to hide it from her and wash it on his own. This time it was draped across the bumpy metal exhaust hose near the bottom of the dryer, low to the floor and almost out of sight; she spotted it when she hopped onto the washing machine and turned to pick up her sandwich.

Her eyes scan the stains all over the sweatshirt in her lap, urgently trying to connect specific memories with the small dark splotches near the neckline or with the two long lines on the left sleeve that are a shade lighter than the thinning gray cloth. Her fingers run over them again and again, her mind searching for a memory of them together, until she finally gathers it up and inhales deeply—expecting the salty, musky odor of his skin. But it only smells faintly of Tide, and dust.

"I miss everything," Katie says out loud, then waits for a sound, any sound, to answer her in the house they once shared. When she hears Nick's voice coming from just a few feet away, loud and clear, she almost falls off the washer.

"Hi, you've reached the Burrellis' residence—"

She hops off the washing machine and grabs the cordless phone from the counter before the answering machine beeps. Her mother hates it when she turns down the ringer, hates it when Katie picks up the phone mid-message, so she isn't surprised when her mother doesn't bother with a greeting.

"I'm not kidding," her mother says. "If you don't change that message, I won't call anymore. It's disturbing."

"How are you, Mom?"

"I just got off the phone with your sister— No, don't interrupt me, I want to know what happened in court with that girl today. She's the high-strung one from the cookout, right?" her mother asks.

Despite the battle ahead of her, Katie smiles. She remembers her mother's face when she was leaving a cookout Katie and Nick had years ago, after the Warwick Center clients had all gathered around, touching and kissing and offering her mother various homemade gifts made out of leaves and rocks (and in one case a small, semihardened piece of dog feces with twigs sticking out of it). Her mother's wig was on crooked, her clothes creased and stained. "They're really quite affectionate people, aren't they?" she'd said, walking away with her gifts, her step a little wobbly. Katie would never forget her mother's face that night—she had never looked happier.

"Kate?"

"Yeah, Mom, Carly's the one you called the bulldog, remember?"

"You know, she kicked me that day. All I did was try to wipe some mustard off her face."

"Well, I told you when you got there. She only lets a select few touch her."

"Right," her mother says, and Katie realizes that her mother has set her up perfectly, once again. "So what about that?"

"I didn't know he was going to do that, I'm not psychic."

"Kate."

"Look, Mom, it's not a good time right now. I'm about to begin some work on my documentary—"

"Katie," her mother interrupts, "please don't dismiss me. I'm asking you a question."

"I don't know, okay?" she says. "Nick is everywhere in this house tonight, and—"

"Hold on a sec, hon."

Katie hears the staticky sound of her mother covering the phone with her hand, then her muffled voice asking her father a question. There's a deep rumbling from her father and then more static.

"*Katie?*" her father bellows into the phone.

"You don't have to yell, Dad."

"Did you hear about what happened to me and your mother at the Rhode Island Mall yesterday?"

Her father, retired for five years and quickly bored with the many hobbies he took up right after, had finally turned his attention to the endless supply of people in the world who were capable of doing great harm to him and his wife. The only hobby, apparently, that stuck.

"You told me about it already, Dad. Twice."

"Your mother thinks those men were okay, but I saw the way they were eyeing us. Especially the tall one. I didn't like the way he was staring at your mother's purse."

Katie hears her mother's impatient sigh in the background. "Jimmy," her mother says in her warning voice. There is more static, her father's muted voice.

"Okay, Grace, but you weren't paying attention like I was."

"*Jimmy.*"

Her father clears his throat, booms back into the phone. "So, sweetie, you know we have snow coming tonight, right?"

"Actually, I didn't."

"You have antifreeze in your car? And a good, dependable scraper?" he demands.

"Yes, Dad, you came by last—"

"And what about lunch meat? And bread? Do you have bread?"

"I'll buy some."

"Because you *need* bread," he says, "It's a staple." And then there is more static and a short, muffled struggle, and her mother is back.

"Okay, *okay,* Jimmy, she heard you—yes, *bread,*" she says. "It's me again, hon. So you've been to the market, then?"

Katie knows that she should let it go, but she can't. "Why do you do that, Mom?" she asks quietly.

"Do what? Your father wanted you to know that it's going to snow."

"You do it every time now. Every time I say Nick's name. You put Dad on, or you change the subject."

There is a brief, surprised pause before her mother answers. "Well, it certainly isn't intentional, Katie, and if you want to talk about him, you know I'll listen. I *want* to listen, you know that." Her mother's voice suddenly eager.

"I don't want to *talk* about him, Mom. I just want to be able to say his name."

"You can, Katie, you can say whatever you want. But I do think the focus should be on *you* now—"

"Oh, okay," Katie says, the anger growing. "You want me to sit through Nick's trial but never mention his name. Got it."

There is another pause, an astonished snort. "Oh, no, I'm certainly not doing this tonight, Katie, really. I called—we called because we wanted you to know that we're thinking of you. And we love you." A third pause. "And they're calling for snow, okay?"

"Okay."

Katie clicks the phone off without saying good-bye.

She moves toward the slider doors and looks into the dark sky, at the oak trees that are silent and unmoving tonight, like they're waiting for something to happen. She's suddenly exhausted, so she turns to pull out a chair from the table—catches herself just in time.

In the living room, she lets her eyes drift around the corners and curves and spaces in this room—the small place between the end table and the wall, the white ledge of the bay window that looks out onto the quiet street, the narrow walking space between the entertainment center and the plant stand with the fern cascading from it. She gathers up all these places that she must eventually conquer by herself, little by little, and takes a deep, labored breath.

"Everything, Nick," she says loudly, impatiently.

She turns back to the kitchen, to the closet near the sliding doors where she stored her equipment the night before.

•

Arthur and Sarah are back on the white shed, their small bodies and spider-lined faces so big and clear that Katie feels that same pang for them tonight—that same spasm of intense loss when their son, Ben, called to tell her how he had found them: both dressed exquisitely— Arthur in his best black suit and tasseled loafers, Sarah in her favorite blue satin dress and expensive stockings, not a hair out of place—lying side by side in their bed, their hands crossed peacefully on their stomachs. The two empty bottles of Percocet on the nightstand, like paperweights, holding in place the letter to their son. *They must have been saving it up for months*, Ben had said, his voice finally breaking.

"You see," Arthur is saying to Katie from the shed, his bony frame leaning forward, big oval glasses in place, "most people, they believed it all began much later. When the Germans crossed into Poland in '39. For us it happened much, much sooner."

Sarah nods into the camera with pressed lips. She shifts slightly to the right to get a better look at Arthur, who is staring intensely into the camera, but this motion of Sarah's lengthens the chasm between their bodies even more. Katie stares at the space between her friends, shakes her head; she hops off the deck railing to push some buttons. There is a quick squeak of the film as it jumps, then the comforting buzz of it moving forward.

Her parents are right, the dark sky looks almost green from holding back snow. Katie gazes at the clumped, dead leaves in the backyard, knows she should have walked across the street to the Legares' to see if their grandson would rake the lawn this year. She could have gone over a dozen times, but each time something held her back, something she couldn't quite name about her interactions with all the neighbors, actually. Not that they were rude, she couldn't even imagine that on this quiet, dignified street. But something about them was just . . . *uninviting*. Like Mrs. Grima from next door—how long has it been since she teetered over on her silver cane with a plate of pumpkin bread, or raisin bread, or zucchini bread, depending on the season? And gossipy but gorgeous Sandy, three houses down on the left and loaded with those small kids—always giving Katie that broad, wide wave now, rather than scooping her arm in her favorite "get over here and have some coffee" gesture like before. And even the Legares, who fussed over Katie whenever Nick was away at a conference ("Come for a small meal, we could all use the company," Mr. Legare would say, Mrs. Legare nodding and beaming beside him), even they only nod and wave now, faces square and unsmiling—as though Katie's misfortune will somehow contaminate them if she stands too close. *Everyone deals with uncomfortable situations in their own way,* Dana has said more than once. *Maybe they think you want to be left alone.* What was left unsaid: *Maybe they know by now that you won't confide in them anyway.* Maybe, but Katie still has the urge to sprint over to Sandy as her kids and their little terrier pile out of that bulky SUV, as Sandy grabs the endless shopping bags and swings her baby daughter onto her hip. She wants to stand too close to this woman with the perfect face and body, with the beautiful children and the biggest house on the block and the handsome cardiologist husband, and shout, *You won't lose your husband, too. If we have coffee and gossip about the neighbors again, it won't all go away, too!*

Katie wears Nick's tattered sweatshirt over her own shirt, wraps the blue plaid blanket around her shoulders. She looks up at the sky, wonders how much snow is expected. Probably not much, she thinks, or someone would have mentioned it today. Still, she wishes she had asked her mother before she hung up on her, because she knows better than to turn on the news these days. Not just because she doesn't want to see herself rushing from the courthouse, pale and clumsy, or Richard's earnest face in a circle of cameras and microphones, but because she can't stand to hear her husband's name issued so casually from the mouths of the nightly newscasters anymore—newscasters who once seemed so familiar and comforting as they joked about the weather, or reported the local news, or tallied the death toll in Iraq with solemn faces, but who now just seem like impertinent strangers. The first time she heard the six-o'clock anchorwoman say it—*Nicholas Burrelli, the speech pathologist shot to death two days ago in Warwick*—she had to lean against the wall to keep from falling down.

She can't watch the news with the volume off, either, because she never knows when the screen will suddenly fill with Nick's smiling face, from that small black-and-white photograph the press has, one of her favorites. The first time she saw it on the news, all she could do was squint and wonder, *Is that dark streak in the left-hand corner the sleeve of my red T-shirt?* The photograph was taken on their trip to New Hampshire, and she remembered exactly where they were: reclining on the huge sand-colored rocks in the river that wound side by side with the Kancamagus Highway, where that lone male hiker snapped their picture. *I just had to,* he told them without smiling. *You looked so happy. Why don't you give me your address?* He didn't introduce himself, just pulled out a pen and paper from his weathered canvas backpack and handed them to her. The man had frizzy dreadlocks, pockmarked and scarred skin, and the clearest green eyes Katie had ever seen. And yet there was something unnerving about all that mess and his crystal stare, about the frowning look he gave her when she passed the slip of paper back to him. Katie was surprised when she received the photo in the mail almost a year later, without a note and bent at the corners, as if it had been handled too much. "Oh, cool," Nick had said, but something about it creeped her out. It creeped her out even more that *that* was the picture her mother had picked out from all the albums Katie had hurled onto their bed the day after Nick had been shot, because the TV stations and a reporter from the *Providence Journal* had asked for a photograph.

She stops the film, gazes at the shed. Arthur and Sarah sit closer now, and Katie is amazed once again at how familiar she is with this footage; it's almost exactly where she wants it.

". . . we saw each other only once in a while, you know, because our barracks were so far apart. But there were times, yes," Arthur says, smiling, and Katie's eyes well up at the delicate way he takes Sarah's hand, at the way his other hand comes up to cradle it. Like he is holding a tiny, frail bird between them.

"It was mostly at night," Sarah says. "Sometimes we could only nod and smile as we passed by each other, but other times, who knows? Maybe our hands would meet for a second and there would be a small present that made sleep come faster."

When they both turn their heads to look into the camera, Katie mouths the words she asked them—*What kind of present?*—and watches the cold air meeting her breath in puffy clouds.

"Oh," Sarah says, and she takes her free hand to pat Arthur's arm, "nothing big, really. What did you have in a place like that?"

Arthur laughs, a cloggy little rumble, and nods. "Sometimes a little discarded piece of red cloth. Sometimes just a smooth stone that I found in the yard," he says. "It was not the gift that counted, you understand. It was the giving."

Sarah nods, her face growing still. "At night, when we would pass by each other, we knew how lucky we were to still be alive. The others—so many others, *friends*—" Sarah coughs, lowers her head.

When she looks back up, her eyes do not meet the camera but wander to a space beyond it. "At night," Sarah says, "that is when the ovens came to life. They waited until nighttime, but the sound, it was always in your ears, even when you woke."

Arthur leans over, captures her hand once again. His voice trembles, but it is full of bravado. "When this beautiful girl passed by and I could see her eyes, when I could see she was still alive," he says, nodding briskly, "I thanked God for one more day, one more day. For her life."

Sarah closes her eyes, smiles faintly.

Katie clicks off the sound, closes her eyes, too.

She pictures them there, the long line of men walking one way, the women coming from the opposite direction, the lines passing each other at night between the rolling barbed-wire fences. She sees Arthur's and Sarah's eyes meet as they locate each other, the relief right there at the surface. As they pass by each other, their fingers flutter and reach out bravely, urgently, and Katie watches their hands suddenly grip, and then, just as suddenly, release.

Outside, the smoke pours straight up from the smokestacks that are like giant barrels reaching into the night sky. The others—the others who are not so lucky, who did not pass by each other tonight and feel the warmth of a hand pressing their own—begin to softly feather down from the sky, their ashes landing on the hats and broad shoulders of the guards, who talk and spit and laugh.

When the first snowflakes touch Katie's cheeks, she raises her face to the sky and inhales deeply. She listens to the silence all around her, and she can almost feel it—she can almost feel the small stone being pushed into her palm with love.

7

The first thing Katie sees when she walks into the almost deserted Super Stop & Shop at 9:15 P.M. is that young checkout girl (Stacey or Tracy or something like that), the one who's always so happy and likes to chat it up and make lots of eye contact. *Not tonight,* Katie thinks, and then smiles and nods at the girl's energetic waving. She shakes the snow out of her hair, scoots down Aisle One to take the back way to the freezer section.

Always the night owl, Katie used to look forward to the girl's silly chatter and laughter, but back in June, just a month after Nick's murder, their light banter took an unexpected and unwelcome turn that still makes Katie squirm in her presence. The girl was packing up Katie's groceries and taking her money, all the while keeping up a steady patter of gossip about her boyfriend, who never had the time to do anything romantic.

"Like sitting there and watching him work on his stupid car all day is fun," she grumbled, but her pretty, smiling eyes said that it probably was, or at least she didn't mind it as much as she was expected to.

What a luxury, Katie thought as she gazed at the girl, to actually look for things to complain about. And then the longing for Nick's touch came again, vicious and breath-stealing, and she had to lean against the counter to keep from falling down. She blurted it out before she could stop herself.

"My husband's dead."

But the girl didn't cringe or look away; she nodded sadly, handed

Katie her change. Let the tips of her fingers rest in Katie's palm a beat longer than necessary.

"I know," she said. "I saw it on the news."

At first Katie was relieved that it was out in the open, but by the time she reached her car with her plastic bags, she felt betrayed. All along, this girl knew who she was, and she never said anything, never gave one single indication? Katie realized that it wasn't logical to be upset—after all, what was the girl supposed to say to her anyway? But despite her better judgment, Katie still can't help but feel a tinge of resentment every time she sees this girl's bright smile and larger-than-life wave. And ever since that night, too, she hasn't been able to shake the feeling that all the people around her—complete strangers—are watching her, discussing her life, thinking they know everything about her from just a glance.

She's leaning deep into the ice-cream freezer, trying to decide on either Breyer's cherry vanilla or mint chocolate chip, when she hears a familiar, happy voice.

"Katie? Is that you in there?"

Katie extracts herself from the freezer. Dottie Halverson, the short, portly nurse from the Warwick Center, stands a few feet away, smiling warmly at her.

"Oh, hey. Hey, Dottie."

Her heart instantly thumps like crazy, but Dottie's open and unguarded look quickly reminds Katie of the motherly nurse's kind nature, of the card she sent after Nick's funeral. *I'm sorry I couldn't be there, but I'm thinking of you. We are all thinking of you.*

"Stocking up for the weather?" Katie asks in a bumpy voice.

"Well, we *are* expecting a whole inch of snow, so of course Fred sent me out for critical supplies." Dottie shakes her head, laughing, and tilts her basket forward so Katie can peer inside: a clear plastic bag filled with sesame-seed hoagie buns, two packages of pink, slippery-looking deli meat, and a box of Ring Dings.

"I keep saying, 'Fred, what happens when you have a massive coronary from eating all this stuff? What about me? Do you realize how *embarrassing* it will be? I'm a nurse!'"

Katie tries to laugh along, then asks in a shy voice, "How *is* Fred?"

Dottie pats her hand. "Oh, you know Fred. Still the same. Still good for nothing," Dottie says, deadpan. Her eyes crinkle up, and she is laughing again, stepping forward to tug at Katie's coat sleeve.

Katie finally relaxes a little, smiles at the picture of Dottie and Fred together—how they walked with their bodies so close, Fred's hand resting lightly on Dottie's lower back. Fred always referred to Dottie as "my girl" to people, which made Dottie roll her eyes and click her tongue, but Katie also saw the blush of happiness that reached her cheeks every time.

"So I see you're stocking up on snow supplies, too," Dottie says.

"I've been making big decisions tonight," Katie says, trying to sound lighthearted. She holds up the carton of Breyer's. "Mint chocolate chip."

"Fred will be *so* proud when I tell him you were out buying ice cream instead of milk and bread." Dottie laughs, motions to the top of the aisle with her chin. "Are you ready to check out, lady?"

Katie nods, the use of Carly's nickname for her making her heart squeeze like a fist.

They walk up the aisle without speaking, turn left at the top, and begin the long walk toward the only lit register. Katie tries to slow their pace, to think of something cheerful and carefree to say, but the words and memories jumble inside her head, solid and strangling.

"Dottie," she says in a too-loud voice, stopping.

Dottie stops also, face expectant. Katie sees the sympathy there when Dottie recognizes her pleading look, but it's impossible to miss the uncertainty and hesitation lurking in her eyes as well.

"Oh, Katie," Dottie says, and takes a step toward her.

"No, no, don't—" Katie says, shaking her head, but she has no idea what she's trying to refuse.

Dottie nods. "Okay."

They stand like that for a moment, staring at different places on the floor. It sounds like someone has turned the Muzak up too loud; a bouncy version of "Little Jeannie" by Elton John bubbles down to them from the ceiling, airy and oppressive. Katie hears the squeak and whoosh of the automated doors opening, feels the short burst of cold air at her side and back, listens to the click of determined heels and the metallic sound of a woman's bracelets jangling into each other as she walks past. Everything around her seems magnified, loaded with a bewildering significance.

"We should probably—" Dottie says, turning and pointing to the register.

"Right."

Katie makes it only a few steps this time. "It's just—" she says, struggling, "just that—"

Dottie stops again, turns halfway to her.

"It's—" Katie gives up, lets out a frustrated breath and looks at the display of shampoo at the end of Aisle Eight. The bright fluorescent green and pink and orange bottles are garish, almost dizzying. IS YOUR HAIR TIRED? STREZZZZED OUT? the sign above the bottles asks her. There's a woman standing to the side of these words, her mouth wide open in a happy scream of elation, thrusting forward a pink bottle.

"I don't know, either, Katie."

She turns to Dottie.

"About everything," Dottie says. "I don't know what to say about it either." Another few seconds pass, more concentrated attention on the dirt caked into the blocky cracks in the linoleum floor. When Katie raises her head, she sees Dottie staring at the lit register.

"Don't do that, okay?" Katie says quietly.

"What?"

"That." Katie points to the register. "Don't want to get away from me, too. Not you."

"Oh, Katie," she says, flushing deeply.

"I couldn't handle that, because . . ." Katie trails off.

"Katie, I'm so sorry." Dottie smiles sadly. "But I do, I have to go," she says, turning away.

And then the months without Nick turn into a concentrated liquid inside Katie's legs, fingers; it's difficult to stand, to even hold the ice cream anymore. She knows she's going to lose it, really lose it, if she doesn't say something—*anything*.

"It's gone!" Katie shouts at Dottie's retreating figure.

Dottie stops, turns around slowly.

"It's like . . . like everything good is gone," Katie says, scratching at her forehead with her free hand, the ice cream numbing her fingers on the other. "But . . . but I keep thinking that maybe if I were good enough—if I were *different*—then maybe . . . maybe I would have found a way to keep it."

She nods hopefully at Dottie, waits for her acknowledgment, her understanding. The struggle is playing across Dottie's face, her eyes blinking quickly. Maybe it's a legal issue, maybe it's something Donna Treadmont has advised the employees of the Warwick Center (*Whatever you do, don't talk to her!*), but Katie knows, she just knows that when Dottie walks away now, another part of her—another big, irreplaceable part of her—is going to evaporate, just *vanish*.

When Dottie moves to her side, Katie can't help it—a quick, grateful sob comes bursting out. She clamps a hand over her mouth.

Dottie's voice is soft, earnest. "No one knows what to say anymore, honey. It all got so complicated, so quickly." Katie allows Dottie to take her free hand. "But sometimes I think—no, I *know*—that no matter how complicated it is right now, some parts don't have to end. Some parts are still there."

"I don't . . . do you mean . . ."

Dottie lowers her head, choosing her words. When she looks back up at Katie, her face is determined. "You could be a part of Jerry's life again— No, please, Katie, listen," she says in a rush. "If you would just go see him, just once, I know you'd feel better. He's like a frightened child right now, and he needs you, you're the only one he wants right now—"

Katie yanks her hand from Dottie, backs away shaking her head.

"There's a list of people who can visit him," Dottie says. "They only allow so many, but Patricia could get you on that list, I know she could if you wanted to see him—"

"No—" Katie says, taking another step back, her heart roaring inside her ears.

"They finally allowed a night-light," Dottie says. "We gave Donna the Bugs Bunny one, that one you bought him years ago when you moved into the house? Bedtime is even worse now, because he's thinking of his mother all the time, and how God is going to come and punish him. You've seen it with your own eyes, Katie. If you could try to remember—"

Katie backs into the bright shampoo display, feels the heavy bottles crashing down around her, on her thighs, her left foot. Before Dottie can say another word, though, Tracy, or Casey, steps out from behind her register in her green apron to flag them down.

"Over here, ladies! Only one open!" she yoo-hoos. "Don't worry about the *bot-tles!*"

"My God, Dottie," Katie whispers. She turns, walks briskly in the direction of the register, almost trips over a rolling green bottle.

"Katie," Dottie says behind her, "he's scared, but—but Jerry thinks he did a good thing. He thinks he *saved* Nick."

Katie's entire body jerks at these words, one violent internal wrench. She shakes her head and waves Dottie off without turning around. *Too much.*

When she reaches the counter, she drops the ice cream on the conveyer belt and focuses hard on the girl's name tag: Tricia. *Tricia.*

"Hey, you," Tricia says happily, reaching for the carton of ice cream. Katie's face must be panicked, because Tricia's eyes go wide and she sucks in her breath. Katie looks helplessly at her, pulls her purse onto the counter as the girl scans the ice cream. She keeps her head lowered and tugs at the zipper, but it's stuck; there's white tissue woven into the teeth from the inside and it won't budge. Dottie's footsteps come up behind her.

"Hey, Justin?" Tricia says in a smooth, professional voice Katie has never heard before, "Are you able to take a customer?"

Katie turns to the front of the store, sees the pimply kid behind the customer-service desk looking around the empty store. He humps his shoulders up.

"Sure," he says, and then Tricia is smiling big over Katie's shoulder.

"Ma'am? Justin will take you over at the customer-service counter so you don't have to wait."

Katie lowers her head gratefully, keeps tugging at the zipper with trembling fingers.

"Katie?" Dottie says behind her, but Katie keeps her head down and shakes it slowly this time. "Okay. Okay," Dottie says and moves away.

"Here," Tricia says gently, and takes the purse out of Katie's fumbling hands. She jiggles the catch a little, unzips the purse in one fluid motion. The girl reaches into the purse, shuffles around, pulls out Katie's wallet.

"Cash?" Tricia asks.

Katie nods without looking up, watches Tricia's perfectly mani-cured fingers unsnap the wallet, flip through the bills, pull out a five. The polish is a deep, shiny red, with alternating white X's and O's in the center of each nail. Katie closes her eyes, listens to the beep of the register, to her heart pumping, pumping.

She's not sure how long she stays like this, only knows that when the girl finally speaks, her rib cage doesn't feel like it's going to explode or collapse anymore.

"She's gone," Tricia says, and Katie opens her eyes. The girl puts the change into her wallet and the wallet back into her purse. She zips up the purse and pushes it toward Katie.

"Thank you," Katie says quietly.

"You're welcome." They hold each other's eyes for a few, quiet beats.

"She worked with my husband," Katie says.

"I figured it might have something to do with that."

"Yeah."

"It must be, like, so hard all the time," Tricia says.

"You can't imagine."

"Guess not."

Another small beat.

"I . . . I like your nails," Katie says.

The girl looks down at her nails. She takes a little step back and flares her fingers against her green apron. "*Très chic,* no?" she says with a grin in her voice.

Tricia flutters her fingers, and it is only then that Katie notices the swell under the green apron.

"Almost four months," Tricia says, nodding and resting her hands on top of her stomach.

"Oh, my God."

"I know," the girl says, "Kenny is *so* freaked."

Katie pulls the straps of her purse over her shoulder, speechless.

"My mom's refusing to help now, too. She's all like, 'You play, you pay,' but I don't really care. She's always been a wicked jerk to me any-way. That's why I'm in my own place already."

"What about—what about your father?"

Tricia shrugs. "I haven't seen *him* in ages."

Katie knows that she should say something encouraging, but all she can think is that this world, this whole *stupid* world, is hopeless. Tricia pops the ice cream into a beige plastic bag.

"So what will you two do now?" Katie asks.

Tricia shrugs again. "I don't know what *Kenny* will do, but I'm having a baby," she says.

Katie blinks at her a few times, shakes her head. "But—but won't it be so difficult, all by yourself?"

"I'm not saying he's refusing to help, and believe me, I'll be totally freaked if he bounces. But what can you do?" She pushes the plastic bag toward Katie.

Katie just stares.

"Be careful out there," Tricia says, "because even, like, this little bit of snow makes the roads pretty slick."

8

By the time Katie rounds the corner and turns onto her street, the snow has slowed to barely a trickle, but she keeps her wipers on full blast anyway. Tears pool at the back of her throat, inch upward with every swipe of the blades that seem too close to her face.

Jerry thinks he did a good thing. He thinks he saved Nick.

In an instant all the whys inside her head doubled, tripled—killing Nick was *good*? Jerry wanted to *save* him? From *what*? And then always back to this, the fear coiling up tightly inside her: Where do I fit into this picture, into that day in the gym?

She swerves into her driveway, nearly slams into the rear of her parents' gray Chevy; she backs up, tires spinning and shooting rocks out into the street, and then pulls alongside their car.

Her mother is in the passenger seat, arms crossed, her platinum wig almost touching the roof of the car. Her eyes are stuck on the windshield, lips pressed tightly together: the perfect picture of parental indignation. Upset, Katie assumes, because she hung up on her earlier.

"Way to pick your battles, Mom," she mumbles. She grabs the bag of ice cream, shoulders the car door open, almost falls out onto the slick rocks.

Her shoes slip and slide as she charges past the Chevy and up the walkway toward her father, who is packed into his bulky blue Eskimo coat, the brown fur around the hood framing his long, angular face. He digs into a bag of rock salt with a blue plastic cup, spreads it generously onto the bottom stair.

"Just in case," her father booms, holding up the bag with a gloved hand.

She pushes past him onto the stairs, the salt crunching underfoot. "It isn't a good time," Katie says in a strained voice.

"Took the driveway there a bit quick, didn't you, sweetie?"

She whirls around on her father from the top step, her warm breath exploding into the frosty air. "It's barely snowing, Dad!" she shouts at him. She swipes at the thick coat of salt with the side of her shoe. "What the *hell*?"

Katie's heart sinks at the shocked look on her father's face, her fury instantly evaporating. She lowers her head apologetically at this betrayal—she's the one who doesn't yell, the one with infinite patience for him, the one who listens and nods and never questions his actions, no matter what. She inhales deeply, feels the cold air enter her lungs. Counts to three.

"I'm sorry, Dad," she says in a choked voice, turning away and ramming her key into the front door.

"It was your mother's idea," her father says behind her in an unusually quiet, confidential tone. "She insisted we come over. Got me out of my pj's and everything."

Katie turns back to her father. He motions with the plastic cup toward the idling Chevy. Her mother hasn't moved an inch, but her window is a quarter of the way down now. Katie skips her eyes to the dark street, to a patch of melting snow glistening under the streetlight.

"She's worried, sweetie," her father says, his hazel eyes slanting up at her.

Katie isn't sure what's worse, the curious, greedy stares of strangers and reporters, or this—a wounded look of love from her dad, who stands shivering on her walkway. She looks at her front lawn, at the wet tips of grass that sparkle and bend. Somewhere in the distance, a dog barks to be let in, short, mournful pleas that echo into the night.

"Dad, I didn't mean it—"

Her father holds up one finger, wiggles his nose; he lets go of a string of noisy sneezes with gusto. Pulls a white handkerchief from his coat pocket.

"Bless you," Katie says.

He nods, trumpets loudly into the hankie. "Tough day, huh?" he says, swiping the cloth back and forth under his nose.

"Yeah."

Her father stares intently at her for exactly two seconds, and then his face does that thing it always does when anyone around him shows too much emotion: it fills with alarm, then almost as quickly shifts to a look of pure concentration—eyes suddenly heavy-lidded and trained on a spot on the ground. *It's your father's "need to split the check" look,* Nick used to say, and then he'd scrunch up his face like her father's and scratch his chin with his index finger. *Let's see, twenty-four fifty for my veal parm and Grace's shrimp scampi . . .*

Her father slowly folds his handkerchief into a square, his long fingers smoothing the cloth with each crease. After he makes a fold, he strokes the cloth carefully, uses his index finger to make a crease for another fold. The movements are exact and meticulous, soothing in their repetition.

Although the snow hasn't quite stopped, there is a stillness in the air, a motionless calm that falls around them. It suddenly feels okay, standing here now and watching her father's precise motions, like the world has finally shut down for the night, has closed in around her and her parents and these small, deliberate gestures; a respite, then, into something solid, into familiar relationships that aren't perfect, but recognizable and constant. For the first time today, she feels the muscles in her lower back give a little.

She smiles at the reverent way her father finally offers her the square of cloth when he's done pressing it. Katie shakes her head no, shifts the grocery bag onto her forearm. Her father's face brightens, eyes locking onto the bag as he stuffs the hankie back into his pocket. He clears his throat, winks at her.

"You know," he begins in his normally loud voice again, "you can always *freeze* that bread. Your mother does it all the time. No harm in it, and we always have it when it snows and we can't get out." Her father peeks over at the car, and Katie turns, sees her mother nodding in agreement from inside.

Katie turns back to her father, to the hopeful look he gives her. It's the same one he's used since she and Dana were children, the one that says, *Why not just get it over with so we can all move on?*

"Okay," she says, "I'm going." She drops her purse and the grocery bag onto the heaping salt, takes small, crunchy steps down the stairs.

"Good girl," he says, patting her arm.

By the time she gets to the car, the window is rolled back up. She listens to the motor rev from the heater kicking on, watches her mother stare stonily ahead. Fat snowflakes sputter onto the windshield and instantly melt into tiny puddles. From a few houses away, the dog barks again, this time more urgently, a steady stream of indignant yelps.

Katie leans in until her face is only inches from her mother's on the other side of the window. She taps the glass twice with a fingernail. Her mother turns her head, stares at her with raised eyebrows. She rolls down the window.

"Kate," she says in a crisp, matter-of-fact tone.

"Mom," Katie says, matching her tone exactly.

Her mother leans back, startled. "Oh, no, do not mock me in this moment, Kate," she says, "you don't want to do that." She pulls the collar closed on her coat.

"Sorry," Katie says. "And I'm sorry about earlier, too. Okay?"

Her mother lifts her chin. "For what?"

"I'm sorry for hanging up on you, Mom."

"It wasn't right."

"No, it wasn't."

Her mother nods, finally appeased. She shifts her body all the way around to face Katie. "It's just rude, hon."

"I know."

"Your father was beside himself," her mother says.

Katie turns to check on her father, who is slowly salting his way back down the walk. The layer of salt, even thicker than the one on the top stair, twinkles in the light. He sees Katie watching, grins and raises the plastic cup like he's making a toast to her.

Her mother scoots Katie out of the way with her hand, leans out the window. Her wig shifts up on the left, and she tugs it back down, shakes her head impatiently.

"Not so thick, Jimmy," she calls out. "We aren't in a *blizzard,* for God's sake."

She rolls her eyes at Katie. "More is always better with that one."

Her mother gives her a lopsided smile, reaches up to tuck Katie's hair behind one ear.

"Mom—"

"No, hold on," her mother says. She dips her head toward the driver's side. "Hop in."

Katie walks around the front of the car, slips into the driver's seat. She shuts the door behind her, feels the heat press into her like a thick woolen blanket—it must be a hundred degrees inside the car.

"Whoa," Katie says, and reaches for the heater before remembering how cold her mother gets these days, an aftereffect of the chemo even though her last session was nearly five years ago. "Doctor says her internal temp is off, probably permanent," her father told Katie over the phone last month when it first started to get chilly at night. "But everything's good. Blood work, levels, everything," he said. "Except this cold thing." And then, in a loud, magnified voice meant for her mother: "But I told the doc, 'Hell, we'll take her any way she comes, hot *or* cold.'"

"You can turn the heat down a little if you want," her mother says, motioning to the dashboard, "Or crack your window."

Katie rolls the window open a little, unzips her coat and stares at her mother's wig, which has shifted up on the left again.

"This one never stays put," her mother complains. She slaps down the visor, tugs both sides of the wig, and scans her face in the mirror.

Though neither one would admit it, her mother and sister are alike in so many respects that it amazes Katie at times. The way they move and behave even in small moments like this—like they've always known their place in the world, are comfortable with themselves and their bodies in a way that boggles Katie. Sometimes she still catches herself in a room with both of them and one word forms clearly about herself: "incidental."

"The tacking is *still* too slippery on this one," her mother says.

Katie looks past her mother toward her father, who is up to his elbow in the bag of salt. So different from all of them, Katie thinks, a sweet man with too much time on his hands, who loves to alter little everyday events with his wife into grand tales full of peril.

"Jimmy, please," her mother had said just last week, waving

him off. "We did *not* almost die at the Citizens Bank drive-through yesterday."

It amazes Katie that while her father enjoys nothing better than to tell his stories to an audience now—a simple trip to the grocery store will stretch out to a half hour—he still can't understand Katie's need to listen to other people's stories. To hear the inflections or the wavering in their voices, to watch the way they move or sigh or keep their eyes lowered, to witness how their bodies shift when their words won't come out the way they want.

She's nothing like either of her parents, Katie thinks now, fanning herself with one hand against the heat. So who, then, is she like?

"Two things," her mother says, flipping up the visor. "One, Michael and Dana are coming to Thanksgiving this year, because his parents are going on a cruise, even though it's their turn to have all their kids for the holiday." Her mother lowers her voice, face clenching up with annoyance. "You just know they're going to expect Michael and Dana at Christmas now, but I won't give in on this one, Katie, and I've already warned your sister. I won't go two Christmases in a row without them, just because his parents have decided to be spontaneous for the first time in their lives."

"I don't think it'll be a problem, Mom."

"It better not be," she says, shifting in her seat to regard Katie for a few seconds. Her face loses its harsh edges. "And I know things are stressful right now with this court business, and it certainly isn't going to get any easier, but we want you there, too, hon. Your Aunt Ginny will be there this year, and she misses you. She said so just a few days ago. We all do."

"Maybe for a little while," Katie says, running her sleeve across her forehead.

"Good," her mother says, nodding. "And two," she says, and here her voice becomes gentle, almost hesitant. Her hand travels up and rests on Katie's upper arm and stays there—never a good sign. "I know it's going to be difficult to get through this trial, but I want you to consider something."

Uh-oh. Katie pinches the front of her shirt, makes a tent, and pushes the fabric in and out.

"It's about these films," her mother says.

"What about them?" Katie asks, ready for the brief peace to crash down around them again.

"Now, I know we don't talk a lot about your work, because it's private and yours and we had *that* discussion years ago. But you just spend so much time watching these people," her mother says. "And I just think that they take away from what should be essential right now."

Katie can see from the look on her mother's face that this is supposed to be a Big Moment between them, a Mother-Daughter Event of Great Importance, the real reason her parents are here tonight and why her father is still salting the walkway, even though the snow has finally tapered off completely.

"Is this about the Nick thing, Mom? Why you don't want me to mention his name anymore?" Katie hates that she can't let it go, hates how her voice sounds, filled with childish defensiveness.

Her mother rolls her eyes, waves at the air with her free hand. "No, not exactly, Kate."

"Then what?"

Her mother's brow furrows momentarily, and she casts her eyes to her lap, struggling for words, it seems, a vulnerable, foreign look on her face that instantly reminds Katie of childhood. Katie sits very still, watching her mother's internal battle, and suddenly remembers, with bizarre but startling clarity, a school project in the fifth grade where students made small holes in the bottoms of eggs. They emptied the contents, leaving the fragile skins of the empty eggs thin and brittle. When Katie was halfway through painting her shell, she saw the long crack snaking up one side. Her mother's face looks just like that fragile egg now—delicate, as if it could split open at any minute.

"Mom?"

"Okay, well, I'm trying, Katie, give me a break." Her mother pulls the collar on her coat together, lets out a small sigh. "Well, it's almost like—it's almost like you become *consumed* with these people, Kate. And I think, especially now during the trial, that it takes away from what matters the most."

"I told you already, I thought it would help me avoid reliving the emotions of the trial every night. A way to work and also escape—"

"Exactly," her mother almost shouts, slapping the dashboard. *"Exactly,* Kate."

Katie shakes her head. "Exactly what? You want me to spend my nights replaying everything that happens in court?"

"No, not replay the days," her mother says. "But now that Nick is gone, now that another chapter is beginning in your life, just try to pay attention to what really matters."

"Which is what, Mom?"

Her mother leans back to stare at Katie. "Well, *you,* Katie," she finally says in a surprised tone. She reaches over, pokes Katie twice in the chest. "Just *you.*"

"I don't even know what that means," Katie says, frustration making the words thick.

"Yes, that's my point *exactly.*"

"I'm fine, Mom, if that's what you're getting at. Everything is just fine."

"You're always 'just fine,' Katie."

"Shouldn't that make you feel better?"

"I don't need to feel better. This isn't about *me.*"

They both turn when they hear Katie's father clear his throat outside the car. He stands in front of the hood, hands locked behind his back.

"Well, that ought to do it," he says loudly, surveying the walkway and the stairs with approval.

Katie leans over and plants a quick kiss on her mother's cheek. "We can finish this tomorrow, okay?" She doesn't wait for an answer, pops open the car door.

She steps out into the freezing night too fast—her left heel skids forward on the slick rocks, but her father is there in a second, his hand underneath one elbow.

"Steady there," he says.

She stares at the lumpy salt winking up at her from the walk, at the wet, patchy drifts of snow on her front lawn. The dog is still barking somewhere, a mournful sound in the distance. Katie steps back from the car, watches her father put one leg inside.

"I hooked your purse and grocery bag on the doorknob," he says.

He looks like he's about to fold his tall frame into the Chevy, but instead he leans toward Katie. She starts to offer him her cheek, but her father just looks at her, his hazel eyes full of concern.

"Ice cream, Katie?" he whispers. "I thought you went to the market for bread?"

•

The house is completely dark inside. Katie keeps her back against the door, watches the headlights of her parents' car crawl up the wall and zip away. She has needed this silence all day, has craved it ever since she stumbled out of court this morning, and yet now that she's by herself, the full weight of it settles down around her. And then Dottie's words come again, puncturing the thick quiet. Jerry saved Nick? What happened in that month of her and Nick's trial separation? And then a familiar darkness sweeps through her body: What if Katie hadn't asked Nick to leave? *Would he still be alive?*

In the kitchen she pulls a serving spoon out of the silverware drawer, tears off the cardboard zipper on the ice-cream carton, picks at the extra cardboard that never comes off. Carton in one hand, spoon in the other, Katie walks to the blinking answering machine, shoveling a towering spoonful of mint chocolate chip into her mouth. With the handle of the spoon, she pokes the red message button, then digs into the ice cream again.

There is a long beep, and then six messages: a reporter from the *Providence Journal,* wondering if she can "chat" with Katie for a few minutes; Dana, reminding her to call if Katie wants her in court tomorrow; Todd, a grad student from RISD who helped Katie years ago with lighting, hoping to pick up some extra work; a perky woman from Whirlpool who enunciates her words with a sinuousness that makes every *S* snake out a few seconds too long (Nick would have loved her); and her friend Jill, her voice way too casual, asking when they can grab lunch and catch up. Katie deletes each message as soon as she gets the gist of what they want from her, and she's about to delete the last one—the telling air space and a bit of static must mean a telemarketer—but freezer head hits her full blast. She drops the spoon and the ice cream into the sink, sandwiches her head between her palms. A man's tentative, feminine voice fills the kitchen.

"Hi, this is Paul Minsky from Oceanside Realty? Not sure if I have the right number, but if this is the same Nick Burrelli that visited last spring, I have great news about that cottage on Topsail Island? North Carolina? It's up for sale again, and the owner asked if you might be interested. If you are, give me a call at the office at 9:10—"

Katie fumbles in the junk drawer for a marker, one hand still glued to her temple. She scribbles the names and number on a yellow Post-it with the word "cottage" beside it. She presses the sticky part of the paper across the top of the answering machine and slowly draws a big question mark beside "Topsail Island." Last spring? She stares at the Post-it, the questions rising, until she hears the metallic sound of garbage cans clanging into each other in her backyard.

Out on the deck, she peers into the night, suddenly bright with moonlight. Her two metal cans are lined up neatly by the shed, the sides wet and glistening. She crosses her arms against the cold, walks to the edge of the deck. The moonlight pushes through the barren branches of the trees, casting striped blocks of light and shadow onto her lawn and shed. There is a fine mist on everything outside, a hazy fog that settles onto the grass and the dead leaves and the branches above her head. Katie leans over and rests her elbows on the railing, feeling sleepy finally, grateful that the day is at last winding down, but then Nick joins her once again. *It wasn't anyone's fault,* she hears him say, and suddenly the moonlight loses its soft edges, makes the beads of water everywhere look like tiny drops of glass, like one good wind could shatter it all, splintering her backyard into a million pieces.

9

They had been lovers for only four months, but Katie could already sense when Nick wasn't beside her at night; sometimes his absence pulled her up from her dreams, arms paddling wildly as if from a great depth, until she surfaced and called out to him.

She felt it now, just before she took in a deep breath and opened her eyes. He was by the window that looked out on the hospital's expansive parking lot, sitting in a boxy chair with his long legs dangling over the arm. Half his body in the moonlight that shone into the darkened room, the other in shadow. Her chest stretched with tenderness.

—Hey, she whispered.

He turned to her. —Hey, he said, hopping up. He moved to her side. —How do you feel?

—Sleepy, she said, motioning to the bag of Demerol hanging by the side of her hospital bed.

—No more cramps?

—Almost gone, she said. And then, taking another deep breath: —I guess—I guess we didn't have to get married after all, huh?

Nick squinted down at her. —Dana and your parents just left, he said. —They'll be back in the morning.

Katie nodded, concentrated on the bumps her knees made from underneath the scratchy white sheet.

—The doctor came in earlier, too, Nick said, his voice softer. —It wasn't anyone's fault. It's called a spontaneous abortion. Probably meant there was something really wrong with the baby.

Katie nodded. She wasn't brave enough to look at Nick—the loss felt like a punishment for her infinite craving for him to be close, to have his hands stealing over her body.

—Do you regret it? she asked.

Nick shrugged. —It was too soon to be thinking about kids—

—No, Katie interrupted, finally looking at him. —I mean the wedding. Do you regret getting married?

—It was the right thing to do, Nick said with conviction.

She laced her fingers into his, watched their hands become one. —But now? she asked.

There was the briefest pause, the briefest hesitation—so brief, in fact, that she could almost ignore it, could almost pretend that it didn't happen. She could almost fool herself that his fingers didn't loosen inside hers for a quick, barely perceptible beat.

He looked up, smiled in that shy way that always pulled at her. —Of course not.

Katie lay back and closed her eyes. Stopped herself from tearing the hospital sheet off and pulling him closer, from pulling him down on the bed with her and saying, *It would have worked better if you said it right away. If you moved your eyes to mine, and pulled our hands up to your chest, it would have been perfect.*

10

The equipment is cumbersome and the light at the top of the base-ment stairs is out again, but Katie's feet have trudged up and down the carpeted stairs so many times that they know the way by feel. To-night, before she finally ends her day, she needs to see Arthur cradle Sarah's hand in both of his again, to see Sarah's shy smile once more when Arthur teases her in his gruff voice about their courtship—to at least try to make some order of all this footage she knows so well. *Not just an escape, Mom,* she thinks, *but my profession.* The perfect response, but only when her mother isn't there to hear it.

At the bottom of the stairs, she elbows on the bright overhead lights and pads onto the cold tile in her thick wool socks. Her workstation is exactly as she left it two nights ago: a disaster. Strewn across her desk are dozens of papers, sketch pads, markers, videotapes, cutting scissors, reels of film, and paper plates with globby piles of drying ketchup or half-eaten sandwiches on them. Her editing board is no better, cov-ered with more of the same. Beside it are stacked boxes filled with re-search papers, books, a turned-over garbage can with small cellophane squares spilling out.

Katie eyes the other half of the basement with longing: completely empty except for an old red beanbag chair in the center—what Nick always referred to as "his side." Katie walks to her desk, the cold pen-etrating the wool and seeping up into the soles of her feet. She dumps the projector onto her desk, snaps on the space heater, and rubs her hands together.

This basement, so open and full of possibility, was the selling point of the house, or at least that's what Nick told people. *It's perfect for Katie, for her work,* he said to her parents, and showed them where he planned to install the pull-down screen on the wall. *We'll put a comfortable chair here, her editing board and file cabinets there,* he said pointing, her parents nodding in agreement. Nick may have convinced them, but Katie knew that the real sticking point with the house was the neighborhood in Warwick Neck—stately, distinguished, jam-packed with doctors, lawyers, and businessmen respected in the community. It was the prestige that Nick craved, the image he wanted to project to the world, but with Katie's never-ending filming expenses and Nick's salary, they couldn't really afford it. And then Nick's mother came through as she always did since they had married—with a grudging generosity that didn't seem to faze Nick at all and made Katie cringe whenever she called. *It's a gift. You don't have to pay me back,* Candice said on the phone after they returned from the closing. But every time Katie thought of the amount of that check—big enough to make their monthly mortgage payments manageable—every time she heard the satisfied tone in Candice's voice, she understood that her mother-in-law was trying to prove something, to show Katie up in a way that Katie could never quite figure out. And every time she gave them a small loan for more filming supplies (saying, before Katie could hand the phone off to Nick, *I hope you have enough supplies to see this one through*), Katie wondered what she had to do to show this woman that she loved Nick the way he deserved. On her rare visits, Candice watched Katie closely when Nick turned away or left the room, her dark eyes tripping over Katie's body, quickly assessing, while the sunny smile remained on her face. Katie was grateful when her mother-in-law moved to California shortly after she and Nick were married—almost like a jilted lover, Katie had wanted to say to Nick more than once, but she knew better by then.

She walks over to the three long shelves that Nick installed into the wall beside her editing board just last winter. There, lined up in no particular order, are canisters of all sizes and colors, waiting for her. Katie flips through the ones on the top shelf, searching for the reel where Sarah describes Arthur's marriage proposal, when she hears a small creaking noise. And then, before she can get her hands to the end of the shelf where it meets the wall, the top shelf bumps down to the second shelf, and the canisters skid down and crash, one by one, onto the floor. The tinny sound of metal striking metal reverberates off the basement walls, rings in her ears; one smaller, rust-colored canister breaks free and rolls across the floor before bumping into a stack of newspapers. Katie watches it wobble in circles, then slap sideways onto the tile floor. Then, only silence.

"Perfect," she mumbles, kneeling down to pick up a large silver canister from the middle of the mess.

She snaps the reel onto the spool, feeds the film onto the spindle. The film catches, hums forward, and she flicks on the bulb. She reaches for the sound machine, pulls back on impulse: she only needs to see Arthur and Sarah together before she ends this night and, she hopes, falls into a gray, dreamless sleep before starting all over again tomorrow.

At first there's just a fuzzy image, but then the focus adjusts. Instead of Sarah and Arthur waiting to greet her, though, there is an extreme black-and-white close-up of Nick's face.

"Shit."

Katie's eyes skip to the jumbled canisters on the floor, then back to the screen. The basement shrinks, the darkness deepening outside the projector's light. She watches as the camera angle widens, and then there is Nick in his dark suit and striped tie, holding a small plaque against his chest. The Warwick Center employees and clients stand in a semicircle around him, smiling and clapping. Nick dips his head modestly as the applause continues. Eddie Rodriguez, the director of the recreation program, is on the right, two of his fingers in his mouth for that shattering whistle of his. The cameras flash and wink all around Nick, and he shakes his head, runs a hand across the back of his neck.

An award ceremony from years ago, one in a long line of gatherings to reward Nick's devotion to his clients. Katie remembers this one (something to do with his new methods in speech-articulation work), and she remembers how she felt, too, standing across the elegant conference room at the Marriott Hotel, feeling miles away from the action as she filmed— longing to clap along, to join everyone in the half circle surrounding her husband. But most of all she remembers wanting Nick to look her way, to look directly into the camera and see her there behind the lens, recording his success on film. She yelled *Over here!* at least three times, but he couldn't hear her above the clapping and shouts of congratulations.

"Over here, Nick," she calls out now, her voice hollow in the cold basement.

The camera sweeps to the right and there is the program director, the normally stern Patricia Kuhlman, looking relaxed for once as she crosses her arms and cradles both her elbows in her hands—the admiration in her face unmistakable. In the background the camera catches Dottie Halverson's husband, Fred, bending over a steaming tray on a long banquet table, plate piled high. Chafing pans are lined up on top of a white tablecloth, a long flickering candle between each one, but the view is suddenly blocked, because Nick's colleagues and clients, as if on cue, are closing the gap around him to shake his hand, embrace him.

Katie remembers this moment perfectly now, rests her hand on her stomach and presses down.

The camera jostles, and then there is Jerry, turning back to mouth *Sorry* at Katie for bumping into her as he moves away from her side. The camera follows his lumbering walk into the center of the crowd, the direct path he makes toward Nick. It captures the way the employees and clients automatically shift aside to allow Jerry into the fold, hands reaching out and slapping him good-naturedly on the back. And then there is Nick, stepping forward, his dark eyes catching Jerry's; it's impossible to miss the pride in Nick's face as he slings an arm around Jerry's neck and pulls him in close. The camera zooms in, frames Nick and Jerry smiling—Nick's face even more handsome because of his happiness, Jerry's face pudgy and filled with childlike joy. And then the camera pans back, catches Jerry suddenly squirming inside Nick's arms.

Jerry swerves his large body halfway around, his face scrunching up, looking for the camera—searching for Katie, to share his happiness with her. He finds her, stares directly into the lens from across the room, his reaction instant: a dazzling smile lights his entire face, makes his eyes fill with delight.

She abandons the projector, telling herself it's the sound of trash cans banging into each other outside again that urges her back up the basement stairs, two at a time. She twists her ankle on the last step, limps through the kitchen and out the slider door.

The weather has shifted—a little warmer now. She heads across the deck toward the stairs, a quick check confirming that one of her trash cans is knocked over. Too cold for raccoons, she thinks, and stops short at the stairs: her neighbor Sandy's dog, a terrier with a black head and white body, and a long snout, stands on the matted lawn next to the deck, one paw resting on the bottom step. The dog gazes up at her with perfect innocence in his black eyes; he scratches once on the wood, his stubby white tail sticking straight up in the air.

"Jack?"

This one word sets his tail wagging, his head turned sideways.

"What are you doing here?"

The dog places his other paw on the step, whines softly. Was that Jack barking earlier when her parents came by? Katie wonders. Has he been out in the cold this entire time?

"Go on home now."

Jack's head twists the opposite way. He whines again, eyes begging. The smooth white fur on his back shivers.

"Oh, okay, fine," Katie says, and Jack bounds up the deck stairs, bumps into her shins and runs into the house.

Inside, Katie checks the clock on the stove—10:33, probably too late to call a house with small kids and a baby—and watches Jack click his way back and forth in the kitchen, his long black nose stuck firmly to the floor. The dog raises his head quickly—he's caught the whiff of something good—and makes his way to the sink, where the ice cream sits in a goopy mess, half in the carton, half in the basin. He jumps up, two front paws resting against the cupboard, and turns hopeful black eyes her way.

"I don't think so. C'mon."

She walks over, grabs Jack by his collar, and pulls. The dog's front paws hit the floor, and he takes two steps before extending his front legs and putting on his brakes; he suddenly pants like he's been running for hours. A metal tag on his collar burns into Katie's knuckle—it's like a thin wafer of solid ice.

"Don't worry, I'm not throwing you out."

Jack follows her to the kitchen closet. She finds a length of rope in a box hidden at the back, kneels down to thread it underneath his collar. Jack's body spasms at the close contact, and he covers Katie's face and hands with kisses. She scratches behind his ears, smiles.

"C'mon. Your mom must be worried."

•

The walk to Sandy's house is short and wet. All the houses are dark now; the only sound comes from Jack's nails clicking on the pavement and the faint whirring of a sanding truck in the distance. Above them the wet tree branches glint in the light cast from the moon and a streetlamp. A cold drop escapes from one, falls down the back of Katie's coat and splashes onto her neck. She shivers, pulls her collar tight. Jack looks over his shoulder at her, happy smile in place.

"What are you looking at?"

It's been months since Katie has walked up to Sandy's door and knocked, and even though she actually has a legitimate reason to be here this late at night, she hesitates on the top stair. Through the bay window, she sees Sandy move into view with her baby daughter in her arms, bumping her up and down, her lips *shhhhhshhhh*-ing. Even at this hour, even with a crying baby and a worried expression on her face, Sandy looks beautiful: thick dirty-blond hair tied back in a ponytail, flawless, peach-colored skin, and full, pouting lips. More like a teenager playing house than a woman only a couple of years younger than Katie's own thirty-two years.

When Katie first moved into the neighborhood, she was flattered by this woman's attentions, her desire to chitchat and speculate about the people who lived around them, but tonight seeing Sandy has the opposite effect on her. She feels awkward and plain, wonders now if it was just her ability to engage in this gossip, to listen to Sandy's drawn-out ruminations, that was the real attraction in the first place. And then Katie has an unexpected but intense desire to talk to Jill, to finally ask her about Amy—if Jill would still be her friend today if Amy hadn't married and moved all the way to Michigan years ago.

Sandy turns, paces back. The baby's face is pleated with red blotches of rage, her tiny fingers balled up into fists. Katie stares at this woman who has so pointedly avoided her since Nick's death, and she wonders if anything worse than a colicky baby has ever intruded into her ideal, protected little world. *It could,* she wants to say to Sandy now. *Shit happens, you know.*

Jack barks up at her, breaks her reverie; she bends down to pet him, tries to compose a casual expression before she knocks softly, but the door is already opening. Sandy stands in the doorway, holding the baby far back on her hip, away from the cold. The little girl takes one puckered look at Katie and turns her head to howl in protest.

"Katie?" Sandy says in a voice soft with surprise. She looks down at Jack. "I thought I heard you out here, bud."

While Sandy leans down to pat Jack, Katie peeks into the home that used to be so familiar—the expensive leather furniture littered with coloring books and cookie crumbs, the lush plants escaping their pots, the ficus tree that reaches halfway up to the cathedral ceiling. Scattered along with the blinking electronics and knickknacks from trips abroad are stuffed animals, racing cars, and tipped-over game boxes with the pieces spilling out onto the hardwood floors. A big flat-screen TV flickers in the background, muted.

Sandy rises, bumps the baby up and down on her hip, and the little girl's crying settles into a grating whine. Sandy sneaks a look at Katie, turns back quickly to kiss her daughter's head, and Katie thinks how tired she is of this: the way people look at her all the time now, their faces filled with hesitation or confusion about what they should say—or the way Sandy's face is right now, filled with almost childlike guilt. Katie looks down at Jack as if to say, *Don't worry, he's the only reason I'm here.*

Sandy smacks her forehead. "Oh, God, I'm sorry, you must be freezing out there. Come in, come in," she says, taking the rope from Katie. Sandy points a finger at Jack. "Not you, bud. *Stay.*"

Katie watches as Sandy hooks the rope around the outside door handle and shuts the door firmly in Jack's face.

She turns to Katie, tries a bright smile, fails. She dips her head down and picks at the baby's yellow sock. Katie shifts from one foot to the other, waiting.

"God, you must hate me, huh?" Sandy finally says quietly, peering up at Katie through long lashes.

Instead of answering, Katie strokes the baby's pajamaed leg with one finger. "She's so big now."

"I'm pretty sure she's allergic to the dog," Sandy says, gesturing with her chin toward the door, and now Katie can see that the blotches on the baby's face and neck are hives. "We didn't know what it was at first, because Jack's a smooth-haired fox terrier, so we figured hair, not fur, you know? *But.*"

"He came to my house."

"Oh, right," Sandy replies, "Thanks. I put him in the garage, you know, but he hates it in there, and there's a dog door. What can you do?"

"Not much," Katie says, shifting her weight again. "Well, it's late—"

"So how are you?" Sandy says, and takes a step toward her. She looks at Katie's face, looks down at the floor, shakes her head. "Dumb question, huh?" she says.

"It's okay."

Sandy transfers the baby onto her other hip, raises an arm at Katie. "Well, come here already, I haven't talked to you in ages, girl."

Katie walks into the half hug, pats Sandy awkwardly on the back.

"You do hate me, huh?" she whispers into Katie's ear.

"No, of course not."

They pull back, Sandy tracking her face for a second. "Well, you should."

"I don't," Katie says firmly.

Sandy nods, tugs the baby's pajama top down. The baby makes wet, burping sounds, gearing up to cry again.

"God, Emily, you're a mess," Sandy says, trying to laugh. "I beeped Rick, and he's supposed to be getting back to me after he talks to the pediatrician on call, but with this weather . . . "

"I'm sure Rick is okay."

"Oh, I know, it's just that everyone pitches in in the ER," Sandy says, "so who knows when he'll get back to me?" Her eyes stray to the bay window, back to Katie. "So, really. How are you? The truth."

"You have a few hours?" Katie says, trying to laugh her off.

But Sandy's face grows serious. "Yes," she says with such sincerity that Katie finds herself grateful and embarrassed at the same time. "Yes, I *do*."

•

After Sandy ties Jack securely in the garage, it doesn't take much time for Katie to catch her up on the trial. There isn't much to say, after all, and she's thankful when Sandy doesn't ask any questions or push for more information. Katie transitions to a question about Sandy's older son for a quick sidetrack, a short respite so she can gather her thoughts about the days and nights since she and Sandy last talked. Wishing, despite herself, that she could explain, as soon as Sandy stops talking— finished now with her son and launching seamlessly into poor Mr. Peterson across the street and two doors down—how she felt after Nick moved out, when Sandy first started to pull back, and then soon after the funeral, when Sandy stopped talking to her altogether.

"I'm pretty sure Mr. Peterson's having problems with prescription medicine now, too," Sandy says, rolling her eyes. "He was out raking leaves yesterday, and he was wobbling over all the place. He looks so thin, too, and I told Rick . . ."

Please, Katie wants to say into the blur of words, *do you remember Nick? Me and Nick? Will you talk about that now?*

" . . . then I saw him at CVS yesterday," Sandy says, "and I was actually *frightened*—"

"Shouldn't you try Rick again?" Katie suddenly blurts out.

Sandy leans back, startled. "Oh. Oh, maybe I will," she says, and gazes down at Emily, who is snoring softly on her shoulder now. The hives are better, faded pink. "Let me put her down first."

After Sandy leaves the room, Katie wants to flee, to run out the front door and sprint home, but the nightly news is flashing right in front of her on the silent TV. A young male newscaster stands in front of the Providence courthouse, bundled into a long beige overcoat, microphone raised and lips moving. Katie picks up a huge remote with dozens of colored buttons, pushes "off." Nothing. Picks up another one, pressing buttons, and watches the scene shift back to the studio.

"Thank you, Andrew," comes the female newscaster's voice, loud and grave.

In a box at the top right corner of the screen is that same black-and-white photograph that was taken in New Hampshire, Katie's favorite, and this time it isn't just Nick there: Katie stares back into her own smiling face in the photo, traces the contours of her body and the way it rests against Nick's as they recline on the huge, sand-colored rock.

" . . . Nicolas Burrelli's wife, Katie, seen here as she rushes from the courthouse this morning," the newscaster says, and then the picture shifts again and the screen fills with Katie in front of the courthouse, ashen-faced, pushing through the extended microphones and cameras, "after the first day of testimony ends almost before it begins."

The walls jump in, out. Her legs drain, chest ballooning as if she's been underwater for too long and needs to surface for air. Her fingers roam over the remote, searching for the "off" button.

The picture shifts again—there is the somber newscaster behind the desk, and there is Jerry's grinning face, at the corner of the screen in a box.

". . . Jerry LaPlante, the mentally handicapped man who is charged with the murder of the speech pathologist this past spring. LaPlante is being held at the Adult Correctional Institution in solitary confinement, at the request of his lawyer."

The newscaster turns to her male coanchor.

"Where he'll remain, I understand, until a verdict is reached," the male coanchor says. "You know, Carol, it isn't a secret that the Burrellis were like surrogate parents to LaPlante, so sources are now questioning if Mrs. Burrelli is actually cooperating with the district attorney at all. Whether or not her personal relationship with the mentally handicapped defendant is interfering with her ability to seek justice for her estranged husband—"

The TV finally snaps off. Katie stares at the blank screen, the remote still pointed at it.

"Oh, God," Sandy says, and Katie turns, sees her standing with the phone in one hand, the other one covering her mouth.

"It's a lie," Katie says. She barely recognizes her own voice. "They're lying."

"Who would tell them that?"

"I don't know, I don't know who—" Katie begins, but it's too much.

"What can I do?" Sandy says. *"Anything."*

"I want him convicted. It's all I've ever wanted."

"I believe you," Sandy says. "You know how reporters are—"

"He would have come back," Katie says. She places the remote on the coffee table, carefully lines it up with the others.

"Who?"

"Nick. If Jerry didn't kill him, we would be together now."

"Of course you would."

"I should have told Richard about Carly today, but that doesn't mean I'm not cooperating."

Sandy's face fills with confusion. "It's probably just a misunderstanding—"

"I have to go, Sandy."

•

The conversation at the door is short and perfunctory. Yes, Katie says, she will take Jack temporarily, until Sandy and Rick can figure out if Emily is allergic to him. No, she won't let Jack have any dairy, because it makes him vomit. Yes, she understands that she should call if she needs anything, anything at all.

There's a crate at Katie's feet, filled with dog food, bowls, things that squeak.

"He'll be good company right now," Sandy says, handing her Jack's leash.

"Okay, right."

Before she can escape, Sandy gets her in a death-grip hug.

"You call me if you want to talk, girl," she says. "I mean it."

"Right."

•

Minutes later Katie is back in the basement on her knees, adrenaline pumping as she tears through the metal canisters of film on the bottom shelf. On some of the lids there is a strip of masking tape with a name written on it in faded marker: HOUSING CRISIS. ANIMAL RESCUE. SAVE THE BAY. The lids come loose as she tosses them like Frisbees across the tiled floor; the canisters clang and crash into each other, the lids skidding across them, the films unraveling and wobbling up to tangle into one another and the ones already on the floor from earlier. Jack watches nervously, shifts his weight back and forth on his front paws and snaps at the canisters halfheartedly as they pass by. Finally Katie finds what she's looking for, the first one—a green canister with a long piece of masking tape across the lid. JERRY AT THE WARWICK CENTER. And then another. JERRY/GROUP HOME. And another. JERRY/MISC.

No, she didn't forget them, of course not. And the question—why she didn't tell Richard about them before—isn't important anymore. Only this: they exist.

Katie presses the curling masking tape down on the top canister. Nick *would* have come back, it is the only thing she is certain of at this point.

You want to see cooperation? I'll show you fucking cooperation.

And then there is finally that pulse of excitement she's been waiting for since the trial began, a frigid, stone-size feeling of satisfaction that starts to grow in the center of her heart, replacing everything else.

11

At 7:45 the next morning, she's sitting in Richard's office waiting for him, her compact video camera by her side. Richard stands outside the door with his assistant, Kristen, who had let her in only minutes before. Katie sees the young woman flipping her long blond hair over her shoulder now, shrugging at Richard. Her small, watchful eyes squinting behind her black-framed glasses, her expression easy to interpret: *Don't ask* me *what she wants.*

Richard walks into the office, sits down behind his desk. He picks up a pen, studies the tip before looking at her. "What can I do for you, Katie?"

She knows she's only one short step away—she just needs that last final push to truly join forces with him, to accept who he is inside the courtroom. She leans forward, elbows on the desk, fingers laced. Face like stone.

"Yesterday you said Jerry was a very dangerous man. Do you really believe that?"

He looks only a little surprised. "Don't you?"

"He still believes in Santa. His favorite show is Bugs Bunny."

"He shot your husband point-blank in the face. After warning him that he was about to execute him."

"And if Jerry was confused? If he thought he was doing something good, like he was somehow helping Nick?"

"By murdering him? Then that makes him even more dangerous, doesn't it? Suppose he wants to 'help' someone else?"

It's clear by Richard's demeanor—his eyes narrowed, his head bent slightly, the stillness of his body—that he knows what's expected of him here. "Jerry was upset with your husband that morning, and he acted on it," he says evenly. "Whether Jerry's complicated history played into his motives is almost irrelevant at this point. And you've witnessed his violent nature firsthand. He is a volatile, dangerous man."

"He draws pictures of stick people," Katie says, her eyes never leaving Richard's. "Someone has to remind him every morning to wash his hair when he's in the shower."

Richard puts the pen down. "He stole a gun, then walked into the gym with the sole purpose of killing your husband. According to the law, that's premeditated murder."

Katie searches his face. "I ran into a woman from the Warwick Center last night, Dottie. Dottie said Jerry thinks he saved Nick."

Richard nods, scribbles on his pad. "Well, it might be a tactic to throw us off, but even if he actually said that, it doesn't change the facts. We have corroborated evidence proving that Jerry was incited by his past and that he acted on it."

Richard watches Katie closely, too, now, as if he can sense the small hesitation inside her. "Even though your husband left—"

"I *asked* him to leave. Just for a short time."

"Exactly."

"We never thought it would be permanent."

And then the final push, the exact words she needs to hear from this man, the genuine outrage in his eyes: "You never had the chance to find out, did you, Katie?"

And there it is, the confirmation once again. Jerry's fault that Nick will never walk through the front door of their home again, Jerry's fault that the chance, the certainty, was taken away from her. All of this on Richard's face as he meets her gaze.

"You have something for me?" He pulls the writing tablet closer.

Katie squares her shoulders; she drops the recorder onto the desk, surprised and pleased when Richard startles back into his chair.

"What's that?"

"I had to use the recorder to film off of the screen. I didn't have time to get a working print to the lab, so the images are a little fuzzy."

"What images?"

"I told you about the documentary I started when Jerry was admitted into the program?"

"Yes, but—"

"I have hours and hours of him on film."

"I know," Richard says.

He leans into the desk toward Katie, the pen suspended vertically in the air. There's a probing look on his face that gives Katie a surprising shiver of power; it's completely unexpected, the sheer force of this moment, how she feels with Richard's attention focused so entirely on her. To be the one who is watched like this, the one who is listened to so intently.

"Then you know that most of the footage looks like home movies, something a mother or father would take. I already told you that sharing the film with an audience felt very much like a betrayal, so I abandoned it. The reels have been gathering dust for years."

She is ready for Richard's confused look. "The problem with this—" he begins.

"*Most* of my footage looks like home movies. There are other things on the film, too. Jerry at the center, working with Nick and with the other clients," she says, then stops for effect. "And the incidents I told you about, when he first came to the program."

"You have some of them on *film?*"

Kate nods, hooks a thumb at the TV standing in the corner of his office. "It works?"

"Yes, yes, go ahead." Richard thumps his pen against his palm.

Katie sets up the recorder, feels Richard's entire focus on her, on what she will give him. Another acute shudder of pleasure passes through her body. "I didn't feel like playing with sound, but you'll get the point."

The TV fills with static, and then Jerry is grinning in his thrift-store clothes, oversize khaki shorts and a faded T-shirt. His hair is combed neatly to the side, blue eyes wide with suspense as he hunches over a feeder at the Roger Williams Zoo, hands cupped underneath the small metal door. A little girl in a yellow jumper stands beside him, looking up with confused but inquisitive eyes: *Is he a grown-up?* Jerry's grinning face is focused on the feeder, his hands shaking with excitement. Nick pops quarters into the feeder and says something to the girl—probably that Jerry is special, a grown-up but different from the kind she knows—and twists the knob. The little girl is nodding, looking from Nick to Jerry, and then suddenly Jerry is swirling away from them, eyes lifting to the sky. His face seizes up, arms instantly striking out. He ducks his head under, but his arms still swipe and attack the air. Nick tries to grab hold of his hands—Jerry wrestles clear, teeth clenched, his fist pounding into Nick's neck. The little girl's mouth is wide, howling—she's frozen until her mother darts into view, yanks her away. Jerry kicks now, fists hammering the air, as Nick lunges and throws his arms around Jerry's middle. For an instant, Jerry looks in the camera's direction—there, right *there,* his face: not the one Richard has seen, not the one the jurors sneak peeks at in court.

Another burp of static, and there is Jerry again, at a birthday party at Nick and Katie's apartment, sitting at the head of the table. A paper crown on his head, beaming with anticipation. Her family standing beside the table, smiling. The screen goes dark—someone has turned the lights out—and then the camera moves to capture Nick walking in with a huge Bugs Bunny cake, a forest of candles burning on top. Nick places the cake in front of Jerry, and the camera pans up. Jerry stares down at the candles, face filled with terror. His lips start to mumble, slowly at first, then faster.

Katie leans over, presses the pause button.

"Sometimes when he does that with his lips, it's a sign," she says in a dispassionate voice. She pushes the play button.

Jerry raises his head, and his face is completely transformed again: no sign of the normally pudgy innocence or confusion or happiness that is usually there; it has mutated into something horrific, his eyes pinpoints of rage—almost feral, focused on destruction. Not a mentally handicapped man anymore, not a harmless adult with the IQ of a child who loves Saturday-morning cartoons. Just a man, a grown man warped with anger and prepared to inflict violence. His hands seize the table, ready to flip it over. The screen fills with snow again.

Katie hits the stop button. "I have a couple more on film."

"Holy shit."

Katie unplugs the cord, winds it around her hand. Tries to quiet the victorious shaking of her body.

"Why didn't you tell me about this?" Richard asks, much too softly.

She turns quickly to him—it's the last thing she expects, this look. She stops winding, her voice smothered by his angry disbelief.

"Why would you withhold something this important, Katie?"

Katie lowers her eyes. "I don't know."

"Do the Warwick Center people know you have these incidents on film?"

"Yes."

Richard shakes his head slowly. "Well, *now* at least something makes sense."

"What?"

"When you first told me about the footage, I thought it was only a matter of time. I thought Treadmont would request them in discovery, but she didn't. She hasn't."

"But why would she? He looks inhuman, like an animal—"

He shakes his head impatiently now. "Well, I didn't know that, did I? And if we introduce this footage into evidence, the jurors have a right to see *all* of it."

"I didn't think—"

"*Right,* you *didn't,*" Richard says angrily, then catches himself.

He breathes in deeply, attempts a smile. "Okay, hold on, give me a minute here," he says. "I'm sorry, my mind is moving too quickly now." He swivels away from her in his chair, eyes flicking around the room. "Just a minute to process."

Less than a minute later, he rotates back to her, relaxes into his chair, his face completely altered: smiling easily now, giving Katie that look again, the charming, grateful one that says he *does* need her.

"Okay, sorry about that," he says. "You're right, Katie, these images *are* important. They're so much better than you up on the stand, describing them. You know that no other witnesses have come forward, but with your family, and even *you* up there talking about them, I worried about the jurors thinking you were biased, that all of you might be exaggerating. And I was a little concerned, too, because if you and Nick were the only ones who witnessed all of them firsthand, there might be more room for doubt, for the intensity, or misinterpretation—a way for Donna to deflate some of them. The brief one from his intake at the police station would have helped, but . . . So this is really great, Katie. Great."

"But why—"

"Well," he says, shrugging casually, "we'll have to deal with the flip side. You don't get to edit this at home, Katie. If we introduce the footage as evidence, a biased party can't simply string these moments together and take everything else out. The jurors get to see it *all*."

Richard opens a side drawer, pulls a folder onto his desk. "I wondered why the defense hadn't taken advantage of the film," he says almost to himself as he flips through papers inside. "Home movies of Jerry," he says, then looks up at Katie. "What better way to humanize this man?"

"I'm sorry, maybe that was my doubt. I don't know."

He starts to scribble notes. "Don't be. It's okay, really, I just got a little ahead of myself. I understand now why the defense wouldn't be eager to share this, but I wondered why no one else mentioned it."

Katie squints at him. "Who else would have told you?"

"Oh," he says, looking up and shrugging again, "I don't know. Your family. Your sister, if she knew."

"I thought you interviewed my family about Jerry."

"Well, yes," he says, staring blankly at her. "This footage is of Jerry, right? His behavior?"

"Yes, but—"

"Listen, I'm sorry, I really am. My reaction was uncalled for. I wasn't prepared, but I want to reassure you—I can definitely see now how this is going to work to our advantage." He shakes his head in wonder. "I don't know how to thank you, Katie."

"I *do* want to help."

He places his hands flat on the desk, leans forward. "I know," he says. "And you have. This is good, Katie. Better than good. You may have just secured this man's conviction."

TWO

1

Katie peers through the open courtroom door. Dana is late this morning, not a big surprise, but there's still time. Donna Treadmont stands alone at the defense table, shuffling through some papers, her matronly body encased in yet another gray suit. A court officer approaches from behind, and Katie steps aside. He nods at her.

"Soon," he says.

She nods back, watches him walk into the courtroom and up the aisle toward Donna and Richard. Richard is sunken down in his chair, steepled fingers against his lips and watching Donna intently. To anyone else it might look as if he's worried about facing Carly again today, but Katie knows these gestures by now; he's excited to begin, trying to keep his emotions in check. Donna looks up from a folder, smiles at him. He nods at her, swivels back to the table, and presses a key on his laptop.

The front row is empty except for Detective Mason, who leans down to shuffle through a box at his feet. Behind him are a few familiar faces, old colleagues of Nick's, some of his college friends, a young male paralegal from Richard's office. Not enough, Katie thinks, though it's clear why the crowd appears so meager: most of the people who loved and supported Nick are still on the wrong side of the courtroom.

Behind the defense table it's the same as yesterday—the Warwick Center employees are crowded into the benches, their bodies in constant motion. In the front row, Daniel leans in close to Veronica and then turns to speak with two women dressed in crisp business suits— probably from Donna Treadmont's office. Behind them Jan Evers,

Jerry's supervisor from work, consults quietly with Judith Moore, who nods every few seconds, her lips pressed together. There are several other cafeteria workers beside Judith, too, sitting closely and whispering, along with an administrative assistant who quit a year ago to be a stay-at-home mom—she grasps the hand of a girl who works part-time in the summer and nods confidently.

Office workers, laborers, full-time and part-time employees from the center—even Alicia, the silly college girl who worked for a single semester last spring—all of them talking, heads nodding, lips moving, eyes skipping repeatedly to the side door where Jerry will emerge. All this concern, all this love and attention and energy. All for Jerry.

Katie turns away, checks the hall to her left. She hears a quiet ping behind her and turns toward the three elevator banks on the right, expecting Dana to come rushing off one, full of apologies and trailing cigarette smoke. But when the middle elevator door opens, Patricia is standing alone in it, reading from an opened folder. She looks up briefly, steps off the elevator, her attention immediately sucked back to the pages inside.

It seems impossible that this woman and all the employees of the Warwick Center were once Katie's friends. But even before Nick had packed his things and moved out of their house, there was a noticeable change in their behavior toward her—stilted conversations, air space on the phone, eyes averted when Katie showed up at the work program unannounced. It seemed as though the moment she and Nick started to have problems, the entire staff not only knew about them but felt the need to take sides. Suddenly it was just Nick who was their friend, just Nick who was the one they cared about and supported. As if all the cookouts and holiday parties and time spent laughing and talking in one another's homes were erased, forgotten.

She turns back to the courtroom. *Look at them, Nick. Now we're both erased—*

"Katie?"

Patricia's deep voice is right at Katie's ear. Katie spins around, and there Patricia is, towering over her, the folder tucked under one arm; the woman gazes down at her without blinking, and Katie thinks that just yesterday the thought of coming face-to-face with Patricia made her stomach lurch. Now she returns Patricia's insistent stare.

"How are you, Patricia?" she asks.

"Dottie told me she ran into you last night at the market," Patricia says. An annoying habit of Patricia's, not answering questions or bothering with small talk.

"And?"

"And of course I want your reaction," Patricia says, thrusting one foot forward.

"To what?"

The skin around Patricia's mouth tightens. "Visiting Jerry."

"I thought my reaction was pretty clear last night."

Patricia frowns at her. "I didn't expect any of this from you, Katie. I honestly didn't. I thought I knew you better."

"Yeah, me, too," Katie says quietly, turning back to the courtroom.

Inside, Jerry materializes from the side door, and the rows behind Donna Treadmont collectively shift and come to order. He shuffles to the table, a sleepy, drugged look on his face as Donna gathers him into a bear hug. Veronica reaches over the banister to touch his arm and speak softly into his ear, and the rest of the Warwick Center people lean forward with encouraging smiles. Jerry rests his head on Donna's shoulder and a confused half smile forms as he looks at his eager audience.

Patricia's hand lands on Katie's shoulder. "Katie," she says in an unsteady voice, "look at him."

Jerry's chubby face becomes serious, and he lifts his head to scan the rows behind Richard, eyes squinting; he doesn't have his contacts in again, but he's still searching for Katie, for the fuzzy outline of her body in the front row. And then his eyes settle on the floor, where her feet should be, and Katie sees him squint even more: looking, apparently, for her shoes. A quick tug of guilt comes—*has he told anyone about the shoes?*—but then she takes in a deep breath. They have nothing to do with all of this, she thinks, and pivots out from underneath Patricia's grip.

Patricia's eyes are like rifles, pointing her out. "You still have the power to help him. You could turn this whole thing around if you wanted to."

"What exactly are you asking me to do?"

Patricia's eyes narrow. "This isn't just about Nick. You know that."

A man from inside the courtroom walks through the doorway, regards both of the women with open curiosity. They step aside.

"Katie, if Jerry did this to someone else from the program, if he walked into my office and shot *me,* you and Nick would fight tooth and nail for him. And that's what I'd expect from both of you."

"Don't presume—"

"You have a responsibility to do what's right here," Patricia says. She shoves a finger toward Jerry. "Look at him, Katie." A command now.

Jerry draws on his yellow notepad, face close to the page, his tongue sneaking out of his mouth as he concentrates. Donna points to something on the pad, and Jerry giggles, covers his mouth with one hand.

"We *all* loved Nick," Patricia says quietly.

Katie turns, sees Dana finally rounding the corner, smiling at her; her sister's eyes instantly shift to Patricia, and she speeds up her step. Katie turns back to Patricia, expecting, if not a fumbling apology, at least some sort of recognition of Katie's grief. But Patricia's gaunt face is hard and unforgiving.

"This isn't about you, Katie," Patricia says.

"Excuse me?"

"None of this is about *you.* And it isn't about Nick leaving you, and it certainly isn't about this need of yours to reclaim him somehow through this trial—"

"I asked Nick to leave."

Patricia waves away her words. "None of that is important anymore. This is Jerry's life we're dealing with, his entire future. You honestly believe he belongs in a jail cell for the rest of his life?" Patricia's face is red with indignation. "Where is your heart, Katie?"

Katie glares back at her. "Where the hell is *yours?*"

•

It's difficult to keep her attention at the front of the room, to completely ignore the Warwick Center people whispering to each other across the aisle. Katie fights the urge to turn around and face them, maybe even cut her eyes at Patricia just for effect.

"I can't believe she'd confront you like that," Dana whispers a little too loudly beside her. Detective Mason glances over at them from the end of the row.

"I took care of it," Katie whispers back.

"Listen to you," Dana says, eyebrows raised. She examines Katie's face closely. "Hey, are you wearing blush?"

"Huh? Why?"

Dana moves in closer. "You *are.*"

"So?"

"You never wear blush."

"Richard said that the jurors will be watching me," Katie says, "and that during dramatic testimony they'll turn to me to gauge their own reactions. Richard said this morning that I'm a vital presence in this courtroom. So I am."

"Okay, sorry," Dana says. "You just never do, that's all."

A woman in the row behind them taps Katie on the shoulder. She introduces herself—a childhood friend of Nick's—and tells Katie how sorry she is, asks how Katie is holding up. This woman knows Richard a little, a friend-of-a-friend sort of thing, and she knows his skills in the courtroom. "We'll be just fine," she says, and Katie's head reaches out and embraces the word "we," a confirmation that she's an integral part of this process, too.

One of the bailiffs moves across the front of the room with determination—any minute now. The anticipation makes the quiet descend, amplifies every small sound; behind them someone coughs, and a few seconds later another person slowly unwraps a candy or mint. Heads turn at the loud plastic crinkling that draws out forever. *Just rip it open,* Katie thinks. *Jesus.*

"You look pretty," Dana says beside her.

"Thanks."

"You're welcome. And by the way, Mom called me before she went over last night, and for the record I told her it was really shitty timing."

"I don't even know what all that was about. Do you?"

"Sort of."

Katie shifts to face Dana. "Well?"

"Maybe we should get through today before we tackle that, huh?" Dana's tone is too casual.

"Just tell me."

"It's a little complicated."

Katie holds her palm up, looks around the room and at her sister: more complicated than this?

"Later, okay?" Dana turns her attention to the front of the room, a dismissive gesture that reminds Katie of their mother.

Katie sits back, has a fleeting feeling of being a child again, sitting in church: the same restless shuffling, the same hard, pewlike benches, Dana's hand finding hers. When they were younger, their ostensibly pious hand-holding quickly degenerated into thumb wrestling, or their favorite game, tracing letters into each other's palm. *T-H-I-S S-U-C-K-S.* Back then it seemed like it was always Katie's turn to guess and Dana's right, as the older sister, to offer the words.

She wriggles her hand away from Dana, turns her attention to the defense table. Jerry's wearing a new suit today, a shiny blue one that hugs him tightly at the shoulders. He flips the end of his wide burgundy tie back and forth until Donna whispers something to him; lower lip pushed out, Jerry drags his yellow pad closer to him. At this angle Katie can see just the hint of something blue in his left ear. Earplugs? She'll have to tell Richard about this: not only is Jerry sedated and virtually blind without his contacts, but he also can't hear most of what takes place in the courtroom. Donna hands him a pencil, pats his hand.

Katie turns to Dana. "Richard got a letter from Candice yesterday."

Dana shifts around to face her. *"And?"*

"She isn't coming. He only read one line from it. 'Why would I want to relive my son's death?'"

"I can't believe she wouldn't want to be here. Are you surprised?"

Katie crosses her arms. "It's her life," she says, shrugging indifferently.

The side door at the back of the room opens, and the bailiff steps forward.

"Are you okay?" Dana whispers.

"I'm fine."

"Kate?"

"Let it go, Dana."

"All rise."

•

The jurors look almost festive as they file into courtroom, legal pads pressed against their chests. The only person who seems even remotely somber is the tall, elderly gentleman who moves into the back row and bends himself into his chair with difficulty—the same man who held his hand over his heart when Richard summoned the picture of Jerry and Nick standing face-to-face in the gym that day, only the barrel of the gun between them. The women on either side of him lean across to whisper to each other, and the man glances in Katie's direction, nods slightly before turning away.

The jurors have been sequestered at the Radisson Hotel in downtown Providence—no TV, no newspapers—so this man can't possibly know about the newscaster's speculations regarding Katie's cooperation. Still, it's a good sign. So are the small smiles she gets seconds later, one from the juror in the center of the front row, the heavyset woman with too much eye makeup, the other from the youngest juror, a Hispanic man in a tight blue T-shirt who sits at the end of the front row, closest to the prosecution table. He shoots a guarded look at Donna and Jerry, who lean into each other, their heads lowered over Jerry's pad.

Of course Richard doesn't miss any of this. He swivels in his chair to the front row, raises his eyebrows at Katie.

"You catch that?" he whispers.

"It's good, right?"

"You're the filmmaker," he says. "You know how to read people. What do *you* think?"

"They're sympathetic?"

"I think you're right on the money," he says, smiling.

Katie feels her face flush with pleasure, turns to her sister. But Dana is glaring at Richard.

He catches this look, gives Katie a quick smile, and moves back to the table.

"What's wrong?" Katie asks her sister.

"Nothing."

"He respects my opinion, Dana. Why would that bother you?"

"It doesn't," she says uncertainly, her eyes moving back to Richard.

"We're a team now. We're in this together."

"That's great, Katie," she says quietly, her gaze dropping to her lap.

Carly is back on the stand, arms crossed, her thick brown hair pulled into a stubby ponytail; the frowning glare she gives Richard is softened only slightly by the wispy ringlets framing her face.

"Good morning, Carly," Richard says. He stays seated, elbows on the table.

Carly just stares.

"First of all, I want to tell you how sorry I am about yesterday. And I want you to know that nothing like that is going to happen again. Okay?"

Carly sucks her teeth and rolls her eyes in the direction of the defense table. The hushed laughter dissipates as soon as Judge Hwang reaches for her glasses and aims a sour look at the benches behind Jerry. Jerry peeks up from his yellow pad, squints around the room; Donna pushes her shoulder gently into Jerry's, and he lowers his head again, puts pen back to paper.

"Carly, do you remember that day on May fifth of this year when you were playing basketball with your friend Nick Burrelli?"

Carly shrugs. The court reporter looks past Carly and up at Judge Hwang and mumbles something. The jurors to her right strain forward to hear, and Carly spins around to stare at her, too. Judge Hwang nods at the court reporter and leans forward toward Carly.

"Miss," she says, "you'll have to speak up so the court can hear you. Can you answer Mr. Bellamy's question?"

"Yah, okay," Carly says.

Judge Hwang nods at Carly. "Go ahead, Mr. Bellamy."

"Thank you, Judge," Richard says, and folds his hands together. He gives Carly a gentle smile. "Do you remember that last day when you got to play basketball with your friend Nick?"

"Little bit."

"Okay, good. Now, I know you talked to a whole bunch of people on that day and that you told them some things about what happened. Right?"

"Yup."

Richard rises, holding a piece of paper. "May I approach, Your Honor?"

"With *caution,* Mr. Bellamy."

Judge Hwang doesn't try to stifle the small pockets of laughter this time. Richard smiles good-naturedly at the jurors, then steps over to Donna and hands the paper to her. She examines it briefly, hands it back, and Richard walks it over to the court reporter. Carly strains backward in her chair, away from Richard, but he pretends not to notice. He keeps his hands locked behind his back while the court reporter attaches a circular red sticker to the reverse side.

"Your Honor, the state offers Exhibit One."

Judge Hwang lifts her glasses at Donna. "Does the defense have any objections?"

"No, Your Honor."

Richard glances at the report, then at Judge Hwang. "Permission to hand the witness State's Exhibit One?"

"Careful, Mr. Bellamy."

"Of course."

Richard keeps his body as far away from Carly as possible; he stretches forward, places the paper on the banister, takes a step back. "Do you recognize that piece of paper, Carly?"

Carly leans forward and scrunches her face over it.

"You can pick it up, if you'd like."

Carly snatches it up, her tongue pushing through her lips. She looks over at Donna, at Richard.

"Do you know what that is?"

"Nope," Carly says. "Some words."

"Are there any words, or anything on it at all, that you recognize?" Richard asks.

Carly holds the paper a few inches from her face. After a moment she slaps the paper against her forehead. "Oh, yup, right there." Pointing, she holds the paper up.

"And what's that you're pointing to?" Richard asks.

"My name," she tells him.

"You signed that piece of paper, Carly?"

"I don't know."

Richard smiles. "Is that how you write your name?"

"Yah."

"Your Honor, would you let the record show that the witness is pointing to her signature at the bottom of State's Exhibit One, which is a report from the Warwick Police Department."

"Noted."

"Carly, can you read this statement to the jurors?"

"Who?"

"To our friends here, beside you," Richard says, fanning his hand out at the jurors.

The jurors watch Carly staring at them, amused eyes flicking from her to Richard. She raises the paper in her hand. Lips pursed, she pulls it close to her face.

"Wwwwwwwwww. Wwwww." Carly puts the paper down on the banister, locks her arms around her body. "I don't read good."

"That's okay," Richard says. "Would you like me to read it for you?"

"Okay, yup," she says. She thrusts it out toward Richard, who steps right up and takes it; their hands almost touch, but Carly doesn't seem to notice, just nods in relief at him. "Thank you," she blurts out suddenly, and Richard smiles.

"My pleasure."

Richard reads each detail from top to bottom—case number, people present, time of arrival. He pauses for a moment, scratches at his forehead like he's uncomfortable; he takes a deep breath, and the jurors zero in on him, Carly completely forgotten now.

"'Witness reports that her friend Jerry came into the gym. She says he pulled a gun out of his jacket and held it up. Witness says that she tried to say hi to Jerry when he got close, but he didn't look at her. Witness says Nick said hi and that Jerry told Nick it was "time to go." Witness said that Jerry was smiling, then shot her friend Nick. Witness says she was scared at the loud noise at first but then she laughed because she thought Jerry and Nick were playing a game.'" Richard stares at the paper for a moment, then looks up at Carly.

"Do you remember telling the police that?"

"Little bit."

"Do you remember why you thought Jerry and Nick were playing a game?"

"Jerry was happy."

"Objection. Goes to state of mind," Donna says, half rising out of her chair.

"Sustained."

"He *was,*" Carly insists. "He smiled happy."

"Your Honor," Donna says.

"Move along," Judge Hwang tells Richard.

"Yes, Judge," Richard says. He walks back to the table, sits down. "Carly, do you remember who else was there the day Jerry walked into the gym to shoot Nick?"

"Objection!"

"Sustained."

"Okay, well, Carly, do you remember who else was in the gym when you were playing basketball with Nick?"

Carly looks up at the ceiling, counts on her fingers. "Um, was me and Joey, and Billy Z, too. Three people."

"And Nick, too, right?"

"Oops! Yah, and Nick. Four," she says, and bends back her ring finger. *"Four."*

"And you were all playing basketball?"

"Um, nope, not Billy 'cuz of he is our janitor."

"So Billy didn't play with you that day?"

"No, stupid, 'cuz of he's the *jan-i-tor.*"

"Miss, I'm going to have to ask you not to call Mr. Bellamy names."

"Oops."

"That's okay, Judge." Richard smiles sheepishly. "Unfortunately, it's not the first time I've been called a name."

Judge Hwang frowns at Richard, but some of the jurors give him appreciative grins.

"Okay, Carly, so what was Billy doing that day?"

"He was, um, he was—he sweeps and cleans," she says. "Spiders live in Billy's beard."

Richard laughs, and Carly leans forward, defiant. "It's *true.* He eats them for snacks."

"I believe you," Richard says respectfully, and Carly sits back. "So Billy was cleaning, and he wasn't standing near you on that day?"

"Yeah-huh."

"Can you show us how close he was to you?"

"Um, this far," Carly says, and stretches out her arms.

"That's pretty close."

"Yah."

Donna scribbles on the pad in front of her.

"Carly, have you ever seen Jerry smile before?"

"Course."

"Do you know how many times?"

Carly looks at Richard like he's crazy. "Only about a gazillion."

"That's a whole lot, I guess."

"Yup."

"So you know what it looks like when your friend smiles."

"Duh."

"And he was smiling on that day in the gym?"

"Yup."

"Thank you, Carly, that's all the questions I have. Thank you for coming in again today. You've been very brave. No further questions, Your Honor."

"Defense?" Judge Hwang asks.

"Thank you, Your Honor," Donna says. She rises out of her chair, rests a hand on Jerry's shoulder. "Only one question, Your Honor." She squeezes Jerry's shoulder, and he folds his hands together on top of the table. "Carly, are you afraid of Jerry?"

"No way." Carly emphatically shakes her head back and forth, the little ringlets flying.

"Thank you, honey," Donna says, and starts to lower herself back into the chair. She stops midway, leaning on Jerry for support.

"Oh, one more thing. Carly? Do you have a nickname for Jerry?"

"Who, Jerry right there?" Carly says, pointing.

"Yes, this same one." Donna smiles, and her other hand comes up to Jerry's shoulder.

"Yah."

"Can you tell us what it is?"

And there it is, the rare, sneaky grin that Katie has seen only a handful of times. Always unexpected, it's almost a shock, this silly happiness that shines in Carly's normally sullen face, how the dimples magically appear and her eyes become crescents of laughter.

"Jerry Bear." Carly giggles. Both hands come up to muffle her mouth.

"Is that sort of like a big teddy bear?" Donna looks down at Jerry affectionately. Even Katie knows that this question is leading, but Richard doesn't move an inch.

"Yup," Carly says through her fingers.

"And is he *still* your Jerry Bear?"

"Oh, yeah," Carly says, "you bet."

•

Billy Zahn looks strangely out of place without his blue work jumper on. As he hooks his middle finger underneath his starched collar and pulls, Katie realizes why he looks so different: for the first time, his thick, wild brown hair and long beard have been neatly trimmed. *Hey, it's Grizzly Adams,* Nick would tease, and Billy would chuckle and stroke his beard with satisfaction.

"So you've worked at the Warwick Center for how many years, Mr. Zahn?" Richard says.

"Going on about fifteen."

"In all those years I guess you get to know a lot about the way things run there."

"You could say that," Billy says stiffly.

"Your Honor, may I approach?"

Richard walks to the front of the courtroom, picks up a large cardboard placard. He walks it back to Donna, who looks at it briefly and nods; Richard takes it to the court reporter, and she tags it.

"Your Honor, the state offers Exhibit Two for illustrative purposes only."

"Defense need to be heard?" Judge Hwang asks Donna.

"No, Your Honor."

One of the bailiffs moves forward with a tripod and sets it up next to Billy and facing the jury.

"Mr. Zahn, will you take a look at State's Exhibit Two, which is not drawn to scale, and tell the court if you recognize what is represented here?"

Billy's eyes travel around the placard. "Looks like the Warwick rec center."

"And would you say this diagram is a fair and accurate representation of the recreation building at the Warwick Center on May fifth?"

"Yeah, I guess."

"And do you think you could use this diagram to help illustrate your testimony about the layout of the building on that day?"

Billy nods, pulls at the back of his collar. "I think so."

"Here you go, sir," Richard says, handing Billy a pointer.

Richard walks Billy through the diagram, has him identify the gymnasium and the figures of Carly, Joey, Nick, Jerry, and himself. Richard has his own pointer, asks endless questions about windows, doors, where the small kitchen and coatroom and back office are located in the building; just about every time Richard points to something on the board and tries to name it, he gets it wrong.

"So then this is the doorway that leads to the kitchen," Richard says, tapping the board with his pointer.

"No, that door," Billy says poking, "leads to the coatroom."

"*Oh.* So then this is the window between the kitchen and the small office."

"Right."

Some of the jurors appear bored, and even Donna looks like she's scribbling listlessly on her pad, but Katie watches Billy, notes the way his shoulders are straighter now, how his voice is less defensive, even mildly patronizing as he corrects Richard or points out another seemingly insignificant detail of the recreation building. He looks Richard in the eye, strokes his beard from time to time.

"So you were standing just inside this closet while Nick and the two clients played basketball nearby?" Richard asks.

"Yeah, right there," Billy says, pointing.

"So you didn't see the defendant walk into the gym?" Richard's voice, which had taken on a rhythmic drone before, is noticeably louder.

Billy checks on Donna, pointer raised.

"Mr. Zahn?"

"No."

"From your position you couldn't see the defendant or the raised gun, correct?"

"Yes."

"Mr. Zahn, in your statement you said that the defendant did not smile before he shot Nick. Is that also correct?"

"He's a good kid, and he—"

"Objection," Richard says.

"Sustained. Witness will answer Mr. Bellamy's question."

"I did *not* see Jerry smile. No, sir."

"Because when you finally stepped outside of the closet, Mr. LaPlante's back was to you?"

"No—well, yes, his back was to me, but that's not why. I could see his face a little."

"'A little.' Okay. So then by your own phrasing you admit that it was virtually impossible to see any clear facial expressions? Even though you were so close?"

"I wouldn't say impossible—"

"But you *did* at least clearly hear the exchange between Nick and the defendant?"

Billy's eyes dart to Donna, back to Richard. He pulls at the knot in his tie. "Yes."

"Well, did he sound angry to you?"

"No, Jerry wasn't"—he clears his throat, shoots a look at Jerry—"Jerry *isn't* an angry guy."

"As a matter of fact, he was great friends with Nick, wasn't he? Nick was like a father to him, wasn't he?"

"He was."

"Okay, well, Mr. Zahn, if you know that Jerry isn't an angry guy and that he didn't sound mad, is it at least possible that Jerry did smile and you just couldn't see it?"

"I guess."

Richard steps back to the placard, holds his pointer between his hands. He stares at the placard as if he is confused. "So can you show us again how people enter the recreation building, Mr. Zahn?"

Billy shrugs, hits the diagram with the pointer. "There's a door here and here."

"So there's an entrance at the front of the building and one in the back?"

"Yes."

"Who normally uses that back door?"

"I do. Sometimes Eddie, the recreation director, and his assistant, Daniel. The shed is out there—" he says, and stops.

"So most people enter through—" Richard leaves the sentence open, and Billy pokes the board with the pointer.

"This one," Billy says, clearly relieved that Richard isn't going to ask questions about the shed.

Donna leans over to consult with the two women in the front row.

"So why do most people come in through this front door?"

"If you walk out this door of the gym," he says, "then you're facing the side door of the work-program building. There's a walkway in between."

"And how many feet would you say it is between both buildings?"

"Thirty, thirty-five."

"And how many feet would you say it is from the front door of the work program to this back door of the gym?"

"I have no idea."

"Can you estimate?

"Maybe eight hundred feet or so."

"So when you're working in one building and you're called into the other, it's safe to say that you normally use that walkway to get back and forth?"

"Yes."

"And can people see you walking back and forth between the two buildings?"

"Yes," Billy says, turning to the jurors, "but we don't have the windows cleaned very often. The budget gets tight."

"But the traffic in between both buildings is still noticeable, even if the windows are dirty?"

"I don't know—"

"Is it fair to say that if you were to walk from the gym to the work building, or vice versa, a number of people would probably see you?"

"I guess so."

"Mr. Zahn, using the pointer, could you show me what door Jerry used when he walked into the gym on May fifth?"

Billy's pointer barely touches the placard. "This one."

"And you're pointing to what door right now?"

"The back door."

"So if the defendant left by the front door of the work-program building and used the back door of the gym, is it fair to say that he wanted to travel undetected—"

"Objection. Speculation," Donna says.

"Sustained."

Even now Katie can't picture this—Jerry so methodical, systematically sneaking into the building, but there is relief, too. He must have been capable of it, she tells herself, because he did it. Richard has told her this all along, and Katie finds herself nodding now: capable all along, a darkness hidden inside him that she never detected.

"Mr. Zahn," Richard says now, "If you yourself were determined to sneak into the gym without being seen by anyone—"

"Objection!"

"Sustained. Move on, Mr. Bellamy."

"Mr. Zahn, to your knowledge have you ever seen Jerry, or *any* of the Warwick Center clients, ever once use that back door in the almost fifteen years that you've worked there?"

Billy's face flushes a deep crimson. "I don't think so."

"Thank you, no further questions."

•

Katie doesn't wait for the Warwick Center people to filter out of the courtroom at the lunch break; she slides toward the middle aisle today and immediately comes face-to-face with Veronica Holden and Jan Evers, who look shocked to see her this close. Katie keeps her glance casual, flicks her eyes away only as she turns up the aisle. Dana rushes behind her into the lobby.

They wait until the hallway clears, until the last Warwick Center people duck around them and leave. Dana pulls on her coat, checks her watch.

"I can't stay for the afternoon session. I have a client at one-thirty I can't miss," she says.

"I'm fine," Katie says. "I have a handle on it. Go."

Dana raises her eyebrows. "Everything okay today?"

"Of course. Why?"

"I don't know, you're just acting . . . different."

"You mean confident?"

"I guess, but—"

"Get used to it," Katie declares.

"*O*-kay," Dana says, drawing out the word and studying Katie's face. "I just don't want you to implode or anything, honey. Between this and the film stuff at night—"

"I'll call you when I get home tonight."

"Oh. All right," she says. "I just want you to be—just be careful with Richard, okay?"

"What do you mean?"

"You said he was slick, right? That he's up there playacting all the time? I just don't want you to get too sucked into it."

"With the jurors, Dana. He isn't acting with me. He trusts me."

Her sister looks away for a moment.

"What?"

"Just remember that this is his job, okay? That he'll do whatever it takes to convict Jerry."

"That's a good thing, right?"

"Sure, Katie," Dana says quietly.

Dana holds her in a hug too long.

"Richard's waiting on me," Katie says, pulling away roughly and ignoring Dana's soft exclamation of surprise.

•

After Dana rounds the corner, Katie steps into the lobby and pulls out her cell phone. She checks to make sure no one is listening—only a lingering court officer and a girl pushing a cart full of cups and water decanters—and pulls a paper out of her purse. She dials, waits.

"Oceanside Realty, this is Elizabeth, how may I help you?"

"Paul Minsky please."

"May I tell him who's calling?"

"Burrelli."

"I'm sorry, what was that name?"

"Burrelli."

Katie only has to wait about five seconds.

"Hey, Nick, I hoped I had the right number," comes the same feminine-sounding male voice from her machine last night.

"Actually, this is Nick's wife."

"Oh—"

"You said last night that the cottage is still available?"

"Yes," the man says slowly. "Yes. It is."

"I suppose we'll have to take a look at it again."

Katie can hear him flipping papers around. "Right," he says. "Okay."

"This is the one that's on Topsail Island, I think you said? Nick and I have looked at so many it's easy to lose track. I'm not even sure I saw that one myself, to be honest."

"Yes, Topsail Island. That's right." He sounds slightly less ruffled. "Mr. Barber—that's the owner—he liked Nick and asked me to track him down."

"Well I'm glad he did," Katie says, and writes down the name: Mr. Barber. "Nick might not be able to make the visit, but I'll certainly plan to see the cottage the long weekend after Thanksgiving, if that's good for Mr. Barber."

.

She sits in Richard's office, watching him flip through folders in the tall filing cabinet behind his desk.

"I don't think Donna's recross of Billy did much damage," Richard says, turning to the desk with a file. "If anything, his insistence that Jerry is a sweet kid, as he put it, will help in the end, especially when we show the footage." Richard sits back in his chair, thumbs through the file.

"How do you do it?" Katie asks him.

"What?" he says without looking up.

"How do you catch them like that and make them forget themselves?"

"I don't know," Richard says distractedly as he turns the pages. "Practice." He pulls a piece of paper from the file, rolls over in his chair to a bookshelf, and runs his finger down the row of book spines.

"You get them to talk when they don't want to," Katie says.

"It doesn't happen every time," Richard says, his back to her, "but there are techniques." His finger stops on a thick blue binder. He pulls out the book, rolls his chair over to the desk again. Starts to thumb through it, his attention riveted to the pages. As if Katie isn't in the room, sitting right across from him, waiting for more.

After a moment he looks up at her, sees her staring. He smiles apologetically. "Sorry, you were saying?" He puts the book on his desk. Gives Katie his full attention now.

"The witnesses. How you make them talk."

He nods. "Right. Well, sometimes they find themselves saying the exact thing they wanted to keep hidden, because you've led them up to it slowly," he says. "But I'm sure you've experienced this before with your documentaries. You must have your own techniques with the people you interview. Ways to help them relax and open up?"

"Yes, sure. But most of them . . . well, they *want* to talk," Katie says slowly. "But when Nick was alive," she says, "well, I guess I—or I wish I just knew . . ."

Richard watches her struggle, waits patiently, like he knows what she's going to say next.

"I guess— I just wish I knew how to do that," she says.

"What?"

"Make people talk about the hidden things."

2

—Look, Katie said to Nick, pointing. —Do you see it?

The projector hummed beside her on the floor, the dense blackness in their living room broken only by the cone of light leading to the wall. Nick stood with his arms crossed, peering at the footage playing on the wall: a young couple arguing in the George's parking lot in Galilee, one of Katie and Nick's favorite restaurants on the Rhode Island coast. When Katie had first spotted them yesterday afternoon, she'd found herself instantly scrambling for her camera, wishing the small microphone on it could pick up their voices; now, on the wall, their mouths moved silently, simultaneously, their faces full of stored-up resentments.

Nick studied them for a few seconds, and then his eyes strayed to the chair and couch cramped together against the opposite wall, at the photographs and paintings scattered all over the carpet. With the side of his foot, Nick pushed away a framed Ansel Adams that Dana and Michael had given them for their third wedding anniversary.

—What am I looking for? Nick said, crouching down close beside her, his hand coming up to rest lightly on her thigh. But his tone asked other questions. When will the lights come up? When can I rehang the pictures and move the furniture back? When will we talk about *my* day?

It wasn't completely his fault. Every night Katie sat at the kitchen table with Nick, listening to stories about his workday, to the progress he was making with his clients at a local high school. It fascinated her how Nick could transform simple problems like a leftover stutter from childhood or a pronounced lisp into complex speech issues that spilled over into every facet of his clients' lives. She loved when he narrated his sessions with a fifteen-year-old boy whose father bullied him about college, or a flirtatious but troubled eleventh-grader who was pregnant and fighting to stay in school, but most of all she loved her part in this nightly routine; for once her normally reticent husband spoke freely and passionately, always taking care to gauge Katie's reactions. She waited for his expected pauses, eagerly filling in the spaces with her praise.

—You help them express themselves, not only in speech but in life, she would tell him. —They confide in you, Nick, because you are such an important presence for them. You change their lives, their *futures*.

And Nick would nod, and listen closely to her, and eventually smile—his eyes finally filling with these exalted visions of himself. And then he'd pour out more of these kids' lives to Katie, a long, sweet elixir—complicated stories about the pressures of fitting in and teenage love triangles and experimenting with drugs that sometimes left her breathless with wonder.

But then there was this: looking at Nick now, who stared obstinately at the wall, sighing and waiting for this chore to end. With his gaze turned away, his hand was suddenly heavy on Katie's thigh, and she felt a familiar weight descend, so that every part of her body felt pushed down, held in place by the light touch of Nick's fingers. *Her* work, *hers,* and he couldn't even summon the patience to pretend it was something real to him, something important in their lives, too. Katie had felt this pressure before in Nick's presence—sometimes, even, during those long talks at the table where she filled him with his own glory—and was able, like now, to thrust it aside quickly. Understanding the dangers of probing too deeply, the terrifying reality if her vague fears were confirmed: simply not enough room in this marriage for both of them at times, not enough room for *Katie*. But in those ephemeral moments before she pushed this away, she at least recognized the dazzling incongruity—this leaden feeling with Nick so close, wanting him closer still. Waiting for him to remember that with each other, at least, they could share everything.

Katie placed her hand on top of Nick's. —See the woman on the left?

There in the background, if you looked closely enough, was a witness to the couple's fight. A middle-aged woman in a long, flowing white dress, waiting at the takeout window. Oblivious to her presence, the young couple stared each other down, their mouths contorting with anger.

—I wish we could hear what they're saying, Nick said.

—Yes, but focus on the woman.

—What about her?

—What do you think is going on with her? Katie asked him.

—I have no idea.

—Try, okay?

—Sorry, he said, his fingers squeezing her thigh.

The couple, in their late twenties and with preppy sweaters knotted across their chests, took up most of the frame. The man turned to watch a white pickup truck snake around them as the woman gestured angrily with both hands, the arms of her sweater slipping back until the knot was at her throat; she jerked it down, kept a tight fist around it. In the background to the right, a tugboat slowly cruised into the Point Judith–Block Island channel.

—Well, she's pretty pissed about something, Nick said. —Her husband or boyfriend there—

—No, not *her.*

The woman Katie wanted Nick to see wasn't the woman arguing (now turning away, then taking an aggressive step toward the man, who pushed his chest up, refusing to step back), but the other one, barely in the frame. The witness. Katie stood and threaded her way carefully to the wall, placed her finger on the middle-aged woman in the white dress.

—*Her.*

The older woman's long, peppered hair flew into her eyes, and she lashed it away, her mouth clenched as she watched the young couple fight. Her focus on the two lovers was startling in its intensity: eyes slit and trained on them, body rigid except for an angry, robotic swiping at her hair. Her other hand held a bill flat on the counter under the window, and after a few seconds she pushed it forward and backward repeatedly—mechanical movements that made the violent emotion in her eyes seem even more disconnected from her body.

—God, Nick said, letting out a low, shocked whistle. —She looks like she's going to explode.

—Yes, but why?

—I don't know. I mean, you know how slow they are at that take-out. Remember a couple of weeks ago when we waited forever for our chowder?

—No, Katie said. —See where her attention is? And see—

Katie pointed at the woman again, watched a tanned arm poke out from the window, pushing a cardboard box of clam cakes onto the counter. The woman didn't notice. She leaned forward as the couple squared off, their faces hard and unbending.

—See how she's watching them, Nick? That couple is having a horrible fight, right? It looks like they want to hit each other, but this woman is completely racked with jealousy. She's lonely, and she wants to be with someone, even if it means causing a scene in the middle of the day in a parking lot. I mean, she might *have* someone in her life, who knows, but that's how alone she feels.

Nick screwed his eyes up, and Katie held her breath.

—Did these people know you were filming them? he asked.

—That's not the point.

—I don't get it, then, he said. —How is this part of your Save the Bay project?

—It isn't.

—So what *is* the point?

Almost as if the couple could hear Katie and Nick arguing now, they turned in the direction of the camera. The man looked confused and then annoyed, took a step forward. The woman, their fight immediately forgotten, placed her hand on his back, ready to follow. In the background, the older woman zeroed in on where Katie sat on the hood of her car, her face filling with guilty shame.

Katie clicked the projector off.

—You can learn so much from watching people, she said quietly.

The excitement gone from her voice, she watched Nick, the way he stubbornly kept his eyes away from her.

—Sometimes, Katie said, —if you're lucky and you pay attention, people reveal themselves without knowing it.

—How is any of this important to your documentary?

—It's important in life, Katie said. What she left unsaid: *Sometimes you can know the most important things about people, about your own life, if you watch them closely enough. If that's all you have.*

But Nick was done, was flicking on the lights and eyeing the mess on the carpet with a frown. Katie watched him, her shoulders bending under the weight.

• • •

Three years. Sometimes Katie said it out loud when she was alone, a way to make it feel more real. *Nick and I have been married for three years,* she'd say to herself while grocery shopping or driving to the bank or cleaning their apartment, and then allow the days and weeks and months to unwind inside her head, a running montage of their life together. Always beginning with the same scene, though—a darkened beach, flames reaching into the sky, the shadows stretching across her husband's bare back. And then a quick fast-forward, a blur of snapshots until she slowed down the scenes at will again, the luxurious moments when they came together—bodies moving against each other so effortlessly, so perfectly. Nick's face and his breath and the way he felt above her, beneath her. The way he touched her.

When darker scenes asserted themselves, demanding recognition, the film inside Katie's head would shoot forward, stubbornly hunting down the years for happier moments. *Love isn't supposed to be perfect,* her mother had said soon after Katie and Nick were married, then went on to describe the hills and dips of marriage, how the best anyone could do was get a firm grip and hang on. Dana had smiled, said, *Keep your arms inside the car at all times,* and Katie nodded at both of them—not comprehending for a single second how difficult it would be to navigate the disappointments, the unwritten, ever-changing sets of laws for sharing life with another person. The bewildering, splinter-thin lines between loving and fighting.

The minor fights they dismissed easily. Nick's refusal, for no apparent reason, to wash two forks for dinner one night, and Katie's unexpected, lightning-quick response: reeling back and hurling a raw meatball at him. How it slapped onto the wall right beside Nick's head, flat as a pancake, then plopped onto the floor at his feet; Nick's eyes growing as round as the flattened meat. The few shocked, solemn seconds—the eventual eye contact—and then the release: laughing until their eyes watered and they had to lean into each other to keep from falling down. So many of these little fights, the kind Katie would take to Dana as they shopped, or ate lunch together, or chatted on the phone. Amazing, how they were almost *good,* these disagreements. Not only for Katie and Nick to laugh at later, but for Katie and Dana as well—the knowing looks and language and touches that passed between two women who understood the sweet, messy implications of loving—the difference in their ages no longer defining their relationship or feeling so enormous.

But then.

The kinds of fights she would never include in her running tableau of their life together, would never share with Dana or Jill or *anyone* over a cup of coffee. The kind you kept to yourself. Starting soon after they married, impossible to predict because their beginnings were so pedestrian, too.

—Have you seen my keys, Katie?

Katie, from the bedroom, under the covers. —In the candy dish?

—Nope.

—On the bathroom sink?

—Are you going to keep naming places or get up and help me look?

—They're around somewhere, Nick, we don't live in a mansion.

And then Nick, thundering into the bedroom, fists bunched at his sides. —Then get out of bed and look for a real job, and we'll have enough money to live in a place where there are plenty of fucking places to lose my keys.

—Whoa . . .

— I have an early appointment, so get up and *look,* he said, ripping the covers off her. His face doing that thing, what Katie distractedly referred to in her own head as "gearing up."

—Maybe you left them in the door again?

—Unbelievable. You're really *that* fucking lazy?

—Nice, Nick. Pulling the covers back over her, despite the growing dread. —They're *your* keys, so you find them.

—You can't help me look, you can't get out of bed before ten, you can't shoot on certain days because of lighting, or you're not inspired, or you have cramps, or some other excuse to lie around all day—

—I get up every single morning about a half hour from now—

—and you can't cook or clean or do anything around here, really, except this, so why am I even shocked that you can't get up for five minutes and help the person who actually *works*.

—Potshots at my cooking? How original.

—You know what makes it worse?

He poked her hip lightly, menacingly, through the covers, waiting for an answer, but Katie only pulled them tighter around her body and tried to sink deeper into the bed.

—You don't even realize, he said, what it's doing to your body. I can't even look at you when you undress lately.

—Keys, Nick. This is about *keys*.

But it was too late. He towered over her, sneering his disgust. —You know how embarrassed I was at dinner the other night? Running into my colleagues like that? "I'm so proud to introduce you all to my ambitious, *beautiful wife*."

—Nick . . .

—What I should do is just point at you, tell them the condom broke and before I knew it we were in a church. Then they'd get it.

There was always this threshold, the anger ending suddenly, the tears rising.

—Why are you such an asshole? she whispered.

—Better than being a *fat, lazy cunt*.

Later Katie would stand in the mirror, eyeing her trembling body, or review footage of her work, vainly trying to see the potential she had seen only the day before. Or call her mother just to check in, her hand shaking as she held the phone tight to her ear. This after she had forgotten to pick up his pressed shirts from the cleaners. Nick reminding her, only minutes after her admission, that her mother didn't even seem to *like* her sometimes. *Who could blame her, really, Katie? When she has Dana for a daughter?*

Hating him at that moment, hating *herself* for revealing so much about her life, her fears and doubts. Hating that she felt this way about the one person who was supposed to understand and then help chase them away.

Such innocuous beginnings. Why couldn't Katie fill the gas tank once in a while? Why did Nick throw his sweaty workout shorts right next to the hamper instead of *inside* the hamper? And yet at times these small arguments would ferment and explode, and soon Katie was the one watching with round, shocked eyes: Nick looming over her, hurling petty insults and accusations with an instinctive, explosive rage that startled her each time. Nothing was off-limits, and her husband fought like a cornered dog, chewing his way into every soft, vulnerable spot Katie had ever revealed to him in the shadows of their bedroom. Tearing into susceptible places he had intuited on his own, or even—after time—created himself. (Was Katie really getting fat? The scale said only five pounds in over three years, but her thighs . . .)

Whenever their minor fights turned into this—not often, but enough, *enough*—Katie couldn't take her eyes off Nick. Furious and wounded, she was also eerily fascinated by the way his body seemed to change right before her: face twisting up, shoulders an inch higher and pushed forward, legs firmly planted. As if *he* were the one being attacked with words sharp as slivers of glass. Her husband, fists tight at his sides, offering new glimpses of himself—spawning even more questions about the life he kept from her.

No, Katie never laughed about these with Dana, rolling her eyes and brushing the fights away like crumbs. Because they gathered inside her—Nick's cruel words, the cheap, exacting shots finding their mark again and again.

Only after he left, only after she had thought of her own punishing words (too late), would she wonder: where did it come from? But only after she could stop hating him long enough to understand that she didn't do anything, really, to provoke him to such an extent. Or did she? She wanted to ask Dana these questions, because it was Dana's job to understand people, to understand the source of pain and fear and therefore anger.

Still, Katie was too embarrassed to ask Dana anything, to tell her sister how heartless Nick could be simply because she had forgotten to roll up the car windows before a thunderstorm. *That's the difference between going to college for a real degree and going to college to watch movies. Simple intelligence.* Tapping his head, his thin, knowing smile before he turned away.

And.

And she never told Dana how easily she accepted Nick's tormented apologies later, the way he would hover around her, his body quivering, begging for her forgiveness. *I'm so sorry, I don't know why—Katie, no please look at me—I don't know why I do it—I love you—*

She didn't tell Dana how completely she loved her husband back in these moments, how her heart and mind wrapped around his unspoken pain and what he said, how his love for Katie shone in his tortured, beautiful eyes—how this proof of his feelings for her made Katie feel more at home in the world than she ever had before. Not alone anymore, never alone again, she would think, as he pressed for her forgiveness.

And she never told her sister how they would eventually come back together, their bodies tangling into each other, their mouths and fingers searching each other's flesh as if for the first time. Nick's pleading and moaning and grasping at her skin, the sheer relief and exhilaration of pure fucking, but with love and need and forgiveness all scrambled into the licking and biting and slapping of bodies.

When it was over, bodies spent, she would cradle her husband in her arms. Stroke his hair, whisper her forgiveness in his ear.

No, Katie never told her sister how powerful, how omnipotent, she felt in those moments either.

3

After the 911 operator's brief testimony in the afternoon, Judge Hwang calls for a fifteen-minute break. Katie signals to Richard, and he rolls his chair up to her; she looks at Daniel in the second row behind the defense table, then at Kirsten, who's sitting beside Detective Mason and talking quietly with him at the end of her row.

"Remember," she says to Richard, "Daniel gets very flustered around beautiful women. Nick told me once that he was painfully awkward with them, like he didn't have a right to be in the same room." She doesn't add that Nick had only said this—during one of their explosive fights—so he could also tell Katie that Daniel was always perfectly at ease with her. "Your assistant," Katie says, motioning in Kirsten's direction, "she's got all that gorgeous blond hair."

"That's a great idea, Katie," Richard says. "I should have thought of that. I could have her move to the center of the row. She'd be more visible there, don't you think?"

"Right—" Katie says, turning to the girl. But Kirsten is already standing, already making her way to the middle of the row, toward Katie.

"Oh, did you already—" Katie begins.

"No, no, hold on." He waits until Kirsten is standing right in front of him, looks up at her. "Don't move around again," he says firmly to her. "Stay right here throughout this testimony."

Kirsten's face is full of confusion. "I—"

"Katie just had a great idea," he interrupts quickly. "I want this witness to see you the entire time. I'll explain later."

Kristen looks at Katie, turns back to Richard. Smiles faintly and sits down.

"I won't move an inch," she says.

•

"Mr. Quinlin, were you inside the courtroom earlier when the 911 operator, Ms. Delory, identified State's Exhibit Five for the jurors?"

Daniel sits perched at the edge of the witness chair, holding the cassette tape between his thumb and middle finger out in front of him. His eyes dart quickly to Kristen, who leans forward over the banister, staring intently at him.

"I am—I was. Yes."

"And you were, in fact, the person who called 911 on May fifth?"

"Yes."

"You were the first one, besides the two Warwick Center clients and the custodian, Billy Zahn, to see Nick lying facedown on the floor?"

Daniel struggles for a moment, his face flushing slightly, and Katie turns to Kristen. She is twirling her hair absently and smiling at him. Across the room Patricia frowns deeply at Daniel, then turns in Kristen's direction.

"Mr. Quinlin?"

"Yes. Yes, I was there."

"Can you tell the jurors what led up to that moment?"

Daniel breaks eye contact with Kristen, turns to the jurors. "I heard the gunshot. I . . . I jumped up. Billy met me in the doorway. He said Nick was shot. I could hear Joey howling," he says, "so I grabbed my cell phone and ran out there."

"And Joey is the client who can't speak, is that correct?"

"He could a little, but mostly he made noises to communicate," Daniel says, and then blurts out, "But he was getting better."

The jurors eye him curiously—Daniel's behavior appears oddly defensive, like he's hiding something.

"He was getting better with Nick's help?"

"Yeah."

"And now?" Richard asks softly.

Daniel lowers his head, examines his splayed hands.

"Objection, Your Honor. Relevance?" Donna says.

Richard turns to Judge Hwang. "Your Honor, without Nick's constant attention and professional help, this unfortunate boy had to be removed to an institution—"

"Objection, Your Honor! What does this have to do with—"

"Yes, okay." Judge Hwang waves a hand in Donna's direction. "Stick to the relevant issues, Mr. Bellamy."

Richard nods and proceeds to walk Daniel through the crime scene, how he told Billy to get Carly and Joey out of the gym, what happened once the paramedics and police arrived. After a few minutes, when they get into the logistics of the 911 call, Daniel starts to stutter slightly, and Katie has a moment of regret: it was Daniel who fought to keep Nick in this world, Daniel who pumped Nick's chest and put his lips against Nick's and shared his breath until the EMTs arrived.

"Mr. Quinlin," Richard asks, "how far is the gym from your office in the recreation building?"

"Down a long hallway, at the very back."

"And how much time did it take you to get down that hallway and into the gym on May fifth?"

"I don't know."

"No? Well, in fact," Richard says, "Detective Mason timed both you and Billy running to and from your office from the gym, didn't he? And he figured that the time between the actual shooting and the time it took for Billy to tell you about it and for you to get up and race into the gym was approximately twenty-five seconds, right?"

"Something like that," Daniel answers.

"Okay. Can you tell me what that defendant"—Richard stabs his finger toward Jerry—"was doing when you entered the gym and saw Nick lying on the floor, facedown and dying?"

"He—Jerry wasn't there."

"Less than twenty-five seconds after the shooting, and the defendant wasn't anywhere to be found?"

"Objection, he's answered the question."

"Sustained."

"Okay, well, Mr. Quinlin, did you wonder where the defendant was?"

"There was so much going on—"

"And the defendant was smart enough to take advantage of that chaos and get out of there before the police arrived?"

"Objection!" Donna roars, rising.

"Withdrawn," Richard says. "Thank you, Mr. Quinlin."

•

Donna stands in front of the jury, her hands clasped in front of her, blocking Daniel's view of Kristen.

"Did you eventually get to see Jerry after the police arrived, Daniel?"

"Yes, I did," he says, more confident now.

"And will you describe his demeanor at that time?"

"He was a mess, he was so confused—"

"Objection," Richard says, "goes to state of mind."

"Sustained."

Donna shoots a look at Richard, turns back to Daniel. "Where *was* Jerry then?"

"He was in the time-out room in the work program."

"And can you describe that room?"

Daniel describes it—a narrow, empty room, more like a long closet with bright fluorescent lights overhead. *Like something in a psych ward,* Katie had complained to Nick once, but he had only shrugged.

"And did you ask Jerry why he was in the time-out room?"

"I didn't have to."

"Why is that?" Donna asks, looking meaningfully at the jurors.

"Because Jerry always went to the time-out room when he felt confused or scared."

"Do you know why that was?"

Daniel explains how Jerry retreated to the time-out room because of its size, because there's only one way in, because it's so bright and Jerry is afraid of the dark.

Donna locks her hands behind her back. "It appears that he felt safe there."

"Yes, definitely."

Donna purses her lips, looks contemplative for a moment. "No further questions, Your Honor."

"Redirect?" Judge Hwang asks Richard.

"Thank you, Judge," Richard says from the table. "Mr. Quinlin, why are clients sent to this time-out room?"

"Well, if a client took something that didn't belong to them," Daniel says, struggling to keep his eyes on Richard, "like another client's candy bar, or if he or she said something inappropriate, they'd spend some time there. Little things like that."

Richard nods thoughtfully. "So if a client broke a rule, or they did something wrong and they knew it, they'd also know about spending some time in that room? Thinking about their mistake?"

"I guess," Daniel admits with a blush. "But it's usually only small—"

"Thank you, sir," Richard interrupts. "Nothing further."

•

Richard stands facing the rows behind the prosecution table, addressing the spectators quietly.

"I just want to warn you all again about the nature of the 911 tape," he says. "Some of you might consider leaving the room before we play it."

More than once Richard has offered to let Katie listen to the tape, to prepare herself, but she refused each time; she could already see that day too clearly in her head, didn't want to add the sound track to accompany it until necessary.

Richard leans down to Katie. "It will be better with you here, but I'll understand if you want to leave."

"I'm fine," she says.

Richard waits on Judge Hwang, his finger suspended over the button on the tape player. Two speakers sit on a cart facing the jurors; one of Richard's paralegals stands nearby.

"Jurors will raise their hands if they can't hear it clearly," Judge Hwang instructs, and motions to Richard.

At first there's just static and then the sound of ringing.

"This is 911 Dispatch, what's your emergency? ... *There's been a shooting, a man has been shot* ... A man has been shot? ... *Yes, you need to get here, three thirty-three Post Road in Warwick, around the back, the blue building* ... That's 333 Post Road? ... *You have to hurry, please* ..."

There's a low howling sound, like wind rushing around tall buildings. It takes a few seconds before Katie realizes that it's Joey, moaning in fear.

" . . . Do you know who's been shot, sir? . . . *He's my friend, it's Nick, Nick Burrell* . . . Sir, can you tell where he's been shot? . . . *I don't know, in the head or the face, I can't tell* . . . Is he breathing? . . . *Yes, no, I don't know* . . . Is the shooter still there? Do you see the shooter? . . . *He isn't, he wouldn't know* . . . *I can't tell if he's breathing or not* . . . *Nick?*"

The sound of tapping keys, the female dispatcher's calm voice trying to reassure Daniel, and Joey's howling, which overwhelms everything else for a few seconds.

" . . . *Get them out of here!*" Daniel yells, and then Carly's tentative voice comes from a distance: "*It's not a game?*" The howling fades away. More static, the sound of Daniel crying now, his panicked voice.

" . . . Sir? . . . *Jesus, oh. God, there's blood spreading all over* . . . Sir, can you get a pulse, is he breathing? . . . *I can't tell, I don't know, this is wrong, it's so wrong* . . . Sir? Hello? Sir, can you hear me? . . . *I don't think he's here anymore, I think he's gone, you need to hurry* . . . An ambulance is en route right now, just keep talking to me . . . *Jesus, Nick* . . . What's happening right now, can you tell me? . . . *I turned him over, there's so much blood I can't even see his face. I'm going to give him CPR, but I need something to wipe off the blood, it's everywhere* . . . *Nick?* . . ."

Static, and the sound of Daniel's sobbing.

" . . . What's happening there? Can you tell me what you're doing? . . . *I'm wiping his face with my shirt* . . . *It's, his face is* . . . *it's* . . . *Oh, God* . . ."

· · ·

She isn't ready to go home yet, so she takes a left off Warwick Neck Avenue onto Rocky Point Drive. At the end of the road is the entrance to the Rocky Point Amusement Park, shut down and abandoned for over seven years now. The gate is open, so she steers her way into the park, blinking into the darkness on both sides of the tall metal fence. It's eerie driving through like this, without the carnival noise and bright lights to greet her.

The summer they were married, Katie asked Nick to take her out on the boat so she could see those colored lights flashing into the sky, to see the yellows and reds and blues rippling over the water and touching up against their hull. They rounded the Warwick Neck lighthouse, saw the crumbling mansion that stands less than three hundred yards from the park on the narrow, rocky beach leading to it: a seminary built sometime in the 1800s, only four deteriorating walls and a couple of arched windows at that point. Nick cut the engine, and the sound of Katie's past rushed into her ears—the same faint music she heard that first night she met Nick. He clicked off the running lights, jumped up onto the bow, and threw down the anchor. Watching him there on the bow, silhouetted by the lights of her childhood, Katie was suddenly overcome by the terrifying, hopeful power of living in this world, with the promise of finally sharing it with a man who truly loved her. —Nick, she said, and he jumped down instantly at the quavering in her voice. —Nick, I can't even put it in words, I don't know how, she said, reaching for him. —I've wanted you my whole life, she said, her voice choking up. He grabbed her hair, then, a fistful in both hands, and pulled her to him. Pulled her face right up to his. —You mean that, he said quietly. —You really mean it. And then they came together, they collided into each other, undressing themselves and each other with stumbling fingers. At one point the sides of Katie's mouth filled with the metallic taste of blood—gone before she could ask whose it was, if it was his blood or her own they passed between them, unacknowledged.

She rounds the corner where the flume used to be (just some girders and a couple of brown plastic logs turned upside down now), hugging the winding road that follows the coastline on the right. The ocean is invisible except for an occasional whitecap, and in the rearview mirror Katie can barely make out the outline of the mansion on the beach. She winds up the hill, past the Shore Dinner Hall on the left, and then down the hill, past the takeout window where her family used to get clam cakes and chowder after church every Sunday in the summer. The same takeout where she and Nick would go when the weather turned and the crowds gathered: dozens of people milling around them, but they were the only two there, leaning into each other and listening to the cries of the greedy seagulls circling above. Now, on the other side of the road and across from the takeout, all the picnic tables are gone and the long dock has boards and big signs nailed across the front: KEEP OUT, DANGER.

She curves around again, passes the Palladium Hall on the left, where both she and Dana had their high-school graduation banquets, and then there is only parking lot on both sides of the car; she leaves the ocean behind her, still unseen.

Close to the exit, right before the road dead-ends into Palmer Avenue, is the plunging hill that her father would race over when they left the amusement park after a long day—a lifetime ago. He'd slam the gas pedal, and they'd cruise over it like they were still on the Cyclone, and lose their stomachs for the last time of the day. Dana would throw her hands up in the air every time, and Katie would hug herself, already nauseous from so much spinning and falling. But she loved what came right after, and it made getting a little sick worth it: her mother grumbling (*For God's sake, Jimmy, haven't we been on the verge of vomiting enough today?*) and looking into the backseat to trade a disgusted look with Katie. Katie, who would wait for that look, the perfect way to end the day. For once she and her mother teamed up, while Dana rolled her eyes at their father, who only smiled and shook his head, unrepentant. Years later, a whole lifetime later, Katie would see this same look on Nick's face as he zoomed over the hill, laughing at her, his warm hand on her leg.

Katie floors the pedal at the last second, feels her stomach bounce as she flies over the hill. Back when she was a teenager and Jill and Amy were off together, meeting boys or trading secrets that didn't include her, she'd get into her secondhand Buick Skylark and sail over this hill—picturing her mother's face, feeling that secret thrill again of being in total concert with her.

She reaches Palmer Avenue, gives one last glance back at the park in the rearview mirror. She'll have to call her parents when she gets home, fill them in on the trial, ask them if they'll come by to let Jack out during the days. But she won't tell them about this trip through the park, because her father has told her about the rumors more than once over the phone; she doesn't need to hear again how the park will be closed up completely soon, how the owners will sell it to developers. Tearing everything down to build condos, or auctioning it all off into private lots. *And don't even think about protests or petitions, sweetie,* her father told her. *You don't want to mess with these guys. I've heard they're linked to the mob.*

•

Her breath fogs the windshield as she stares up at her house: total darkness inside. Katie wonders how Jack is making out in there, how he's finding his way around the unfamiliar rooms and corners.

Her eyes travel over the door, the windows, the small red maple that bends toward the side of the house where the gutter empties onto the lawn. —*Feels like home already, doesn't it?* Nick had said one night, soon after they moved in. Just sitting in the car like this, staring up at their new house. —*Ours, Katie.*

Katie pops open the car door, listens to Jack barking inside—hoarse, like he's been stuck on autopilot all day. She stares at the bay window on her way up the walk, looks for signs of the little dog in the blackness inside.

Katie crunches up her front stairs, still thick with salt, and kicks her shoes into the cement below the door; Jack's barking grows urgent until she inserts the key and it stops altogether.

"Jack?" She snaps on the lamp by the door.

A pile of damp and chewed up envelopes is on the floor in front of her. Jack cowers into the curve of the blue sofa, ears flattened. His toys are spread out from the living room to the kitchen, a line that begins with a squeaking newspaper and ends with a purple stuffed elephant wearing a maniacal ear-to-ear smile.

"All these toys, and you decide to play with the mail?" she asks him. His nose dips down an inch. *"That's a good boy."*

Jack shoots forward, flings himself at Katie, who is already kneeling down and ready for him. She hugs him up into her arms, deposits kisses into the thick white fur around his neck. Jack waits impatiently for his turn to love her, body squirming; he gives a soft yelp of pain, and Katie unlocks her hold, accepts his frantic kisses.

"I'm sorry," she says, "and I'm sorry I forgot to leave a light on, too." Jack twists inside her arms, tongue dancing out. Katie stares at him, at the happiness in his black eyes as he wiggles, determined to get his face even closer to hers.

"Dumb dog," she says, swallowing hard. She carries him into the kitchen, pursing her lips against more sloppy kisses.

By the refrigerator, Jack's food and water bowls are turned over, a small puddle of cakey dog kibble between them. Katie pats him, puts him down. He stands next to her, body touching up against her leg, suddenly solemn. They're both eyeing the clump silently when the phone rings.

"Hi, you've reached the Burrellis' residence, please leave a message for Nick or Katie at the beep."

"Hey—hey, girl, it's me," Sandy says in an unnaturally bright voice. "I forgot to tell you, Jack just *loves* to munch on mail, so you might want to leave a box or something under the slot. Okay, call me if you want to talk tonight. Thinking about you," she singsongs before hanging up.

Jack looks up at Katie, and she shrugs at him. "It's the thought," she says. "C'mon, let's go pee."

•

Back inside, she pours Jack a fresh bowl of food, checks the blinking answering machine—a good sign tonight, only four messages besides Sandy's. Richard asking in a concerned voice if she's okay, and her father yelling into the phone about the dangers of salt and car rust. The third rambling message is from Dana—she can't meet Katie tomorrow, she's so sorry, because she knows they'll show the photographs in court and how hard that will be, but Michael needs an emergency root canal, it's so unexpected, he can't drive, and has Katie considered letting someone else be there for her?

The last call is from Arthur and Sarah Cohen's son, Ben, who says in that leisurely way of his that he is just checking in with her, everything is fine with him, he is just wondering how Katie is doing today.

"There is no rush to get back to me. You call me if and when you have the time, dear," he says in his slow, ultracasual voice. "If and when, dear, if and when."

She hits the delete button before the beep—there's no way she's ready to do battle with guilty feelings tonight, and besides, she has every intention of bringing some order to all those canisters of film, of continuing the process of screening his parents' footage and making sense of it all. She still has to finish sketching the storyboards, to figure out if she will use the clips of the concentration camps she purchased from the National Archives, and if and how she will introduce the Library of Congress photographs—how all of it will eventually come together to tell the story that needs to be told. Ben will have to wait a little longer to hear from her, something he is certainly used to by now. Still, Katie does feel a small pang—Arthur and Sarah's son is already in his sixties and not the healthiest man since his wife died two years ago. *It is all this takeout food that Margaret did not allow,* he told her the last time he called, around the end of September. *I am a horrible cook, dear, and I'm afraid I have discovered the pleasures of the Burger King.*

The last time Katie shot footage of Arthur and Sarah, over a year ago, she met their son Ben for the first time. Since then Katie and Ben have talked on the phone every couple of months—long, meandering conversations that she always dreads, because she's waiting each time for Ben to ask her how the documentary is coming along; he has never asked, not once, and the unspoken question stays between them until Katie comes up with a reason to hang up first. Ben never says a word about this, either. He is nothing like his outspoken father, and Katie still remembers how surprised she was when she met him—his tall, slight frame and the hesitant way he ducked around her and the equipment; even when he moved forward, Ben somehow gave the impression of retreating. Though he did surprise her later, when she tried to explain to his parents why it was so important that they change back into the clothes they had worn for the previous interviews.

"So it doesn't distract the viewers," Katie told them, eyeing Arthur's silk tie and suit jacket. Sarah was all elbows, reaching back to hook her pearl necklace.

"We are talking about life and death here, and people are worried about the color of my pants? And my shirt?" Arthur said, eyes darting between Katie and Ben. "This makes sense to anyone?"

Katie looked to Ben for help, but he was already turning away to hide the mischievous, delighted smile on his face; he looked so much like Sarah at that moment, the younger Sarah whom Katie always pictured on the screen inside her head as the Cohens told their stories, that Katie turned to her for help. But Sarah was looking around her living room like she suddenly didn't understand what they were all doing there, surrounded by the bright lights. And then Arthur had burst out with a long bout of coughing, and finally, with a strained look on her face, Sarah revived and moved into action, passing Arthur a handkerchief. Arthur nodded his thanks, swiped it across his lips.

Three days later and they were gone, and Ben was calling her for the first time to tell her the news, to thank her for her interest in his parents, for her kindness. *Your film is their gift,* he said, and then there was a long sweep of silence.

• • •

The beanbag chair on Nick's side of the basement has a fine layer of dust on top of it. Katie kicks at it, picks it up and shakes it out, which turns out to be a mistake: Jack is beside her in an instant, teeth sunken into the red plastic. Katie drags the chair across the room with one hand, Jack attached to the other end.

"Quit it, Jack."

He snaps his head back and forth, tries to wrestle it away from her.

"Here, I was going to wait on this," she says, pulling a rawhide out of her pocket. Jack releases the chair, nose up and sniffing. He trots over to her, and she kicks the beanbag chair the last few feet, in front of the pull-down screen.

"Okay, let's see what we have here," she says, settling into the chair. She picks up her sketch pad and rests it against her knees. Jack saunters over and plops down on her feet with his rawhide.

Arthur's voice fills the basement before the film catches up. "When I first saw her there, in the general's kitchen," he says, and then there they are, on their brown couch, looking at each other, "my heart, it lifted right up inside my chest."

Arthur beams at his wife, and she bumps her shoulder into his, a surprisingly youthful gesture Katie had forgotten.

"It was the first time in over a month," Sarah says, "and all that time I did not get word that he was alive. All I knew was that he was not digging the ditches like before."

"But I was very much alive, no?" Arthur asks in his teasing voice, and Sarah smiles again at him. "God was keeping his eye on both of us, I am sure," he tells his wife.

Are you sure God was watching? Katie asks him. *That He could even see you?*

He turns to Katie. "Yes, of course. Always," he says with confidence, and Sarah nods along.

But it must have been so difficult to believe with everything around you.

Arthur taps his knee thoughtfully. "Is this not the nature of faith? Not just this believing in what you cannot see, but even more difficult, as you say, to see everything in the world with your eyes, and then trust what is in your heart instead?"

Yes, I guess so. And . . . and how long did the two of you work in the same house? she asks both of them. *At the general's house?*

Arthur turns to Sarah, and she does that thing wives do with their husbands—she says to Arthur, *Go ahead, you tell her* just with her eyes.

"Almost until the end—" he says, then interrupts himself to cough into his handkerchief. Sarah peers at him, but he waves her off. He tucks the handkerchief back into his front pocket. "You see, Sarah's father taught her how to bake, and I," he says, puffing out his bony chest, "I could do anything."

Sarah shakes her head at him. "*Arthur.*"

"What, I'm lying?"

Sarah turns to the camera. "The woman who supervised us, the kitchen workers, Adele, she told me that the general liked Arthur. His sense of humor."

Arthur feigns indignation at his wife. "So now it is only humor that keeps a young man alive?" He looks into the camera, taps his head with an arthritic finger. "Ingenuity. I was quick in the brain, a smart man who knew how to keep things running in any situation."

Sarah pulls the tapping hand into both of hers. "Funny *and* smart. Now, tell me, how can you ask for something more?"

"You see?" Arthur says, all cocky self-assurance.

Katie asks them about the nature of their contact, how often they came together in the general's house.

"Do you mean face-to-face?" Sarah asks.

Yes.

"Oh, only once or twice in those first few months," she answers. "And we did not dare speak to each other. But we found ways."

How?

Sarah shifts forward as if she will tell a secret on Arthur, and Katie thinks of their son in a flash, because there on Sarah's face is the same mischievous smile she remembered seeing on Ben's face when Arthur complained about the change of clothes. Now it's Arthur's turn to watch Sarah closely.

"It was winter, and Arthur arrived at the house every morning before me," Sarah says, "to light the fires. I would come later, through the same door at the back of the kitchen. Every morning, drawn in the dirt beside the steps, would be my message from him."

Arthur is nodding, face intent on Sarah.

Wasn't that dangerous?

"Not the kind of message you think," Sarah says, and then she stops, looks at Arthur. "Once, I think . . . I think it was . . . no. Wait." Her eyes drift to the left of the camera, and she pulls herself forward, to the edge of the sofa, her fingers working over the pearls. Her wrinkled face twitches with confusion.

Arthur coaxes her to sit back, and she relents, sagging against him briefly.

"I was not foolish," Arthur says. "I made sure only my Sarah would understand. Maybe a sun scratched into the dirt, small, so no one would notice," he says. "And if they did, what harm?"

"Yes," Sarah says, reviving, her hands clapping together once. "Yes, I remember that. Arthur's way to ask how I slept. And I would leave at night and draw a small curve into the dirt, a smile to say, 'Yes, yes, Arthur, I am warm enough at night and I can sleep.'"

Arthur beams and nods along, then pulls his handkerchief out of his pocket. He holds it over his mouth, clears his throat.

"The next morning," Arthur says, "I started my day with her answer. And then, fast so no one could see, I would ask her something else. An oval for bread, maybe: 'Do you have enough to eat, Sarah?'"

But how could you both understand things like that? Ovals and smiles?

Katie listens to her bewildered voice coming from the sound box and feels it again, the frustration welling.

"You learn because you must, yes?" Arthur asks. "An understanding grows quickly."

Sarah is nodding. "Yes, but you start with what is important, what you already know about each other," she says. "What you have learned before war, before hunger and all this craziness."

Katie's voice is insistent: *But it must have been hard on both of you anyway, the coded messages and the few seconds here and there, without any physical contact?*

Arthur turns from Sarah to the camera, bushy eyebrows knit together. "You need to touch someone to know how they feel? How *you* feel?" He swipes the air with a spotted hand. "It is only one of many ways to show how much you love," he says with finality. "Only one."

4

The celebration took place in a banquet room at Cappelli's restaurant, a crowded space filled with huge, too-green artificial plants, plastic brick walls, and loud Italian music that violined out over their heads. Katie sat at the small horseshoe-shaped bar alone, staring into the gilt-framed mirror right above the bottles of liquor. In it she watched Nick winding around the white-clothed tables, a beer in one hand, a slight, private smile on his face. This party was for him, a time to celebrate his winning the contract at the Warwick Center, but as Katie tracked his movements, she sensed the restless contradictions inside him. It was something about his smile—introspective but also a little arrogant—coupled with the way he carried himself around the room: an uncertain, speculative stride, trailing his fingers over chair tops, tables, and at one point the rim of an ashtray. As if there were answers about himself, this new success that had nothing to do with commonplace lisps or stutters, to be gleaned from the Braille sweep of his fingertips. From time to time, a group of Katie's relatives tried to catch Nick's eye, to offer their congratulations once again, but Nick kept on his thoughtful path, the smile intensifying, his hand moving cautiously over surfaces. From somewhere in the room, then, possibly a clue; Candice's laughter reached Katie's ears despite the loud music and rumble of conversations around her. Nick's smile deepened, his walk slowed, the tips of his fingers lingering on a gleaming metal lid at the corner of the banquet table.

Katie sighed. It was one of her mother-in-law's gifts, this laughter.

It issued from the very back of her throat, a low, undulating laugh that was confident and coy at the same time—the kind of laugh that seemingly offered instant intimacy. Katie was grateful at least that Nick's mother only made the visit from California every couple of years, that Katie had to pretend just fleetingly that this intimacy was openly offered to her, too. She shifted her eyes away from Nick to hunt down her mother-in-law: across the room with three of Katie's uncles, who were at that moment forming a semicircle around the woman. Candice was overdressed for the small Italian restaurant, her trim figure tapered into a backless silver dress, her hair pulled up in a complicated twist; her ears twinkled with huge diamonds that caught the light when she bent to extract a cigarette from her purse. Katie's uncles buzzed around her glittering mother-in-law like dazed and dazzled moths, each craning forward for a chance to touch a sliver of her light. Captivated by her—*stupefied,* really—but Katie understood it, too. The power of that evocative, dulcet laugh. She had fallen for it at first, too.

When Candice turned away to exhale a thin line of smoke, Katie caught a true glimpse of the mother-in-law she barely knew. She watched Nick's mother survey the room quickly with determined, hooded eyes, her indomitable jaw like stone. So like Nick's, those large, dark eyes that stood out from her lightly tanned face as they canvassed the room expertly, finally locating Nick by the buffet; Candice nodded faintly to herself, then turned to Katie's uncles, her face adjusting instantly. Less than ten seconds from that first exhale of smoke until she turned back to the men—if you weren't watching carefully, you'd miss the real woman hiding behind the smiles, the inviting laughter.

At the banquet table, Katie's father strolled over to Nick, grabbed his hand and slapped his shoulder. Nick smiled broadly, pumped her father's hand in return, but there was that familiar embarrassed tilt of his head, the same look of claustrophobia whenever the two men met face-to-face. Katie wondered, not for the first time, if this had anything to do with being raised by Candice alone; if this and Nick's stilted reactions to older men had anything to do with the fatherless history he kept from her over the years.

Katie's father drifted away when Candice moved into the mirror's frame. Nick smiled at his mother, held up his crooked arm to her; Candice wrapped her arm around his, and they wandered the length of the buffet together.

Katie watched Nick guide his mother through the buffet, his hand moving to her lower back now—the gesture so intimate, so self-assured and proprietary that Katie had to look away. They were a family, Nick and his mother, a whole, complete family of two, sharing the past and every little thing that came with it. Candice's presence and their mysterious history so important that they made Nick's body move in strange, irreconcilable ways—egotistical and unsure all at once.

Watching them together summoned a sudden, intense paroxysm of loneliness from the very center of Katie's body, eerily like the ones she experienced as a child and right up until the time she met Nick. She flicked her eyes away from them, turned from the mirror to see Dana approaching with a smile

—Still here? Dana said, plopping onto the stool next to her.

—I think I'm a little drunk, Katie said, her voice like cotton.

—That might be a good thing, her sister said, pointing, because Mom's got that look in her eye.

Their mother stood by the entrance of the room, next to a framed aerial shot of Italy, her eyes stalking the crowd. They finally settled on Nick and Candice.

—Lucky you, Dana said, and giggled. —Poor, poor Nick.

Their mother plowed through the crowd. She was wearing one of her new wigs tonight, a jet-black one that would have looked stylish with her normally dark complexion but now only highlighted how pale her face had become. She exchanged a few words with Candice, who smiled that enormous, sun-drenched smile, and then pulled Nick away, a hand clamped possessively around his wrist. She dragged him into a crowd of her neighbors then—neighbors who were invited tonight only so Katie's mother could brag about her son-in-law's challenging new job working with the mentally handicapped.

It was a familiar sight, instantly sobering: Katie's mother hauling someone into a crowd to boast, though usually it was Dana who was put on the spot like that. Nick handled it well enough—he smiled, shook hands, managed to look humble and appreciative at the same time. Her mother smiled proudly, threw her arms out wide. *He's taking care of the whole world,* Katie imagined her mother saying, and she felt the sting again. Not once had her mother bragged about Katie or her documentaries—not *once*.

Dana turned to her, misinterpreting the look on Katie's face. —She's going to be okay, Katie, she said. —They caught it very early.

Katie felt her face grow hot with shame. Of course their mother would survive her cancer; the doctors had given her an excellent prognosis, and her mother had announced that nothing, especially not a tumor the size of a pea, for God's sake, would be enough to kill her. But what kind of daughter was Katie anyway? Instead of trying to cherish this time with her mother, she was nurturing old resentments that seemed to grow with each passing year. Just a few weeks earlier, when Katie was planning a trip to celebrate Nick's new job and his thirtieth birthday, her mother had stepped in, proclaiming that the entire family should be involved with Nick's success. Before Katie could object, the pamphlets for Hawaii had been swept aside and her mother—fragile and pale from her third week of chemotherapy—was stubbornly calling restaurants and consulting about menus. Instead of being grateful, or asking if she could help, Katie had slumped into the recliner in her parents' living room, stewing at her mother's interference.

There were so many things Katie wanted to tell her sister in this moment, not just about their mother but how Nick turned on her sometimes, expertly cutting her down before she even knew what they were fighting about; the parts of himself he kept hidden from her, as if there were a whole other person inside him. And what she really wished she could say to Dana was how twice now—*crazy, crazy*—she had started fights over a wine stain on the counter, a mislaid credit-card bill, hoping they *would* catch fire, detonate inside Nick's brain and body. Actually *hoping* he would attack her with words like razors, because then there was afterward—his quivering apologies, Katie's absolute love for him and from him, their bodies crashing into each other. Katie built back up again for the moment.

But not all the way. No. She learned that quickly.

Afterward, no matter how powerful she felt with him inside, on top, behind, she felt the cuts inside her body, pieces of her chipped away for good. Gouges too deep to fill no matter how many times he whispered his apologies and her name and took her body back into his.

·

—We were hoping you'd stay with us, Mom, Nick said. The look on his face was suddenly boyish and shy.

Katie could sense her mother-in-law staring at her, so she turned her eyes to the parking lot, to her relatives saying their noisy good-byes.

—That would be so lovely, sweetheart, but as I've said, the arrangements are already made at the hotel.

—Katie and I don't mind huddling up on the couch. You could take the bed, and in the morning I'll make us a huge breakfast and we'll catch up. Nick said this with such an earnest expression on his face that Katie had to look away a second time.

Candice laughed, a deep, rolling wave of sound, and Nick automatically moved closer to her. —You're both so sweet, she said. —But I think I'll probably sleep in a little, so why don't we meet for an early lunch? My flight leaves at three o'clock, and it will give us plenty of time for a nice long sit-down.

—Great. Nick walked into his mother's outstretched arms.

—You should be so proud, Nicky, she murmured into his ear. —I never had any doubts. You have been brilliant since birth.

Nick blushed, his arms tightening around her. Candice turned half-way in Nick's arms to face Katie, sparkling smile in place. —Of course we would love for you to join us tomorrow, Katie, she said. —Please say you'll come?

—No, that's okay, why don't the two of you catch up? I have some work to do anyway.

—Yes, your documentaries. They must be so exciting and challenging, Candice replied, her eyes turning hard and mocking before she returned to her son's embrace.

·

Before they even drove out of the parking lot, Nick fell into a moody silence. He stared blankly at the cars passing on Post Road.

—Your mother could have canceled her reservation if she wanted to.

—I'll see her tomorrow, he said, pulling in to traffic. Both hands wrapped tightly around the wheel.

—I just don't understand why she doesn't like me.

Nick kept his eyes on the road, shook his head. —Nope, I'm not going to do this. I barely get to see her.

—And what did she mean by that—my documentaries are "challenging"?

—Jesus, every time, Nick muttered, glaring into the rearview mirror.

—You just don't see it, Nick, the way she looks at me sometimes.

—She hasn't *seen* you for over two years, Katie.

—So now she doesn't visit because of *me*?

—I didn't say that.

—I know, because you never say anything.

He shook his head, sighed dramatically.

—I'm just trying to get it, Nick, that's all.

—Get what?

—Everything. *You*.

—And we're off, he said in that tired voice she hated.

—Then let's do it! Let's go! I don't care if it gets messy, just talk to me.

He flicked his eyes at her quickly. —I talk to you every day.

—You know what I mean. She strained against her seat belt to face him. —Tell me something, Nick, she said. —Tell me about him. Your father.

—I met him twice, Katie. Twice. You know that.

—But how does that make you feel? How did that affect you—

—Isn't this Dana's job? Making people talk about their feelings?

—Don't do that. Don't make it a joke.

—I'm laughing?

They drove in silence for a few minutes. Out of the corner of her eye, she watched the lights of passing cars glide across Nick's face. His handsome, indifferent face.

—This is it, isn't it, Nick? she finally asked quietly.

—What?

—It's going to be like this forever, isn't it? she said. —Waiting. That's all I do. I wait for you.

—So stop, then. What do you want me to say?

—*Anything!* Say anything at all.

She steadied herself for his insults, her palms sinking into the cushioned seat on both sides, but his only answer was a thin, cruel smile. She stared at him, the profile of his face, how this smile altered him so completely. So unknown—so unwilling. She wasn't sure which was worse, Candice's phony smile or Nick's heartless, dismissive one. *Both of them,* she thought angrily, *with their secrets and superior smiles and contempt!* Something inside her snapped wide open.

—Fine, then I'll say something! she shouted. —Your mother hates me, Nick, and you don't even see it! You don't *want* to see it. You're so stuck up her ass that you can't even see *you*—so full of yourself you can barely hold your head up straight, but walking around like the floor might crack underneath you when she's in the same room. Can you honestly say that has nothing to do with her? She's a *phony,* Nick! You want to know why your father left both of you, take a good look, because she's a fucking *phony,* and you know it—

He slammed the brakes, hard. The front end swerved, back tire clipping the curb on Katie's side. Nick's teeth were exposed and clenched, dark eyes rigid on the road. She tried to say something—nothing came. He kicked the gas pedal, careened into an empty parking lot. Hit the brakes hard again—Katie's body jerked forward, the seat belt biting her shoulder. She crashed back into the seat, the air in her lungs pushed out.

Before she could compose herself, before a word would come, Nick calmly released his seat belt and leaned toward her, his fingers lightly closing around her throat. There wasn't any pressure in his touch—but his fingers were around her throat.

—Why do you always have to ruin it? His breath hot on her face.

—*Nick.*

—You're supposed to be happy for me.

—I am. She pried at his fingers. —Please.

His eyes drilled into hers, unseeing, so dark they looked black.
—Aren't you proud of your husband? Aren't you proud?

—*What are you doing, Nick?*

And then his face turned suddenly—a closed look that Katie knew well. Like fingers quickly curling under, hiding the palm beneath.

Nick finally released her, sat back in his seat. Her heart kicked a steady, violent rhythm against her ribs.

—Jesus, he finally said, blowing out air. He placed his hands carefully on the wheel, stared straight ahead.

—Nick, she whispered, her hand rising to her throat now.

He wouldn't look at her. —Did I hurt you?

—No. No, of course not.

He nodded slowly. His chest quickly rising, falling. He adjusted the rearview mirror, hooked his seat belt. —I can't believe I did that.

—You didn't hurt me.

He nodded again, exhaled loudly. Adjusted the rearview mirror again with a shaking hand.

—Why? she said.

He splayed his fingers, studied his hand like he didn't recognize it. —I'm sorry.

—Okay.

—I just don't like, he began slowly, —I just don't want to keep defending her. Defending myself.

—You don't have to.

—I don't?

—I just want you to trust me.

He stared out the windshield, pulled the gearshift into drive. —You just can't imagine, he said slowly, deliberately, —how fucking exhausting this has become.

•

At home they walked around each other, nursing their anger and embarrassment; they undressed in different rooms, waited politely for the other one to finish in the bathroom. In bed they kept their backs to each other, until Katie grabbed a pillow and headed for the living room.

She waited for him then—for the conclusion of this routine of pain and forgiveness, for the chance to feel connected to him again, to feel *herself* again. From the stifling living room, she listened to the air conditioner humming in their bedroom. Pictured Nick sleeping contentedly, the blankets tucked up around his body. After an hour she gave up, peeled the sweaty sheet off her, and headed for the shower.

The water was too hot, but Katie bent her head under the stream anyway, felt the rivers of steamy water curling down her face, around her nose, and onto her lips. Stayed like that, her belly and thighs and the tops of her feet scalding, trying to contain her fear, the implications of Nick's absence. She replayed the past few weeks since he'd started working at the Warwick Center—seeing now, suddenly and clearly, the importance of the changes. Nick, no longer waiting for her words of praise and recognition. No longer embellishing stories about cleft palates or lisps to make his work appear more important than it was, or leaving long pauses for Katie to fill in with her gushing admiration. Now he sat across from her at their dinner table, visions of his own glory filling his eyes without her help. He had long days full of real challenges now—adults with speech disorders complicated by learning disorders, cerebral palsy, and all the idiosyncratic methods of communication that each client brought to his sessions. Now Katie's job was to simply listen. She wished she could go back just a few weeks—regain her coveted position in their nightly discussions at the dinner table, even if it meant still silently resenting his ongoing, barely concealed indifference for her own work. What a minor issue his apathy seemed now. Nick had found the important job he'd always wanted, and her part in his days—maybe even his life—seemed small and insignificant.

Fear curled up inside her, cold and choking despite the steaming water, but then she heard the plastic crinkling of the shower curtain; she almost collapsed in relief. Nick's cool skin pressed against her spine and legs. He pushed his knee into the back of her right thigh, reached around her for the bar of soap.

At first she had to put her hands on the tile to steady herself against his vigorous washing, but soon enough one hand came up flat and pressing against her soaped shoulder. He swirled the foam across the expanse of her upper back, down her spine and onto her butt, making leisurely, wide circles on each cheek.

—We could still huddle, he said quietly.

—Back there, in the car, she said, shaking her head.

—I know.

—We can't add that, she said. —All the little things, the big things already—we can't add that.

—We won't. *I* won't.

He pressed himself against her, their wet bodies sealing. Traced a line from her elbow down to the knuckles of her hand.

—But you can't be like that either, he said quietly.

She whipped around to face him, falling backwards into the tile.

Her fears instantly forgotten, she glared at his lowered head through the running water that separated them now. —Me?

—What you said about . . . the things you said. It isn't you.

—You say things like that to me, Nick. *Horrible* things.

The water worked parts into his hair, ran down his face and into his eyes. He let it, arms hanging at his sides. —But that's *me,* he finally said. —Not you.

—That isn't fair. You can say hurtful things, but I can't?

—It isn't you, he insisted, his voice tremulous. He finally met her glance, placed his hands on both her shoulders. She saw the love, the need in his eyes. He pulled her forward, until their faces were only inches apart under the water. —It isn't *you,* Katie.

He turned her abruptly by the shoulders, so she was facing the tile again.

—I never would, you know, he said, his body shuddering as he tucked himself up against her. Hurt you . . . I . . . never could—

She leaned into him, pulled his arms around her. —I know. I do know that.

He nodded against her, gulping air. —Without you, he said. —If you weren't here, if I didn't have you, I wouldn't be anyone.

He cupped her ass and pulled, fingers digging into flesh.

Easy then, to remember the ways they *were* together—his hands moving roughly against her burning skin. She placed her hands flat on the tile, and his teeth bit into her shoulder.

—Gentle, she said, and he obeyed, his tongue licking into the water pooled in her collarbone.

—I'm so sorry, Katie. Right now, this is us. This is the part that's real.

She nodded, turned for the last time to face him. Nick covered her breast with his mouth, and she spread her legs wide, guided him inside her. Used one hand to steady herself, the other to push the back of his head into her.

From the shower to the floor in the living room to the bedroom. Almost the entire night, both of them tireless. When the sun finally started to rise, Katie held him inside her arms.

—No more apologies, she said when the sun finally slanted into the room and across the sheets. She allowed herself a small, teasing smile. —You have the rest of your life to make it up to me.

The EMT has been on the witness stand for almost an hour, describing the details of the day Jerry shot Nick, confirming the chaos he and his partner walked into inside the gym. Every time Richard asks him a question, he grabs his knuckles in one hand and swivels in his chair to answer the jurors directly.

There isn't anything remarkable about the way this man looks—slight and in his mid- to late twenties, with glasses and adolescent acne—yet his direct stare and deep, confident voice have the jurors paying close attention after all this time. Whenever he answers one of Richard's questions in detail, he watches the jurors with a serious look until Richard asks him another one; then he swivels back slowly to face Richard, as though he's tearing himself away from what's really important. The jurors watch him carefully, bend their heads to scribble his words onto their pads.

"So it's standard procedure, then, to use this cardiac monitor on unconscious clients?" Richard asks him.

The EMT grabs his knuckles, turns to the jurors. "Yes. In this particular case, however, we used the monitor solely to establish asystole, or what is commonly known as a flatline."

"And once you established this?"

"We did not attempt to resuscitate the victim at that point."

"You knew you couldn't save him?"

"We knew the victim's situation was not conducive to life."

Richard sighs heavily, lowers his head to think. "Up until that point, had you seen the defendant?"

For the first time, the EMT doesn't turn toward the jurors—he keeps his eyes locked on Richard, which causes a ripple of fidgeting among them. The Hispanic man in the front row frowns slightly, the two young women on either side of the elderly gentleman in the back row angle their heads to get a better look at the EMT's face.

"Not on the scene, actually."

"Then where?" Richard asks.

"I encountered the defendant out in the parking lot."

"And would you describe that, please?"

"The police were having a hard time containing him, so my partner and I went over to assist."

"And is that normal procedure? For an EMT to help restrain a suspect?"

"No, but they couldn't get control of him."

"Can you tell the jurors who 'they' are?"

The jurors don't seem to realize, or they are just too fascinated now to care, that this back-and-forth has been rehearsed. Without the EMT's serious face turned toward them, they strain forward, eyes moving between the two men. Their restless anticipation boils inside Katie, too—she is eager to replace pictures of Nick's lifeless body with Jerry's bulking rage, ready to break the stillness of death with the violence of Jerry's impending capture.

"'They,'" the EMT says, and finally turns to the jurors, who crane toward him as if one, "were the police officers, about five or so, and a firefighter. I think there were two or three people from the Warwick Center trying to help as well."

"So possibly nine people, and they still couldn't get him into the squad car?"

The EMT stares at the jurors. "They couldn't even get him on the ground."

"Please describe what happened after you jumped into that mess," Richard says wearily.

•

Donna doesn't try to prolong the image of Jerry's violent flailing, of his striking out at Veronica, who sustained a broken arm from the fall, or of the police officer who finally used his Taser to get him to the ground. While Donna thanks him for coming in today, Katie closes her eyes and flips back and forth between two images: Nick, pale, still, *gone,* and Jerry, face bloated with pain, his massive body convulsing on the pavement.

•

It surprises Katie how many people come in and out of the court-room during Officer Marzelli's testimony. Judge Hwang has warned the courtroom about the gruesome nature of the photos, has asked anyone unprepared to view them to leave before Richard introduces them on the overhead projector. There is a hushed nervousness in the air as Officer Marzelli confirms the EMT's testimony, a buildup that urges people to find reasons to rise from their seats and leave, then sidle back in.

Katie keeps her eyes toward the front. She wants the jurors to know that she is unconcerned with these movements, that what is happening up on the stand is the only thing worth her attention. *Your reaction is important here, Katie,* Richard told her earlier. *I'm counting on you.* She feels strong, visible, ready for what is to come, so she is surprised at the relief she feels when, seconds after the familiar squeak and rush of air from the courtroom door, her father slides into the front row beside her. He gives her a calm smile, drapes his arm on the bench behind her. She eases back, feels her father's fingers kneading her shoulder.

There are two TVs in the courtroom, one in the front for the specta-tors and lawyers, the other beside the front row near Katie, facing the jurors. Richard walks with the stack of photos to the projector.

"Officer Marzelli, can you tell us what we're looking at here?" Rich-ard says, and places the first photo on the projector. There are audible gasps throughout the room: Nick appears for the first time in a close-up, his face masked in blood, a small black hole between his right eye and the bridge of his nose. There are swipe marks across his lips and chin, where Daniel wiped away the blood to give him CPR.

Katie feels her father's fingers squeezing into her neck as Officer Mar-zelli confirms that the photo identifies what he witnessed in the gym.

The second photo shows Nick's face and chest, the dried, clotted blood on his neck and the thick pool of it underneath his head.

"This one shows the extremity of blood loss, there on the victim's body and around the head."

One by one, Officer Marzelli identifies the photos taken by the CSI investigator, and each time Katie's stomach contracts, her heart skipping, before she flicks her eyes from Nick's face and body to the corner of the judge's bench.

The last photo shows Nick's entire body, the awkward angle of his left leg from Daniel turning him over, his arms limp by his sides.

"That's the bullet casing by his arm and the murder weapon by his left leg."

Richard lingers over the photo for a moment, then asks Officer Marzelli to confirm the previous description of Jerry's behavior in the parking lot.

"We very reluctantly agreed not to handcuff him inside, but as soon as we stepped out the door, it was chaos."

"So it's safe to say that the defendant was violent and out of control?" Richard asks.

"Yes."

Donna objects to the term "out of control," but Richard doesn't miss a step; he hands her a piece of paper, has it tagged, gives it to Officer Marzelli.

"Can you read the fourth line of your arresting report, Officer?"

" 'Suspect was violent and out of control at the time of arrest.' "

"Thank you, Officer."

•

Donna stands at the defense table, legal pad in her hand.

"After you brought Jerry out of the work-program building, he became violent?"

"Yes."

"Besides flailing around because he was scared and confused—"

"Objection to the question."

"Okay," Donna says, "okay." A woman in the front row holds a pad up to her. Donna scans the pad, nods, turns back to Office Marzelli with a smile.

"When you first approached Jerry, was he violent and out of control?"

"No."

"He was actually very calm, wasn't he?"

"Yes."

"You didn't even feel the need for handcuffs at that point, did you?"

"Well, we did, actually. But the director of the program pleaded with us to cuff him outside, away from the other clients."

"And you agreed because Jerry was cooperating fully?"

"Yes."

Officer Marzelli gives short, clipped answers, but it's clear that Donna is gaining ground. The violent picture of Jerry is slowly being replaced with a docile, cooperative man who was only "set off" when he saw the police cars in the parking lot—an understandable reaction, given his history.

"Why isn't Richard objecting?" Katie whispers to her father. She shrugs away from his answering nudge to sit back.

"So up until that point out in the parking lot, he was a model suspect?"

"I suppose so."

"Thank you, Officer Marzelli," Donna says with a satisfied smile.

•

At Hemingway's, Katie's father hovers behind her in front of the hostess stand, his hand resting lightly on her back. She watches the hostess studying her face, pencil poised over a clipboard—the older woman clearly trying to place Katie, why she looks so familiar. She makes a decision, places her pencil carefully on the stand.

"There's a twenty-minute wait," she says quietly, eyeing the crowd at the door, "but I can seat you now." She swipes up two oversize menus, nods respectfully at Katie and her father. "Right this way, please."

A young waiter immediately steps up to their table, pours them water from a glistening metal decanter. He nods importantly at them as they order, like they are making crucial life decisions by requesting a turkey club and a cup of tomato basil soup.

"Special treatment, huh?" her father asks with a wink after the waiter walks away. He lifts his water glass.

"You're doing a good job, Dad."

He holds the tipped glass in front of his mouth. "With what?"

"You know, all the hugging and everything. It looks good for the jurors, like you're here to support me."

He puts the glass down. "I *am* here to support you, sweetie."

"Just keep doing it, okay?"

"Okay, Katie."

Their food appears minutes later. Her father digs in, happy to have something to do with his hands. "Your mother is going to let Jack out," he says, and takes a big bite of his turkey club. "She'd kill me if she knew I was having bacon."

"I can't believe Richard didn't stop her," Katie says, pushing her cup of soup away.

"Your mother?"

She doesn't try to hide her impatience. "Donna Treadmont, Jerry's lawyer."

"This guy knows what he's doing. The *Providence Journal* said today that he's building up a strong case."

"He should have recrossed or something. Those jurors need to know what kind of person Jerry is," Katie says.

Her father eyes his sandwich like he's trying to memorize the contents. He looks up at Katie, his face hesitant; he puts the sandwich down, wipes his mouth with his napkin. "He's that kind of person, too, Katie," he says gently.

"What do you mean?"

"I don't know Jerry like you do—" he begins, picking up a small piece of tomato off his plate.

"But," Katie says, leaning forward.

Her father flicks the tomato back onto the plate, then slowly pushes the plate to the middle of the table. "But when they talked about him earlier, the way he acted, I could see him then, too."

"You mean calm and cooperative? You think that's who he is?"

"People aren't just one thing, sweetie."

"He *murdered* Nick!"

Heads turn toward their table. Her father looks around the restaurant, nods slowly, like someone acknowledging old friends at a class reunion. He waits for the curious strangers to return to their meals, then rests his gaze at a spot on the tablecloth.

"Whenever you brought him to the house, he was a gentleman. A good kid."

"He isn't a kid, Dad. He's a man."

Her father reaches across the table for her, but Katie pulls both hands into her lap. He picks up her soup spoon, taps the table with it.

"Remember the game we used to play on Sundays, me and Jerry?" he asks her.

They'd go almost every Sunday for dinner at her parents' house—Nick and Katie and Jerry, and Dana and Michael, too—and soon after the meal was served, her father would eye Jerry's heaping plate with a grave face. —You have some money on you, Jerry? Got a way to pay for that meal? And Jerry, who loved her father and all his teasing, would hide his smile behind his napkin. —Bad service, he'd say, trying to hold in the laughter. —No good. Too slow.

"Is that who you see when you look at him?" Katie asks her father now.

Her father examines the spoon. "I don't know what to think, Katie. I've tried to understand, but I don't know what happened that day."

"He shot my husband in the face, and he took everything away from me, in a matter of seconds. He took away my life. That's what happened."

He looks her in the eye now, hands her the spoon; Katie takes it without thinking, like she's accepting a present.

"Not all of it," he says, "Right? Not every single thing?"

"Not everything, no, but—but how would you feel if the cancer came back, Dad?"

The reaction is instant, expected: fear fills his hazel eyes, makes his chin quiver. She feels the cruelty behind her words, yet she can't help herself. "I know it's been almost five years, Dad, but it happens."

He draws his hand down his face with a sigh. "I would hope," he says, "that if I lost her, I would find a way to go on. That there would be other parts of my life worth living, and that my family would help me." He looks around the restaurant, and Katie watches as thoughts of Jerry filter away. "But we'd fight it until the last day, the last second."

"That's what I'm doing. I'm fighting."

After a pause he leans toward her. "But Nick's already gone."

"Not yet," she says, "not until Jerry is guilty."

The waiter approaches the table, takes a step back when he sees Katie and her father squaring off.

"Just the check," Katie says, turning away from her father.

6

Katie stood at the front reception desk at the Warwick Center, waiting for Veronica to get off the phone. She could probably just grab a visitor's pass and log in to the work program herself, but Veronica was making dramatic eyes at her, which usually meant that she had some gossip or news to share. Katie wondered absently if it had anything to do with Nick's moodiness this past week—the reason she was visiting for the third day in a row.

—I understand, Mr. Lunderville, Veronica said into the phone. —And I'm so sorry. Our custodian, Billy, explained to your daughter just this morning that he was only joking about walruses living in toilets. Veronica shook her head, not unkindly.

Katie smiled, then scanned the hallway to the right, toward the administrative offices. Patricia Kuhlman's deep voice trailed out into the hallway, so Katie wandered in the opposite direction. Down the hallway on the left—where the nurses' station, employee kitchen, and more offices were located, including Nick's—Katie could hear the program nurse, Dottie, laughing. Judith emerged from the kitchen and puffed her way down the hall toward Katie with a tray of boxed juices, the straws poking up.

—Hey there, she said, giving Katie a bright smile.

—Hey, Judith.

—Can't keep away from us, huh?

—Guess not.

Katie checked the flyers on the bulletin board near the reception desk. Colorful sheets of paper announced upcoming events (a chili cook-off for the staff next week, a roster to sign up for volunteer work at the Special Olympics at URI in June), surrounded by pages of the clients' wobbly drawings. Easter was over a month away, but every picture was bursting with red and blue and green colored Easter eggs—messy, zigzagging designs filled with stars and diamonds and patches of color that reminded Katie of her own childhood, of dyeing eggs with Dana as their mother looked on and warned them not to touch the shells before they dried. Some of the clients *were* like children, Katie thought: sweet and loving and innocent, and sometimes balding and middle-aged and paunchy, too, but children just the same. Katie wondered, not for the first time, what it was like to be trapped in childhood like that—if their adult bodies rebelled occasionally, if they ever recognized the incongruity of their age and the way the world treated them.

In the seven months Nick had worked as their primary speech-language pathologist, these clients, and most of the staff, had embraced Katie as one of their own. Even when she showed up unannounced for three days in a row like this, no one seemed surprised or irritated that she was back again. Instead they fussed around her and asked her questions about her projects, made her feel almost as loved, almost as necessary to their lives, as Nick. She turned and watched Veronica wagging her head over the phone.

—No, I really *can't* imagine what it was like fishing all those sandwiches out of your toilet last night, she was saying. —Oh, dear, Jeanne threw in a can of corn, too?

As soon as Veronica hung up, she signaled to Katie. —Don't ask.

—Bit of a clog at home?

Veronica grinned. —Leave it to Billy.

She stood, placed the BEE RIGHT BACK! sign on the desk—a smiling bumblebee with a pink ribbon in its hair and dashes behind it to show it flying away.

—I want you to see something, Katie.

She followed Veronica into the workshop. Inside this vast room that looked like a warehouse, the clients sat at long benches assembling boxes or grappling with menial tasks that seemed to fascinate some of them. The clients looked up with expectant eyes at their arrival; seconds later a group had gathered around Katie and Veronica, touching and hugging.

—You stay? a slender, balding man named John asked, petting Katie's arm. —You stay today and tomorrow?

—Pretty hair, a woman in her mid-thirties with cerebral palsy said, resting her head on Katie's other arm. —Want to watch me put labels on the boxes?

—What color do you feel when you're unsad? asked a girl in a wheelchair, one hand curled at her side, the other around the chair's control. She scowled at Katie, waiting.

—Do you love chocolate? asked another.

Katie answered them all, and Marty, the elderly supervisor who was always threatening to retire, nodded his approval.

—Okay, guys, Katie didn't come here for a party, he said mildly, scooping them away with his arm. They scrambled back to their seats.

—She's here to kiss Nick, a boy with Down syndrome taunted loudly, and then there were fits of giggling at all the tables.

—This way, Veronica said quietly, grabbing Katie's hand.

They walked to the back of the room, down a short hall, and past the cafeteria, to the opening of a small vestibule. Veronica ushered Katie into a room with a two-way mirror, then checked to make sure the intercom was off. Inside the adjoining room, Nick sat at a table with a client Katie didn't recognize.

He was enormous.

A tattered T-shirt stretched across his wide chest, his fleshy upper arms pushing against the thinning material. He watched Nick, his light blue eyes terrified, his pendulous lower lip pushed out like a shelf.

—His name is Jerry, Veronica whispered. —He started about a week and a half ago. File thick as an encyclopedia.

Katie's eyes moved to Nick. He held his body very still, hands folded on the table, his mouth moving in silent conversation with the man.

—Nick's trying like hell, but he can't even get Jerry to talk to him.

Katie moved to the mirror, placed her hand on the glass.

Nick kept his head bent forward slightly, a compassionate, paternal look on his face as he spoke. Jerry continued staring, wide-eyed, and then his body suddenly jolted. He lowered his head, cradled himself in his arms. A quick flash of anger sliced across Nick's face, pulsed momentarily inside his eyes. Gone an instant later, easy to miss, Katie thought, if you hadn't before tracked that same anger in his eyes as he formed his punishing words.

—Nick never mentioned him, Katie whispered.

—Jerry won't communicate with anyone unless prompted, word for word, by Patricia, Veronica whispered back. —It must be driving Nick crazy, but you'd never know it.

—Why Patricia?

—I don't know, something to do with his past, his mother, I think. I haven't read the file. Nick spends all his downtime with it. Looking for clues, I guess.

Nick leaned into the table, slowly reached toward Jerry. In a flash, Jerry jerked away, his large hands pushing the air in front of him, eyes clamming shut. Nick sat back, and Katie almost gasped: there, on Nick's face, was an emotion utterly unfamiliar to her, a raw, exposed fear that was gone before she could fully register it.

—Hello, Katie.

She hadn't heard Patricia's approach. Katie didn't turn to the director, just mumbled a greeting and kept her eyes on Nick.

—I wanted Katie to see Jerry, Veronica said apologetically, as if she'd been caught doing something wrong.

—That's okay, Patricia said, in a tone that said it wasn't okay at all. —Though perhaps we should give them some privacy.

•

They made dinner together that night, Katie brushing orange glaze onto two chicken breasts and waiting for Nick to mention Jerry, his fear of failing to connect with a client for the first time. Instead, Nick talked about the home they would purchase in the next few months, his attention focused on the small russet potatoes he peeled into the sink.

—We can't afford anything palatial, of course, he said. —But I'd prefer something dignified, like that last one we saw. But in a better neighborhood. He kept his eyes on the small potato in his hand, as if he were addressing *it* rather than Katie.

Katie listened to the confidence in his voice, watched how it contrasted with his actions—the haphazard, nearly frantic peeling, the red skins flying and sticking to the sides of the sink and the faucet.

—I stopped by the center to see you today, she said casually. —But you were busy.

He stopped peeling, gave her a blank look. —When?

—Around two? Veronica said you were in session with a new client.

He scowled, started peeling again. —I'm talking about a house here, Katie. *Our* house. Am I the only one interested in getting out of this little shithole apartment? His face doing that thing. *Gearing up.*

She dropped the brush with glaze on it, moved behind him quickly, and wrapped her arms around him.

—I can't wait for us to move into a new house, honey. But I just had to tell you. I walked in that front door today and I got this huge burst of pride that I know you. Veronica says almost every time I visit that you're the best speech pathologist they've ever had.

Peeler raised, Nick peered into the sink full of wet, red skins. He turned around in her arms, slowly. Looked at her carefully, his eyes tracing her entire face—almost as if he were tracking his own features in a mirror, unable to recognize them.

—I can't imagine the pressure, she said, resting her head on his chest. Listening to his heart thrumming against her ear.

She felt him shrug in her arms.

—Is it a man or a woman? she asked.

Nick stepped back, out of her arms. Looked closely at her again. —Who?

—The new client.

—Man.

—Big speech issues?

He shrugged again. —Too early to tell yet. He turned to the sink again, shoulders thrust back. —Shouldn't be a problem, though.

—At least not for you, she said lightly, and walked to the stove. She pushed the chicken into the oven.

He stared at the potato in his hand. —This one might take a little time. He's got this very messed-up past, and he has trouble communicating.

—Well, thank God you're there, right? she said. —Chicken's in, so you better move it with those potatoes.

Nick watched her adjusting the heat on the oven, finally smiled.

—You look pretty tonight, he said.

Katie raised one eyebrow at him. —Just tonight? she said. —What about last night? Or the night before that?

He shook his head at her, finally grinned. —Idiot, he said, and reached for her.

•

Just before bed, as Katie brushed her teeth over the sink, she suddenly felt Nick's hands on her hips. It unnerved her sometimes, the way he would sneak up on her like this, but there was comfort, too—this need for her, the way it would come so unexpectedly. The understanding between them that she was always ready for him. His thumbs pushed against her lower back, bending her forward. She rested her elbows on the sink, her toothbrush still in one hand, and Nick lifted her nightgown and hooked his fingers onto her panties. He pulled them down to mid-leg, and Katie waited for him to kiss her neck, to cup her breasts in both hands or run his tongue between her shoulder blades. Instead he drove himself at her, missing, and then again, until he was inside her. Katie gripped the toothbrush to stop from screaming out in pain.

—Nick, she said, or thought she said. When he didn't answer, she tried to pivot away, but Nick's hands tightened on her hips, holding her in place. She watched him behind her in the mirror, his closed eyes, the look of intense concentration on his face.

—*Katie.*

She smiled and slumped over all the way, moved in time with him. Listened to her name, his need for her. His voice shaping her body.

7

"I'm not sure what you're asking me to do," Katie says to Richard after the lunch break. "You want me to act for the jurors?"

"No, of course not," Richard says, placing a comforting hand on her arm.

They're standing near the bathrooms opposite the courtroom, bodies huddled in consultation. Over Richard's shoulder Katie sees Veronica walk inside, followed closely by Daniel.

"But you know how important your reaction will be when Agent Fortier shows it to them," he tells her. "Think how it will affect these jurors."

"But I don't know how—I don't think I can pull it off."

"Okay, well, there are ways to get into this. Think about when you were a kid and you'd react so strongly to what an actor was going through on the screen, how you'd really *feel*—"

Katie takes a quick step back. "Who told you that?"

"No one." For a split second, Richard looks guilty, like he's accidentally discovered something about Katie he shouldn't know. "But don't all kids do that? Get lost in the main character of a book, or even in a cartoon animal from a movie? And then experience the same emotions?"

Katie eyes him warily. "I guess so."

"But I'm not asking you to act or even pretend here. I just know that sometimes it might feel like all of this isn't real anymore, and it's easy to lose some of what actually happened and the natural emotions that go along with it due to this long process. And we have to find ways to get ourselves back into it—"

"I haven't forgotten Nick once in this. I've never stepped outside of it, not once."

"I'm sorry," he says, pressing her arm again. "Of course you haven't."

"If I do this, then it will be real."

"Look, Katie, I've counted on you for so much, and maybe it isn't fair to ask you to really put yourself back in that moment."

"I've been inside that gym every day since this trial began," she says. "Every moment of every day since Nick died."

"So—"

"So if it happens, it will be *real*."

•

The CSI agent, a hefty bald man with a perfectly groomed goatee, blows air into the opening of two surgical gloves and snaps them onto his hands. He waits for Richard, who is in deep consultation with Detective Mason at the right side of the room. The two men talk quietly, surrounded by cardboard boxes marked LaPlante Evidence.

"Mr. Bellamy?" Judge Hwang prompts.

Richard nods and accepts a small manila envelope from Detective Mason. He walks over to Agent Fortier, hands it off. "Do you recognize that envelope, Agent Fortier?"

"I do."

"And would you identify it for us?"

"The label has my initials on it right here," the agent says, pointing with a gloved finger, "and it reads that it contains a hair sample."

Agent Fortier confirms that he was the one who collected it from the crime scene and then sent it to the Warwick Police Department, who in turn sent it to SBI for testing.

"Would you open it, please, and confirm that the label and contents match up?"

Agent Fortier tears open the top, pulls out a small plastic envelope that looks empty. Holds it up to the jurors, confirming that it is Jerry's hair sample, taken from the scene.

Richard treks across the room and returns with envelope after envelope, a steady stream of evidence the CSI agent gathered at the scene. At first there isn't much interest on the jurors' faces: the agent pulls out a letter, another hair sample, the broken doorknob from the shed behind the Warwick Center. But even the jurors are able to read Richard's movements now—when he strides purposefully across the room with a large envelope in his hands, they sit up straight, suddenly attentive.

Up until this point, Agent Fortier shook each envelope until the contents settled at the bottom, then carefully tore off the top. This time he pulls a knife out of his front pocket and snaps it: a long blade scissors out with a loud click. The heavy woman in the front row gasps, then flushes; she hides her embarrassed laugh behind her notepad. Agent Fortier shakes the envelope, slices the top open. He pulls out a rolled-up shirt.

"And what is that?"

"This is Nicholas Burrelli's shirt." He holds it up, and the cloth unfurls. Dark brown stains saturate the thick collar, bleed into the entire top half.

Katie's eyes travel all over the shirt—the last piece of clothing Nick ever wore—and wraps her arms around herself.

"And is this shirt in the same shape today as when you took it into custody on May fifth?"

"Yes."

"And was this in your exclusive care, custody, and control from the time you collected it until you turned it over to the Warwick Police Department?"

"Yes."

The shirt still held high, he explains the staining process, the chemical investigation from SBI, the DNA testing. That the blood is Nick's.

A few minutes later, there is only silence as Richard stands with Detective Mason near the boxes, consulting. The jurors stretch forward when Detective Mason hands Richard a medium-size envelope. Richard crinkles it inside his hands as he slowly makes his way across the room.

Agent Fortier slices open the envelope, pulls out a clear plastic bag. Inside, a small .22 revolver.

"Will you take it out of the plastic bag, sir?"

Agent Fortier pulls it out, holds up the small gun in both gloved hands.

It looks like a toy, Richard had said earlier, outside the courtroom. *I don't think it will have the punch we need. Maybe . . .*

I'm not sure what you're asking me to do.

"Will you let the jurors get a better look?" Richard asks the agent.

Agent Fortier rises, holds up the gun. He walks past the jurors, and a few half rise out of their seats to see it. When he gets to the end of the row he turns slightly in Katie's direction, and Katie half rises, too. She stares at the gun, and then her hands slowly come up to cover her mouth. She nods at Agent Fortier, sits down with a long, shaky exhale. Feels the jurors' eyes on her, stares at her lap.

As she keeps her eyes trained on her folded hands, she wonders what Richard's face looks like right now—what *his* reaction is. She wonders if what she just did was for him or if it was real. Wonders if, by the time the trial is over, she'll be able to tell the difference.

•

Donna stays seated at the table for her questioning, her forearm touching Jerry's. Jerry has a pencil in his hand, the pad in front of him, but his eyes seem to be fighting sleep; his lids droop, snap open, flutter again.

"Part of your job is to take photos of the crime scene?" she asks Agent Fortier.

"Yes."

"Once you book and fingerprint a suspect, I understand that sometimes you also take additional photos. Can you explain this to the jurors?"

Agent Fortier turns to the jurors. "If the suspect has tattoos, or any distinguishing marks, we take photos of them and keep them on file."

Donna glances at Jerry, pushes her arm into his before she rises. Jerry, well trained by now, pulls the pad in front of him and stares at it. But his lips begin to move slightly.

"And did you take any such photos of my client after his arrest?"

"I photographed some scars on his body."

Donna picks up a folder on her desk, walks it over to Richard; he flips through the photos inside, nods at Donna, hands the folder back.

"Your Honor, the defense would like to admit Exhibits One through Nine."

While the court reporter tags each photo, Donna checks on Jerry. She turns away immediately, touches her hair, fusses with the sleeve of her suit jacket. The jurors watch her nervous movements, their faces curious, but it isn't the photos that provoke Donna into action. Back at the defense table, Jerry's lips move faster, his face wrinkling up like he's arguing with himself. A woman in the front row finally notices and scoots over to him. She talks softly to him, discreetly pulls something out of her pocket. Pours water into a small cup, hands the cup to him, and then places what Katie assumes is a pill in his palm.

Donna carries the stack to the overhead projector. She places the first one on the glass. The TV screen fills with a close shot of Jerry's torso—three bumpy scars, about two inches long, stretch across his stomach in a neat row.

"What is this we're looking at?"

"These are three scars on the defendant's torso," Agent Fortier says.

Donna removes the photo, places another one on the glass: a shot of Jerry's leg, revealing six circular white indented scars.

"And this one?" she says in a soft voice.

"These are scars on his left calf."

"These are burn marks on Jerry's leg?"

"Objection. Agent Fortier isn't a scar expert."

"Sustained."

"Okay," Donna says, tapping the glass. "Did you ask Jerry how he got these marks?"

"Objection. Relevance."

"Overruled."

"He said his mother burned him with a cigarette," Agent Fortier says, "because he was bad."

"Objection, Your Honor. I don't see how scars from over thirty-seven years ago have anything at all to do with the murder of Nick Burrelli six months ago."

"Overruled."

One by one, Donna places the photographs on the glass, and Agent Fortier identifies them.

"Those are scars on the defendant's ankles and feet. He said his mother made him stand in the kitchen sink while she poured boiling water into it."

"That's a photo I took of the defendant's chest. He said his mother hit him with an extension cord."

"And did he tell you why she hit him with an extension cord?" Donna asks.

"He said his mother told him he had to be punished. Because he had sinned."

Donna pauses before she puts the last photo on the glass—she stares at it, flicks her eyes to Jerry, lips compressed in a grim line.

The TV screen fills with a close-up of Jerry's back. There are sounds of distress from some of the jurors, who look away and then at the TV again. Katie eyes the long white crisscrossing lines that fill the expanse of Jerry's back, at the dozens of pink divots in his flesh and the large arrow-shaped pink scar in between his shoulder blades.

Donna points to the pink divots. "These?"

"The defendant said his mother poured hot oil on him because God was angry with him."

"And these?" Donna's finger trails the white lines.

"Radio antennae," Agent Fortier says, looking away for a moment.

"And this," Donna asks, her finger trembling right above the arrow-shaped scar.

Agent Fortier shifts in his chair. "The defendant said his mother tied him facedown on the bed and put a hot iron on his back."

Donna shakes her head, her fingers hovering over the photo as if she's afraid to touch it. "Thank you, Agent Fortier."

•

"Just a couple of questions on recross, Your Honor."

"Go ahead."

Richard rises, walks around the table, and smiles confidently at Agent Fortier. "You realize that this is a trial about Nick Burrelli, who was shot point-blank in the face just over six months ago?"

"I do."

"And that the defendant's mother isn't on trial here?"

"Yes."

"And according to the defendant, most of the scars are over thirty-seven years old?"

"Yes."

"That's quite a long time ago, isn't it?"

"It is."

"Thank you, sir." Richard saunters back to the table, nodding with satisfaction. He stops, turns around. "Oh, one last question, Agent Fortier. Did the defendant say anything else about the scars all over his body?"

"Yes."

"Can you tell us what he said?"

"He said when someone does something bad, God wants them to be punished."

Richard waits for the murmurs to die down. "And did Mr. LaPlante share with you what Nick Burrelli did that warranted *his* punishment?"

"Objection!"

"Withdrawn."

. . .

Katie left her father outside the restaurant right after lunch, assuring him she was okay before heading back to the courthouse alone, so she's surprised to see his car parked in the driveway, right behind Dana and Michael's Jeep—another surprise. It looks like every light is on in the house, and Katie's first thought is Jack—something has happened to Jack. She rushes up the walk, barrels through the door.

The living room smells like Lemon Pledge and there are vacuum tracks in the beige carpet. Katie strides through the room toward the kitchen, notices that the knickknacks on the mantel are rearranged and that the fern by the entertainment stand has drops of water budding on its leaves.

Katie reaches the archway, steps into the kitchen. "What's all this?"

Her mother stands at the stove, one hand on her hip as she stirs a wooden spoon inside a pot. The kitchen is rich with the smell of her mother's Bolognese, Katie's favorite.

"Surprise," her mother says, turning with a bright smile. "We've invited ourselves over for dinner."

Michael is slumped at the kitchen table, his eyes glassy; he waves at Katie, winks in slow motion. "Surprise," he echoes, grinning at her. His left cheek is puffed out, and Katie remembers: root canal.

Her mother points at Michael with the spoon. "Vicodin," she states.

The counters have been scrubbed and Windexed, and the floor is gleaming; the light reflects off of Jack's metal food and water bowls, pushed off to the side of the stove near the louvered doors that open up to the washer and dryer. Beside them the dog toys are stacked neatly inside a wicker basket.

"You didn't have to clean," Katie says to her mother's back.

Her mother stays focused on the pot, dismisses her with a wave. "It was no problem. Your father dropped me off on his way to court." Strands of gray hair peek out the sides of her mother's platinum wig.

Dana emerges from the half bathroom, a slightly guilty look on her face as she wipes her hands with a towel. "Hey," she says, walking past their mother to the laundry doors. She opens them, throws the towel into the washing machine.

"Hi," Katie says. "Did I get any mail, Mom?"

"I sorted it, hon. I threw out flyers and anything that didn't look important." Her mother turns around. "Did you know that that dog likes to chew on it?"

"You didn't have to do all this." Katie should thank her, yet something about having everything in its place, sorted through and cleaned by her mother, feels like an accusation.

"I answered your phone today, too. The messages are over there." Her mother aims the spoon at the answering machine—even the black casing shines now—but there isn't any paper bearing messages next to it.

Katie's father emerges from the basement. "Hey, sweetie, there you are!" He snaps off the light, slams the basement door. "I put in a new bulb at the top of the stairs and checked the heater. You can't be too careful this time of year." He turns to Katie's mother. "Did you ask her about this guy? What's his name?"

"Paul Minsky," Michael says slowly. He rests his palm on his good cheek and gives Katie a sleepy smile.

"How do you feel, babe?" Dana asks her husband. Michael gives her a thumbs-up and closes his eyes.

"Your mother said this Paul guy sounded a little . . . *you know,"* her father says, raising his eyebrows meaningfully.

"Dad," Dana says, in a tone that sounds too much like her mother's warning voice.

"What?" he asks Dana innocently. He walks past her, ignoring her indignant frown, and peers over his wife's shoulder to inspect the inside of the pot.

"Jimmy, we don't mind the gays, remember?" her mother says, sneaking a peek at Dana. She shoulders him away. "Why don't you get the water started?"

Dana gives Katie a look: Patience. "Dad told us about this morning, and Mom thought it would be nice if we all had dinner together." Dana gives her a bright smile. "Wasn't that a great idea?"

"You looking at property in North Carolina, Katie?" her father asks from behind the counter.

"What? Oh, no," she says. "I was thinking of making an investment with some of the insurance money. You know, before it runs out."

"Paul Minsky is gay?" Michael asks, eyes still shut. He scratches his beard, the tip of his nose.

They all ignore him, except for Dana, who smiles indulgently at him. "The Realtor from Topsail Island, honey?"

"Mmmmmm, right."

"Hey," Katie says suddenly, "where's Jack?"

"Oh, I let him out, hon. That dog has to urinate every two seconds."

Katie rushes to the slider door. "You can't just let him out, Mom, you have to keep an eye on him." She steps outside, marches to the edge of the deck. Scans the backyard, panic rising, when she sees Jack sitting by the trash cans, ears lowered.

Dana walks up behind her, lights a cigarette. "It's Mom," Dana says, blowing out a long stream of smoke. "I'd be hiding out there, too."

"It's okay, c'mon, Jack."

Jack takes a step forward, stops.

"He's kind of cute," Dana says.

"Jack." Katie squats down, holds out her arms. "Come *here*."

The dog charges to the deck, bounds up the steps and into Katie's arms.

"Are you going to keep him?" Dana asks.

"For now," Katie says, picking him up. He licks her face wet, wiggles his body over to give Dana some attention.

Dana allows his frenzied licks for a few seconds; she steps back, scratches his long nose, raises her cigarette to her mouth. "Hello, Jack."

Katie turns toward the slider: Michael is resting his head on the table now, and her mother is directing her father to the dish cabinet with the wooden spoon.

"Okay," Katie says, looking Jack in the face. "Let's get this over with."

•

She feels a little indulgent during dinner—ungracious, even—but everyone is so attentive as Katie relays the details of the day, and what will come next, that she feels an unfamiliar stirring of self-assurance sweeping through her body, urging her on. Her confidence grows throughout the meal, until she finds herself using a slightly superior tone with her mother.

"Well, of course they're allowed to open up all the bags of evidence, Mom," she says, buttering a piece of bread with impatient strokes. "How else will the jurors get to see them?"

Her mother takes in this information silently, with arched eyebrows.

After the table is cleared, she watches her mother and Dana quietly skirting around each other to clean up and make the coffee, their movements brisk and economical. Michael snores on the sofa in her living room, and her father, who sits across the table from her, seems entirely captivated by the small silver spoon in the sugar bowl. As he taps it on the bowl, Katie skips her eyes between all of them, the suspicion mounting with this uncharacteristic silence in the room.

Jack lies beside Katie with his body pushed into her leg; every so often, he sits up and pushes at her hand or thigh with his snout, like he needs reassurance that everything is okay. He turns his head toward the living room, where Michael's snores have suddenly kicked up a notch. She pats Jack distractedly, watches Dana's smiling approach.

"So I can be in court tomorrow," Dana says. She places the coffeepot on the table, pulls out a chair. "Mom promised to check on Michael, but I'm sure he'll feel much better by then."

Her mother cuts her eyes at the living room "He'll be fine," she says, joining them at the table with a pint of half-and-half.

"You don't have to come if you're busy."

"No, I put in for some personal days today," Dana says casually.

Katie's mother gazes at Dana, and her father sneaks a look at both of them: Dana only takes personal days when there is an emergency, and apparently Katie has become just that; it's clear now why they're here—rather than feel relief or admiration that Katie is trying to take control of her life, they're panicked. Her father dribbles more cream into his coffee, and Dana and her mother concentrate on their mugs, their spoons twirling almost in unison.

"Okay, *what*?" Katie says.

They all stare. Jack, startled awake, nudges her leg with his nose.

"I know it feels like a gang-up," Dana begins—and this is when Katie's father gives her an apologetic smile, *What can you do, sweetie, you know how this goes*—"but have you considered what you'll do after the trial, honey?"

They wait for her answer, another too-familiar sight: even Dana, looking at her like she's a puzzle with too many pieces, or pieces that don't quite fit and never will. Jack bumps her again with his nose, then gives up and tramps off to the living room.

"It's only going to last a few weeks or so, right, hon?" her mother asks. She takes a delicate sip of her coffee, peers over the rim. "Then what?"

"The trial just started," Katie says.

"But what about after, honey?" Dana says.

Katie wants her father to say something—*My Katie will find her way, she always does*—or she wants Dana to answer these questions for her, instead of stubbornly aligning herself with their mother. The truth is, though, that for the past year her life has been figured out in her head by "when" stages—when she and Nick would get through their rough patch, when Nick would move back home, when the trial would start—that she hasn't even considered the "after" part.

"I'll finish the Cohens' documentary," she says, shrugging, "and then poke around for a new project. Why?"

"What if you don't finish it, Kate?" her mother asks, face full of doubt.

"Grace," her father says, the first thing since dinner. They all look at him and wait for him to finish, to add something. He opens his mouth, closes it. Goes back to stirring.

"I know the insurance money will run out and things will get tight—" Katie stops when she sees Dana shaking her head.

"That's not it," her sister says.

Her mother mimics Dana's placid tone. "Do you remember what we talked about in the car last night?" She doesn't wait for an answer, just plunges right in. "Well, Kate, when we see this new side of you, all riled up and such, we're all just afraid." Her mother darts her eyes to Dana, back to Katie, and suddenly blurts out, "Afraid that it's just more of the same, but *worse.*"

Dana gives her mother an exasperated look. "Mom."

"I'm sorry," her mother says to Dana, "but I've tried to talk to her about this before, even before she met Nick, and she just shuts down on me every time." She turns to Katie. "We were hoping that with Nick gone, it might give you an opportunity to really look at your life, Kate, to start coming around a little—"

"To what?" Katie asks, throwing Dana a poisonous look.

"To your own life, to *yourself*!"

"Mom, *please,*" Dana says, then turns to Katie. "Honey, this may sound crazy, but it might be the perfect timing after all."

"Again, for *what?*"

"A chance to get in touch with yourself, with what *you* want. Just you, honey, independent of Nick or anyone else."

"I do know what I want," Katie says in an even voice.

"Do you?" her mother demands.

"*Mother,*" Dana says. And to Katie: "Tell us."

"I know what I want tonight. I want you all"—and she looks at her father, too, who refuses to trade glances—"to remember that I'm trying to get through—"

"Yes, Kate, that's *it*— No, Dana, you're not saying it right, I'll do it. Kate, it just seems like for a long time you've been 'getting through' with other people and *their* stories. You're so worried about what's important to *them*—"

"It's my job—"

"Yes, but that's it, it's not just about your job, it's *always* about someone else. What about you?" her mother says.

"What about me?"

Her mother gazes at her for a long, quiet moment. "What about *your* story?"

"This *is* my story, Mom. Nick was and *is*—"

"No, Kate, I think you're purposely misunderstanding—I mean what's important to you, just you?"

All three stare intently at her, waiting, and the air in the room grows thin, needling. She stares back at them, her head swimming with confusion, and then anger. She stands.

"I don't understand what you're asking, why you're attacking me, when you know I have—this trial—" She chokes out these last words, her hands flat on the table.

They hop up, too, her father sliding around the table, his arm curving around her waist.

"We aren't trying to attack you, sweetie. We love you," he says simply, his eyes watering.

"I think—I think I need to lie down for a minute," she says, turning from the pity in her father's eyes.

"Okay, honey, it's okay," Dana says, glancing at their parents. "Another time. C'mon, let's get you upstairs."

.

Later, after they've tucked her into bed like a child, after more coded words from her mother—*No one expects it to change overnight*—and they've reluctantly left the house, Katie lies with the comforter up to her neck, the sheets below bunched inside her fists. Replaying their conversation over and over, seeing again their worried expressions.

"I don't get it," she says to Jack, who lies at the end of the bed, his head nestled between his paws.

And then, before the anger comes back, before the frustration starts to well up because they've only added to the questions swirling inside her head: "What were they saying, Jack?"

She asks this in a whisper, watches the dog angle his head at her, staring back. Like he doesn't understand her family one bit either.

8

The cafeteria at the Warwick Center was deserted except for the women wearing hairnets in the kitchen, chatting back and forth as they cleared away the morning snack trays and rinsed large plastic bins in the sink. It reminded Katie of her own elementary-school cafeteria—the bumpy concrete walls painted a light yellow, the faint scent of Salisbury steak and ammonia—but it was Nick, sitting beside her at one of the long tables and silently examining his fingernails, who occupied most of her attention.

—This isn't a reflection on you, Nick.

He turned his head sideways at her. —Who said it was?

—No one. But no one expects you to have all the answers either. It's been weeks, and if he's still not talking—

—Please don't lecture me on failure, Katie. Not *you*, Nick said, his mouth twisting with sarcasm. He went back to his fingernails, leaving Katie to absorb his words.

Composing herself took a few minutes. She stared down at the floor, caught the fluorescent lighting sparkling off the sequins on the sides of her black pumps. Shook her head ruefully—so much attention to what she wore today, as if the right pair of shoes would make this meeting perfect, despite Nick's resistance.

—Jerk, she finally said quietly.

—I'm sorry, okay? he said. —But this is ridiculous.

—What if Marty is right? I've seen Jerry watching me, too.

—And that's going to convince him to work with me?

—It might, if he—

Conversation stopped with Patricia's entrance; she gave them a brisk nod and turned back to the door. Nick sat up, folded his arms.

A few seconds later, Jerry's thick body filled the narrow doorway— his thin brown hair combed to the side, a crisp button-down shirt tucked neatly into his jeans. The only sign of trepidation showed in his chubby, storming face: trying hard, it seemed, to arrange itself for this new situation. He finally ducked his head in, looked directly at Nick with wide blue eyes.

—*Uh-oh,* Jerry said. —Him.

—It's okay, Jerry, Patricia said. —There's someone else here I want you to meet.

Jerry reluctantly tore his gaze away from Nick; his eyes pulsed in recognition at Katie for a second before he hung his head.

The floor absorbed all his interest for a full minute. Patricia stood patiently by, whispering words of encouragement, her hands folded in front of her. With his chin remaining securely tucked against his chest, Jerry finally lifted his eyes to Katie for a brief moment—face still struggling, lips moving silently.

—You can do this, Patricia told him.

Another minute watching the floor, arms clamped to his sides like a soldier, his lips continuing to move in silent argument with himself. Patricia coaxed and encouraged, and suddenly Jerry's right arm twitched, a little jolt of electricity. Katie watched in fascination: it twitched again, and then, slowly, it started to rise up. When it was straight out in front of him, Jerry closed his eyes tightly, pushed his arm through the doorway. Fingers reaching for an invisible rope to pull him into the room.

—Good, Jerry. Keep going.

He placed a tentative foot over the doorjamb, carefully tested the floor with small steps, arm still extended.

—You've seen her around here an awful lot, and I think you'll like her.

His face flushed deeply at this, but then his other arm came up gradually, hand reaching.

—Almost there.

He rocked in the doorway, pelvis swaying back and forth, fingers pulling at air, eyes squeezed shut. The one sneakered foot already in the room taking quick slaps at the floor.

Finally, with a small grunt and a hop, his other foot landed in the room; he stood bent in half, his arms extended and his lower half jutting back toward the door.

—Good job, Jerry!

Katie waited until Patricia led him to the table; she stood slowly, said in a neutral voice, —Hello, Jerry.

Jerry looked at her, jaw dropping, then stared at her feet.

It was all scripted beforehand by Patricia—when Katie should stand, how much eye contact she should make, when and how she should respond directly to Jerry. Nick's job, on the other hand, was easy: sit quietly and let Katie and Jerry interact as naturally as possible.

—Katie is Nick's wife, Jerry. Can you say hello to her?

He towered over her, his lips whispering without words.

—Hello, Katie, Patricia prompted. —Nice to meet you.

Lips working faster. —Meet you, Jerry said without looking up.

—Can you tell Katie what you do here at the center?

Nick closed his eyes, pinched the bridge of his nose.

—Sometimes, Patricia coached, —I put backs into earrings.

—Put da bags in, Jerry repeated, his voice like a boy approaching adolescence, high-pitched one moment, deep and guttural the next.

—And I eat lunch with my new friends here in the cafeteria.

—Lunch-teria.

Patricia nodded at Katie. —That's great, Jerry, Katie said.

Jerry's head snapped up. He stared at Katie, slowly lowered it again.

—Do you want to tell her about your new house? Patricia said. —I live on Dixon Street now.

—Dison.

—And I have two roommates, Bobby and Victor.

Lips practicing the words first. —Woom-mits.

—Bobby and Victor.

—Viter.

—I like Bobby and Victor very much, Katie said, smiling. —Do you?

Jerry stared at her, openmouthed. He turned to Patricia, and she nodded and smiled at him: *Go ahead, talk to her.*

Jerry turned back to Katie, closed his mouth, opened it again—his light blue eyes fastened on her. After a moment he started making small panting sounds, his head pulsing forward with each exhalation, eyes growing big with urgency. Katie had to fight to keep the smile on her face: he loomed over her, his stare unnerving.

—Viter *cook,* Jerry finally said, face red with the effort. —Cook *macwoni.*

Patricia beamed at him, at Katie, her eyes skipping between them triumphantly.

—*Good,* Jerry, that's right. Sometimes Victor helps cook dinner at your new house. Good job!

One of the rules was no quick movements, to keep her body as still as possible, but as Patricia continued to coach Jerry, Katie watched him more closely. Was it her imagination, or was Jerry staring at her shoes? She carefully tilted her left foot one way, then the other, thinking of sequins and light. Jerry's eyes widened, his mouth opening, until Patricia spoke again.

—Can you tell Katie what Nick's job is here?

An instant frown, lips pressed together. But still trained on the shoe Katie displayed for him.

—Nick helps us try to speak clearly, Patricia said.

Nothing.

—Katie is Nick's wife, and she loves him very much. She trusts him, and she isn't only his wife, she's his friend, too. Katie told me that she hopes you'll let Nick be your friend.

A doubtful look directed at Katie.

—It's true, Jerry, Katie said. —And I hope you'll be my friend, too.

Almost a smile for Katie then, but Nick shifted quickly in his seat and Jerry's eyes were back on the floor, filled with impending terror.

•

Patricia's office was a surprise, a sort of structured chaos—thick files piled on the corners of her desk, blue Post-it notes stuck to her computer, the windowsill behind her desk, and on the oversize day planner; phone numbers and names and meetings crowded each square on the planner, a few triple-circled in red ink.

—I discussed the possibility with Nick, and now I have no hesitation, Patricia said to Katie. —I think you both should be his resources.

—What's that? Katie asked, turning to Nick.

Nick ignored her, his arm draped across the back of his chair, one leg thrust forward—a posture of studied detachment.

Patricia looked from Nick to Katie, said, —Some of our clients have elderly parents or, like Jerry, no family at all, and we match them up with what we call "visiting resources." They take the clients out to eat, to a movie, that sort of thing. Over time the bond can become pretty strong. We have a few clients now who do sleepovers, spend the holidays with their resources. I'm hoping Jerry will be open to it.

—One meeting, Nick said. —That's what we're going on here?

—I've seen it, too, Nick, Patricia said. —He follows her with his eyes. Something about her has captured his interest. She shrugged. —It's a start at least. We need to connect with him soon, or we might lose him.

—You really think Jerry is going to sit in a restaurant with me? Nick asked.

Patricia smiled sympathetically at him. —Maybe if Katie is there.

· · ·

For their second visit with Jerry she wore bright red sling-backs with three-inch heels, the kind of narrow, teetering shoes that took painful bites of her feet with every step. Completely inappropriate for Pizza Hut, though Nick didn't say a word about them. Since their meeting with Patricia, Nick had been either short and dismissive with Katie or infuriatingly polite. After the first visit, she thought of reasons to back out, rehearsing her excuses in the shower. *You're the expert here, honey, not me. I know that Jerry will come around with your help. You don't need me.* And it was true, too—she saw signs of it on their very first visit to Newport Creamery. Jerry sneaking quick looks at Nick when Nick dropped his long ice-cream spoon onto the floor, or when he pulled money out of his wallet and calculated the tip. Both times, in just those few seconds, there was an unexpected, open curiosity in Jerry's light blue eyes, the fear completely gone. He caught Katie watching once, smiled shyly at her instead of glancing away.

But Katie didn't tell Nick about these looks or the smile, and she didn't back out of the visits. Because his mother had called once, twice, a third time. And each time Nick mouthed "busy" at Katie before retreating to the kitchen table with the thick textbooks Patricia had given him.

—Is something wrong, Katie? Candice asked on her third try.

—This isn't like Nicky.

—No, Candice, he's just very busy with work. He's been exhausted.

—Maybe I should try him in the morning?

—Okay, then, I'll let him know you called.

But if Katie was honest with herself, she knew that it was more than this mild triumph that kept her silent. She could still see that look of vulnerability and fear on her husband's face with Jerry close by, so alien and telling. Was it a clue, this fear of failing with Jerry? A hint about the things Nick kept hidden from her?

Katie spent her days visiting the Warwick Center, watching Jerry watch her, watching Nick watching them both, and—in her spare time—shopping for just the right pair of shoes.

On their way into the Pizza Hut, Jerry loped beside her, Nick striding ahead of them to the door. It was only the second time they'd picked him up from the group home on a Sunday afternoon, but Katie was ready for Jerry now, remembered not to swing her arms, or walk too quickly—impossible in these shoes anyway. A calculated pace so Jerry could find her hand and capture it for those brief moments before they stood beside Nick, and Jerry took his hand back.

Nick stood at the entrance, staring at the space between Katie and Jerry where their hands had been linked only seconds before.

—Age before beauty, he said to Jerry, smiling.

—Oh, Jerry said, stepping back to let Katie go in first. —Oh.

—I think he meant you first, Jer, Katie said. She tried to catch Nick's eye, but he was watching Jerry's nervous movements—hands slapping at his thighs, taking a giant step back, two small steps forward, another big step back.

—It's okay, buddy, Nick said gently.

Jerry took one more step back, then suddenly shot through the door, head tucked down. He stopped short, eyes widening, and turned around to look at Katie. The dining room was teeming with loud, hungry families, with waitresses weaving through the tables, pizzas held high to avoid darting children. Jerry turned to the room again, lips mumbling.

—Why don't you two get a table? Nick said to Jerry, the frustration clear on his face. —I'll be right back.

Jerry waited until Nick disappeared up the hallway toward the bathroom, moved closer to Katie. He stared wide-eyed around the room, then looked down at her shoes.

—Pity, he said.

—Pretty?

Jerry nodded.

—Thank you, Jerry. She turned her foot to the side for a better look.

He stared, then looked up at her and smiled. —Day hurt you?

—No, not really.

—Oh, he said, looking disappointed. His lips moved in that familiar way now, like Patricia was coaching him. —Dem shoes old? His face suddenly hopeful.

—I've had them forever, she lied.

—Old, he said, nodding. —Good. You wear a lot. Jerry looked back at the shoes.

—You sweat in dere?

Katie hesitated for a moment. —A little bit.

—Dat bad?

—No, not at all.

—Oh. Okay. Day pinchy little? he asked, with that sudden, eager look again.

—Sometimes, yes.

His mouth opened, closed. Opened again, face pink. —May-be, Kay? May-be—I—

The hostess interrupted them, arms loaded with menus and a brittle smile on her face. —Two?

Jerry hid his blushing face in his arms.

At the table Jerry inched his chair closer to Katie's, just in time for Nick's reappearance. He pretended not to notice, but his nostrils flared in annoyance.

—Waitress come yet? he asked the space right above Katie's head.

—Not yet, she said lightly, trying to catch his eye again.

Nick pulled out his chair, careful to keep his glance away from the thin sliver of space between Jerry and Katie.

A few minutes later, a flustered young waitress rushed to the table with apologies, water, and—after Nick's obvious, appreciative gaze at her—a special smile meant just for him.

—How about a large deep-dish with extra cheese and banana peppers? Nick said, touching her arm. —But I can see how busy you are. No hurry at all.

The waitress smiled at Nick, headed back to the kitchen with a walk that was somewhere between a saunter and a strut.

—Peppas? Jerry asked Katie.

She glared at Nick.

—Haven't you ever had them, Jerry? Nick asked.

Jerry turned to him. He watched Nick carefully, switched his eyes to the table, and shook his head.

—They're delicious, he said, looking straight at Katie. —I think you'll love them.

—Nick knows I don't like them, Jerry, she said, staring back at Nick. —He knows I think they're pretty gross.

Jerry looked from Katie to Nick and back again. —Gwoss?

—Disgusting, Katie said directly to Nick. —And childish.

—Oh, *please.*

When the pizza came, Nick beamed at the waitress, then served Jerry, who stared down at his pizza as if it were trying to communicate with him.

—Peppas, he said. —*Oh.*

Katie served herself, took her time flicking off the banana peppers one by one and sliding them to the side of her plate. Jerry watched her and followed suit, used two fingers to pick them off like bugs.

At first Nick scowled, but then he reached across the table, lifted one of the peppers off Jerry's plate, and raised it to eye level. Turned it around slowly to inspect it.

—Hmmmm. Yes, this one will definitely work, he said, studying the pepper.

He caught Jerry staring. —Okay, buddy? Nick asked, and Jerry nodded shyly.

Nick curved the pepper against his teeth, pressed it down, tucked the ends into the corners of his mouth. Opened his lips for a wide, waxy yellow smile.

Jerry stared. Nick's lips stretched, and then he munched the pepper, swallowed.

—Crunchy smiles, Nick said. —Dee-licious.

Jerry's mouth dropped open.

—Yup, Nick said, reaching for another one. He fit it into his mouth, smiled big again and raised his hands. *Ta-da!*

Jerry peeked at Katie. She shrugged, and he picked up a pepper with two fingers. Looked at Nick, who nodded his encouragement. Jerry lifted it up to eye level for careful inspection, but then his elbow dropped, landing squarely in the center of his piece of pizza. Like a sudden sting—Jerry flung the pepper onto the table, turned his arm sideways. Stared at his elbow in horror.

—*Uh-oh!*

—Man, I hate when that happens, Nick said.

He looked at his piece of pizza, looked at Jerry. Plunked his elbow into the very center of his own slice. Smiled a waxy, banana-pepper smile.

Jerry's lips moved as he looked at Nick's mouth, his elbow firmly planted in the pizza. And finally, what Nick had waited for, had clearly hoped for, since his first meeting with Jerry. A slow grin spread over Jerry's face.

Giggling, Jerry reached for another banana pepper—watching for Nick's approval.

—Dis one good, Jerry said, holding it up for Nick. Nick nodded, and Jerry dropped his elbow back into the pizza. Giggled again.

—Wait a minute, buddy. Someone here is holding out on us, Nick said.

Katie and Nick held each other's eyes for a moment. —Do I have to? she said, shaking her head with a smile.

The pepper in Jerry's mouth was crooked, hanging halfway out of his mouth.

—'*Mon,* Kay, he said. —You, too!

Katie picked up a pepper from her own plate. Plopped her elbow into her pizza.

Jerry's squealing laughter filled the restaurant.

9

Eddie Rodriguez, a normally youthful and athletic man in his mid-fifties, looks as if he's aged twenty years since May. His thick brown hair has new patches of gray on both sides, and his shoulders are rounded as he makes his way up the courtroom aisle with a studied gait.

Eddie doesn't look at the jurors as he answers Richard's questions; instead, he explains his duties as the Warwick Center's recreation director in a soft, faltering voice, his eyes glassy and focused on the floor. Judge Hwang asks him twice to speak up, and both times he stops his narration to cast a wary glance in her direction before beginning again.

"So you were away from the building when the shooting took place?" Richard asks him quietly.

"Yes," Eddie says.

"And Detective Mason eventually brought you to the shed that day?"

Eddie nods, then mumbles another "Yes" after Judge Hwang asks him to speak up again.

"And how did the defendant know that the gun was in that shed, Mr. Rodriguez?"

"We had a game—we tried to sneak up on each other. I didn't know he followed me outside. If I knew he saw it . . . if . . . I didn't intend on leaving it there—"

"But you did leave it there."

A guilty crimson steals over Eddie's face. "I only planned to keep it there overnight. I just picked up the permit—"

"There had been some robberies in your neighborhood?"

Eddie nods, catches himself. "Yes."

"So you purchased the gun for protection?"

"Yes."

"But you didn't want to take it home that night because . . . "

Eddie steals a look at Donna. "I was picking up my sons at school that day," he says quietly. "My wife wasn't crazy about them being in the car with a gun."

"So you were going to store it in the shed and take it home after work the next day?"

"Yes."

"And then the next day the defendant broke into the shed and stole it."

"Yes."

"Did the defendant ask you why you had a gun, Mr. Rodriguez?"

Eddie turns to Donna again, eyes beckoning.

"Mr. Rodriguez?"

He clears his throat, a high-pitched cracking. "Yes."

"Can you tell us what you told him?"

"I told him . . . I said that I bought the gun," Eddie says, "because there were some bad men in my neighborhood."

"And what did Jerry say about that?"

Eddie looks to Donna again for help. She shakes her head slightly at him, and Eddie's hands come up to cover his face. Richard could prod him to answer again, but it's the exact buildup he wants: the only sound that breaks in to the layered silence is Eddie's stifled attempts to hold back his tears.

"He said . . . he said that bad men . . . belonged in hell," Eddie says. "He said it's okay if I—if I shoot them. Because God would want that."

As Judge Hwang bangs the gavel for silence, Eddie lowers his head, the tears finally escaping. Only then does Katie realize she's been holding her breath. She lets it out, sits straighter on the bench. This was all about Jerry's history, his confusion about God and sin from when he was a child, she tells herself. Things taught to him by his mother, long before Katie ever met him.

•

Judge Hwang calls for a fifteen-minute recess, asks the jurors to step across the hall. Katie takes the stairs to the ground floor, pushes her way outside and into the frosty morning air. She sits on the stairs, pulls out her cell phone.

"Oceanside Realty, Elizabeth speaking. How may I help you?"

"Paul Minsky, please. This is Mrs. Burrelli, returning his call."

It takes longer for Paul Minsky to answer this time.

"Hello, Katie," Paul says in a falsely cheerful voice.

"Good morning. My mother said you called the other night?"

"Yes, though I'm afraid it's bad news."

"Oh, no."

"I'm afraid that the owner simply isn't willing to wait for your visit."

"May I ask why?"

"Well, it's simple, really. Mr. Barber is motivated to sell, and there's a list of eager people with offers already on the table. There's virtually no chance that the cottage will stay on the market another two weeks."

"But you said Mr. Barber liked my husband. I thought he wanted—"

"Yes, I did. Listen, Mrs. Burrelli," he says crisply, "something isn't adding up here, to be honest. Nick—your husband—never mentioned he was married when he came for his visit last spring. He . . . well, let's just say that Mr. Barber is an old southern gentleman. Male alliances and all that. He's a little twitchy now."

"Twitchy?"

"Yes. He's eager to sell, and he doesn't like entanglements."

"If you could just send a property package, I could give it to Nick and see if he could meet with Mr. Barber right away and clear up any misunderstandings."

"Again, there are already offers on the table."

"Please," Katie says, trying not to beg.

She listens to the Realtor's sigh. "Okay. I suppose that can't hurt. But please be aware that by the time you get the package it might already be off the market."

"I understand."

A long pause, then: "Could I ask you something? I don't mean to pry."

Of course you do. "No, it's okay."

"Well, Nick told Mr. Barber that he needed to get away from New England. That it had become too claustrophobic?"

"Yes?"

"Well, we were under the impression . . . well, I don't mean to be insensitive. But he didn't have on a wedding ring, so when you called . . ." He lets the question hang in the air for a moment. "It's just a little confusing, because Nick didn't mention a wife."

"I don't know, Mr. Minsky, he may have been distracted," she says, "but if you have a pen handy now, I can give you our address."

"Oh, of course. And please, will you tell Nick hello from both me and Mr. Barber?"

"I will. I'll see him in about a half an hour, and I'll pass it on."

"Lovely."

•

After the SBI investigator's testimony—long and tedious descriptions about formal protocol and the detailed measures used to confirm Jerry as the shooter—Richard calls Jan Evers to the stand.

Jan has traded her normally hippie-chic clothes today for a blue button-up shirt and stiff black pants that swish noisily as she makes her way to the stand. Other than her short salt-and-pepper hair, which is spiked straight up in the air, there is no trace of what Nick always referred to as Jan's "earthy-crunchy look."

"Will you introduce yourself to the jurors, please?"

"My name is Jan Evers," she says. "I'm Jerry's work supervisor at the Warwick Center."

"Could you please describe your duties as a supervisor at the center?"

Katie has informed Richard about Jan's talkative nature, her need to overexplain a natural by-product of working with a mentally handicapped population. Richard stands quietly by the jurors and listens as Jan explains, in excruciating detail, the simple factory work the clients perform, not trying to reel her in. Given free rein, Jan starts to relax— sitting forward, smiling a little as she launches into another anecdote about putting labels on boxes. Richard takes advantage of one of her pauses, steps toward her.

"Ms. Evers, I'm sorry to interrupt, but I understand that Jerry left his workstation to attend a speech-therapy group the morning of the shooting?"

"Yes, he did," she says eagerly, then seems to catch herself.

"And what was his behavior after that group meeting?"

"He was a little quieter than usual."

"Actually, according to your initial statement to Officer Devine," Richard says, picking up a piece of paper from his desk, "he seemed 'very troubled,' didn't he?"

"Oh. I guess so."

"And what happened next?"

Later, Jan tells the courtroom, Nick returned from an individual session to see if Jerry would like to have lunch with him. Jerry's reluctance to join Nick for lunch, she says, was such a surprise to both of them.

She stops at this point, looks over at Donna as if she's said too much.

"And why would both you and Nick be surprised if Jerry didn't want to have lunch with him?"

"Well, Jerry and Nick, they were pals. Jerry loved Nick, *adored* him."

Richard pauses thoughtfully, turns to the jurors. "But maybe not on this day?" he asks lightly.

Judge Hwang sustains Donna's quick objection.

"Ms. Evers," Richard asks, "did you have to convince the defendant to have lunch with Nick?"

"I did. I spent some time encouraging him, telling him how fun it would be."

"Before this day had you ever been in the position where you had to actually *encourage* the defendant to spend time with Nick Burrelli?"

"Oh. Well, not that I can recall, but—"

"Thank you," Richard says, walking over to the jurors. "Now, Ms. Evers, you also saw the defendant when he returned from lunch with Nick. Could you speak about that, please?"

Jan visibly wilts on the stand. "He came back and went straight to work."

"Well, did he appear angry to you?"

"Angry?" Jan sits up a little straighter. "No. Not at all."

Richard looks at Jan as if he's confused. "He didn't seem angry?" he asks with a hint of surprise in his voice.

"No," Jan repeats, "not at all."

Richard contemplates this for a moment. The jurors watch him pace away from them, pace back, unmistakably distracted. "Okay, well could you tell the jurors what happened next?"

Jan is more relaxed now that it appears she has caught Richard off guard; she explains how Jerry worked diligently for the next hour, placing earrings into cardboard backings with ease.

"Pensive," she says, turning to the jurors. "Jerry seemed pensive, but not angry, no."

"Not upset, or irritated?" Richard asks.

"Not in the least."

"'Not in the least,'" Richard repeats thoughtfully, and now Katie can see that Jan's insistence that Jerry wasn't angry is exactly what he expected—what he wanted. "And after the shooting, when he was out in the parking lot, Ms. Evers. Did he seem angry then?"

"At that point I suppose so."

"Thank you, Ms. Evers. Nothing further."

•

Donna spends an inordinate amount of time asking Jan to describe Jerry's usual behavior in the work program. Jan is only too happy to tell the jurors how, in the last three years as his supervisor, she has never had to speak to him once for inappropriate behavior.

"Not once?" Donna asks.

"No."

"Never had to confront Jerry for outbursts of anger or anything like that?"

"Never," says a smiling Jan.

"Now, Ms. Evers, according to your earlier testimony, Jerry adored Nick. Is that correct?"

"Absolutely. He *worshipped* him."

"And on the day of the shooting, besides a reluctance to have lunch with Nick, did Jerry show any outward signs of malice toward him?"

"No, he just seemed upset, but definitely not angry."

During this easy back-and-forth, Katie thinks of Richard's brief update this morning—*We need to end with a bang this afternoon, so the jurors have an entire weekend to ruminate over what they've heard.*

"Thank you for your time, Jan."

"Prosecution?" Judge Hwang asks.

"Yes. Thank you, Judge." Richard says. "Just to clarify, Ms. Evers, when Jerry returned from his lunch with Nick, he went straight back to work? He was 'pensive' and 'diligent'?"

"Yes."

"Thank you. No further questions."

•

The sight of Alicia, an assistant who worked part-time at the Warwick Center last spring for college credit, sends a thrill of fear through Katie. She hugs her arms around her body, steeling herself against what this girl will reveal to the jurors. *It's okay,* she tells herself, *none of this is news to you.*

Alicia settles herself on the witness stand, her face full of adolescent insolence; she sits primly in the chair, chin raised slightly, and watches Richard flip through the pages of his notepad.

Richard uses an overly deferential tone as he questions Alicia about her relationship with Nick, and Alicia, guarded look firmly in place, describes the way Nick encouraged her in her studies, how he was a mentor to her.

"And a friend, too," Alicia adds, "a *good* friend."

A lengthy discussion follows about Alicia's job at the center; Richard locks his hands behind his back and nods respectfully, murmuring his appreciation at all of Alicia's responsibilities until Alicia's body language slowly transforms. After ten minutes, there is no trace of the defensive college student anymore—Alicia leans forward, eager to answer his questions, almost vibrating with enthusiasm under the watchful and supportive eye of Richard.

"So part of your duties at the Warwick Center included assisting your friend and mentor Nicholas Burrelli?"

In a self-important voice, Alicia explains that while she didn't attend any of Nick's sessions, her responsibilities included typing up his notes for individual sessions and weekly group-therapy meetings. She was going to be a speech pathologist one day, too, so she made it her business to know everything that took place behind closed doors with his clients—*everything.*

Donna lets out an audible sigh of frustration, shakes her head.

"Speech pathologists also do group work?" Richard asks.

Yes, she tells Richard, part of a speech pathologist's job is to also help the clients simply express speech with their peers. Sometimes they work with cue cards to get the clients to express emotions verbally—showing a picture of a woman's angry face, or someone who looks happy or sad, and then asking the clients to verbalize to each other what the person is feeling. Or they employed a social-functional story, one of Nick's favorites, as a way to express speech in a social setting using full sentences.

"Nick would set up a story, like, suppose a client went outside to throw away garbage and a stranger approached them asking for money? He'd ask them what they would do and what they would say to the stranger. Things like that."

"And can you recollect if Nick used this story technique on the day of the shooting?"

"Yes, he did."

"And can you tell us the topic?"

You know this already, this isn't a big deal, Katie admonishes herself. But her body is trembling.

The girl hesitates a second under Richard's steady gaze. "It was about love and marriage," she says. "And sex." She raises her chin, manages to keep her glance level with Richard's.

There is some shifting and movement across the aisle as the line of questioning becomes more apparent, but Katie barely hears it, because the fear is singing through her body again—in an instant she sees Jerry's flushed, determined face, one of her shoes mangled and torn inside his hands, but then she pushes the image away. *This isn't about me, it's about his mother,* she tells herself sternly. *His mother.*

"With Jerry's history—" Richard begins.

"Objection," Donna says, rising.

Richard turns to Judge Hwang. "I haven't asked a question yet, Your Honor."

"If I'm correct," Donna says, "Mr. Bellamy is going to ask this witness about my client's history, and as a temporary, part-time secretarial assistant she is in no position to discuss that sort of information."

Alicia unmistakably bristles in her seat and flicks indignant eyes from Donna to Richard. Richard gives Alicia a look of sympathy and support, and the girl, eyes locked on Richard, squares her shoulders.

Judge Hwang turns to Richard. "Mr. Bellamy?"

"Your Honor, this witness was privy to all of Nick Burrelli's therapy notes, which naturally included some of the defendant's history at times. I'm not going to ask her for interpretations or explanations, just some basic information she typed up for him."

"I'll allow it, but be careful," she says, touching the rim of her glasses.

"Did you ever, in the course of typing Nick Burrelli's case notes, come across information that spoke directly of the defendant's past abuse?"

"I did come across quite a bit," she says, nodding.

"And so you were aware that the defendant struggled with his past abuse and that Nick thought that some of his speech issues might be connected to that?"

"Yes."

"Does it make sense to you, then, why a discussion about sex might upset, or might even enrage, the defendant?"

"Your Honor—" Donna says, rising.

Alicia leans forward, defiant: "I can definitely see why he'd become *totally* infuriated—"

"Your Honor, this witness is a student and not an expert on physical abuse or behavior!"

"Sustained."

At this point the jurors can't possibly understand Richard's intentions or what Jerry's anger about sex entails, but they sense the importance of this testimony: all twelve heads are bent over their pads, their pens moving quickly across the pages.

You weren't there when Jerry was incited, and you couldn't have stopped it. This is what Richard's staff told her in the days following the shooting, what they believed. What Katie so urgently needed to believe then—what she needs to believe now, as the panic continues to pulse through her body.

•

Detective Mason's initial testimony centers exclusively on describing proper procedures, the collection of evidence, the confirmation of testimony given by other officials at the scene—a necessary process that drags out for over an hour. The courtroom doors open and close constantly, and each time most of the jurors turn to cast longing glances at the back of the room. Richard's intention to end the week with a bang is suddenly failing; he should have ended with Alicia, because Detective Mason's testimony is slowly putting them to sleep.

Katie checks the clock at the front of the room: only twenty minutes left until they adjourn for the week—he's running out of time.

"Detective Mason, you were the one who processed the defendant at the Warwick Police Department?"

"Correct."

"And part of this procedure is to videotape the arrest interview?"

"Yes."

Some of the jurors perk up at the mention of a videotape. As Richard and one of his paralegals set up the video equipment, Judge Hwang informs them that the sound on the tape is of poor quality and requests that the jurors speak up if they need the volume adjusted.

The footage looks like it was shot from a distance, probably a ceiling camera, and is too grainy to capture facial expressions. Detective Mason and a stocky female officer sit on either side of Jerry, who slouches down in his chair, his arms hanging dejectedly by his sides. Detective Mason reads the arrest report to Jerry, who is completely nonresponsive at first: chin tucked under, body so still it would look like a freeze-frame if he were the only one in the room. But as Detective Mason reads the list of charges—breaking and entering, felony theft, first-degree murder—there are little movements from Jerry: a sudden jerk in the neck, shifting in the chair, hands meeting on the table, knuckles bulging. Jerry mumbles something unintelligible on the tape, and a hand is raised by the elderly juror in the back. But before the intern can turn up the staticky sound, Jerry is rising out of his chair on the screen, ripping the report away from Detective Mason, crushing it into a ball with his hands. He hurls it across the room with his whole body, clutches the table as though he will flip it over—Detective Mason and the policewoman are by his side in seconds, struggling to pry the table from his grip, and then they are all falling to the floor, the policewoman's arm hooked around Jerry's neck. From the back of the room, out of the camera's view, a string of officers file in—they join the melee of arms and legs on the floor, partially hidden by the table. Through the gasps and mutters of the jurors, and the muffled static of the struggle, one sound is crystal clear: Jerry's infuriated screams echo inside the small interview room and into the shocked courtroom.

Bang.

•

Later she's waiting in Richard's office, the three reels of Jerry's footage on her lap. For once Richard ignores her completely, his pen blazing across his notepad. The ticking of the small clock on his desk is like a pulse inside Katie's head—the seconds slowly clicking away, one after the other, before she hands Jerry's past off to a complete stranger. Outside the window the darkness is punctuated with the lights of downtown Providence, little stars blinking into life in the city's skyline.

They're waiting for the agreed-upon third party to pick up the reels, to do whatever it is they'll do with the moments Katie has filmed from Jerry's life. Over the weekend, Richard has explained to Katie, they will watch the footage from beginning to end—Donna Treadmont, Judge Hwang, Richard, and other "involved parties"—and they will decide among themselves what the jurors will see in court. For now it's all still cloudy to Katie: what moments Donna will fight for, which ones have the potential to deflate Jerry's rage on the screen. The only thing Katie really understands at this point is that the jurors will not be subjected to over seven hours of footage, that strangers will decide the relevant moments of Jerry's life, and that his life can and will be edited for time and content by a roomful of professionals.

"Katie?"

"Huh?"

"I asked if you needed anything. Water?"

"I'm okay."

Richard checks his watch. "He should have been here by now. Look, why don't you just leave them with me. I told you, you don't have to wait."

"I don't mind."

"All we're going to do is hand them over to this guy."

"I know."

"You don't have to verify you're the filmmaker until we get into court. He's just picking them up."

"I know that."

"So—"

"I'll wait," she says, and pulls the reels closer.

· · ·

Katie checks the bulb in her flatbed, snaps on a reel of film, and toggles forward through black space until Sarah and Arthur emerge on the thirteen-inch monitor stationed above it; they stand in front of their couch, facing each other and preparing for a new interview. Katie freezes the frame just as Sarah reaches up to brush lint off Arthur's shirt— Arthur's eyes stay fixed on the fingers resting flat against his chest, where Sarah's eyes also rest. It's the first time Katie has seen them on such a small screen, yet she can make out every detail of their features: the fine lines around their eyes; the trace of a smile at the corners of Arthur's lips as he gazes at his wife's hand; the small, fussy crease of skin on the bridge of Sarah's nose as she frets over her husband's appearance.

Katie toggles forward until she sees Arthur and Sarah on the couch, their hands folded in their laps and ready; she cues up the sound, listens to the casual banter between husband and wife. Back when Katie started this project, she quickly realized how important it was to get the elderly couple on track, to move them along by helping them recall where they left off the last time she visited their home. Otherwise, right at the beginning of filming, they would interrupt themselves and chew up valuable minutes to quiz Katie about her own life, her relationship with Nick. To appease them, she would chat with Sarah and Arthur for fifteen minutes or so before she turned her camera on, though even then, after she tried to get them on track, their questions still spilled over at times.

Katie digs through a large cardboard box and listens to her own mild prodding with the couple: *Last time you told me about some changes in the house you both worked in?* Within a few minutes, the couple begin to describe the change of command in the house, how the old general— transferred to a new camp—was replaced by a much younger one.

"He is a good man, Nick? A good husband to you?" Sarah suddenly asks, interrupting Arthur's harsh assessment of this new general.

Katie looks up from the box and sees the concern and curiosity playing across Sarah's wrinkled features. Arthur turns his eyes in Katie's direction, too, waiting for her answer.

Yes, Katie answers from behind the camera. *He's a wonderful man, a great husband. You were saying that this new general was much younger?*

Katie pushes the box aside, rolls her chair to the flatbed and toggles back.

"He is a good man, Nick? A good husband to you?"

She watches Sarah and Arthur closely. How did she miss this? This look of doubt that passes between the couple right after Katie answers? And then Arthur, worrying a crease in his pants.

He's a wonderful man, a great husband. You were saying . . .

Katie sighs. She doesn't have time for this now. Maybe when their film is finally finished, she'll review these moments alone, figure out what all these little gestures mean, but for now she toggles forward until she sees a familiar break in the film. Sarah and Arthur reappear, bodies close.

"It was on Sundays," Arthur says into the camera, "when the new general attended church with his wife. Do you remember, Sarah?" Arthur asks softly, his hand cupping her shoulder, and Sarah turns to stare blankly at him for a moment before she responds.

"Arthur?"

"The stories?" he says gently. "On Sundays?"

Her slow, demure smile is Arthur's answer.

"He should have written books, this man," Sarah says. "The things he would come up with, like fairy tales."

"Oh, Sarah," Katie says sadly, and Jack looks up from the center of the beanbag chair, where he is curled up in a ball. He wags his tail, tucks his head back into his paws.

Can you give me an example? Katie asks from behind the camera.

Arthur describes the place where they would meet on Sundays—Arthur sitting on one side of the wall in the hallway outside the kitchen, Sarah crouched close to the corner on her side. There, for ten minutes every Sunday, Arthur and Sarah would go on their "dates," whispering back and forth while the kitchen supervisor, Adele, smoked cigarettes just outside the kitchen door.

"Sometimes we would have a long dinner together," Arthur says, "and we would talk about happy things, serious things. I would describe our children, how smart they were in school."

Sarah is nodding. "Arthur said he wanted ten children. And he wanted them all to have my eyes."

Arthur watches her, lowers his voice. "We wanted a son first, a strong man. We told each other what he would do one day so that nothing like this could ever happen again. You see, we were proud of this boy before he was even born."

And are you proud of your son now?

Sarah smiles remotely, her attention focused on a space above the camera.

"Always," Arthur says, turning away from Sarah. "He is a clever man, just what we expected." He adds in a soft voice, an afterthought: "And our Ben, he has his mother's eyes."

Sarah's wrinkled face has glazed over, lost in the past.

"One Sunday," Arthur says in a loud voice, "we went on a trip together, to Venice—"

Katie pauses the film, rises. Walks slowly to the shelves, eyes the reels with a sinking heart. She picks up a new canister, brushes the dust off the lid with one finger. She hasn't revisited this footage once since filming it, unsure how to work it in with the romantic scenarios Arthur and his wife exchanged to make their weeks, their months, pass more quickly. Hoping she could ignore it completely, work her way around it. But it's a part of their story, too. *An important part,* Sarah says on this reel, despite Arthur's resistance. But Sarah was right. Katie knows that now.

"That's the problem with fairy tales, Sarah," Katie murmurs, pressing the canister to her chest.

10

Jerry's transformation had an almost storybook quality to it, the kind Katie was used to seeing in movies from her childhood. On their visits now, he would buddy around with Nick and tease back and forth with both of them, and he was finally working hard in his speech-therapy sessions. He was starting to make friends in the workshop, too, talking with the clients on either side of him as he worked steadily to wrap pipe cleaners with rubber bands or pack pencils into boxes. In the cafeteria Jerry started helping the workers hand out the midmorning snack, his face beaming with embarrassed pride as he placed a yogurt cup or a banana on a client's tray. When Katie visited and found Nick at the rec center, shooting hoops between sessions, it was only a matter of time before Jerry burst in. —You play me, Nick? he'd say, out of breath as if he'd raced all the way from the work building. And then his eyes would move to Katie, who sat in one of the folding chairs on the sidelines. —Oh! You!

Sometimes Katie had to remind herself that this was the same man who had been so terrified of Nick that he had to cajole his own body to step into the same room with him; the same man who had to be prompted word for word by Patricia to communicate with anyone. Now, Jerry had no problems speaking to Nick, no hesitations when he looked at Katie and said,—It May, Kay-tee. You tell it again? And Katie would smile and think of chance meetings with a small shiver.

She loved visiting the center even more now—so many of the staff members eager to talk to her about Jerry, cornering her in the hallways or in the workshop, or pulling her into the employee kitchen to share their news about his progress.

—I'm so glad you're here, Katie, listen to this—

—I was hoping you'd stop by! You aren't going to believe this—

And then Dottie Halverson or Marty or Eddie Rodriguez would grab her hand or wrap an arm around her shoulder, and lead her to a private space usually reserved for the employees.

Sometimes, when Katie was at home alone and reviewing footage of her current documentary in the darkness of her living room, she'd find her attention wandering, dreaming of Jerry—of the way he impulsively grabbed at her hand on their visits, or how he looked at her at times, like she was the most important person in the room. Or she'd recall how happy the employees seemed when she arrived at the center, how eager they were to swap stories with her, and within minutes she was in her car and on her way.

One afternoon Katie and Nick stood at the entrance to the workshop, watching Marty give Jerry a quick hug for a job well done. For just a beat, Jerry rested his head on the elderly man's shoulder, and then he was squirming out of Marty's arms and heading back to his place on the bench. Patricia walked up behind them just in time to see Jerry sit down and peek over his shoulder at Marty with a shy smile.

—It's amazing, Nick, Patricia said quietly. —I never imagined that it would happen so rapidly. All your hard work and effort has really paid off.

Katie waited for Nick to mention something about *her* influence in Jerry's life, but Nick kept his glance on Jerry.

—He's working so hard, Nick said modestly, and Patricia rested her hand on his shoulder.

—Well, whatever you're doing, keep it up.

•

Jerry came to their apartment for lunch for the first time, looking around their home with worried, questioning eyes.

—You okay, buddy? Nick asked, and Jerry nodded, suddenly shy.

He waited until they had all finished their tuna melts and chips, until Nick had left to get them a movie, and then he stood from the table where he was drawing quietly. Handed an entire folder of pictures over to Katie. She opened the folder, turned the pages slowly: different scenes of their visits to restaurants, or parks, or out on the boat, but all with one recurring image—three stick people holding stick hands and smiling, the middle stick figure towering over the other two. Connecting them.

—Beautiful, Jerry. I love them all. So will Nick.

—Not for here, Jerry said, his face grave for the first time in weeks. —For dat new one.

—Our new house?

He nodded, wouldn't meet her eyes.

—We're moving soon, but you know you'll get to visit us there all the time, too, right?

He looked right at her then. —*True?*

—So true, she told him, laughing at the relief in his face, at the awkward way he grabbed her into a hug. She patted his back. —You aren't getting rid of us that easy, buddy.

—Love Kay-tee, he whispered inside her arms. —*Love* her.

· · ·

The first time it happened was at the indoor playland at McDonald's in Cranston. The rain hadn't stopped for days, and it pounded the roof and swept across the windows, rattling their tall frames. In the parking lot, young trees bent over in half, their tender, exhausted leaves ripped off by the relentless wind. Mothers who had herded their fidgety children inside sat together in clumps, sipping coffee. Their kids screamed to each other from the bin of bouncing balls up to the twisting, colorful tubes, and slid around the floor in their socks in a whirling blur.

That afternoon Katie's gaze was fixed on the pile of little shoes and sneakers by the pink entrance tube, thinking how odd it looked to see Jerry's size-twelve-and-a-half hiking boots in the middle of the mess, when a long branch from one of the trees outside broke loose and slammed into a window. The leaves were fanned out and stuck to the glass, and for a moment they looked like fingers, and the branch like a long, skeletal arm—a huge hand holding the building in place. Katie saw Jerry standing in the middle of the children, staring at the branch. His fingers gripping the black netting on the ladder to the slide.

At first Katie thought he was simply caught up in the netting and was trying to untangle his hands. But then his face turned puffy and red, his fists curled up, and she understood: he was trying to tear it off.

She grabbed Nick's arm. —Look, she whispered.

Jerry's socked foot punted out a plastic window on a tube filled with children—their terrified screams echoed inside the room. Mothers were on their feet in seconds, bolting into action. Katie watched Jerry's arms swinging through the air, his fists full of black netting.

—Someone stop him! a mother cried, and then Nick was by his side, talking in his ear, his hands wrapped around Jerry's fists. Ignoring the mothers who stood in a mass now, watching, their arms protectively hugging their small children.

—*Kaaaaaaaay!* Jerry howled.

He ripped himself out of Nick's grasp, came charging at Katie, the tears streaming down his face. She couldn't move. Nick was right behind him, but Jerry reached her first; he hurled himself into her arms and Katie teetered for a few seconds on her high heels. They crashed to the floor, Jerry's arms fastening around her so tightly that she had to fight for breath.

For a few seconds, there was only Jerry's loud sobbing, the pain on the side of her face where it lay on the sticky floor, her thigh throbbing where it had knocked into the corner of the plastic picnic table on her way down. One of her shoes lay beside her head, twinkling in the light.

Nick stood over them, speechless.

—It's okay, Jerry. You're okay, she said, untangling an arm to pat his back.

After a few minutes, they guided him to a sitting position, one of his arms still locked around Katie.

—What's wrong, buddy? she asked, and then his other arm closed around her. She listened to his wails, his incoherent babbling—a string of muddled noises and words that sounded like he was talking in tongues.

—What's he saying? Katie whispered to Nick, who crouched beside them.

But Nick couldn't answer, just watched Jerry inside her arms, a helpless look on his face.

•

They drove a silent Jerry back to the group home, where Patricia and his social worker waited. Patricia ushered Jerry inside, and he followed obediently, meekly, his lips moving in silent conversation with himself.

After they described the incident to the social worker—a young, mousy woman who nodded too much, unable to keep the confusion from her face—they waited in their car for the storm to slow down before heading home. The rain and wind rocked the car right to left, the windshield wipers utterly ineffectual: it looked like someone was pouring bucketfuls of water from the roof of their car.

—It was Scripture, Nick said at last, breaking a long silence.

—What?

—What Jerry was saying, Nick said. —While you were holding him. "The Lord hath his way in the whirlwind and in the storm." It's Scripture.

—How do you know?

Nick kept his eyes on the windshield. —There are things in his file. I've been doing some research.

—This happened before?

—Once. Not the violence, just him babbling Scripture during one of our sessions.

—Why would he do that?

Nick shrugged. —Part of his history catching up, I guess.

—But his social worker just said he's never been violent.

Nick shrugged again, fiddled with the keys hanging from the ignition.

—Some of the staff mentioned that his mother abused him, Katie prodded. —But I don't understand the religious part.

—You know I can't get into that. It's confidential.

—It's *me,* Nick.

—Look, Katie, there's this, Nick said, holding his hand up toward the house. —Picking Jerry up for these visits, and taking him out, helping him socialize and have fun. And then there's the professional side. My side.

—What just happened was *fun?* she said. —He wanted me back there. He needed *me.*

—I know, Nick said, fixing his gaze on her. —I know he did.

• • •

Michael and Nick wouldn't be long—probably only an hour or so to help Katie's father pick up his new leather recliner and let his son-in-laws haul it into the house.

—I can't see paying eighty-five dollars for delivery when I have two strong son-in-laws! he had yelled over the phone to Dana. Loud enough so they all heard, even though they were spread out in Dana and Michael's huge kitchen.

It was the first time they'd brought Jerry to Dana and Michael's house, and it was clear that Michael was hesitant to leave his wife alone with him. But Nick was already grabbing the keys of Michael's Jeep and turning to check on Jerry, who sat at the table drawing, his tongue poking out in concentration.

—Go help Dad, honey, Katie told him. —I can handle Jerry.

Nick still barely talked to her father, was awkward around him in small ways that were probably obvious only to Katie, but the second her father needed anything Nick would spring into action like this.

—We'll be right back, Nick said quietly to Katie.

—Jerry'll be fine with me, Katie assured him.

She didn't miss the passing look of annoyance on Nick's face as he nodded and turned to the back door. —Ready, Michael?

At least an hour, plenty of time. As soon as Michael pulled out of the driveway, Katie turned to Dana.

—Do you have a pair of shoes I can wear home? she whispered.

—What's wrong with the shoes you have on? Dana asked, eyeing Katie's black pumps.

—*Shhhhh*. Nothing. Do you?

—Yeah, but why?

—You'll see. And to Jerry: —We'll be right back, Jer. I have to change my shoes.

Jerry's head jerked up, and he looked at Katie. Stole a quick look at Dana.

—Two seconds, okay, pal?

—Oh. Okay.

Jerry's pencil stayed suspended over the paper.

•

Dana and Katie crouched by the back door of Dana's house, peering through the window and onto the porch where Jerry sat on a bench with Katie's shoes: one by his side, the other held up at eye level so he could inspect it from every angle. His mouth hung open and he squinted fiercely, turning the shoe from side to side.

—It's a fetish, right? Katie whispered.

—Definitely, Dana said, mesmerized.

Her sister lit a cigarette, her first since they'd brought Jerry over. Nick still wouldn't divulge Jerry's specific history to her, but there were rules that hinted at his past abuse: no smoking around him, no loud noises or crowds during thunderstorms, no ironing with Jerry in the same room, and—after a disastrous thirty-eighth-birthday party for Jerry two weeks earlier at their apartment—no lit candles.

—How long? Dana asked. She blew out a stream of smoke, and they both ducked as Jerry snuck a look at the house. He turned back, head lowered.

—A couple of weeks, about an hour after the birthday-party episode. Nick was writing up an incident report on the computer in the bedroom, and Jerry asked me if I was done with an old pair by the door. Katie shrugged. —I just gave them to him. He took them into the bathroom.

They couldn't see the floor of the porch, but they both understood by Jerry's movements and lowered head: he was trying on Katie's shoes now. His mouth formed silent words, as if he were struggling to coax his large feet into the shoes.

—Did he talk to you about it? Dana said.

—No. He was really awkward and embarrassed when he asked, but afterward he was relaxed, and it was like it never happened.

—Any more violent episodes?

—No, just those two. Otherwise he's following Nick around like a puppy, and he's working really hard in their sessions. And he's so sweet to me, Dana, he's like a little kid sometimes.

Dana kept her eyes trained on the window. —Makes sense. He feels safe with you and Nick. You've become parental figures, probably the first positive ones in his life. His past is finally coming out, because he knows he's safe.

—That's what Patricia said to Dottie. Dottie told me a few days ago that Patricia thinks the incidents were actually good.

Out on the porch, Jerry's lips moved slowly, his plump face deathly serious. He held one shoe up with both hands now, a black pump with strappy sides and a pointy heel.

—But I haven't told anyone about this, Katie said. —I don't know why.

—You have to, Dana said, turning quickly to her. —I mean, it clearly isn't hurting anyone right now, but his social worker needs to know, given his behavior lately.

—Maybe they're not related.

—Everything's related, Katie. Believe me.

—But telling someone might break his trust with me—

—*Wow,* Dana said, her voice soft with shock: Jerry's hand was wrapped around the side of the shoe. He pulled hard, teeth clenched with effort, ripping at the leather. With a low grunt, he finally tore it loose from its backing

—Why does he do it? Katie asked. And then more quietly: —It's sexual, isn't it?

—Probably. Yes. Maybe not this part, Dana said, motioning to the window with her chin. —But trying them on? Yes. The sexual part doesn't have to be directed toward a person, though. It doesn't mean he has sexual feelings toward *you.* Only that he trusts you.

They watched Jerry's fist close around the heel. He pulled, forehead scrunched up, and tried to break it off.

—He probably doesn't even know why he wants to do it. It's probably an unconscious thing that gives him relief.

—You mean he— Katie stopped, embarrassed.

Dana shook her head, blew out a stream of smoke. —No, he doesn't necessarily ejaculate or anything like that. But he feels the need, has to act it out, and it probably releases tension.

Jerry held the broken heel in his palm now, staring at it, lips mumbling quickly.

—I take it he's been abused? Dana asked.

Katie shrugged. —His history is confidential. Some of the staff have mentioned bits here and there about his mother abusing him, but I'm not allowed to read his file.

Jerry had the other shoe in his hand, both strappy sides in his fists, pulling in opposite directions. His face turned a deep maroon, both eyes locked on the shoe.

Dana's eyes narrowed as she watched. —I tell my clients who have fetishes that it's typically associated with someone they were close to in childhood, even if that person was abusive. Acting it out as an adult is equated with love and being needed.

Over on the bench, Jerry examined one of the broken straps in his hand, talking to himself.

—But this is a little out of my league, Kate. With his past trauma and his handicap, it takes on a very complicated nature. It's not necessarily "bad," but if it starts to affect his overall daily functioning . . .

—It hasn't, Katie said firmly.

—And maybe it never will. But you never know.

—I wonder if a part of destroying them might be that he's punishing the shoes? Like *they're* bad and maybe a kind of stand-in for his mother?

—Definitely a possibility. A good one. Dana stubbed out her cigarette. —But I told you, it's complicated. There's this element of sexuality and destruction that people who work with him should know about. Including Nick.

—You can't mention this to him, okay? He gets angry when I try to discuss Jerry's past.

—Sure . . . oops, I think he's done.

Jerry rose from the bench, and Dana jumped up, waving the cigarette smoke away. She spritzed the air, scooted to the other side of the kitchen.

Jerry knocked softly on the door, and Katie opened it, smiling.

—Hey, Jerry. All set?

He nodded, avoided her eyes. —You tell Dana? he whispered.

—No, of course not.

—Oh. He gazed at his hands.

—Jerry? It's okay.

—Oh.

—It's private, and you aren't doing anything wrong.

He finally met her eyes. —It bad, Kay-tee? he whispered. —I *bad*?

—No, buddy. Of course not.

—You not tell? You please not tell no one?

She watched the torment playing on his face, hesitated for only a second. —No, she said quietly. —No, I won't tell anyone.

—*Swear?*

—Cross my heart. You can trust me.

—You? he whispered, staring. *Sure?*

She didn't hesitate this time. —One hundred percent sure. I promise, Jerry.

He finally smiled. —You are my good friend, Kay-tee, he said, enunciating carefully. His eyes skipped back to the bench.

—Don't worry, I'll take care of them, she said.

Jerry nodded, pushed past Katie into the house.

Katie walked to the bench, picked up her destroyed shoes, and moved quickly to the garbage can out back. Buried them deep at the bottom.

• • •

That night they drove Jerry back to their apartment for his first overnight. As soon as they stepped inside, he became quiet, hugging his backpack to his chest and looking around the apartment.

—You'll sleep on the couch this time, Nick told him. —But we'll be moving very soon. And you know what? I think there's a spare bedroom at the new house with your name all over it.

—My name? On walls? *Uh-oh.*

—No—no, it's just an expression, Nick said, leading Jerry to the living room.

—You'll sleep right here, okay? And we'll leave all the lights on.

—Oh.

Katie dropped a pillow and a blanket on the couch. —It means when we move into the new house, you'll have your own room there, Jer. And you can fill it with all your own stuff.

His eyes opened wide. —Real?

—Yes, Katie said, turning to Nick with a smile. But he was staring at Jerry's hand, reaching for Katie's.

—Okay, Jerry, Nick said, pulling his backpack out of the one arm that still held it close. —Let's get your pj's out, and then we'll get you set up on the couch.

·

In the middle of the night Katie woke with a start. She turned on her side, checked on Nick: snoring loudly, one arm thrown across his face, elbow pointing at the ceiling.

—You're snoring again, she grumbled, pushing at him. —Roll over.

He mumbled, turned onto his side. She closed her eyes, half asleep, when she heard the sound again. But it wasn't Nick snoring. And then she remembered—*Jerry.* Jerry was in their living room. And he was moaning. A low, feral sound, like a trapped animal.

Katie sat up to prod Nick awake, then stopped herself. All those meetings about Jerry's violent behavior, all behind closed doors. *I should know more,* Katie said to Nick more than once. *I'm a part of this, too.* And Nick, looking in that slightly haughty way at her across the table. *I've told you already, it's confidential.*

Jerry lay like an ironing board on the couch, arms by his sides, the pillow over his face. The living room was bright from the overhead lights and a lamp right beside him on the end table.

—Jerry? You okay?

He stopped moaning.

—Jerry? It's Katie. What's wrong?

—It dark.

—Well, let's take that off your face.

—Oh.

She sat at the edge of the couch, pulled off the pillow. His light blue eyes were stretched wide.

—Do you want me to stay for a while?

He nodded.

—Here, sit up.

He obeyed, and Katie placed the pillow behind his head. She pushed him back against it gently.

—Were you afraid?

—I am.

—Nothing will hurt you here. And Nick and I are just in the next room.

He nodded doubtfully.

—Do you want to read? She leaned over to the side of the couch, grabbed a book out of his backpack. Held up his "best": *If You Give a Mouse a Cookie.*

Jerry shook his head.

—How about some water?

—I not dirsty.

Jerry stared at her, his lips starting to move in that familiar way, talking without sound.

—What is it, Jer? You can tell me.

—Kay?

—Ka-tie, she corrected without thinking.

—Kay-*tee*?

—What is it, buddy?

He practiced the words first again, but this time it was a little different: eyes moving back and forth, as if he could actually see the words, but had no idea what they meant. As if the words were in a language he didn't understand.

—You . . . you like to look at me? he said at last.

—Of course, you handsome guy, she teased lightly, and pulled the covers up to his chin. —And that was a great sentence, by the way.

He didn't smile. —My mom don't. She say I sin before me.

—Sin before you?

His face turned urgent, eyes suddenly round with fear. —Dat *me,* Kay-tee. *Sin.*

—No, no, you're not sin, honey. You're—you're a gift, Jerry. Absolutely the opposite of sin.

—Uh-huh. My mom *say.*

—Then she was wrong. I know it.

Jerry turned away, faced the back of the couch. He curled his huge body up into a ball, knees touching his chest.

—Jerry?

—*My fadder come,* he said in a low whisper, a voice that reminded Katie of campfires and ghost stories. —He come and see Mom. God got *mad.* Sin is *me.* His body started shaking, and he curled his fists and mashed them into his face.

Shit. But no—she could handle this.

—Your father and mother made you, and God got mad?

He nodded at the back of the couch. —*Sex,* came his terrified whisper.

—Do you know what that is, Jerry? Sex?

—Someding too bad.

Katie thought about the shoes then, about her role now in the entire hazy mess that was Jerry's past.

—Jerry, am I your good friend?

—You?

—Yeah, me.

He turned his face toward her. —You, Kay-tee?

—Yeah.

He turned over. —You, he finally said, face crumpling with a sad-happiness she had never seen. —You da *bestest* in da world.

Katie's heart swelled, and it came to her, quickly: like a son—this troubled, enormous man was like a *son* to her. She put her hand on his shoulder.

—Then listen to me, okay? I will never, *ever* be mean to you. Ever, she said. —Not like your mom. This last sentence tentative, more like a question.

He nodded, started gulping air. —She hurt.

Katie rubbed his shoulder gently. —I thought so, and that makes me so sad. You didn't deserve to hurt.

He shook his head, sat up suddenly, his fists pushed into his chest. His face was too close to Katie's, and she forced herself to stay seated, to keep her hand on him.

—Yes, Kay, I *do.* Tears springing in his eyes. —God tell her. He *want* it.

—No, Jerry, you did not deserve it. God couldn't want that. He doesn't want to hurt anyone.

—He *mad* for me. At night He *come.*

Jerry raised a fist, and Katie held her breath—but he only wiped his knuckles against his wet face.

—God is not going to come, and He isn't mad at you.

—*Is*. He make my fadder go to hell because of *me.*

—No, Jerry, you haven't done anything wrong—

—Me, Kay! he said, and threw his body into hers, almost knocking her off the couch. —*I* wrong! Sobbing now, clutching Katie, his body racked with tremors.

She wrapped her arms around him, held him tight. Forever, it seemed, she held on tight.

.

After he finally fell asleep, she tiptoed into the bedroom, checked on Nick: on his back, again, both arms slung over his face now. She walked into the kitchen, to the small table by the door where Nick kept his brief-case. One quick look confirmed that Jerry was still asleep, too, his arms hugging the extra pillow Katie had slipped there to replace her body.

She clicked the briefcase open. The sound, amplified in the quiet apartment, made her freeze for a full ten seconds.

She looked off toward the bedroom door. Nothing, just soft snor-ing. Katie slid her hand inside.

—Ow.

She popped her finger into her mouth—a paper cut from a piece of paper sticking out of a book. She eased it from the briefcase with her other hand. Not a thick textbook on speech-language therapy as she expected, but the Bible; not a piece of paper either, but one of a dozen yellow Post-its poking out.

She sucked at the thin line of blood on her index finger, flipped to one. In the Old Testament, from Nahum, chapter 1, Nick had under-lined parts of Scripture in verses 2, 3, and 6. *The Lord is furious . . . will take vengeance . . . will not at all acquit the wicked: the Lord hath his way in the whirlwind and in the storm, and the clouds are the dust of his feet . . . his fury is poured out like fire . . .*

She flipped to another one, also from the Old Testament, Psalm 68. Underlined in verses 2 and 5: *As wax melteth before the fire, so let the wicked perish at the presence of God . . . A father of the fatherless.* Katie read it again, thinking of birthday cake and candles.

And another, Psalm 51:5. *I was shapen in iniquity; and in sin did my mother conceive me.*

And still another, Psalm 51:3. *For I acknowledge my transgressions: and my sin is ever before me.*

She heard Jerry's words again: *Sin before me.*

—Holy shit.

.

She slept in the next morning, found Nick's note taped to the door. *Taking Jerry to breakfast. Call you later.*

She tried Nick's cell phone, left a quick message, jumped in the shower. Checked the answering machine and her cell after she was dressed and done drying her hair, but there was only one message, a return call from an old classmate who worked at PBS in Boston. Katie had called him over a month ago, and she listened to his apology now, his sudden awkwardness.—Um, so, sure, I guess so, Katie. I might be able to take a look at your work at some point, but I'm pretty busy over here. He paused. —Do you think . . . could you just remind me who you are again?

She looked around the apartment, hands on hips. She folded Jerry's blanket and plumped the pillows, stored them back in the linen closet. She vacuumed all the rooms, dusted every surface in the apartment, used a sponge to clean out the glass shelves and the rounded egg cups in the refrigerator. In the bathroom she scrubbed the sink and the tub with Clorox, then got down on her hands and knees to clean around the toilet with a Brillo pad. She washed their bedding, organized their CDs and DVDs alphabetically, watched an episode of *Little House on the Prairie* while she paid the bills. By two o'clock she had called Nick's cell phone a half dozen times, had left as many messages. *Where are you guys? Is everything okay?* But the phone never rang.

By four o'clock she was sitting at the desk cramped up against a wall in their bedroom, staring at the computer; the cursor winked at her, waiting. She didn't think Jerry would mention their conversation last night with Nick, but what if he did? She imagined Nick's reaction, how their conversation would most certainly degenerate, within minutes, to his scornful, explosive observations about Katie's intelligence, her body. She typed her name onto the computer, stared blankly at it.

When Jerry had acted out at McDonald's and at his birthday party right here at the apartment, Nick had sat at the computer just like this, writing up incident reports for Jerry's file. Of course Katie wasn't allowed to read the final drafts—*Confidential,* Nick had said both times, even though Jerry eventually ended up in Katie's arms, mumbling Scripture and sobbing into her hair, both times.

She pictured herself handing Nick her own report from the night before, immediately saw his reaction: that same expression whenever Jerry suddenly reached for her, in fear or in happiness, the same one whenever Nick saw Katie whispering with the staff in private places at the center. She turned the computer off, watched her name disappear.

She stared at the blank screen, saw Nick's hands fisted by his sides, his chest pushed forward. She swiveled in the chair to look at her closet, at the shoes spilling out of it.

For the next hour, Katie reorganized the closet—jeans and cargos folded neatly on the wire shelves on one side, shirts hung by color, dark to light—then sifted through and weeded out the shoes she didn't mind giving up. The shoes Jerry would take into the bathroom when Nick was out running an errand, or to the bedroom while Nick was showering, and rip to pieces. The shoes he would try on first, then tear apart and destroy with his hands, while Katie waited patiently for him to finish so she could bury them at the bottom of the trash.

Reassuring him each time, It's okay, Jerry. I won't tell anyone. You have my word, you can trust me.

•

Nick finally called her around six-thirty, on his way back from the group home.

—You took him home already? she asked.

—We had a big day. He was tired.

—Why didn't you call me back?

—I was thinking, he began slowly. —I was thinking about the visits. I should have told you this sooner. But I think I should take Jerry on them by myself for a little while.

—Why?

—Just until we get a better handle on his recent behavior.

—Did you talk to Patricia about this?

—I'm going to, tomorrow. And his social worker, too. Maybe it'll help if he has some alone time with me, just a male presence to interact with. If they do agree, it will probably be better if you lay off on the visits to the center for now, too. It might distract him.

Just like that. In less than a minute, Katie felt herself thrust back in time, to a life filled with restless tiptoeing around the outskirts of everything that felt important.

—I kept calling, Nick, because I wanted to tell you, she said quickly, struggling to sound casual. —That old college friend called me back this morning.

—Yeah?

—The guy who works at PBS?

—Great, Nick said. —Hey, did you eat yet? I could pick something up.

—No, but listen. He said he's busy, but he's willing to look at my work. I was going to call him back and pitch this idea I've been throwing around, but I wanted to talk to you about it first.

—Okay, shoot.

—Well, I've been thinking about you and Jerry a lot lately. How there'd be a huge audience for this sort of thing.

—What sort of thing? Nick's voice unmistakably defensive.

—Your relationship with Jerry, how much you're helping him, how much progress he's making. It would be the focus of the film. I think PBS would definitely pick it up, possibly even enter it into some film festivals or something. But if you think Jerry should spend time alone with you . . .

—You think this guy would be interested?

—Definitely.

—Hmmmmm.

—I'd have to be around for the filming, although I'd be behind a camera most of the time, so I wouldn't be in the film at all. But if you don't think it's a good idea for me to be around Jerry right now, I'll show him something else. I just thought it would be so cool to see you on TV, Nick. How all these people you've never met would see you working with Jerry, too . . . She trailed off again, waiting.

Only silence then, but she knew Nick by now. His silence, for once, enough—an answer. Her legs nearly buckling with relief, she sat down on the couch, waited for his spoken confirmation.

11

On Saturday, Katie finally calls Jill back, and they meet for a long lunch date at Twin Oaks. Sitting across the table from her friend, she thinks what a relief it is to replace her family's interrogation and a sleepless night of foundering with Jill's steady patter about the man she's breaking up with, the one she wants to date next, the deranged woman who cut her off and almost killed her on Route 6 the other day.

"This woman had all this crazy hair, sort of spiky and all in her face," Jill says, motioning to her own long hair, "you know, like that girl in high school, the one who wouldn't change in front of anyone in the locker room, Lacey, or Nellie something?"

"Nancy. Nancy Cummings."

"Yes, *Nancy*, God, I haven't thought about her in years, but, Katie, this woman in the Volvo looked *right at me,* and I swear she stuck her tongue out right before she swerved her car at mine! And then I was flying into the other lane, and a couple of seconds later I hopped the curb and was heading right for a tree!" Jill laughs as if this is the funniest thing that could have happened to her on a Thursday afternoon during the five-o'clock rush.

Katie picks at her chef salad, smiling and nodding every so often at Jill, who is like a windup toy with a broken string today; the tales pour out of her mouth through the entire meal, until she finally pushes her plate away.

"Whew, I'm *stuffed,*" she says. "So that's *me.*" Jill grins, props her elbows on the table. "Should we try to squeeze you into this conversation or what? What's going on with the trial?"

"It's going," she tells Jill vaguely, and then reassures her friend that she still doesn't need any company. "It's not as bad as I thought it would be," Katie says, looking for the waiter. She catches his eye across the room.

"Look at you, Katie," Jill says, staring, "You are *so strong.*"

Don't believe everything you see, Katie thinks, but she just smiles at Jill, asks her if she's heard from Amy lately.

"A few weeks ago," Jill says, less animated now. "They're already buried in snow up there." Her face clouds over as she reaches into her purse for her wallet.

"You know," Katie begins, her heart starting to race as she watches the melancholy deepen on Jill's face, "I was just wondering something the other day. It's sort of silly."

Jill tips her head up, stops flipping through credit cards.

Katie lines her plate up to the very edge of the table; her skin tingling, her legs a little wobbly, she forces the words out. "But, you know how you and Amy were so close in high school?"

Jill squints at Katie, a small crease forming between her eyebrows. "Well, we were all close, right?"

"Yeah, of course," Katie says, trying to assemble the words that suddenly feel adolescent and foolish: *Did you like me as much as her back then? And if Amy hadn't moved to Michigan, would you be here right now?* But then an urgent voice drowns them out, warning—do you really want these answers *now?*

"I was just wondering," Katie finishes brightly, "if you thought Amy was happy up there. Married and with kids."

Jill doesn't answer right away. She sits very still, looking at Katie. "Seems like it," she says. "You should call her sometime."

The waiter comes, and Jill reaches for the check. "My treat," she says in the same subdued voice.

Out in the parking lot, they hug, and Katie promises to keep in better touch.

"I know that your life is nuts lately," Jill says, opening her car door. "But you can call me anytime. And I'll still come to court if you change your mind."

"Thanks," Katie says.

"Don't thank me, you idiot, that's what friends are for," Jill says, smiling, but there's an impatient edge in her voice that Katie doesn't recognize.

"I'll call you," Katie says, nodding, "I will."

But Jill's door is already shut, the engine humming to life.

• • •

By Sunday evening Katie is more than a little surprised. She has received only one phone call from her family all weekend—from her father—and then just to tell her about the robbery at Gregg's restaurant, where her parents and their friends go every Saturday night for one of their famously rich desserts.

"We missed them by minutes!" her father had yelled into the answering machine after Katie ignored the ringing, content to sit on the floor with Jack and share her turkey and cheese grinder. "Only *minutes,* Katie!"

She felt a little guilty sitting there on the floor, ignoring her father's call—or she did for about one minute and ten seconds, the time it took for her father to use up the minute he was allotted to leave a message and call back to further speculate about *what might have happened.* No mention of the trial, no mention of the failed intervention to help Katie understand why she had recently become "worse."

Worse than *what?* Katie had wondered again, seeing the pity in her father's eyes as Jack nudged closer. What did they want from her? *Change,* their faces seemed to say as they talked about Katie's job, her life, *change who you are.* She remembered her mother's words from so long ago—*You need to make more of an effort*—and her own frustrated wish to be different. To be better.

"Just four minutes, five *tops,* and me and your mother and the Potters would have come face-to-face with these thugs at the door!" her father had yelled into the phone.

Katie peeled off the heel of her sandwich, put it on the floor for Jack; she rose and turned the volume down on the machine, cutting off her father's sad observation that it was, after all, a very troubling comment about the world when you couldn't even eat a piece of strawberry cheesecake or coconut cream pie without risking death.

Now that Jack is, she hopes, done vomiting all over the kitchen (the Swiss cheese from the sandwich causing his spine to bow as he hacked up the mess in little puddles, Katie remembering Sandy's warning about dairy too late), she wanders aimlessly around the house, contemplating the decisions that were made about the footage this weekend, the finished tape the jurors will see in court. What happy moments will make their way onto this tape, how they will dovetail with Jerry's anger—what it will feel like to see Jerry's love reflected back to her through her lens in front of an entire courtroom. And Nick. To see him again, to hear his voice and see the camera close in on his face, to witness him once again embracing Jerry, laughing with him, encouraging him. But maybe Richard was right about this; even Donna would understand the dangers of showing too many shots of Nick alive, eagerly helping Jerry. Loving Jerry.

She ignores Jack, who trails behind her, whining insistently. "Go on out," she tells the little dog in the kitchen, and opens the slider for him.

Outside, long, slow gusts of cold wind rock the tops of the trees in her backyard. Jack trips along the lawn, nose close to the ground, then disappears behind the trash cans.

The phone rings inside again—the fourth time in a row—and Katie's glad she turned down the volume. Despite her protests, Richard informed Katie on Friday that he wouldn't bother her this weekend with the details of the final footage, so it wouldn't be him. *It can wait until Monday morning,* he insisted. *Try to enjoy your weekend.* With any luck the person calling is just her father, still ruminating about his close call, and not Ben Cohen again—though she doubts that Ben would call repeatedly like this after leaving another message this morning. Still, she really should return Ben's phone call, because it's clear that something must be wrong. At first his message hadn't troubled her—it was left in the same casual voice he always used—but later Katie wondered at his persistence. It wasn't like Ben to call twice in the same month, never mind the same week. She had missed his phone calls before, back when Nick was alive and after he was gone, and then a month or two later Ben would call again, too polite to mention Katie's slight. But while she should at least acknowledge this change in his behavior, the thought of one of those long, casual conversations with Arthur and

Sarah's son is just too exhausting. All she wants to do now is gather up Jack and cuddle with him in front of the TV, relax a bit before another week in court.

"Jack?"

Either the little dog has found a special treat behind the trash cans or he's heaving up the rest of the sandwich from earlier. Katie can see only the stub of his white tail sticking straight up, stiff with concentration.

The phone rings again, and this time Katie hears two long beeps, which means the caller has decided on this fifth try to leave a message. Just as she is about to turn to the house to investigate, the gate opens on the side of her yard and Dana steps through, her cell phone raised at Katie.

"You are familiar with how this phone thing works, right?" Dana asks blithely. She says hi to Jack, who trots over to greet her, a small, dark lump hanging out of his mouth. "I dial some numbers, and your phone rings, and then you pick up your phone, and then we get to talk?"

"I didn't feel like hearing any more of Dad's drama about last night," Katie says, surprised by the unexpected flood of happiness she feels.

Dana snaps her phone closed. "Forty-five minutes. That's how long I had to listen to what could have happened if the thieves were a couple of minutes earlier. And I blame it on you," she says with a sly smile. "You couldn't take a little heat off me?"

Dana crouches down to Jack, who opens his mouth and lets the lump plop onto the lawn.

"What *is* that?" Dana says, standing and covering her nose. "Ewww. It stinks."

Jack wags his tail, then proceeds to drop to the ground and roll gleefully all over what appears to be a dead bird.

"Oh, shit," Katie says, and rushes down the deck stairs.

"I'll get the plastic gloves from under the sink, you fill up the tub," Dana says, walking past Katie and punching her lightly on the arm.

•

"Jack!" they yell in unison, which does nothing to stop him from shaking off the thick suds from his fur. Soapy bubbles fly in every direction, landing on their arms, shirts, hair. For a few minutes, they dig in and scrub on opposite sides.

"I'm mad at you, Dana," Katie finally says. She pushes away her sister's hand when it creeps onto her half of Jack's body.

"I know."

They massage Jack's twisting body in silence, and then Dana grabs the shower hose. Katie puts her hand up to Jack's face: stay. Dana stands and sprays him off, and then Katie lifts him out of the tub and onto the bathroom mat. They both get down on their knees to dry him off, but Katie tugs the towel out of Dana's grip.

"I can do this part alone."

Dana sits back on her heels, slowly peels off her gloves.

The wiry white fur on Jack's back stands straight up on end as he pants with impatience for Katie to finish. When she stops toweling to face off with her sister, Jack sees his chance; he sprints away and bounds out of the bathroom and up the hallway. Dana keeps her head tucked down, fingering the tips of her wet gloves.

"How could you all gang up on me like that?" Katie asks her sister.

"I told you, it wasn't supposed to be like that. Mom was coming over to continue your conversation from the night before, which is the only reason I was there. To make sure she didn't freak you out."

"Great job."

"I know."

"So care to clue me in now?"

Dana stands and takes Katie's wet gloves, drops both pairs into the tub.

"What did she mean by 'more of the same,' Dana?"

"Mom said she wants to wait until the trial is over to discuss it with you again, and I agreed. It would be too much right now, but it isn't anything horrible."

"No, not horrible, just 'worse.'"

All of a sudden, Dana is intensely interested in making sure the wet towel is hanging perfectly straight over the shower rod.

"Dana?"

"Okay," her sister says, studying the towel. She brushes her hand against it, turns to Katie. "Okay, then let's just do this." Dana sits down on the toilet, places a steadying hand on each thigh.

Katie settles herself on the rim of the tub, ignoring the water that immediately sinks into the seat of her jeans.

"I have to warn you, though, it isn't that simple," Dana says.

"What in my life is simple right now?"

"Oh, honey, I *know*," her sister says, and tries to grab her hand.

Katie shakes her head. "Just tell me."

"Okay. Well," Dana says, and then becomes quiet, as if she's se-
lecting her words carefully first. "Well, do you remember when you
were little? How much you loved to watch movies all the time? And
you—"

"Wait," Katie says, leaning forward. "Why would you bring that
up now?"

"What?"

"Richard said something about me watching movies just a few
days ago."

"He did? What did he say?" Her sister looks at the doorway, like
she's waiting for Jack to reappear.

Katie pictures herself in the courtroom, Richard asking her to act,
her dramatic reaction to the gun. "Never mind, just get to the point."

"Kate, you need to be patient, because I really do feel like shit about
this. I know I should have said something to you a long time ago, and
I was wrong not to. I mean, it's my job—"

"I'm not one of your clients, Dana. I shouldn't be a *job* to you."

"No, you aren't, I didn't mean it like that. It's just the opposite, actually. My training, my objectivity is almost nonexistent with the people
I love. Like that time Michael—"

"Can we just focus here?" Katie interrupts. "How all the trouble
began when I was a little girl and used to watch movies all the time?"

"Kate."

"Sorry. Go ahead."

"Well, so you were obsessed with them when you were little, remember? You'd watch them over and over. One would finish and
you'd rewind and watch it all over again, and you'd cry and get angry
or happy or sad all over again, like everything was happening to you."

"That's what filmmakers want, Dana. They want you to relate to
the main characters, to empathize—"

"I know, but it wasn't just with movies. You'd watch people like
that all the time, too. I don't mean you'd cry or laugh or anything, but
you always had that same incredibly intense look on your face, like

when you were in front of the TV. You do it with your documentaries, and even now you still sit away from the crowd and watch everything happen around you, instead of actually interacting with the family."

"Can you blame me? You see the way they treat me."

"How do they treat you?"

"Everyone in this family, except you, has always treated me differently."

"Differently than what?"

"Oh, c'mon, Dana, don't pretend you haven't noticed. Different from *you*," Katie says.

"Well, we're different people, Katie, and back then just the difference in our ages would—"

"Give me a break," Katie snaps. "You know what I mean. Maybe the reason I watched those movies so much is because I wanted to know what it felt like to *exist*. Everyone in this family has always thought you were perfect. And you love being in the spotlight, completely adored, while I'm—"

Her sister jumps up. "That isn't fair! I never asked to be in a spotlight."

"But you *are*."

"And what, you're stuck in the shadows? Because of me?"

Katie is on her feet now, too. "You're actually going to deny it?"

"This is part of the issue, Kate, sometimes you say things like this and I realize what a skewed perception you have of your place in relationships—"

"Skewed? Are you serious? Do you even *live* in this family?"

They are face-to-face now, only inches apart, Katie trying hard to control her breathing. Dana checks the doorway again.

"This is all wrong, I didn't want it to be like this." Dana shakes her head. "Mom was right, I shouldn't have come," her sister says. "I should go." Like a shot, Dana is pushing past Katie.

Katie follows at her heels. "Are you kidding me? You're *leaving*?"

Her sister skips down the stairs, swipes her purse and coat off the kitchen table, and heads to the front door.

"I came here because I felt awful about the other night, Kate, and I wanted to give you time to think about it."

"Again, care to clue me in before you leave a second time?"

Dana faces the front door, head lowered, taking in deep breaths. She places her purse on the floor and slowly pushes her arms into her coat, then turns to face Katie.

It's the closest Katie has ever come to striking someone—even angry and trying to escape from Katie's home, her sister looks composed, completely in charge.

"I knew you might have felt this way when you were young, but I thought you were over it by now. I thought you wouldn't still try to blame me."

"I'm not blaming you, exactly."

"Yes you are. You're trying to say it's my fault."

"I don't even know what the hell *it* is, Dana!" Katie roars. She is seconds—just *seconds*—from driving a fist into her sister's infuriatingly calm face.

"I'm not in some sort of spotlight, Kate. Our family treats me the same way I treat them," she says. "Even now, during this trial, I know you're taking everything in, you're making your assessments—but then you share only a fraction of what you're feeling. Can't you see how that might make people react?"

"So this isn't about me *watching* people now, it's about the way I treat our family?"

"You were the one who brought them up, Katie, but yes, it's all tied together. It's about your relationship with the family, with people—"

"I'm not worried about *people,* Dana, I'm worried about this trial, about Nick."

"I know, and I know that Nick was the most important person in your life, and without him—"

"Right, without Nick it's just 'more of the same.'"

"Kate," Dana says, "will you please stop getting caught up in Mom's words?"

"She wanted to know what my story was, right? You want to know? This *is* my story! I don't understand why you all think it's so easy to just let go of him. Can't I even wait until the trial is over before I change my personality and go out and get a new fucking life?" She is shaking so hard that her teeth start to chatter.

"I'm so sorry, I didn't want to upset you. This is why I thought you should talk to someone, why I suggested—"

"I'm talking to you right now, aren't I?"

"You know what I mean, Katie. A therapist, someone who's objective and trained to deal with grief and these kinds of issues."

"'These kinds of issues'!" Katie shouts just inches from her sister's face. "I'm fine!"

"Really?" Dana says. "I know you say that all the time, but are you? This is why I came tonight, too. To ask you to consider talking to a professional. Not just about Nick's death, but all of it," her sister says, opening her arms wide.

"So now I need professional help because my husband died and I watch other people and I treat these same people like shit. Great, Dana, thanks for letting me know just how crazy I really am. You have impeccable timing, just like Mom."

"I don't think you're crazy—I really didn't come here to upset you."

"Another fantastic job, Dana, really stellar." She wants to hurt her sister, wants her words to come out like knives, but instead there are bumps in her voice. "How about this? How about you all just steer clear of me from now on," she says, turning away, but Dana grabs her by the upper arm from behind and wheels her around.

"Listen—"

Their faces are too close, and there's something in her sister's eyes—pity or shame or aversion, maybe all three—so Katie tears herself out of her sister's grip and pushes her away, hard. Dana's eyes flare in surprise, and she trips backward, palms smacking against the door, her head whipping back and hitting the wood with a loud thud.

"Oh, God," Katie says, "I didn't mean—"

But her sister shrugs off her sympathy, holds her back with one hand. "Last night," Dana says, barely controlled now, "I was in bed, and I was thinking how good it was that you and Nick never actually had a baby. Because if you did, Nick would always be with you. A little girl who laughed like him, or a boy who had his eyes, or something like that." Her sister's eyes roam all over Katie's face. "But it's more than that. You're never going to figure out what you really want until you take a good look at yourself, until you let him go and you finally—"

"How can I, with this trial?"

"Just *stop*," Dana says, then composes herself, softens her voice.

"Have you ever considered, just once, that none of the answers you need are out there? You're always looking everywhere, you're always looking to other people for answers, but—" Dana sighs, shakes her head.

She moves forward, presses her finger into the center of Katie's chest, softly. "Right here, Kate. The answers have always been right here."

12

For the documentary's interviews, Katie used the room in the War-wick Center with the two-way mirror where Nick met with his clients, because of its simplicity—a table, four chairs, and scenic pictures of Rhode Island meant to calm: Black Point, Narragansett, with its moss-covered rocks meeting the ocean; a landscape of Breakheart Pond in Arcadia, where the water looked like a glass floor extending out from the forest.

Too many faces could potentially confuse viewers, so Patricia and Nick had helped Katie compile a list: Dottie Halverson, Eddie Rodriguez, Patricia, and of course Nick. Patricia had helped persuade Jerry's hesitant social worker to allow the filming, and she even made numerous calls when the necessary permits and permissions were bogged down with red tape. It was the first time Katie had sought anyone's help with a documentary, and she was grateful. She was even more grateful that Nick sat by her side at night, reviewing the footage.

—The first thing I'm going to do in the new house is set up your pull-down screen, Nick told her one night after filming.

—That would be great, Katie said, spooning film onto the spindle.

—Okay, we're all set here. Now, remember, this is just a rough cut of the interviews. I'm still working on how to string them together to get a coherent history. I'll have to edit out initial responses to my questions, repetition of information, and weave actual footage in between.

—And then we do my narration? Nick asked.

—We don't add your voice-over until we're done. Sometimes you don't know what the story is until the very end, so we'll work on that after we're done with all the filming.

The first footage on the wall showed a close-up of Patricia nodding thoughtfully. Behind her and a little to the left, a photograph of Cold Brook in Little Compton, because Katie had liked the effect: stripped branches bent over with snow and reaching across the frozen brook.

—Yes, Patricia said into the camera after a moment. —His mother, Evelyn. She was a deeply religious woman. And yet, despite her convictions, she had engaged in an affair with a married man.

Jerry is this man's son?

—He is. According to the files, Evelyn told the social workers that this man was going to divorce his wife, but when Jerry was six months old, he was diagnosed with mental retardation. Soon after, his father cut off all contact with them.

Did he try to support Jerry financially?

—Initially, yes. But after the diagnosis, all talk of divorce ended. He stopped visiting soon after, and the child-support checks stopped a few months later. Evelyn did some investigating and discovered that Jerry's father had died suddenly of an embolism.

That must have been a horrible shock for her.

—Apparently not. She saw it as a sign from God. Divine retribution for their sins, Patricia said, mouth curving with derision.

Five seconds of blank space on the wall, and then Dottie's face replaced Patricia's. —Evelyn was *very* religious, Dottie said. —But obviously there was a lot more going on there. I don't think she was ever officially diagnosed by a psychiatrist, but it's clear from some of her statements that she suffered from severe mental issues. Dottie shook her head. —When Jerry's father died, it only got worse.

How so?

—She believed that Jerry's MR, what she called his "affliction," was an indictment against her for her adulterous sins. Some of the statements she made to social workers . . . Dottie shook her head again, this time in amazement. Well, it's evident her disturbed mind and stringent beliefs about God turned to a sort of religious fanaticism. And Jerry's illegitimacy and handicap made him the obvious bearer of atonement. The abuse— Dottie said, and stopped. She turned away from the camera to collect herself. —She told the social worker that

Jerry's father was in hell because of Jerry, and her son needed to know that. He should *feel* it.

After a moment Eddie Rodriguez appeared on the wall, a body shot of him sitting at the table. —She abused him all the time, horrendous things. Reciting from the Bible like a high priestess the whole time. She'd recite to the social workers, too. Katie, you wouldn't believe some of the things she said to them. Eddie shifted in his chair, looked off to the side. —Sorry, he said, and cleared his throat. —I forgot not to address you directly.

Patricia was back after a few seconds of blank space. —During his formative years, when most children learn to communicate and establish loving, trusting relationships with adults and other children, Jerry was locked in a dark room with only minimal contact from his unstable mother. And that contact. . . . Patricia shakes her head angrily. —She may have forgotten to feed or bathe him for days at a time, but she never forgot to torture him.

Dottie was back, explaining how Jerry finally escaped this abuse; how, when he was six years old, a nurse at Kent County Hospital went to the Department of Children, Youth and Families and demanded that they take a second look at the numerous medical reports of Jerry's "accidents." Jerry and his mother were woken in the early-morning hours by a social worker, accompanied by two police cars, their lights spinning; afterward, Evelyn made sure Jerry took responsibility for the meddling presence of the police.

—Even now, after all this time and all his progress, Dottie said, when Jerry sees police cars with their lights on, he panics.

—There was a lengthy investigation after that, Patricia said next. —Then, and only then, did some of the neighbors finally come forward.

—Can you imagine keeping that sort of thing to yourself for so long? Eddie Rodriguez asked the camera after a brief space in the footage. He sat back in his chair, shook his head sadly. —All the crying and yelling, and they did nothing.

But obviously some of them had to give statements?

Eddie described the police report given by an elderly neighbor, detailing the haunted look of the small boy who she thought was deaf and mute on the few occasions she saw him being led to and from the house.

—How can you be mute if you spend six years screaming for help?
Nick was the last interview, an extreme close-up of his face.

—Jerry was finally removed from Evelyn's custody, Nick said.
—And then he was shuffled from one foster home to another. As
a teenager, and then as an adult, Jerry was housed in group homes,
where it was easy to get lost in the commotion of demanding, mentally
challenged adults.

It was a miracle, then, Nick told the camera, that Jerry survived at
all, that he was able to communicate or trust adults after so many years
of abuse and neglect.

—But we have hope, Nick said, a confident smile on his face. —His
past is starting to work its way out of him, and we're going to keep him
safe. We're going to make sure Jerry has a very loving, supportive, and
peaceful future with us. Only good things in his life from now on.

• • •

The third time it happened, they were at the zoo, Katie watching
from behind the camera, Nick slipping coins into the feeder for the
baby goats, Jerry giggling in anticipation with cupped hands. Then
a small bubble of thunder in the distance, a mother moaning loudly,
Oh, God, not a storm! and Jerry's instant reaction: eyes lifting to the
sky, lips moving—then fists punching the air, punching Nick, who
had a bruise on his neck for weeks. The fourth time was at Chelo's by
the Sea in East Greenwich, Nick dipping steamers into butter, trying
to persuade Jerry to try one. Jerry laughing, shaking his head, saying,
—No way, day like boogers. And then, at the table right beside them,
too close, a woman clicking her lighter. She lit her cigarette, took a
long drag, stared back at Jerry, whose eyes had attached to hers. She
held the cigarette up for him to see. *What?* her gaze asked. *This?* She
pushed it forward in his direction. *You want one?* And then the other
patrons were rising, standing back and watching in stunned horror
as Nick wrestled a thrashing Jerry onto the floor, the tablecloth inside
Jerry's fists. Their lunch skidded across the table, crashed down on
top of them: plates, silverware, creamy New England clam chowder,
small cups of hot butter, and dozens of tiny steamer shells that crack-
led underneath their rolling bodies (later a trip to the ER, because
Nick needed stitches where a shell had dug in, and a tetanus shot).

Katie glared up at the woman, her cigarette still poised in front of her mouth.

—Put it out! Katie yelled. —This isn't the smoking section.

—It isn't? the woman had asked. And took another long, fascinated drag, watching Jerry sob and reach for Katie, already on her knees beside Nick, who was shaking his left hand in pain (an X-ray revealing his index finger broken in two places).

And then only one more, the last violent episode of his past twisting out of his body, groaning its way into the world. Out on their boat, waiting for the sun to set completely, a time to celebrate the end of summer. Waiting for fireworks, but then that scissor of lightning in the distance. Afterward Nick's fractured wrist, Katie's hip mottled black and blue and yellow from where she clipped it on the corner of the cooler on her way down.

Amid the frantic images of Jerry's anger and whirling fists, amid the footage of Jerry working at the Warwick Center and the interviews with the center's staff and Nick working with Jerry in their sessions (Jerry holding a mirror, watching his mouth stretch wide to train his muscles—*Ohhhhhh, Eeeeeee*—or Nick holding a tongue depressor against his tongue, coaching him: —Say "that," Jerry. "Thhhhhhat"), there was also Jerry, hauling boxes into their new house in Warwick Neck, grinning into the camera. And Jerry, standing in the spare bedroom, *his* bedroom, turning in circles with his arms out at his sides. Staring in amazement.

—*True?* he asked Katie behind the camera. —Mine?

The room bobbing up and down as she nodded behind the camera. —Yours, Jerry.

The camera lingered on his face, on the expression of relief and happiness so potent, so powerful and real that Katie put the camera down to go to him.

—A family, Kay-tee? he said into her hair, buckling her into his arms.

—I told you, Jer, you're stuck with us.

—*Better.* The word like a sigh.

Nick popped his head inside the room. —Let's get a move on, slackers.

—Mine, Nick! Jerry told him, releasing Katie and running to Nick. —*Mine.*

Nick turned inside Jerry's arms, whispered to Katie. —You should be filming this.

•

They set up his bed, plugged in the Bugs Bunny night-light Katie had picked up at Toys "R" Us, taped his pictures onto the wall. Right beside the bed, they filled a small white bookcase with his "best" books, an assortment of drawing pads, and a jar of pencils. On the dresser a framed photo of the three of them squinting into the sun at a seaside restaurant in Mystic, Connecticut, Jerry's stuffed beluga whale from the Mystic Aquarium propped up beside it.

Jerry lay in bed that night, eyes locking onto every object, his hair still wet from a shower.

—Did you remember to shampoo? Katie asked him, sitting at the edge. She ran her fingers through his thin brown hair.

—Uh-oh.

—That's okay. Tomorrow.

—I forget.

—It's okay. We'll have to change your contacts tomorrow, too.

—Yuck.

—I know.

Jerry's eyes were wide as he scanned the walls, the dresser. —Dis *my* room.

—It really is.

—Wow.

—It will always be your room, buddy.

A few seconds of thoughtful mumbling, then looking at Katie expectantly. —God not come here mad.

—Never, Katie said. —No way.

—Oh. I forget.

—That's what I'm here for, right?

—Right, Jerry said, hiding his relieved smile under the sheet.

—Now, what book should we have on your first night? In the mood for a Gruffalo?

He looked around his room again, at Katie. —No book, he said. He wriggled closer to her. —You know.

—Again?

—It May, Jerry said, and waited.

Months later, when the weather turned cold and she started editing the footage in the basement—months later, when they realized that Jerry's episodes had suddenly ended because he finally had a home, a real home with a mother and a father every weekend, and sometimes during the week, too—Katie knew she had the perfect ending to his film: Jerry twirling inside his room, staring in wonder, the kind of amazed relief you could almost touch.

. . .

After the holidays Katie reviewed the final edited footage while Nick was at work. She kept rewinding to that last episode caught on film, Jerry's final outburst of anguish on their boat before the incidents disappeared forever—the only one captured from beginning to end, because Katie had neglected to turn the camera off before she put it down on the cushioned seat of their boat to race to Jerry's side. The camera recording the aftermath for the first time—Jerry clinging to her, gulping his fear into her neck, calling her name. Why, she wondered absently as she looked at the screen, why hadn't she edited herself out? Katie stood in her cold basement, watched herself in Jerry's arms, saw her own arms securely around him. And she knew.

It didn't matter that her old classmate who worked at PBS hadn't returned any of her calls since the initial one, wasn't important that she didn't have any real contacts she could call. Jerry's film was everything a filmmaker could wish for: compelling, sweet, frightening, hopeful—the journey of a mentally handicapped man who had risen above his past, who had discovered the secret to living with his fears. The film would be snatched up, there might even be bidders—but still, Katie knew.

Standing alone in the basement, she replayed this entire scene, again and again—strange to see herself on the screen like this, a part of Jerry's life for the first time on film. Strange that her time behind the camera, and watching and editing footage that didn't include her had in some ways erased her existence in his story. But here she was now, and here was Jerry, holding her, needing only her, and Katie knew in that moment, before she turned off the projector, that she couldn't do it. Knew, for reasons she couldn't explain right then, that displaying Jerry's private pain and offering his tortured history to strangers would be a betrayal. Katie could easily edit herself out of the scene, out of Jerry's story on film, but she couldn't erase those times when Jerry's past came bursting out of him, when the camera was put aside and he fell into her, trusting that Katie would keep him safe. And without the actual violent episodes on film, the entire direction of the documentary crumbled.

She turned off the camera, and the darkness unfolded inside their basement. She pictured Nick's reaction when she told him tonight that they didn't need to do his voice-over after all. When she told him they were done, and started packing the reels away forever.

• • •

They stood in a row, facing the screen. Nick was right beside Katie, but he wouldn't look at her. His eyes skipped from the screen to Patricia, who held her elbows in her arms, watching the footage:

Jerry, sitting on the long cushioned seat at the stern of the boat, smiling up at the sky, his eyes half open—the camera zooming in on the look of blissful happiness on his chubby face. Over his shoulder, sunset on the ocean, haunting and a little sad in its perfection, the sun slowly falling in the pink- and orange-ribboned sky. But then a sudden, dark rumble. In the distance the gray underlining of puffy clouds filled with light from above, and seconds later another shock of thunder—louder, longer, the kind you could feel right in your bones. A bolt of lightning knifed across the sky, and a small child on a nearby boat wailed in fear. Jerry's lips moved, silently at first, and then the words, barely audible. —*Lord come with fire.*

Within seconds, the camera was sideways on a cushion, tracking the lower half of Katie's body, her legs moving quickly to his side, her arms fastening around him. The basement filled with Katie's whispering: —I'm here, Jerry, I have you, you're okay.

—Is God come *now*? Jerry said, his thick arms shaking Katie. Katie, who would not let go, even as the boat lifted up into the water and tipped them over, falling out of the camera's view.

Katie stopped the film, flipped on the lights.

—I just can't, she said. —He trusts us, and—I don't know, but when I picture people watching him, if I even think about Jerry knowing we've shared this—

—We'll explain it to him, we'll tell him why. Nick said this to Patricia, ignoring Katie's pleading look.

Patricia held Nick's gaze for a moment. —We have to trust Katie's judgment, she finally said, then turned to Katie. —Thank you, she said. —Thank you for your compassion.

—But he hasn't had an episode since this last one, Nick argued, gesturing to the dark screen. —Not in months, not since the summer. We show that in the film, how he eventually overcame them.

Katie felt a tug at the "we," how strongly Nick had aligned himself with one of her projects for the very first time. Patricia remained silent as she faced Nick, her mouth pinched—Katie's decision confirmed. The program director turned back to Katie.

—I didn't realize, Katie, she said. —I had no idea how much Jerry relied on you.

Katie was unable to see Nick's reaction to this, because he was already storming toward the basement stairs.

—I don't believe it, he said angrily. —This is what it's been about all along. We knew this from the beginning.

—He can't—I can't share it. It isn't our right, Katie called after Nick tearfully, watching him disappear upstairs. She turned back to Patricia. —He's my family now, I have to protect him.

—I agree, Patricia said. —And I respect your decision, Katie.

•

For weeks she tried to make Nick understand, to explain why she had to abandon the film.

—Even if Jerry never sees it, it'll be out there, she told him. —And we'll know that we've taken the most painful parts of his life and given them away to strangers.

—Aren't most of the people who watch documentaries strangers? Isn't that the whole point?

—But Jerry only showed this side of himself to us, no one else, because he trusted us.

—There were other people around every time, Katie. Every time.

—He didn't see them, he only knew that *we* were there, that *we* would help—

But Nick's dark eyes filled with contempt each time before he turned away.

Her documentary, so close to completion, would never be shown to the world, and this fact ripped into her marriage like a storm, tearing apart the peace and companionship that she had shared with Nick for so many months. Nick looking at her as if she'd betrayed him, no matter how many times she insisted that she loved him more, she wasn't choosing Jerry over him—but she had to follow her heart.

When Candice called (frequently now, her happy voice full of mild victory when Katie answered) Katie would watch Nick standing in the kitchen, the phone crushed against his ear, nodding emphatically at his mother's words. Chewing on the inside of his mouth, skipping his eyes toward Katie, waiting until she found other parts of the house to hunt restlessly. Katie didn't need to hear her mother-in-law's words to know what she was saying; it was written all over Nick's face: *I told you. Selfish woman. A mistake, right from the start.* And she didn't have to look at Nick to understand his angry displeasure, because it radiated from him every time they were close—close but completely separate, the miles yawning between them.

. . .

Jerry still slept over every weekend, and occasionally during the week, but now he watched Nick carefully—seeing but not understanding the tension, the palpable disappointment and resentment Nick's face revealed whenever he walked into a room and found them together. Like he had entered a room in their house that he didn't know existed until that moment—and he wasn't happy about the discovery.

—Nick feel mad?

—No, of course not.

—Sure?

Jerry's eyes always tracking Nick closely now, the questions growing. *Why Nick shower so long? Why Nick not watch movies with us?* And at the Warwick Center: *What Nick do in room with Carly? Why he eat lunch in office today? He mad?*

On the weekends there were ways to make the questions stop. A pair of T-strap silver pumps with clear side buttons, a rounded peep toe, and a wedge heel. Red Mary Janes with an ankle strap and plenty of places to take hold and tear.

Afterward she hid the remains in the garbage can outside, then went back inside to Jerry, who would retreat to his room to draw.

—Your dad say he pay me for to rake old leaves, Jerry said one afternoon, looking up from his pad. —Okay?

—I'll drive you over tomorrow.

—Maybe your mom cook?

He loved her mother's cooking, almost as much as her father's constant teasing about the growing tab he was calculating for Jerry's food consumption. How her father would wink at Katie, so Jerry could see, and pull out a small notebook from his back pocket. *Let's see, a hunk of lasagna that big would be at least six dollars, so I think we're up to one million, four hundred thousand . . . Wait a minute. Grace, did you give this boy garlic bread, too? How much we charging for that now?*

—Nick not mad? Jerry said more and more on his visits.

—No.

—He come with us to your mom's dis time?

—Maybe.

She saw his looks of doubt, tried to ignore the way his eyes trailed down to her feet.

13

On Monday morning Katie wakes somewhere near dawn, kick-ing away the down comforter and the knotted sheets around her ankles. Her foot clips Jack, lying at the end of the bed, and he grunts and hops off the bed. He stands beside it, tail between his legs, looking up at her.

"Sorry," she murmurs, running her hands over her face.

Outside the window the blue-gray morning is beginning to reveal the outlines of the day, the start of another long week in court. But first this, first Nick—so close only moments before that she could smell his skin, feel the silk of his hair between her fingers.

In the spring, when he moved out, Katie's dreams had started to change, so slowly at first that she hardly noticed. She'd wake up the same as always, recall snippets of the vivid images that came from childhood—a birthday party at Judi's, her best friend in the sixth grade until her family moved to California, or swimming at Matunuck Beach with her family, or walking the crumbling military edifices in Beaver-tail with Amy and Jill as teenagers. She'd remember bits of dreams with childhood dogs that bounded up to her, wagging their tails, no signs of the crippling arthritis or kidney failure that took them away years later, or that same dream she still has today, where she's sitting in her senior-year history class, realizing with an acid panic that she hasn't been to the class the entire year; she would fail the final, wouldn't graduate, and her mother would kill her. But then others came, and she'd wake in the morning, rub the sleep out of her eyes, and suddenly remember: Nick had visited her in the night, buried in between the other dreams, his face slowly taking shape.

Nick had made it into her dreams when they were together, but in all those years his image was more like a mirage—his outline wavering, like the camera in her dreams was permanently out of focus. But shortly after he packed his things and left the house for what she thought would be a brief respite, his image started to form completely. A month later, after he had left her world for good, she'd wake in the darkness with a start, swallowing back her tears, her hand sweeping across his side of the bed. She'd remember the dream—Nick whispering her name, his face above hers, Nick laughing at her as she danced under a spray of water on the docks, and, later, Nick lying in a pool of blood, his eyes blank but lips moving and saying something she couldn't hear—and then the bubbling would start on the underside of her belly, and she'd sit up in bed. Dead. Nick was *dead*. Sometimes she said it out loud, and other times she willed herself back into the dream so she could be with him again, feel his body close to hers, even if his head was framed by a dark puddle of his own blood.

But this morning's dream was worse, because it didn't have any of the confusing yet familiar shifts that dreams usually have, the jarring skips in time or location, the sudden replacement of her mother for her eighth-grade algebra teacher. It mimicked reality so closely that the voice inside her head that should have reminded her that she was dreaming was absent, and she felt the full force of the fight inside her, as though it were happening in real time: Charging into Nick's office upstairs, confronting him about the abandoned documentary because the spaces between them were still there, gaping, six months later. *Don't you get it, Nick? I'm your biggest fan,* she had said, and in the dream she saw it again, the light of wonder on his face as he looked at her. *I'm nothing without you, I'm not even here,* she said, and looked up to see Nick's face, so clearly, so clearly right in front of her. *You're everything,* she said, and closed her eyes. She felt him pull her body into his, sank into his embrace. *Katie, Katie.* His voice the same as that night, tormented but with a hint of awe in it, too. *I've been so lost, Katie.* And in the dream, with Nick's arms around her, she felt the hope from that night, the hope in Nick's need to have her see him, to really *see* him and believe in him, how important he was to her—how important she could still be to him.

She wipes the sleep out of her eyes now, and in a wavery voice asks Jack to come back on the bed. The little dog eyes her, still wary. She hugs her knees into her chest, relives the rest of that night with Nick, what the dream didn't capture. Later, in bed together, lying side by side.

—Let's start a family, she had whispered, needing to keep him close, knowing how easily he could retreat again.

—I don't know.

—It will be a boy, and he'll look just like you.

Katie listened to his rapid breathing, the doubt with every inhale and exhale. Said the words he needed to hear: —You'll be an amazing father. He'll make you proud.

Her own breaths matching his then.

—When? Nick finally said, and Katie pulled his hand onto her stomach.

—Now.

Now, she had said to him, and heard Nick draw in his breath as she pressed his hand into her flesh.

A little girl who laughed like him or, better, a boy who had his eyes . . .

She can almost feel Nick's body against hers right now, the hope speeding through him, dreaming of his son. And then Katie sees Dana's arms thrown wide to include Katie's entire life—this moment with Nick, and the years before she met him, the months since he'd left, and everything in between. Wanting Katie to talk to a professional, to tell a complete stranger *all of it.*

"How?" she says, and buries her head inside her hands. Jack hops up onto the bed, pushes his nose into her.

When, Nick had said that night, finally coming back to her all the way. *Now.*

"I didn't know what else to do," she says helplessly to the dog, enough for him to lean his body into hers with a nervous whine. She hugs him into her lap, stares into his black eyes. "What else could I give him?"

THREE

1

On Monday morning Jerry's current social worker, Amanda, is on the witness stand first, immediately floundering under Richard's pounding questions. The young woman's eyes protrude a little, which adds to the dazed look on her face; she blinks at Richard and around the room, struggling to keep her composure.

"So if someone filed an incident report at the Warwick Center about the defendant's violent behavior, your office would be notified and a copy of it would be sent for your files as well?"

"Yes, but Jerry hadn't been violent in such a long time—"

"But the reports should be in the files regardless of time, right?"

"They should be," Amanda says.

"But they aren't, so how have you tried to account for that?"

"I haven't . . . I can't, actually. I thought we sent you the complete files when you subpoenaed them."

Richard raises his eyebrows at the jurors. "As his current social worker, are you aware that the defendant went through a period of time when he was aggressive and disruptive? Or didn't you even read the reports?"

"No—I mean, yes, I knew and I read them, but it was my understanding—"

"That they weren't important anymore?"

"No, not that, it's—"

"And how long ago did you read them?"

"When I was assigned his case, about eight months ago."

"And now they're just"—Richard snaps his fingers—"missing."

"That's what I heard—but I when I sent them, I think they were
in—"

"Your client is on trial for murder, and you didn't check to see if
potentially damaging information was included in his files?"

"I don't—I think—"

"Is it normal procedure at DCYF for records to just disappear like
that?"

Throughout this exchange, Donna's objections are overruled, one
after the other, and she flags at the defense table, shaking her head.
Jerry stares down at his yellow pad, the pencil off to one side. His eyes
are unfocused, bleary, and there are puffy bags underneath them. He
is a statue, solid and unmoving, and when Donna turns to consult with
one of her assistants and accidentally bumps his shoulder—a gesture
that makes Katie flinch on her bench—he doesn't react.

Last week, just *days* ago, Katie would have sat forward, her eyes
hard and unforgiving at this assault, but she recognizes this girl's confusion, her desire to understand. And then her failure, her frustration,
as she checks the defense table for help yet again and sees Donna still
consulting with a woman in the front row.

"Well, I suppose this is just a matter of record keeping, then?" Richard says to Amanda. "That now you can call the Warwick Center administration and have them make copies from their own files?"

No one in the courtroom could possibly believe it's this easy, that the
missing incident reports would be mentioned at all if they still existed,
but Amanda is glad to be let off the hook.

"Yes," she says.

Katie watches Amanda's body go limp with relief, wishing hers
would do the same.

•

One by one, Richard calls DCYF administrators and Jerry's past social
workers to the stand and begins his assault all over again. Katie finds
a rhythm inside her head, a way to shut out the words that come at
her, along with Richard's scathing looks and gestures; she catches herself counting her fingers, slowing her breathing, the way Nick taught
Carly when she couldn't calm herself after her mother's death. It works
for a while, long enough for Katie to understand that what looks like

simple badgering (Richard repeating the same questions to each witness) is actually practiced and has a purpose. Richard shakes his head,
sighs, raises his eyebrows in doubt. As always, it works: when he stands
before the jurors and gives them a look—*Can you believe this?*—all
twelve sets of eyes mirror his frustration.

There is only one interruption in the rest of the morning session,
though not from Donna, who doesn't object any longer. Katie watches
Donna with envy, because she has become as quiet, as unmoving, as
Jerry, which makes the scene even more dramatic: as the last social
worker trudges out of the courtroom, Jerry's body spasms once, torso
twisting, then a second time. And then he is suddenly falling out of his
chair sideways, landing on the courtroom floor with a loud whimper of
pain. As the noise of confused voices intensifies inside the room, Katie
has only one clear thought: she's just glad she wasn't the one to fall
down.

·

"Can I get you anything?" Richard asks at the lunch break. He bangs
his briefcase and laptop onto his desk, sits. "Something to eat?" he asks
without glancing at her.

She can't pinpoint it, but something has changed between them.
She's sure of it. First there was the unsettling way he treated her this
morning when she asked about today's witnesses—his short, overly
formal answers, his scarcely hidden irritation with her, as if she were a
meddling reporter with too many questions. And now, as she watches
him, this: he opens his laptop, hits a key, begins typing. Like Katie
isn't in the room at all—or she's *in* the room, but completely irrelevant now.

"I'm fine," she says.

"Please," he says, jerking open a drawer and rifling through it,
"have a seat."

"I'll stand," Katie blurts, too loud, and Richard looks up.

"Everything okay?" he asks.

"Fine," Katie says, louder.

Richard turns his eyes briefly to where Katie's hands clench the
chair in front of her. His eyebrows rise, and he looks back at Katie.
"You said you have some questions? About the tape, I assume?"

"Actually, no. I just want to know if your strategy has changed."

Richard becomes absorbed in another drawer for a moment.

"Please," Katie says.

He pulls out a legal brief, flips it open. "Last week was a little crazy, for a bunch of different reasons," he says. "For one, the footage of Jerry's violence was brand new to me, and I had to make some adjustments."

"I'm sorry—" she begins, but he stops her with an indifferent shake of his head and scribbles something onto his pad.

"Treadmont might have known about it before me, but in fact she's playing right into my plan. Even with the footage that made it onto the final copy." His voice is defensive, like Katie is challenging his competency.

"So the strategy *has* changed."

"No. We've always needed to show deliberate and premeditated behavior. Still do."

"But you keep talking about his anger, and then you let the witnesses talk about Jerry's compliance, how he wasn't an angry guy."

"I keep pushing them to repeat this for a reason." He lines up his pen with the cardboard binder of the pad. "I want the jurors to believe that Jerry *wasn't* angry and out of control."

"But why the footage then, why—"

"The more I push to show he could become violent, the more the defense pushes back. In the end it will be exactly what I need."

"Which is?"

"He smiled right before he shot your husband, Katie. He didn't strike out, he wasn't aggressive at all."

"But earlier that day, he had the group session with Nick." Katie lowers her eyes for an instant. "About sex and marriage. The defense is going to say it was fear, that he was set off by his history with his mother and how she abused him while she talked about sex and recited Scripture."

"And what happened years ago, when Jerry was 'set off'?"

"You know. He freaked out."

"Exactly," Richard says, leaning forward. "But this time he didn't. He learned to control his rage. He was upset by whatever he heard in that session, and whatever he and Nick talked about later at lunch, and then he acted on it. He seemed preoccupied, but not angry. He was upset with Nick, but not out of control. In his supervisor's own words, he was 'pensive' and 'diligent.' *Planning*." Richard sits back in his chair, folds his arms. "Controlled. Deliberate. Premeditated."

"And when they say he tried to save Nick? That he was confused and tried to help him?"

"I recall Rodriguez's statement. 'Bad men belong in hell.' Jerry thought it was okay to shoot a bad man, because God wanted it."

"But I don't think it's that easy. Jerry *did* love Nick."

Richard shrugs. "Jerry may have loved your husband and still tried to kill him for reasons we'll never understand. Maybe he thought Nick was 'bad,' or he got pissed off at what he heard that day, or maybe he really thought shooting him was a good thing—who knows? The facts are still the same. He stole the gun, hid it in his jacket, then walked into the gym to murder Nick. He smiled and said, 'Time to go.' *Why* he did it barely matters anymore."

"But the tape," Katie says. "They'll see the other side—"

"It doesn't matter how many sugary moments made it on there. Those jurors will still see what this man is capable of, how he hurt Nick in the past."

"But during those struggles, when he was upset by thunder or something, he wasn't purposely trying to hurt Nick."

"Well, they can make that decision for themselves, can't they?" he asks tersely.

"The point is," he continues, "they'll see a man who became enraged when his past caught up with him, someone who would strike out, but only when Nick was around. Even if Jerry learned to contain himself and deal with his past, the images of this rage will affect them. And then, when we put them side by side with his complete restraint on the day of the murder," Richard says, "even when the jurors see the innocuous images of Jerry juxtaposed with the blowouts on the tape . . . well, we've got exactly what we want. A violent man who might have appeared harmless at times but who also became vicious within seconds. A man who eventually found a way to focus this rage in a controlled manner, who was completely aware that shooting Nick from three feet away would kill him. A man who was still able to recite the Bible thirty-some years after he heard it. 'Thou shalt not kill,' right?"

The self-satisfied smile on Richard's face is too much. Katie looks away, mumbles her thanks.

"Anything else?" he asks in a dismissive tone.

"Are you—have I done something wrong?"

"No. Why would you think that?"

"I don't know, you just seem upset with me."

"Not at all," he says with a stiff smile.

• • •

"Please state your name for the jurors."

"My name is Patricia Kuhlman." Undaunted, Patricia keeps her gaze level with Richard's.

"You are the acting program director at the Warwick Center?"

"I am."

"Your duties include overseeing both the work and recreation components of the center?"

"Yes."

"And that includes supervising all the employees, and the clients, and keeping things like accounting and client files updated and organized?"

"Yes." Patricia doesn't break eye contact with Richard.

"You are ultimately accountable for every piece of paper that crosses your desk?"

"Of course. I read each one."

"And that includes incident reports?"

"Yes."

"So how do you account for the missing reports from the defendant's file?"

"I can't."

Richard waits for more, but Patricia just raises her eyebrows at him: *Next question?*

"You understand that removing those reports from his file is illegal? That keeping them from the prosecution is considered an obstruction of justice?"

"I do."

"And that their absence could potentially help the defendant's case because of their incriminating nature?"

"Incriminating?" Patricia asks, musingly. "No. No, I don't believe they are."

"No? Reports detailing the defendant's violent outbursts wouldn't incriminate him? Even if they included medical reports of, say, Nicholas Burrelli's fractured wrist or his broken finger—"

"Objection," Donna says. "Judge, the reports have gone missing, and that is unfortunate, but we can't simply speculate what *might* be in them."

"Sustained."

"Did you remove those reports from the center's file yourself, Ms. Kuhlman, and did you direct or request DCYF to do the same, because you knew that reading them aloud to jurors would be shocking? That Nick's resulting injuries from the defendant's—"

"Objection!"

"Sustained," Judge Hwang says, lifting her glasses at Richard. "Move on, Mr. Bellamy."

"Okay. Well, Mrs. Kuhlman, are you aware, then, that the defendant fractured Nick's wrist—"

"Objection," Donna says, standing. "We've covered this."

"Your Honor," Richard says, "this is a reasonable question. By her own testimony, this woman is privy to every piece of paper that moves within the Warwick Center administration. She's read the missing reports, and she can at least verify what was in them."

"I'll allow it."

"Thank you, Judge," Richard says, and turns back to Patricia. "Did you, in fact, read the incident reports that included medical records of Nicholas Burrelli's injuries?"

"I read Jerry's incident reports, yes," Patricia says, "but there weren't any medical reports attached to them."

Richard stares for a moment. "If a staff member is injured—"

"If a staff member is injured, then yes, medical records are attached to the reports, but that is rare. Very rare. I can assure you that while Nick did suffer minor bruises from trying to contain Jerry, he didn't need medical attention. I assume you subpoenaed his medical records from Kent County Hospital, Mr. Bellamy, so I'm also assuming you know that the injuries you just mentioned had nothing to do with Jerry."

Katie remembers their trips to the emergency room, Nick sitting in the curtained room, charming the nurses who smilingly wrote everything down. *I was lifting the anchor up on my boat, and then I tripped.*

Guess I'm getting clumsy in my old age. Protecting Jerry back then—protecting him now.

"So you're actually denying that Nick's visits to the ER had anything to do with the defendant?"

"I certainly am. It's completely false."

"Even if we have an eyewitness who observed Nicholas Burrelli sustaining serious, multiple injuries at the hands of that defendant?"

He is pointing to Jerry now, but Patricia has finally broken her staring match with Richard. She is looking directly at Katie.

"I can tell you, with utmost certainty, that anyone who claims that Jerry seriously injured Nick is lying for his or *her* own personal, confused reasons."

"And do you also understand, Ms. Kuhlman," Richard says angrily, "that if *you* lie in a court of law, you could be prosecuted for perjury?"

Patricia flicks her eyes back to Richard. "I do, but I can assure you that Jerry never purposely or critically harmed Nick."

"So murdering Nick, intentionally executing him—"

"Objection!"

"Withdrawn."

•

Veronica is on the stand for less than a minute when Richard begins his attack.

"Mrs. Holden, is it true that clients' personal and private files at the Warwick Center are openly discussed with people who don't even work there?"

"Our client files are always confidential," Veronica says.

"By 'confidential' do you mean it allows you to discuss a client's past or progress with people who aren't professionally affiliated with the center?"

"No, we don't. We can't."

"But didn't you and other staff members in fact discuss the defendant's history and his progress with Nick Burrelli's wife, Katie?"

"Oh, well, if people are close to the clients," Veronica says, looking quickly at Katie, "sometimes we would."

"So you and other staff members *did* share information from his files?"

"A little," Veronica admits.

"But I assume that there is a process for this disclosure? A thorough discussion among the staff first to determine that being 'close' to someone is enough to reveal private, legal information? And then meetings with, and official clearances from, their social workers? Lengthy administrative procedures to determine it's okay to break confidentiality?"

"Everyone knew Katie was like a mother to Jerry—"

"And was she also a mother to"—Richard picks up a piece of paper, reads—"a 'Joseph Capaldi'?"

"Joey?"

"Yes, the client who witnessed the defendant shooting Nicholas Burrelli?"

"Katie wasn't close to Joey, no—"

"But you and others at the center discussed Nick's problems with Joey, his communication difficulties?"

"Well—"

"So then you weren't exactly truthful just now, were you? Outsiders don't actually have to be close to a client at all to hear about that client's personal and confidential information, do they?"

One by one Richard calls the staff up to the stand and begins all over again: Did you ever discuss private information about the defendant's therapeutic and social progress at the center? Did you tell Katie Burrelli, before she had clearance to film a documentary about the defendant, that his mother had abused him? Is this normal procedure for staff members to carelessly mention confidential information about the clients to anyone who walks in the front door?

By late afternoon Richard has painted a disturbing picture of the Warwick Center staff—unprofessional, gossiping people who thought nothing of breaking rules that were meant to protect an innocent and challenged population. Donna's objections come frequently, and Judge Hwang dismisses them each time in a sullen voice.

Dottie is the last to take the stand. She settles herself in the chair, looks directly at Katie, and offers her a gentle smile. Before Katie can process this act of kindness, this unexpected generosity—before she can stop herself, her hand comes up to chest level, and she waves at Dottie shyly, as if they are meeting for the first time. Dottie's smile deepens, and Richard's head snaps back toward Katie, who feels the guilty rush of blood climbing up her neck and into her cheeks.

Some of the jurors' eyes follow Richard's, and out of the corner of her own eye Katie can see the staff, across the aisle, turning her way, too. She clamps her hands together, the room contracting inward.

"Mrs. Halverson, can you please tell me what information, if any, you illegally shared with Katie Burrelli about the defendant?"

Suddenly the air in the room becomes thick, strangling—Katie jumps up, scrambles to the end of the row. Comes face-to-face with the Warwick Center employees, stops short: sees, in Billy, and Eddie, and Jan and even Veronica the once-familiar looks of concern playing across their features. Not for Jerry this time, but for Katie—they look like they're actually worried about *her*. Katie stares back until Veronica leans forward, nods, a signal that seems to say, *I'll come with you if you want*.

Katie shakes her head, lurches up the aisle—the stunned silence propelling her onward. Outside the courtroom she bends at the waist, blows out short breaths. When she hears Richard's angry questions— "Did you tell Mrs. Burrelli, before she gained permission to hear the defendant's history, that his violent outbursts were actually good? Did you relay this information that the program director shared with you in privacy?"—Katie races to the elevators, her heart clamping inside her chest.

• • •

Something silly and unimportant, that's what she needs. Not to think, not to remember, not to try to understand why, for one overwhelming moment in the courtroom, she imagined falling into the rows packed with her former friends. Knowing then, knowing right now, that they would have caught her—after everything, *still*.

In Sandy's driveway she plays back their faces, not from today but from last spring, when no one cared, when the faces all seemed to turn away from her. *Remember that!* she commands herself, and jumps out of the car.

She knocks on the front door, realizes only when it opens that her car is still running in the driveway.

"Hey, girl!" Sandy steps back with Emily on her hip to allow Katie in. In the background Sandy's two sons, dressed up as cowboys, chase their way into the kitchen, waving toy bows and arrows.

"I killed you!" the bigger one says.

"You didn't, I ducked!" says his little brother.

"We have a visitor," Sandy says brightly, and the smaller one, slipping in red plastic cowboy boots, throws an uninterested wave over his shoulder before he disappears around the corner after his brother. "Good God," Sandy says, smiling after them. "Well, get in here and make yourself at home."

Katie steps over the scattered toys on the floor, threads her way to the couch. She pushes a Tupperware container filled with cookies off to the side, sits.

"You are exactly on time. I just made coffee." Sandy plops the baby on the couch next to Katie, heads to the kitchen. "Two sugars and extra light, right?"

Katie nods, turns to Emily, who stares back at her, a pacifier working up and down in her mouth.

"Hi," Katie says in a shaky voice, and the baby's forehead wrinkles up.

"Court already done for the day?" Sandy calls from the kitchen.

Before Katie can answer, there is a cry from one boy, protests from the other.

"We do *not* stick arrows in our brother's ear," Sandy says in the kitchen.

Emily stirs on the couch, tired of Katie already; she slaps her legs with her fists, makes a long squeal that grates against Katie's nerves.

In the kitchen Sandy quiets the boys (both crying now, with fresh accusations about other places they've been poked), and Emily sits gurgling and laughing quietly to herself.

Sandy emerges with two mugs, her eyes moving from Katie to Emily and back again. The boys trail behind, shoving each other.

"She likes you, Katie," Sandy says, winking, and hands her a mug. She sits cross-legged on the floor in front of the couch, and blows into her mug. "So fill me in. What's going on?"

Katie shakes her head, one hand coming up like a shield; a bad idea coming here, the mess of toys all over the place, the boys' pushing back and forth, the gold sheriff's badge on one boy's vest too shiny as Emily makes squeaky, scraping noises right next to her. Katie looks at the door: can she just get up now and run? And if so, where will she *go*?

"Okay," Sandy says in an even voice. "Hold on."

She scoops up Emily, tells Katie she'll be right back. The boys are hustled into their room with threats to play nice and to keep an eye on their sister, and then Sandy is back, her beautiful face full of worry. She sits on the couch next to Katie, takes the mug that Katie has been holding automatically, puts it on the floor next to her own.

"Just talk," she says, touching Katie's arm. "Go."

For a couple of minutes, Katie doesn't edit herself, she doesn't try to soften what she's saying or worry about Sandy's reaction; the words come spilling out, the relief almost intoxicating, even if what she's saying can't make much sense to Sandy—the feeling of falling down, and the things her family has been saying to her, and Jerry lying on the courtroom floor, killing Nick, saving Nick, and the baby she couldn't give him, and Dottie's smile, and *Nick,* Nick is dead, really *dead,* he's never coming back, and what else could she do to keep him, what does she do now? The words overlap, crisscrossing over each other and looping back—"I almost fell, I *wanted* to fall," she says—and she keeps plowing on, scratching at her forehead, until Sandy reaches up and takes Katie's hand in her own.

"Slow down, okay?" Sandy says.

She squeezes once, smiles, and this brings Katie back into herself.

"Oh, God, I'm sorry, I didn't want to do this, I didn't," Katie says, taking her hand away. "I should just shut up, but really, it's okay. I'm fine, actually." She clears her throat, tries to laugh at herself. "So—so what's been up around here?"

She's ready for a flood of information—Mr. Peterson, hopped up on painkillers and wandering around the neighborhood, the accountant next door, mostly likely having an affair while his wife is on a Fulbright in Ecuador—but Sandy only looks at her with a hurt expression, drops her gaze to her lap.

"I wish you wouldn't always do that," Sandy says quietly.

"What?"

"I don't know," Sandy says. "Change the subject, I guess."

Katie sits back on the couch to get a better look at Sandy: gorgeous, even with this injured expression on her face. There are strands of blond hair poking out of her ponytail, and Sandy pushes them back over her ear, a small, elegant gesture that instantly makes Katie feel unwieldy and foolish.

"I guess you don't trust me in some ways," Sandy says softly, "but I wish you would."

"It's not trust," Katie begins, a little defensively. "It's just . . . well, all we do is talk about the neighbors anyway, and it's fun sometimes—it *used* to be fun—but then you were suddenly gone, and we didn't even have that."

Sandy takes this in slowly, eyes downcast. "Okay," she says, nodding. She sits back so that they are shoulder to shoulder on the couch, both facing the window.

A crow swoops across the gray expanse of sky outside the window, lands on a telephone wire by the street. Its mouth opens, cawing, unheard in the living room. The boys' laughter cuts into the silence, and Katie listens to toys being plunked into the walls of their bedroom, an excited screech from Emily. Sandy ignores it all, still thoughtful; she picks at the cuticle of her index finger, rubs it with her thumb.

"Katie, please don't take this the wrong way," she says, "because I don't want it to come out as an accusation. Not now, with everything going on. I know you're upset, and I can see you need to talk, but I don't—" Sandy sits up to face Katie, folds a leg underneath her. "I'm just going to say it. Yes?"

Katie nods, trying to brace herself for *more*.

"You know me, I love to gab about anything, I think it's fun and it passes the time. But, well with you it seems like that's *all* we talked about. You know, these people," she says, motioning toward the window.

"I know."

Sandy puts her hand on Katie's knee, an apology. "No, I mean, it seems like that's all *you* wanted to talk about."

Katie starts to protest, but Sandy's earnest look stops her.

"It's like, I know you film people, you watch them for a living," Sandy says, "and I think it's such a cool job to have. And when we first started having coffee and everything, I thought that's what you were doing. You know, just watching people, trying to get a handle on them."

"It's my job," Katie says. "To see things and understand—"

"I know, I know it is. And I'm not going to lie, I loved it at first." Sandy sits back, her eyes on the window again. "But after a while I just sort of took my cue from you. I talked about the neighbors, and when I tried to change the subject a little or ask you something personal about yourself and you didn't budge, I just went along. I mean, I did like laughing with you and hearing about how people say things about themselves just by walking a certain way, or looking at the ground or something like that, but—" Sandy shakes her head.

Katie's pulse is thudding inside her ears now, Dana's words filtering through the noise: *You're always looking everywhere, you're always looking to other people for answers . . .*

Katie sits up, folds her own leg underneath her so she can see Sandy, who won't look at her. "Keep going," she says.

Sandy nods, swallows. "Well, I always just thought you didn't trust me with the big stuff. Here you are, with the important job and taking care of someone like Jerry, and I'm just this housewife who's pregnant half the time."

"You have *everything,* Sandy."

Sandy finally turns to her. "Do I?" she says, and her arms come up to her sides, collecting everything in the house into them. "I mean, you know I love the kids, I wouldn't change that for anything. And Rick, he's so busy with his patients, but he's great. But this life, my life here," she says, shaking her head. "Sometimes it isn't enough, and I just— well, at least for you and me, for our friendship, I just thought you figured I didn't have anything else to offer, you know what I mean? And when you and Nick separated, I thought you had other people, you know, maybe *smarter* friends, who could help you with that. I chickened out, and I backed away, but I was wrong. I'm sorry."

Sandy reaches for a tissue on the end table beside her.

"I shouldn't have ignored you like that," she says, dabbing her eyes, "and when you came over last week, I just wanted to make you happy. You know, gab again about the neighbors because I knew how much you liked to do that before. Because I knew, or I *thought* I knew, that you didn't have any faith in me to discuss the trial, or what you were going through. That you didn't really respect me."

Katie stares at Sandy, hears Dana's words again: *You share only a fraction of what you're feeling. Can't you see how that might make people react?*

"Jesus," Katie says, standing up.

"No, please don't go, I'm not trying to accuse you—"

"I think," Katie says, "I think I'm not sure what to do with myself right now."

Sandy hops up, grabs her by both arms. "Okay, wait. Wait a second."

Somewhere in the back of Katie's mind, things are still working, and she can hear Sandy sprinting up the hallway, a car driving by, and she can see colors, too, the blue jay arcing across the sky outside, the bright green leaves of the ficus tree in the living room that almost touches the ceiling, but nothing is actually getting in all the way.

Sandy comes back, hands Katie a pill with a V-shaped cutout in the center. "Valium," she says, and hands Katie a Baggie with another pill inside it. "It really helped me during a crazy time. I only have two left, but they're yours."

Katie pops it into her mouth, takes the mug from Sandy and washes it down with lukewarm coffee.

"C'mon, come and lie down for a minute."

One clear thought only, suddenly critical. "My car is running. Out in the driveway."

"That's okay," Sandy says, "I'll get it."

Katie allows Sandy to lead her away, past the laughing children and whipping toys, past the master bedroom where Sandy, who used to have it all, sleeps with her husband, Rick the cardiologist.

• • •

Katie stretches in the dark, yawns. Her head is a little clearer now, or maybe "muted" is a better word; it's all in there waiting for her, but for now at least it's churning at a slower rate.

Somewhere in the house, she can hear a man's deep voice, and it instantly evokes Nick, how she felt lying in bed in the morning, listening to him getting ready for work: stepping on that creaky bottom stair on the way to make coffee, the scratchy noise of a knife buttering toast, the splash of the shower turning on—the small sounds of life that reminded her she wasn't alone anymore.

The Baggie is on the nightstand next to her. She gets up on one elbow, pulls out the pill, and swallows it dry. The pill skids down her throat, and she works up some saliva in her mouth, swallows. She swallows two more times, then moves the curtain above the bed to the side: only the black night, waiting.

•

They don't see her at first, standing there in the kitchen doorway and looking in. Rick holds Emily between his legs at the counter, making goofy faces at her, and Sandy kneels down by the table with her younger son and wipes a tear from his cheek.

"Did he hurt your feelings?" she asks the little boy, and he nods, fresh tears falling.

The older son sits in a chair beside them, holding his face up with his hand and kicking his legs, pretending to be bored. Rick sees her first.

"Hey, there she is."

Everyone turns, and Sandy smiles and ruffles her son's hair. "Be right back," she says, and rises. She points her finger at the son sitting at the table, who buries his head in his arms and angrily kicks the table leg.

"Watch it," Rick warns him.

"Did you sleep?" Sandy asks Katie, touching her arm.

"Yeah."

"Good," Sandy says, and turns toward her sons, who take turns poking at each other and then reeling away.

"Boys!" Rick yells, turning from Emily, who starts up a wail.

Sandy turns to Katie. "Valium," she whispers with a secret smile.

•

Sandy has respected Katie's refusal to talk anymore, to hide somewhere in her huge house for some privacy. They stand at the front door, Sandy holding Katie by the arm.

"It's not because I didn't trust you," Katie says. "I do, and I respect you, too."

"I know that now. But I meant what I said," Sandy says, squeezing. "When you're ready, you call here, day or night. Or just stop by."

"I'm sorry about the neighbor thing. I didn't realize—"

"It's over now," Sandy says. "Really."

"I don't know how to thank you."

"You don't have to, you're my friend," Sandy says, and Katie thinks instantly of Jill the other day—how Jill's face had clouded over when Katie changed the subject to Amy, instead of talking about herself or the trial. How Katie had interpreted that look as Jill missing Amy, wishing she were with Amy instead of with *her*.

"Okay, I won't thank you," Katie says.

"Good. And I'm not going to screw things up again, I promise."

"You didn't. It was *me*."

"Then we're both to blame," she says.

"Okay."

"You sure you don't want to stay for dinner?"

"Thank you, no," Katie says. "I think tonight is the perfect night to bury myself in work." As soon as it comes out, she feels guilty, but Sandy just laughs.

"Lucky girl," she says.

"I'll tell Jack you all said hi."

"Give him a big fat kiss for me, will you?"

"Sure."

They move into each other's arms at the same time, and Sandy's voice, close to her ear, is full of mischief. "Screw the neighbors. The next time you come by, we'll talk about the war or some other depressing, worldly subject."

"Right," Katie says, and smiles into her friend's hair.

• • •

The big envelope from Oceanside Realty is full of tiny bite marks, wet at the edges. Katie sits down on the floor beside Jack's food bowl, pushes the dog away, and tears it open. Inside, a brief note paper-clipped to the photo. *Hope this helps, and good luck in your search.* Paul Minsky did not bother to attach a card.

The cottage isn't what Katie expected. It's not a cottage at all, actually, but a two-story white brick house with an expansive lawn, right on the beach. The front of the house is filled with windows topped by red-bricked arches, and two huge dark wooden doors that open up to a circular driveway. On the other side of the house, there's a screened-in porch and, on the lush green lawn, a short picket fence surrounding a white gazebo. Beyond the fence, a long dock and the swelling ocean.

The second Valium has kicked in, which makes the pain of looking at this beautiful home—this beautiful home that Nick wanted to
escape to—a little fuzzy. Her mind drifts to the days after he moved
out. Going to the Warwick Center. Nick not there. Veronica telling her
he took some vacation time. Not brooding inside his new apartment,
missing her, but traveling to North Carolina. All of Veronica's attention on the phone, willing it to ring.

"This," Katie tells Jack, pointing, "is *not* a cottage."

Jack worms closer, sniffs the paper and then Katie's face as she
yawns again.

"I've got work to do," she says, already falling asleep as she stares at
the house, at the ocean and the dishwater-gray whitecaps that rise up
behind it.

2

She tiptoed into Jerry's room to prop the box of chocolates on his dresser, but he was already awake and sitting on the bed, holding the framed photo of them in Mystic.

—Happy Valentine's, Jer. I have a surprise.

He wouldn't look at her. She walked over, handed him the box of chocolates, but he pushed it away.

—You don't want your candy?

Jerry pointed to the photo. —You, Nick, me, he said. His finger poised over his own face.

—What's wrong, buddy?

In the empty bedroom next door, they could hear Nick whistling happily, the pull and zip of a measuring tape. Jerry let the picture fall onto the bed, cradled his body inside his arms.

—Us, he said.

—Yes, Katie said. —We had so much fun that day, remember?

—*Our* house, he said, his eyes skipping to the wall. On the other side, Nick's happy tune whistled on as he measured spaces for a crib, a changing table, and a dresser.

—It will always be your house, she said. —Your home.

Jerry picked up the frame again, his finger pointing to the empty chair in the photo. He tapped it gently. —Him, too.

At first they thought they would wait until she was pregnant to tell Jerry, but Patricia had suggested telling him sooner to give him time to absorb the news. Time to deal with questions and fears that should be addressed before Katie's stomach began to grow.

—It'll get awful busy around here when a baby comes, huh? Katie asked now.

Jerry nodded again, eyes filling with tears.

—We meant what we said, Jerry. We're really going to need your help more than ever.

He looked at her through wet eyelashes. —Sure?

—Very, very sure. This family is going to have to help each other out. We're all going to have to pitch in, and you're not getting out of it.

Jerry's eyes moved back and forth across the photo. —Like a bru-dah, Kay-tee?

—Of course, Jerry. You'll be like a big brother.

—You and Nick love us *both*.

—We'll love both of you, yes.

Katie's hand came up to her stomach, hoping that this would be the month they'd find out she was finally pregnant. Seven months and counting, but she wasn't worried. Not yet.

—Kay-tee? he said quietly, looking away. —You have some for me?

It had become a Saturday-morning routine, ever since they told him about the baby. Katie sneaking off to the bedroom, coming back with the pair of shoes. Bringing Jerry a pair of scissors now, too, or a screwdriver—something sharp to help with the destruction. The guilt rose again, the same as every Saturday morning. How to address this after so much time had passed? And what would she say? But each time she told herself she couldn't lose his trust, and she was assured each time, too, that keeping it to herself was the right thing. Minutes later Jerry would be stretched out on their blue sofa, giggling over cartoons.

—Okay, Jerry. But let's wait until Nick is done and goes downstairs, okay?

He nodded, mouth moving with unspoken words.

• • •

When they'd first started trying the summer before, and the months had passed and she still wasn't pregnant, Katie and Nick thought it had something to do with the spontaneous abortion she'd had years ago. But Katie's ob-gyn told them that many women miscarried their first child—it was more common than most people realized—and then went on to have normal, healthy families. *Go home. Enjoy your time together,* he said with a wink that made Katie blush.

Still, after nine months of trying to conceive and failing, they found themselves back at the doctor's, running over a list of possible reasons. There were more tests than they could've imagined—needles and biopsies and mucus tests—but terms like "inhospitable womb" and "lazy sperm" and "acute endometriosis," were ruled out, one by one.

—Everything seems to be in working order, Katie's doctor said to them in April, flipping her chart shut. —Not time to panic yet. Keep trying, he said, winking.

This time, after he closed the examining-room door behind him, Katie wanted to grab the metal tray beside the bed and hurl it at the door.

Nick squeezed her knee over the crunchy paper gown. —Well, we're good at that at least, he said.

She looked down at his hand on her knee, the tears close.

—Oh, Katie, no, he said, leaning in to her. —Please don't. It'll happen.

She couldn't tell Nick that her tears had nothing to do with having a baby. Not exactly.

Back when they first started trying, it was nearly possible to forget those six months of tension between them, the feelings of her failing Nick with the abandoned documentary. Their marriage, on the verge of collapsing in on itself, had changed in one night, and just last month something happened that Katie still considered a miracle. They were in bed, dreaming of the child that would come, laughing about what he would do and say, when Nick turned his eyes to the ceiling.

—I won't be like him, he said quietly.

After all their silly dreaming (*he will find a cure for hangovers, he will invent a delicious, fat-free chocolate cake*), Katie had misunderstood. —No, but he'll be just like you. What else could we want?

Nick's eyes met hers quickly, and then they were back on the ceiling. —No, like *him*. My father. It won't be that way.

He didn't say anything else, but after all this time the tip of everything that made the world too big for Nick at times had finally broken the surface. Spilling out, after all these years.

Katie *needed* to give him this child, but something wasn't right. The doctors couldn't confirm it, but she knew that the problem lay with her, with her own body. In the shower, while she shopped, even while she was reviewing the footage of her Animal Rescue project, her mind would travel back to that night in the hospital with Nick, soon after their wedding—the doubts that floated up through her Demerol-glazed mind, right after Nick tried to console her with the doctor's words. *He said it wasn't anyone's fault.* Her reaction that night, creeping back to her in the past nine months. God was punishing her for loving Nick so completely.

Every month when she felt the pains in her lower back and the slow cramping that would eventually build up and keep her in bed for half a day, she knew it: My fault. I'm failing him again, and it's my fault.

And maybe this was what really caused the tears. Because even though Katie knew what it meant for Nick, for their marriage, even though her body was betraying her, she finally accepted the truth. It wasn't the baby she wanted at all, it was still Nick—always Nick. Only a few times, in all these months, had she pictured herself holding a tiny infant, or dressing him in little outfits, or watching him sleep in his crib. She wanted this child because she wanted *Nick.* All of him. Only him.

Her tears were for her husband, for what she was going to lose. It wouldn't last forever, this kind solicitousness of Nick's, this revelation that he would finally have a reason to give himself over to her completely. As the months dragged by and she still couldn't conceive, it would end. And then he would turn away from her again, and she would fail him for the last time. Finally and completely.

3

Katie peels herself off the kitchen floor, head still foggy from the Valium, and peers through the window: still dark, but Jack is standing at the slider, sidestepping to go out.

There are only three messages on her machine from last night. The first, from her mother, is casual—she's just calling to check in, to say she is thinking of Katie and misses her (her father yelling out his agreement in the background)—and then there is a pause, and her mother's voice comes back, tremulous in the effort to be controlled. "You know I love you, Kate. You *know* that."

The second one is from Richard, wanting to discuss Katie's flight from the courtroom. "Not cool," he says, then hangs up without saying good-bye.

Ben Cohen is the third message, left at his leisurely pace, as if he is actually speaking directly to Katie: he needs to see her for a moment, would it be possible for her to come by his house tomorrow or the next day, or could he drive to her house if it is more convenient, and when would be good for her?

"I know you're busy, dear, but I do think it's time," Ben says in that slow way of his, which is like metal dragging along asphalt this morning.

There are too many hours ahead of her before she meets Richard in his office to watch the final footage that made it onto the videotape, too many things to think about, so after Jack comes back in, she tramps down to the basement. *Escape,* she thinks, realizing that maybe her mother had a point after all.

•

On the screen Arthur and Sarah sit on their couch, looking as they always did on a new day of filming: a little unsure and self-conscious, Arthur's fingers quickly checking to make sure buttons are buttoned, Sarah picking invisible lint from her shirt.

We left off last time with the new general and your "dates" on Sundays, but I wanted to know if your lives changed in other ways with his arrival? Katie prompts.

In an instant, Sarah's face bunches up, a network of seams. "In some ways," she says, and turns to Arthur, whose body becomes rigid with attention.

"In all other ways, it was the same," he states, both hands on the rims of his thick glasses. "The same work, the long days. We did not know then that our time at the camp was coming to an end, thank God." He turns back to Sarah. "It was almost over, remember?"

"But first," Sarah says nervously, tugging at his arm.

"It is not important," Arthur says, and looks startled when Sarah shifts away from him on the couch to stare at him.

"Oh, yes," she says. "How can you say that, Arthur? An important part." Her voice small but insistent.

Arthur's shoulders sag. Sarah sits forward, at the edge of the couch, her hands flat against her chest. "The general before him, he was an old man. But this new one . . . " Sarah says, and now Katie sees the effort Sarah uses to keep her hands quiet against her chest. Her fingers find her necklace, move over the pearls as over rosary beads. "This new one was very young. His wife was young as well, beautiful, but nothing agreed with her, none of the food we made in the kitchen."

"We eat food they would not give to the guard dogs," Arthur growls, "and this woman complains about steak, and potatoes with too-rich gravy." He directs this at Sarah's back, turns to the camera. "Sarah would throw this woman's food into the trash, she was not allowed to eat the leftovers. I would sneak into the kitchen, whisper before anyone would see us. 'Try, Sarah, be careful. A small bite one night, another the next.' Do you remember that, Sarah? All the food?" But these questions are directed at the camera, not at his wife.

Sarah's eyes drill into the space next to the camera where Katie was sitting.

"The general's wife was beautiful. Long hair, almost white," she says, touching her own gray hair. "He was a young man. Tall and quiet, but strong. And she was sick all the time. She took to her bed, and she stayed there, sometimes for days."

Did he talk to you about her?

Katie remembers asking this question only to fill the awkward silence, the way it felt to have Sarah's eyes on her.

Sarah nods. "He told me one afternoon—I made a pie, apple, he came to compliment me, the first time. And he told me I had a pretty face. Like his wife's around the eyes and nose. He touched my lips, he said his wife was not able—"

"Enough!" Arthur cries, raising a fist in front of him.

For a moment it looks like he will slam it into Sarah's back to quiet her; he fights to control his breathing, his thin chest rising and falling, the spotted skin on his knuckles tightening until the spots stretch and fade. Sarah does not move, and finally Arthur lets his fingers unfurl, his arm drop onto the couch.

"This is not what we want her to know," he says weakly.

When Sarah speaks next, Katie can see that her mind has traveled somewhere else—not in the camp any longer, or in the kitchen with the general, or even in the room with Arthur and Katie; she looks at the ceiling, talks in an odd, high-pitched voice that Katie has never heard before. Like a young girl, speaking to her mother, or confiding in a girlfriend at a sleepover.

"I told Arthur, after it happened, that I pretended it was him. My eyes were closed the whole time"—closing her eyes here, a wistful smile on her face—"and I could see him, I could see my Arthur. We were on a date, and it was Arthur's hands touching my body like that . . ."

• • •

No one says a word while the videotape plays this morning. There are five of them inside Richard's office: Katie, Dana (who had arrived only minutes before they closed the door), Richard, a male intern, and a female assistant DA from across the hall. All silent, their faces taut as they watch the images play on the TV.

Richard was right. Seeing Jerry grinning on their boat, watching him carefully make his bed before the screen skips to one of his explosions, is jarring and utterly effective. A harmless man, a sweet, simple man—*but then*. What was hidden all along beneath the surface.

Only twenty minutes have made it into this final copy, but they're enough.

They've watched it two times before this, but every time Jerry bursts into a violent episode on the TV, their faces still light up with excitement. Only Katie and Dana, whose hand is tucked into hers, appear upset by the swollen fury on Jerry's face.

Richard hits the pause button.

"Okay, Katie," he says, without smiling. "For today we'll just need you to verify you're the one who shot the footage."

It's obviously a signal for the party to break up. The female assistant DA touches Richard's sleeve. "Good luck," she says, and heads to the door.

"Would you check on Dr. Sorenson and tell him we'll need him tomorrow morning?" Richard says to the departing paralegal.

The man nods, and Richard watches him close the door, holds his palm up toward the two chairs in front of his desk.

"Do you mean Andrew Sorenson?" Dana asks, sitting down beside Katie.

"You know him?" Richard asks, pulling out his chair.

"I've met him a few times," Dana says.

"In addition to the history/aggression issue, he's going to tackle Jerry's IQ as well," Richard says. "He'll confirm that Jerry's low IQ of fifty-one doesn't account for overall intelligence, and therefore culpability."

"He's going to argue that Jerry's IQ is actually higher?" Dana asks, turning from Richard to Katie and back.

"Your sister and I have talked extensively about this," he says, looking at Katie briefly. "Even if a person is diagnosed as mentally retarded based on his or her IQ, if they reach a high level of functioning, it proves that the 'label,' if you will, isn't exactly appropriate. If they acquire strong life skills and choice-making abilities, and adapt successfully to their environment, then IQ becomes somewhat beside the point. Plus, we have the added benefit of Jerry's ability to quote from the Bible and understand sophisticated language. All these things should show that he's actually smarter than we think."

"You honestly think Sorenson can prove that?" Dana says. "Talking to Jerry is like talking to a child."

Richard is too caught up to notice Dana's tone or incredulous expression. "Well, if it backfires, we can always use their own argument against them. If Jerry isn't more intelligent than we think, he still acted deliberately, and with the expectation that his actions would result in death. If he's unable to learn from this experience or from his own mistakes, then that makes him even more dangerous, doesn't it?"

"I guess you've got it all covered," Dana says, and this time Richard picks up on her tone.

He turns to Katie. "You ready for today?"

"Yes, but why am I only verifying that I shot the footage now? I'm not testifying?" Her voice high and tight, a stretched violin string ready to snap.

"Change of plans," Richard says. "I want to end the day with these images, let the jurors mull them over tonight. So now we'll have the regional pathologist and the forensic expert today, and then end with you. I'll ask for permission to recall you, which I'll do after Sorenson's had time to deal with the images and the IQ issues tomorrow."

"But what if the defense has questions for her?" Dana asks. "She won't be prepared."

"I've got it timed, so let's just get through today," he says, consulting his watch. "We can always meet later if we have to. If you'll both excuse me. I'll see you down there."

Dana waits until the door shuts behind him.

"You okay?" she asks Katie.

"Fine."

"You look the opposite of fine, honey. Did you sleep last night?"

"I was up early. Working on the Cohens."

"Do you think that's the best—"

"Not now. Please."

"Okay," Dana says. "I'm sorry I just showed up this morning, but I felt awful about the other night. I just wanted to be here with you. I wanted to be here yesterday, too, but I thought you needed a break from me."

"Something's wrong, Dana."

"With what?"

"Richard. I think something happened over the weekend. I don't know what, but he's been so different with me."

"Maybe the pressure is getting to him?" Dana says in an oddly hopeful tone, which makes Katie stare for a moment.

"I don't know. Maybe."

"Let's just get through today, okay? He said we can talk later, so we will if you need to," Dana says, but Katie can hear the worry inside her words.

"I'm glad you're here."

"I'll be here tomorrow, too. If you want me."

"Tomorrow," Katie says heavily.

"Why don't I sleep over tonight? We don't even have to talk. We'll just have dinner or something, maybe practice your testimony a little, and then call it an early night."

Katie finally looks at her sister. "I think I'm starting to get it. What you were talking about the other night."

"That's good, Katie. Really good."

"Yeah? Then why does it feel like I'm standing on a very narrow ledge?"

●

The regional pathologist pushes his square glasses back with slender white fingers that look like they've never been outside the protective walls of a lab and confirms the distance between the gun and Nick's face using one of Richard's diagrams. It's larger than the other placards Richard has utilized in the trial, chilling despite its relative abstractness: a black, almost formless figure pointing a gun at a smaller figure, an arrow drawn between the barrel of the gun and the smaller figure's face. Above the arrow, in red lettering: 3 FEET. The pathologist describes the specifics of the bullet's path, the destruction of Nick's brain, the cause of death—things Katie's heard before, but now it's enough to make her refocus her attention on anything but the diagram, because these abstract figures are taking form, their outlines filling with breathing, moving flesh.

She flips her eyes to Jerry: heavy-faced and morose at the table, Donna's hand on his forearm, moving up and down. Behind them the Warwick Center staff is a solid, quiet mass, their faces reflecting the battering they took the day before.

Katie knows now, in her heart, that Jerry will be convicted. Along with everything else, this pathologist's descriptions of Nick's body, the clinical way he describes his death, is unsettling and potent: Nick has become a scientific specimen, a body on a table with a brain sawed open, poked and prodded, fragments of the bullet that killed him pulled out with long metal tools. The jurors watch with alternating expressions of interest and horror as the pathologist describes Nick, who is simply "the body" now. No longer a man, a speech pathologist, a husband, a son, a coworker, a future father. Just a body, his shattered brain spread out on a sterile metal table for inspection.

At the lunch break, Dana hooks her arm through Katie's and pulls her out of the courtroom, and Katie follows, knowing that someone else is leading Jerry away in the opposite direction, and that he is looking around the room, searching blindly for Katie. Wondering when she will finally come and tell him that everything will be okay.

• • •

Later in the day, there is a short recess after Judge Hwang excuses the forensic expert. Katie checks the clock behind the bench—4:07—amazed at Richard's perfect timing. After the break there will be just enough time to introduce Katie and watch the footage before court adjourns for the day. Tonight, Katie thinks, the jurors will fall asleep with pictures of Jerry's spiraling fury lodged inside their heads, pondering the implications, making subconscious decisions about a man they've never met.

Katie squeezes Dana's hand, leans over to whisper in her ear. "Do you remember when you said that I always know what people will do?" Katie asks her. "If I spend time with them, how I can figure them out?"

"Yes, in the conference room that day. After Richard touched Carly."

"Why did you say that?"

"Because it's true. Most of the time."

"I've lost it, you know."

"What?"

"I'm watching, and I'm paying attention, but I'm getting it all wrong."

"Good," Dana says. "It's a start."

"All rise."

•

Every eye on her now, sitting on the witness stand, the center of the spot-light. She's halfway through the prayer in her head before she realizes what she's doing—asking God to see her, to guide her through this. She folds her hands around the videotape in her lap to stop the shaking.

If she keeps her eyes on Richard, does that staring trick that makes everything around him go out of focus, the rest of the room will stay shapeless. It helps a little, and so do the sympathetic faces and smiles on the jurors' faces after she turns to them and tells them her name.

"You are Nick Burrelli's wife?" Richard asks her.

And just like that, the small comforts are gone—Katie stumbles, the word "are" catching her off guard. *Is* she still Nick's wife? Even if he's dead?

"Katie?" Richard asks.

"Yes, Nick was—*is* my husband."

The brief glint of victory in Richard's eyes explains the wording of the question, how he has achieved exactly what he wanted: her hesita-tion, an opportunity to show his concern.

"We're sorry for your loss, Katie," he says. "Do you need a minute?"

"No," Katie says. "I'm okay." She hates how theatrically brave she sounds.

"Good. Now, you and Nick were very close with the defendant, weren't you?"

"At one time, yes."

"'At one time,'" Richard muses. He walks over to the jurors, who track his progress along with Katie. "Katie, would you please tell the courtroom what you do for a living?"

"I'm a documentary filmmaker."

"And at one point you intended to make a documentary about the defendant?"

Katie looks over at Jerry. He is gaping in her general direction as though he can sense she is in the room, facing him.

"Yes."

"And the videotape you're holding contains footage for that documentary?"

"Yes," Katie says, holding it up for the jurors to see.

It takes a few minutes to cue up the video, and then there is an issue with one of the TVs. When they finally straighten it out, Katie only listens, keeping her eyes just above the top of the TV. She listens to Jerry's laughter, to his innocent question ("We go to a movie tonight?") and to other sounds she heard just this morning, but suddenly she can't recall the order of the footage anymore. Is that Jerry drawing? Making his bed? Jerry stretched out on the floor watching TV, a mesmerized look on his face? And then she hears the children, the sound of baby goats bleating, and, within seconds, Jerry's grunting cry, a struggle, and then Nick's voice telling Jerry to calm down, he's okay, his voice mixing with Jerry's groaning wails and the staticky sound of arms and legs colliding. She hears the shocked intakes of breath in the courtroom, and then more indecipherable noises from the TV—legs stamping (Jerry running through Goddard Park with his kite?), a soft giggle, and then people on the video singing "Happy Birthday," her father's loud voice ringing above the rest. And then the table in her apartment crashing over, glass breaking.

A few minutes later, she hears Jerry out on the boat—"Kay-tee, is God come *now?*"—and she finally looks at the slanted picture of Jerry holding on to her, her holding him back. She sees it on the TV, filling the screen, and then inside her head, her brain automatically plugging in the missing elements. The beautiful sunset over the ocean, the approaching storm. *Here, Jerry, I'm right here.* She sees Patricia in her basement, too, thanking Katie for taking care of Jerry, and then she sees Nick's face, his brooding frustration with Katie because she did not want to offer up Jerry's pain to the world. Knowing that sharing it with strangers would be a betrayal.

Her eyes move from the TV to the jurors, and then to the ceiling. She silently asks the question that used to fill her nights before she met Nick on Patience Island—that summer long ago, when she sat on the dark beach away from the glow of the fire, believing that she was too small for God to see her. *Are You there?*

•

Katie is rising from the witness stand when Donna tells Judge Hwang that she has a few technical questions of her own about filmmaking.

Katie freezes in a half stand, waiting for Richard's heated objection, but he simply turns a composed face to Judge Hwang and half-heartedly argues about timing and finishing for the day. Judge Hwang refuses his mild objections, and then Richard is strolling back to the prosecution table without a glance toward Katie. She sits back down.

Donna consults the legal pad in her hand, looks up. "Good afternoon, Mrs. Burrelli," Donna says.

"Good afternoon."

"Just a couple of questions before we leave for the day."

Katie skips her eyes from Richard to the clock: 4:50. Only ten minutes, but enough time for her to admit it. She decides right then and there: if Donna asks why she held Jerry on the boat, Katie will be honest, she will just say it. *I loved him. He was scared, and he needed me. He was like a son.*

"Now, you said earlier that you're a documentary filmmaker?" Donna says. "That's how you earn a living?"

"Yes," Katie says, the panic rushing up into her chest.

"Could you tell us how long you've worked at this profession?"

"About eight years or so."

"And could you tell us about some of your projects?"

Richard doesn't rise from his chair. "Objection. Relevance?"

"Goes to credibility, Your Honor."

"Overruled."

"Mrs. Burrelli?" Donna prompts.

"I've worked on several. The housing crisis in Providence, Save the Bay—"

"And how much money does a documentary filmmaker earn?"

"Objection," Richard says much too coolly. "How does salary speak to credibility?"

Judge Hwang eyes Katie with curiosity. "I'll allow it."

"Thank you, Judge," Donna says. "Mrs. Burrelli? How much has eight years of documentary filmmaking earned you? Roughly."

"It's very difficult to make a lot of money at first."

"Well, how many projects have you worked on in the past eight years?"

"Five."

"Does that include the one you're working on now? About Holocaust survivors?"

"Yes," Katie says, locking eyes with Patricia in the front row.

"Okay, well, of the four documentaries that you've already completed, how many of those will you or have you sold to earn your living?"

Katie looks at Dana, who is sitting up in the front row, tense, her hands on the banister. Her sister's eyes flash at Richard's back as he idly jots notes.

"Let me word this another way," Donna says, taking advantage of Katie's silence. "Of the all the documentaries that you've worked on in the past eight years, not including the one you're working on now, how many of them have you actually *completed*?"

Impossible to do the trick of staring now, nowhere safe to look.

"Mrs. Burrelli?"

"I haven't."

"Oh," Donna says with artificial shock. "You've worked for eight years on five different projects, and you haven't completed even *one* of them?"

"No."

"In fact, you never even finished your degree in filmmaking, did you? You met Nicholas Burrelli the summer before your last semester and then dropped out of college halfway through the fall, didn't you?"

"I was pregnant, I miscarried and it affected me—"

"I'm sure it was a difficult time," Donna says, "and you certainly have the court's sympathy. But what about afterward?"

"Afterward?"

"Mrs. Burrelli, don't most documentary filmmakers today use computers to make their films? Don't they normally transfer footage directly from a camera onto a computer, and use sophisticated editing and sound programs to produce the final product?"

"I suppose so."

"But you still use storyboards, an obsolete editing machine and sound box, don't you? Isn't that incredibly old-fashioned and outdated?"

"That's what I was taught—"

"Is that before or after you dropped out of college?"

Katie waits for Richard's objection, but he only scribbles onto the pad in front of him.

"Mrs. Burrelli, you use antiquated methods to work on your unfinished documentary films because you don't even know *how* to produce a film using computers and sophisticated filmmaking programs, do you?"

"No."

"Would you tell the jurors, Mrs. Burrelli, how much time you spent at the Warwick Center when your husband was alive? When you could have been working on your documentaries, or learning new and more efficient filmmaking techniques, or possibly even finishing your degree?"

"I don't know—"

"In fact, you spent an inordinate amount of time there, didn't you? Sometimes three or four times a week?"

"Sometimes, yes."

"One last question, then," Donna says. "Mrs. Burrelli, is it fair to say that you were obsessed with your husband and that it interfered with every aspect of your life? And that your judgment has been clouded concerning Jerry LaPlante because you can't see around the extenuating circumstances involved in this case, and you need to blame someone, *anyone,* for your losing your husband—"

Richard rises halfway out of his chair. "Objection."

"—when in fact your husband left you just a month before this unfortunate accident due to your fanatical behavior—"

"She's badgering this witness, Your Honor," comes Richard's calm objection.

"Sustained," Judge Hwang replies, then peers over the rim of her glasses at Richard.

• • •

They're sprawled out on the sofa in Katie's living room, head to toe, Jack wedged in by their knees and gnawing a massive bone Katie bought for him at Stop & Shop.

"Therapy lying down," Dana says, "I can see the benefit." She pokes her head up to check on Katie, who smiles weakly at her. "How're you doing over there?"

"A little better," Katie says. "God, I looked liked an idiot up there."

"You were blindsided, honey."

Katie sits up to get a better look at Dana. "But it's all true. I *am* a failure. Nick saw it, Mom saw it—"

"You are not a failure."

"Then why would Mom ask if I was going to finish the Cohens' documentary last week? She *knew*. Even Nick's mother would call, after she gave us more money for film and bulbs, and she'd ask if I had enough supplies to 'see this one through.' Even Candice knew, and laughed at me behind my back. Like today."

"No one was laughing today. She bullied you up there."

"It was Patricia. She told Donna those things about me," she says. "That's what they all thought of me, all those years."

"They didn't. They were your friends."

Katie considers this, sees Dottie smiling at her from the stand. "He made them all look so incompetent yesterday. With my help."

"That's why you left?"

Katie examines her hands for a moment. "I had to. It felt like . . . like for once *I* was on the wrong side. And then today it was like I wasn't on *any* side. You saw Richard's reaction, Dana. He *knew* what Donna was planning. He knew what was going to happen today. He timed it that way, I'm sure of it. And after we adjourned, you saw him rush out before I could even ask why."

"I know."

"Why would he do that?"

"I don't know. I still can't think of any logical reason."

"Maybe Donna told him about me this weekend, and that's why he's been acting so differently toward me. But I don't understand. Why would she? And why wouldn't he warn me?"

Dana sits up now, too, crosses her legs underneath her. "She didn't tell him about you not finishing your documentaries, Katie," she says quietly. "Or about visiting the center so much. I don't know if she unintentionally let something out this weekend, or if Richard overheard a piece of the defense's strategy, but you're right, something happened. And I think that's why Richard changed his plan with you today. He wanted her to discredit you, to distance himself from you. But she wasn't the one who told him those things."

"Then who? I don't understand any of this."

"I told him," Dana says softly, lowering her eyes. "Before the trial even began. When he interviewed me."

"*You?* Why would you do that?"

"Katie," she says, her eyes pleading for understanding now, "I was trying to protect you. I wanted him to understand you. What you've been through."

Katie stands too fast, her head swimming. She stumbles, paces to the end of the couch, watches Dana shrink into her body.

"I was right on Sunday, wasn't I? The *movies.* You told him about that, too, didn't you? And he tripped up that day?"

"Yes. I wanted him . . . I needed for him to know you, so—"

"What else, Dana?" Katie demands. "What else?"

"Only that you loved Nick—that he was your world. I wanted him to know that you were fragile."

"I can't believe this, Dana. You're my *sister.*"

"We wanted to protect you. Me. Mom and Dad. I told him about the documentaries and about the visits because I thought he would find a way to deal with it in court when it came up. He knew that Donna knew about it, too, because of course Patricia would have told her."

"My own family. *Jesus.*"

"Please, Katie. *Please,*" she says, trying to hold back tears. "I thought it would help. I knew you wouldn't tell him important things and I was afraid he'd find out too late."

"So you told him without warning me, and you told him that I'm obsessed with watching people, right? That I'm this pathetic—"

"No, no, those are Donna's words, not mine."

"But you believe it."

Dana bows her head. "Can't you see why I wanted you to be careful with Richard? Why I was angry with him? He's been playing you, Katie."

"But—but we were working together." Katie slumps down beside Dana, the fight inside her suddenly gone. "He said we were a team."

"He wanted to keep you close, honey. He wanted your help to do his job. Until it didn't work anymore."

Katie sinks back on the couch. "This entire time."

They sit quietly for a long moment, Katie replaying Richard's questions, the respectful way he treated her. How important she felt back then—how *necessary.* Again, she thinks. *Again.*

Katie finally turns to her sister. "What do I do now?" she whispers. "What do I do *tomorrow?*"

Dana tries to take her hand, but Katie crosses her arms.

"Kate," she says, wiping her eyes and sitting up straight. "We have to think. What could he know? What would make him turn on you like that?"

What *did* he know? What could possibly make Katie seem so incompetent, so unreliable, that even Richard had to distance himself so blatantly . . .

"Oh, God." Katie buries her face in her hands. Did he know? Did Richard find out about the *shoes?* But how could he . . .

"What?"

"Nothing—nothing, Dana," she says.

Dana pulls Katie's hand into hers. Katie tries to pull away, but her sister hangs on. "Okay, so we don't know what Richard knows, we don't know anything. But tomorrow—we have to figure out how you'll deal with his questions tomorrow. Because whatever made him turn on you will probably come out then."

"But I have to stick to the script. If I stray from the back-and-forth he planned, he'll tear me apart."

"Katie," Dana says sadly, "I don't think there's a script anymore."

"*God.*" She turns to Jack, whining softly at the end of the couch.

"But it's not too late," Dana says.

Katie turns back, meets Dana's appraising stare.

"What if," Dana says, choosing her words carefully, "what if we knew? I know you're always asking yourself why Jerry did it, but we still don't know. Maybe Richard understands more than we do at this point, and I suppose their experts will try to explain. But what if you did? Right now?"

"Richard said the *why* isn't important anymore."

"Isn't it? Isn't it the one question you've wanted answered all along?" The answer to all of Dana's questions is clear: If Katie knew, it might change everything tomorrow.

"I can't go back, Dana. I can't forgive him."

"I'm not asking you to."

"All of this—all of it's for Nick."

"But is this what he'd want? Jerry in prison?"

Jack picks up the huge bone in his mouth, walks across the couch, and with a wagging tail offers it to Katie.

"I don't know. I thought I did, but now?" Katie says, pushing the bone away. "Now I don't know what Nick would want. Sometimes I feel like I never even knew him. I tried, but—" Donna's words coming back now: *obsessed, fanatical.* "You were right, Dana. I didn't want to get it, but I do now."

"What, honey?"

"Looking at everyone else to figure out my own life," she says, shaking her head. "And when I met Nick, he was so quiet, so unwilling to share himself with me—I went into overdrive, I guess. I thought if I kept my eyes open, I would understand him. I would understand myself."

"And now?"

Katie draws her knees up to her chest, testing the words that are so new. "Now . . . now I can't stop thinking about how I've always kept the biggest parts of what I was thinking, what I was feeling, to myself. Except with Nick," Katie says, and looks at her sister. "Even with you, Dana, even *you* I didn't tell everything. Big things."

"I know."

"And it wasn't just to understand myself, looking all the time, keeping to myself—it was wanting people to . . . I don't know, maybe trust me? *Like* me? Because—because I listen. I'm easy to be around, because I listen and I don't make many demands, right? Maybe I'm not as much fun as you, not as friendly or pretty, but I think . . . I'm beginning to think," she says, "if I didn't ask too much, I wouldn't give anyone a reason to walk away. Because no one ever seemed to like me as much as you, I wasn't like *you.*"

"You never had to be like me. You only needed to be yourself. That's all you need now."

"But I don't even know who I *am* anymore. I don't know what my life's supposed to be."

Dana puts her arm around Katie. "Who you are, and what you do, is up to you, Katie," she says gently. "People will love you for the person inside, the person I see and love right now. That's what we were trying to say. You can have any life you choose, but you have to choose it for yourself."

"For such a long time, Nick *was* my life."

"I know that," Dana says.

"I was so afraid of losing him, I couldn't see anything else."

"I know that, too."

Jack wiggles his nose in between them, whines softly. They make space for him, and he lies down, his front paws in Katie's lap.

Katie pats him absently, turns to her sister. "I don't know what to do."

"You'll know," Dana says. "By the time you get up tomorrow, you'll know."

"How can you be so sure?"

"Because you'll have to," her sister says. "It's up to you now. Despite what Richard throws at you tomorrow, the way you answer and the choices you'll make up there will be up to you. Only you."

• • •

Hours after Katie has left Dana on the couch with Jack, she's still staring at the ceiling in her darkened bedroom. Thinking of choices, trying to make sense of what happened today, what will happen tomorrow. And then: what happened before there was a trial and secrets and lawyers talking behind closed doors.

Always this, no matter what the day brings—every moment always leading right back to Nick. When he was still hers, before it all started to fall apart with him. That moment in time when her own decisions and actions determined her future, her present: lying in bed alone, splicing together her story with Nick, wishing she could hit the rewind button and edit out the moments that led to the final scene with Nick in their home.

I want you to leave, she'd told him that night. After everything, after some of the answers she had waited for were finally revealed, that's what she said. *Just go.*

4

—Who dat? Jerry asked her, and Katie turned around in the booth at Dunkin' Donuts, saw the woman standing beside Nick at the counter. She was digging into her purse, shaking her head and laughing ruefully.

The woman wasn't beautiful, at least not in the traditional sense. She was one of those women who had odd, crooked features—high forehead, with a beaky nose and eyes too far apart—but the way it all came together was startling.

—*Pretty,* Jerry said.

She thought absently of the first time Jerry used that word—*Pity*—and while she should have praised his careful pronunciation, instead Katie watched Nick whisper something to the woman; she looked up and nodded cautiously, put her purse on the counter.

—One more, Nick called out to the girl making his coffee, and the woman tilted her head at him, a little coyly now.

—Nick knows her? Jerry asked, his blue eyes wide, his mouth rimmed with powdered sugar. A glob of raspberry jelly trailed down his shirt.

—He's just being friendly, Katie told him. She handed Jerry a napkin before turning back.

The woman accepted the coffee, and Katie waited for Nick to return to the booth to explain. Instead, he stepped in front of the woman, pushed open the door for her.

—Thanks so much, she said to Nick in a loud, cheerful voice, ducking under his arm.

Nick watched her leave, his arm still holding the door open. He turned toward Katie and Jerry, who stared back at him. He shrugged at them, walked over.

—She forgot her wallet, he said, and scooted in beside Jerry, who moved closer to the wall, eyes on Katie.

In the car on the way to her parents' house, Nick filled the silence with questions about her new documentary, about the elderly couple she'd met a few months ago at Chili's, where she and Dana had a quick lunch between Dana's sessions. Something about the way the man and woman had treated each other during the meal—simple gestures, the woman offering a french fry to her husband with a sweet smile, the man pushing his wife's dish closer to her—had captured Katie's attention as she ate her sandwich and pretended to listen to Dana. After her sister had pulled out of the parking lot, Katie found herself walking back into the restaurant, standing in front of their table. Suddenly too embarrassed to talk. They looked up at her, faces open and curious, and after Katie managed to say something—*I noticed how happy you looked*—they invited her to join them. *Sit, sit,* the man had said, and raised his hand to the seat beside his wife. *There is always room for one more.*

—Holocaust survivors, Nick said. —That's a tough one.

Katie didn't reply. She was watching Jerry in the visor mirror now, sitting in the backseat and staring at the back of Nick's head. Lips mumbling.

—You know her? Jerry blurted out, and Nick adjusted the rearview mirror to look at Jerry.

—You okay, buddy? he asked.

—You buy her coffee. An accusation.

—I told you, Jer, she forgot her wallet. I was being nice.

Nick turned to Katie for help, saw her watching him, too.

—*Shit,* he muttered, and turned the mirror back.

● ● ●

No one mentioned Katie's failure to get pregnant anymore. Only Jerry, who watched Nick tirelessly, who started asking his questions again. *Nick okay?* Jerry would say, as if he were responsible for taking care of Nick instead of the other way around. *He mad about no baby?* And

other questions, ones that recurred too often now. *Nick knows dat lady?*
Why is he talk to her?

At The Inn, where they went for dinner with Katie's parents one
Friday night, Jerry put his fork down every time the young waitress
approached the table and bantered with Nick. And the weekend after,
when they went for doughboys at Iggy's in Oakland Beach, Jerry was by
Katie's side, pointing to Nick by the jungle gym on the beach, chatting
with a young mother who bounced her son on one hip. *Nick knows her?*

Katie, who couldn't keep her eyes off Nick either, who found herself compulsively tracking his movements, too, started asking questions back.

—Why? Did he say something to you?

· · ·

It was almost a year and a half since the doctor had told them everything was okay physically—over two years since they'd begun trying.
And while Nick still told her he hadn't given up the idea of starting
a family, there was a palpable presence in their bedroom at night, especially when they moved into each other's arms. She was used to the
quiet ways he moved around her in the dark, how he reached for her
without words, but now it felt loaded down with something bigger.
Disappointment? Blame? Or was Jerry onto something? Was there
another woman in Nick's life, or the possibility of another woman?

Sometimes she felt this presence outside their bedroom, too, when
Nick caught her staring—in the seconds it took for him to turn away
from her, that look on his face she couldn't interpret.

· · ·

—He come back, Jerry said one weekend, after they had dropped Nick
off at T. F. Green Airport for a conference. —He come back in time
for turkey.

—That's right. He'll be back next weekend, and then we'll all have
a big Thanksgiving dinner at my parents'.

They had watched his plane take off, Jerry waving with both
hands.

—He go by himself, Jerry said. —He alone.

—Of course.

Katie steered the car onto Post Road, pictured Nick miles above them, jetting through the clouds.

Maybe the break would be good for them, she thought. Maybe it's all they needed.

But then she pictured Nick, sitting in his seat by the window, watching the earth disappear below him. Wondering what he was thinking about, how he felt as the miles opened up between them. And then, before Katie could stop herself: She saw the woman dozing lightly in the seat beside him. And then Nick, pulling up the armrest between them, gently shaking the woman's shoulder. His smiling offer. She saw the woman's sleepy surprise, her answering smile. She saw this woman lean across the space separating them to rest her head against Nick's chest.

· · ·

She was standing at the counter, chopping broccoli for a stir-fry, respecting Nick's moody silence. He sat at the kitchen table, drinking a Heineken, one arm draped over the back of his chair, legs stretched out long. She knew that Nick was frustrated with a new client at work, a boy named Joey who could barely communicate. For weeks now it was the same thing when he returned from work: eyeing her briefly before going upstairs to change clothes, sitting around listlessly, snapping at her. She hadn't learned very much about Joey from Nick, didn't prod him into talking about it either; instead, she roamed around the Warwick Center, waiting for the employees to fill her in.

Jerry helped him today, this new kid, Joey, Billy said last week. *Knew Joey just needed to take a leak—oops, 'scuse me, lady. I mean, use the bathroom. But Nick is having trouble with him. All the grunting and whatnot,* Billy said, stroking his beard.

Katie turned away from the cutting board, watched Nick, who kept his eyes fixed on the green bottle as he took another swig.

—Stop it, Nick said.

—What?

—Just stop, he said, voice fat with disdain.

The look on his face frightened Katie.

—You're not hungry?

—Forget it, he said, pushing away from the table. His eyes sliding up and down her body.

She watched him stalk off toward the living room, shoulders squared.

—*Stop,* he said, not bothering to turn back.

. . .

—What are you doing out here? Katie said.

Nick was sitting on the floor of the shed, a wrench in one hand, parts of their lawn mower scattered around him like puzzle pieces. It was mild for February, though not so mild that his T-shirt could be enough to keep him warm. Nick splayed his empty hand at the parts: isn't it obvious?

—I thought you might be cold, she said, handing him his favorite sweatshirt.

—Thanks.

He dropped the sweatshirt by his side, picked up a small motor, turned it in his hand. There were grease marks on his fingers, a streak on his neck. Lately anything in their home that could be taken apart and examined ended up like this: in pieces, with Nick turning them around in his hand, a baffled look on his face.

—We're going to my parents', she said. —We were thinking of watching a movie after dinner. Trying to make it sound fun, inviting.

—Have a good time.

—Want to come along?

—Nope.

Dismissed, again. Ever since he had to call his mother, because Katie needed more film and bulbs for her flatbed—but it was before that, wasn't it?

I want this documentary to be perfect, she had said. *This is the one, I know it.*

You've said that before.

But if you could meet Sarah and Arthur, see how much they love each other, in spite of what they've been through, the way they treat each other—

Fine, he said, stopping her rush of words. The look on his face this time easy to interpret. Scorn.

Nick put the motor on the floor, wiped his hands on the sweatshirt.

These recent projects, Dana had told her, were simply Nick's way of trying to fix things, probably the result of his inability to "fix" Joey, who could barely form basic words to communicate. The Warwick Center staff confirmed Dana's suspicions.

Nick doesn't seem fazed, but things aren't going so great, Veronica said last week. *Still.* And Jan Evers, who believed that anything could be fixed with love and harmony and a good long talk, had to agree. *Nothing Nick tries is working. Though you couldn't tell by looking at him.*

If they saw him now, eyeing the spare parts of their lawn mower, they might change their minds.

And if they saw the way he looked at other women all the time now, Katie thought, the whole picture might come into sharper focus. How his failure with Joey, and her failure to give him a child, has led to this—sitting in the shed in a T-shirt, too proud to admit that he was cold.

—Anything else? Nick said irritably, waiting for Katie to leave. She hadn't realized she was staring.

She followed the streak of oil on his neck to the dark spot on the collar of his shirt. —No.

• • •

At dinner they listened to Katie's father speculating about the new neighbor next door, a strange, quiet woman who barely came out of her house. How he was positive he saw her on *America's Most Wanted* the week before.

—Robbed a bank in full daylight, he told them. He crooked an eyebrow at Katie and Dana. —Still at large.

Her mother wagged her head at him. —Jimmy, that girl had long blond hair and was at least two hundred pounds.

—Haircut and a dye job, he said, ignoring his wife and looking suggestively at Michael and Jerry now. —And a fat suit. You can buy those at costume shops, you know.

Jerry had giggled, turned to Katie.

—Don't listen to him, Jer, Katie had said, and Jerry giggled again, twirled one finger in a circle at his head.

After dinner Katie scooped up the damp patches of crumbs at the corners of the table: wiped by Jerry, who had left long wet streaks over the entire expanse. Katie pulled them into her palm, ignoring her mother's impatient sighs on the phone. She was calling Nick, who was missing Sunday dinner for the fourth week in a row.

—At least he can stop by for coffee and dessert, her mother said, cupping the mouthpiece.

—I don't think he's there, Mom.

It was the second time her mother had tried to get in touch with him, and somewhere between the cleaning of the table and the talk of coffee and dessert, Dana had escaped to the back porch to smoke, Michael tagging along with her.

—Nick? It's Mom. Are you there? Hello. *Hello?* She glared at Katie like it was her fault. —What in the *world* is more important than manicotti and my homemade tiramisu?

Either Nick was ignoring her mother's call, Katie thought, or he wasn't home. Again.

—He's been spending some of his free time doing research on cerebral palsy, Katie said, wishing she believed her own explanation. —He's having some trouble with a client.

—He works too hard, her mother said, raising her eyebrows meaningfully at Katie.

The implication was clear. Katie didn't work hard enough, never had. She spent too much money on her "films" and then abandoned them halfway through, the same way she abandoned her degree, which was useless in the first place.

In the kitchen her father and Jerry prepared the dessert and coffee. Katie turned away to listen to Jerry's giggling; her father probably had his notebook out, tallying up Jerry's bill for the day. A few minutes later, the back door opened, and Dana walked into the dining room, smelling like smoke and fruit spray. Their mother eyed them both, apparently dissatisfied with their company, and picked up the phone again.

—You smell like a watermelon ashtray, Dana, she said.

Dana rolled her eyes at Katie. —She's calling Nick *again?*

—I can hear you, I'm not in another room.

With a small nod of her head, Dana signaled Katie to follow her. They walked through the kitchen to the back door, found Michael, Jerry, and Katie's father sitting on stools at the island, the small notebook in between them.

—Coffee's almost done, girls! her father called to them.

—Kay-tee, Jerry said, grinning and pointing to her father. —He say I own him two million dollars!

Katie's father winked at her. —Oh, wait a sec here! he said, his finger running down the page. —I forgot to add a cup of coffee. That's two million dollars and sixty-five cents. Hand me that pen, will you, Michael?

Out on the back porch, Dana lit another cigarette. —Where do you think he is?

—I don't know. Katie left the back door open a few inches so she could listen to the happy sounds of her father's teasing, to Jerry and Michael's silly laughter. —Wherever he goes these days.

—Be patient, Katie. He'll feel better when he makes some headway with Joey.

—I think it's more than that this time, Katie said. —It's like I'm not even there anymore. He walks around the house ignoring me most of the time, and on the weekends he's barely talking to Jerry either. And I know Jerry doesn't understand what's going on, and his feelings are hurt.

—Maybe Nick only has room for one challenge at a time.

—It isn't just work, Dana, Katie said. And then, more quietly: —We haven't had sex in over two months.

—All couples go through dry periods, honey. Especially when there's stress.

—*We* don't. Or at least we hardly do, Katie said. —How are we going to have a baby if we aren't even trying?

Dana blew out a long stream of smoke. —Did he ever take a look at those pamphlets I dropped off?

—He doesn't want to adopt.

—What about the one on in vitro? I know it's expensive, but it's an option.

Katie watched a squirrel furtively digging for nuts in the backyard. It bounced to another spot, bushy tail swishing, and started digging again.

—Dana, I see him looking at other women all the time, and I don't know what he's thinking. Maybe he wants to have an affair, or maybe he's thinking that if I can't give him a baby, someone else can.

—Nick wouldn't have an affair. That's crazy—

—You don't know that. He could, Katie says. —Sometimes I can actually see him with another woman, and it's like I can't even breathe, Dana. I couldn't handle it if he decided to be with someone else, if he wanted to start a family with another woman.

—Kate, even if that happened, even if there's the off chance he *is* seeing someone else, then you would still live your life—

—No, Katie said. —No, I wouldn't. I wouldn't want to.

Dana sighed, started to lift the cigarette to her mouth, stopped; her face filled with panic. Katie turned, saw Jerry standing at the door, peeking out. His eyes wide with terror.

—Your dad say to tell you coffee is done, he said, covering his face with his hands.

· · ·

She told Nick that she was going to Sarah and Arthur's to film the last interview, and since he never asked questions anymore, he had no idea that she had wrapped up with them in the fall. The strain of the filming schedule had started to show with Sarah—she lost her concentration easily, her focus wavering and wandering back to Katie and Nick's marriage, her questions endless and prying—and Arthur had suggested that they double up on their sessions to keep her on track. Katie hadn't understood how interviewing them two times a week instead of one would help, had her own suspicions about why they were speeding up the process. Arthur had a long bout of coughing one day, and she was afraid that he was sick, that time was running out for him. Sarah's concerned look when he passed a handkerchief across his lips only added to Katie's fears for her friend.

She was parked on Warwick Neck Avenue, a block up from her own street, waiting. *This isn't stalking,* she told herself, *not when it's my own husband.* There were still a few hours until Nick picked up Jerry for the weekend, and Katie's gut feeling was that he would leave the house soon after her, on his way to wherever it was he went these days. She thought of finally catching them, what she would say after she had pulled the nose of her car right up to his, snapping on the high beams blinding them temporarily. And then Nick's face—the quick succession of anger, guilt, and apology playing across his features. And the woman he spent all his time with now, too. Her hands coming up to shield her face. *Gotcha!*

Fifteen minutes later Nick's car turned out of their street and onto Warwick Neck. The darkness settled quickly, the traffic heavy on a Friday night. She kept a two-car distance behind Nick, followed him onto Rocky Point Avenue, and then left onto Palmer. Past the Seven Seas Chowder House on the right, where Nick and Katie had their first official date, Nick devouring a bucketful of steamers by himself, dipping each one in the plastic cup of butter, because Katie was too nervous to eat.

When he turned right onto Samuel Gorton Avenue, toward the Longmeadow Fishing Area, Katie pulled to the side of the road: there was only one way in, and Nick would see her if she followed him.

For the next hour, she tracked his progress around Warwick—next to Conimicut Point then to Gaspee Point, passing Jenny's Ice Cream along the way, Jerry's favorite place to get pineapple sundaes—following Nick's trek to see the ocean from every available access road that led to it. She almost lost him on the way back on Warwick Avenue—an accident near Korb's Bakery had clogged traffic—but she caught up with him again when he took a right onto Sandy Lane, and then another right onto Strawberry Field Road. She thought he might be headed to the airport—Strawberry Field Road dead-ended into Industrial Drive, the access road on the other side of T. F. Green—and wondered if this was it: Nick finally escaping forever, taking flight from his life with Katie. But then he made a sudden left onto Burbank Drive, a quiet, tree-lined neighborhood, and pulled in to the driveway of a blue house.

Katie raced to the curb, threw her car in park. Popped open the door and started to jump out until she realized it wasn't Nick's car in the driveway at all. She had followed the wrong person, had lost Nick somewhere in the dark.

5

After an hour of watching her life behind closed lids, Katie rises, walks to the bedroom doorway. Looks down the hall toward Jerry's room. After all the months of internal remonstrations—*it is the spare bedroom now, the* spare *bedroom*—it is still this: Jerry's room. She trudges to his door, her legs heavy. Takes in a deep breath, opens the door.

The last thing Katie expects is the pungent, clean smell of lemons. She was prepared for the heaviness of stale air, thick and peppery with dust, maybe even a sour odor, because sometimes Jerry would leave glasses of half-drunk milk or juice on the floor. She could have missed it that day in May when she tore the room down, ripping his pictures from the walls, tearing the sheets off his bed—trying to remove every trace of his having lived in it before she shut the door behind her for the last time. But there isn't the clinging mustiness she expected, no curdled milk, just lemons and fresh air, evoking memories of childhood springtimes and her mother's frenzied cleaning and screen washing as soon as the first buds flowered on the trees.

She clicks the light on, sees that her mother has organized this room, too: the pile of Jerry's drawings that Katie had let drop to the floor stacked neatly on the mahogany dresser now, the dark wood polished and shining. The bed that Katie had stripped and shoved against a wall lined up perfectly now underneath the window—the moonlight pushing through the lace curtains and falling across the mattress in patches. Against the opposite wall, Jerry's books and pads and boxes of pens and colored pencils in a row, instead of scattered on the rug beside it—moved back onto the bookshelf, so her mother could vacuum the rug, which still had tracks in it. The big Bugs Bunny pillow Dana bought Jerry last Christmas sits flat on the center of the bed; if Katie flips it over, she'll see the burned Coyote, the Acme dynamite box, the Road Runner's beaky smile that made Jerry gasp in delight when he discovered this favorite character's "friends" on the other side.

Of course her mother would clean this room, too. Katie wonders absently now how her mother reacted to Jerry's possessions as she organized them, placed them in neat piles. If she understood the significance of this room, the backdrop to Nick's accusations, his packing, leaving. But no, of course Katie had never told her mother the details of that last fight.

She turns off the light, lies on the bed. Cradles Jerry's pillow in her arms and breathes in the lemon-filled air as her eyes adjust to the darkness. A weight creeps into her body, slowly crushing.

How many times did Jerry do this, after Katie and Nick had said good night? How many times did he lie in the glow of moonlight across his bed, afraid that this would be the night when God would come, full of blinding vengeance? Reliving the torture of his childhood as he huddled under the blankets, as Katie and Nick wrapped themselves around each other down the hall, greedy for the taste of each other's skin? Or later, lying side by side silently, both pretending to be asleep? And how many times had Katie watched the ceiling like this herself when she was younger, hoping God *was* watching her, praying He would come and show her what was missing in her life, what she could do to make the loneliness go away and stop the endless longing that made her body ache?

She's ready now, finally ready to replay that last night with Nick, to dissect the pieces and examine them. To allow the reel to slowly unwind, the images and words to wash over her. For too long she has kept her eyes wide open, has watched everyone around her, not once trying to see what was right in front of her—within view if she only looked. She's ready to see that night with Nick, to finally see herself, to let the pieces fall where they will.

· · ·

It's April, and she's in Jerry's bedroom, cleaning up the mess from last
weekend and getting it ready, expecting Nick to walk in the door with
Jerry any minute now. The window above the bed is open halfway, and
the fresh spring air ruffles the curtains—there's still a bite to it, but this
is New England after all. By tomorrow it could rise into the seventies,
and maybe the three of them would go down to the dock to get the boat
ready for the season. Katie and Jerry waxing the fiberglass while Nick
tooled around with the engine, and then putting on thick sweatshirts
and motoring around the inlets . . .

    . . . *Is this really what I was telling myself while I waited for them? she
thinks now, lying on Jerry's bed in the dark. Trying to convince myself that
all Nick and I needed was the summer to make things better? But no, Katie
remembers what came after—the creeping embarrassment at herself, the
sensation of standing at a great height and looking down. The weight on her
shoulders, the threat of falling, plummeting* . . .

    She fluffs the pillows, waiting for the sound of Nick's tires crunch-
ing over the rocky driveway. For the past two months, Katie has sent
Nick to pick up Jerry alone like this, and she tells herself that her motives haven't been completely selfish. Jerry has needed this time alone
with Nick, and lately it seems to be working. Nick has been more at
ease with Jerry around the house, and last weekend they went fishing
together at Conimicut Point, alone the entire day for the first time in
months. Katie wasn't asked to go along, but she didn't begrudge their
time together. It was good for Jerry to rekindle his relationship with
Nick, and he had come home smiling, relaxed, ready to draw pictures
of his day at the beach. Besides, it gave Katie more time to search Nick's
office upstairs, to look for clues . . .

    . . . *Donna's words ringing in her ears again . . . obsessed, fanatical* . . .

    So far her efforts in the preceding weeks have produced very little—a
note found in Nick's suit jacket from that college girl, Alicia, thanking
him for all his support, signed with a childish heart over one *i;* a Post-it
note on his home computer, reminding him to "talk to Stephen ASAP";
a phone message in his desk at the Warwick Center to call Robin; and,
last week, Nick's prolonged visit at a Cumberland Farms, though Katie
couldn't see who he was talking to from where she was parked, lights
off, at Brooks Drugs across the street. She still has hopes that the Cumberland Farms incident will pan out (who talked to a convenience-store

clerk for over twenty minutes anyway?), and after a little prying she found out from Veronica that Robin is Joey's mother . . .

. . . She cringes now at the image of Veronica standing at the entrance of Nick's office, catching Katie in the act of sifting through his desk drawer. Was that really her? Snooping through his desk while he was out to lunch? Hunting the hallways even after Nick had packed up and left? Donna's words again: "In fact, you spent an inordinate amount of time there, didn't you? Sometimes three or four times a week?". . .

The sound of Nick's car pulling in to the driveway. The front door opening. Maybe, if Jerry and Nick watch a movie together tonight, Katie can sneak out to his car, rummage through the glove compartment and between the seats . . .

. . . Obsessed . . .

Nick stands in the doorway, alone.

"Where's Jerry?" Katie asks.

"At the group home," he says, staring. "I saw you tonight."

"Where?"

"You were following me. Again."

She turns to Jerry's bed, places his Bugs Bunny pillow in the very center of the pillows. There's a smudge on the top, something Jerry has carelessly spilled, and she'll have to ask him to be more careful if he brings drinks up to his room.

"I'm just finishing in here. If you want me to go for the ride to get him—"

"Jerry's not coming this weekend."

"Why not? He won't understand—"

"Why the hell were you following me?"

She tries to close the distance between them, hand outstretched, and Nick takes a step back into the hallway. Katie stops midstride, wonders when it came to this—her husband recoiling from her touch.

"You never say where you're going. I needed to know."

"There's nothing to know. I just wanted some time for myself."

"You have *all* your time to yourself lately—"

"I can't work through any of it here," he says. His eyes moving around Jerry's bedroom, then down the hallway.

"I know you're frustrated with Joey, and you're disappointed that I'm still not pregnant—"

"You don't know what I'm thinking."

"Then tell me. I'm so tired of watching you and trying to figure it out."

"I'm tired of it, too. Sick of it, actually."

"So you'll try with someone else, is that it? Find a woman who—"

"You aren't listening!" he suddenly shouts.

She's too afraid to speak, because she knows it's one of those moments in life, the kind that determines everything else that will follow. All she can do is stare.

"Right there," Nick says, pointing at her. His lip curling up. "Right there, Katie."

. . . She thought he was pointing at her, pointing out her inadequacies, taking in her whole body in one motion . . .

"I've tried, I don't know what else to do," she says. Hating the whining need in her voice.

"It's not about *you.*"

And it never was, she thinks now. Never. But even this, she knows now, is her fault. Nick didn't ask for her devotion, to be the center of her life. He may have soaked it in, thrived under her encouraging words, but he wasn't the one who put Katie on the sidelines. She did that all by herself.

"If it isn't about me, about us, then what is it?"

"All of it," he says. And when she waits for more, for him to finally reveal something she can hold on to, her eyes searching his face, his voice comes out in a growl. "Stop, okay? Just fucking *stop.*"

. . . She wasn't sure what he meant then—stop what? Waiting for him to talk to her, to open up to her? But no, after all this time something simple, almost absurd really. Stop looking.

"We have to get Jerry, he needs his family."

"Are you that blind, Katie? We are *not* a big happy family."

"How can you say that? Things aren't perfect right now, but—"

"Jerry isn't my son, and he isn't *your* son."

"Is that it? I know you want your own child, and we'll keep trying, we'll have a baby eventually."

"It isn't that. It's you—it's both of you, staring at me all the time. It's suffocating."

"We're worried about you. We love you, Nick. I love you more than anything else in this entire world."

His shoulders slump, and he shakes his head; his face, so angry and resolute seconds earlier, softens a little. "You don't get it."

"I want to—I want to understand. It's all I've ever wanted."

His head dips down, and he stares at the floor, a muscle in his jaw pulsing. When he looks back up at her, his face is pinched with fear.

"Everything," he says. "Right now everything is off kilter."

She watches this raw, helpless look on his face, realizes that she's holding her breath. "Tell me. Please."

He looks down the hallway, looks back at her. "At least Jerry knows, Katie," he says in a whisper. "At least he knows. Did you ever think of it like that?"

"What? What does he know?"

"About his father," Nick says, his voice trembling. "That it was his fault. He left because of Jerry. Don't you think . . . can't you see that there's comfort in that? Knowing?"

"Maybe, I don't know, but not the way his mother told him, how she accused him."

"My mother," Nick says, shaking his head as if he didn't hear her. "She always said—she always told me my father didn't leave because of me."

. . . Finally, Katie remembers thinking, we're here, we're finally here . . . only good things after it all comes out . . .

Katie tries to move to him, to soothe the tortured look off his face, but he does it again: takes a step away until his back is pressed up against the wall in the hallway.

"If she lied, Katie. If she was lying about that . . . then what else?" This in a strangled voice.

"She didn't lie. You were only a kid, it wasn't your fault."

"She used to do that all the time, too, while I was growing up. Stare at me. And I never knew. I didn't know what she saw, what she was really thinking. If she believed what she said. Not just about my father, but about *me*. Brilliant from birth, right?" His face contorts with the effort to smile.

"She didn't lie about that, Nick. I know—I *know*."

"Sometimes I believed her. She said it all the time, Katie. My earliest memory, telling me I was destined for greatness. She made me feel like a fucking giant, like I could do *anything*. But then I'd see her, her eyes were always on me, and I knew. I felt like—I always thought, She's lying, she's just waiting."

"For what?"

He turns away, looks back. "For me to disappoint her, to fall short. It was stupid little things, a C on a math test, or . . . or coming in in second place in an essay contest. Nothing big, but I'd know—bullshit, everything she said was *bullshit.*"

"Nick, look, I won't pretend that I like your mother, but it wasn't—"

"And then something would work out, something good—I'd ace a test, get into the right college—and I'd think, Okay, maybe she's right. Maybe I deserve this, maybe I am just fucking *brilliant.*"

He crosses his arms, his face slowly closing up.

"Nick, don't stop. Please. All these years—all this time."

His voice changing now, too. Becoming harsh, accusatory. "Always, always at the back of my mind, right until I moved out. I knew. It was just talk, she was just afraid that she would lose *me,* too."

"Nick, I know your mother isn't perfect, but I don't think—"

"You weren't there! You weren't in that house, with her eyes hunting me down. Years! Like you, that's all you do. But you, Katie, I *believed* you. From that first night, I thought you saw someone else, someone better. My biggest fan, right?"

"I am, of course I am."

"Really?" Suddenly sneering now. "Still?"

"Yes. Always."

He shakes his head again. "Right."

"It's true, Nick. I swear it," she says. "What can I do? I'll do anything."

"I don't know. I'm trying to figure it out."

"Do you think you just need a little time?"

He stares for a few seconds. Lowers his head. "I found an apartment. I can rent it month to month."

She turns back to Jerry's bed, sits down on it. Tries to draw air into her lungs. "You're leaving?"

"I can't breathe here," he says, looking around the room.

"But—but what will we tell Jerry?" she says.

"You'll figure something out."

"Me?"

But he only glares at her, waiting for her understanding.

... And now she does, after all this time ... Jerry was hers, right from the start ... It didn't matter why anymore, only that he had picked Katie ... It was Katie he wanted, Katie he needed ... And maybe even this, even this, was another failure in Nick's eyes ...

"He'll have to spend weekends with you," Katie says. "You'll have to tell him."

Using Jerry as a punishment, the child in the middle of the divorce.

"Fine."

Her fingers dig into Jerry's blanket. She watches Nick turn now, walk away from her. Listens to the sound of his footsteps as he walks to their bedroom.

She listens to their bedroom closet open, the plunk of the suitcase hitting their bed. "I want you to leave," Katie calls out to him. "Just go."

And then, when he doesn't answer, in a hopeful voice: "Just for a little while."

... Pretending it was her choice, her decision ...

The dry squeak of drawers opening. Katie still on Jerry's bed, cement in her limbs.

She curls up on Jerry's bed now, her body like lead. All this time she blamed Jerry for taking Nick away from her. For losing Nick.

But I lost him myself, she thinks. He was already gone.

6

Jill and Sandy are in the courtroom now, waiting for her, and her entire family is there, too, filling the benches, standing at the back of the room. Dana must have called their parents early this morning, replayed the long conversation she had with Katie on the couch and then later, in the middle of the night—working through that last fight with Nick again. Her mother probably took over from there, burning the phone lines, making demands that no one dared refuse. Katie can hear her now, as she bends over the bathroom sink to wash her hands for the third time. *What do you mean you have to work? For God's sake, Katie needs you there today!*

The rows behind the prosecution table are filled with uncles, aunts, cousins she sees only twice a year and barely knows. Even her parents' neighbors are there, along with Mr. and Mrs. Potter, the couple they go to Gregg's restaurant with every Saturday night.

Her mother didn't say a word when Richard walked into the courtroom earlier—she just touched Katie's arm, gave her a look of teary pride. But Katie could see the fear there, too, and in her father's eyes as well. There would be consequences for what she said today, and Richard would be unforgiving.

It was as if Richard were reading her mind at that very moment; he swiveled around in his chair to check on Katie, his speculative gaze urging her to her feet. "Bathroom," she muttered to her mother, and raced out of the front row.

• • •

Only seconds now before she's called up to testify. Richard and Donna stand in front of Judge Hwang, arguing. She senses Jerry looking at her, turns. Jerry stares, his light blue eyes huge. He's gaping at her, but it's different this time: he *sees* her. He must have his contacts in, because this time he actually *sees* Katie.

"What's going on up there?" her mother whispers to Dana.

Behind her, the sounds of her family's agitation—moving restlessly in their seats, whispering. On the other side of the aisle, only silence. The jurors flick their eyes from the front of the room to Katie, and then to Jerry. Jerry, who doesn't look away, his big eyes asking questions.

Listen, Dana had said this morning. *Listen to yourself. Only you.*

How will Katie lift her body off the bench? Stand? Walk to the front of the room? The jurors, her family, Jill, Dottie, Patricia, even Jerry now—witnesses to her stumbling confessions. Richard will humiliate her, he'll cut her down, disgrace her. He'll have to if he wants to win.

And he will. Even after she tells them everything today, she knows Jerry will be convicted. She knows this now.

Please God. Help me hear.

The courtroom door opens, heads turn. Katie doesn't move—she's trying to will the pressure to lift up and out of her body; she's trying to listen.

Up at the bench, Donna slaps her hands at her sides, and Richard scowls at her, then whispers urgently to Judge Hwang.

Time is jagged now, moving too fast, slowing down, racing ahead. On the other side of the room, bodies are stirring. The people behind Jerry turn to the back of the courtroom. Out of the corner of Katie's eye, she can see them turning to her, too.

She closes her eyes.

Forgive me. Not knowing whom she is asking this of: God? Jerry? Herself?

A dull hum of conversation starts on the other side of the room, grows in volume.

"Quiet!" Judge Hwang orders, banging her gavel.

Instant silence, but Katie is listening now. She opens her eyes, turns. Sees her.

A woman well into her eighties—small, squat, her pink scalp showing through thin tufts of white hair. Leaning on a cane, led to a seat by Patricia. Jerry turns, too, peers. His huge frame jerks once, twice.

Patricia's face is grim as she helps the woman into the row behind Dottie and Eddie. The woman struggles to get her cane into the row, and it bangs the seat. Dottie's body jumps, and she looks at Katie. A frown at first, and then she mouths something to Katie.

"What is that woman saying to you?" her mother asks, and Katie mouths her own silent question back to Dottie: *What?*

This time Dottie forms the words perfectly: *Jerry's mother.*

Katie shakes her head, a refusal. Dottie nods solemnly, and Katie hears her father's voice as if from a distance.

"You okay, sweetie?"

Jerry's mother? Jerry's mother is alive? That's *her?* That elderly woman sitting behind Dottie is the one who beat him and pushed lit cigarettes into his leg and drove a hot iron onto his back and starved him and told him that his existence was a sin? She's in the room right now? That sweet-looking, grandmotherly little woman in the ruffled dress and the white knit sweater who peers around the room with a scared, uncertain smile on her face? That's Jerry's *mother?*

Katie's mother is talking, too, asking something Katie can't hear because her heart is pounding the blood in circles around her head, deafening.

Jerry's mouth is moving now, his eyes frantic as he looks at the back of the courtroom. But how can he recognize her, after all this time? And why would Patricia or Donna Treadmont want him to?

Jerry turns to Katie. Eyes begging.

"Jerry," Katie whispers.

She stands. Stumbles to the end of the row, swipes away the hands trying to stop her. Jerry's lips mumble, mumble, there's only Jerry now, how his eyes narrow at her. The terror and hope fighting inside them.

"I'm right here," Katie says loudly, tripping over Detective Mason's foot at the end of the row.

Judge Hwang's voice echoes, calling out from the other side of a tunnel. "Mrs. Burrelli? We're not ready for you yet."

But Jerry stands, too. He's ripping at his ears. Earplugs—he's pulled them out, two blue sponges. They drop to the floor, his chest heaving in and out, waiting. He can hear her now.

"Everyone sit down!" Judge Hwang barks.

"Jerry," Katie calls out. "It's *me*."

She's at the gate, pushing. Jerry's huge frame starts to spasm, mouth opening wide, eyes flaring. Donna sneaks into the frame, pulling on his arm.

"Everyone, take your seats!"

I'm coming, Katie thinks.

Daniel and Patricia come into focus, too, they pull at Jerry's arms, but he is fighting them, his fists tightening, and Katie pushes at the gate again—stuck, but no, a bailiff is there, blocking her, his arm coming up. Then more arms, touching her, and Dana's voice.

"Honey—"

"Order!" The gavel pounding inside her head.

Richard is rushing toward her, and people are standing, talking, the words growing louder. Katie zips her eyes to the jurors: standing, too, watching. She twists her body left, right, tries to wrench off the hands that keep holding her back.

"Kay-tee!" Jerry screams—trying to rip himself out of the arms that grab at him, too, and then one arm flies free. His fist connects with Donna's face.

They yank at Katie, but she fights, the bailiffs charging at Jerry, then officers in beige, all of them descending on top of him.

"Stop it!"

An arm hooks around Jerry's neck, khaki limbs wrapping around his legs, tackling. People shouting, people pulling at her as she wrestles away from them. Jerry falls behind the table, groaning, screaming, and Katie can't see him anymore. She can only hear him, his choking sobs, her name on his lips, and then she feels it, the heaviness finally slipping free from her body, the sheer weightlessness of falling.

• • •

"Here," her mother says. "Sit up." She guides Katie up from the pillow and hands her a mug of tea. "Be careful, it's hot."

Dana, stretched out on Nick's side of the bed, nuzzles Jack in her arms.

"Is that what you have to do to get a drink around here? Faint?" Dana teases. "Kind of dramatic, isn't it?"

"Not the time, Dana," her mother says. "And get that dog off the bed."

"Has anyone called yet?" Katie asks.

Her mother curls Katie's hair around one ear. "Patricia said she'd call as soon as she can get in to see him."

"She said to thank you, too," Dana says, propping up on an elbow. "For trying to help."

"I think I just made everything *worse,* though, don't you?" She asks this of her mother, whose face flushes guiltily. "Oh, I didn't mean it like that, Mom. I'm not trying to throw that comment about me back in your face. Honest."

Her mother waves her off. "I know it, hon, don't worry about it. I know, this mouth of mine," she says, shaking her head. "Sometimes it doesn't come out the right way."

"You were right, though," Katie says quietly.

"I'll give this bedding a wash when you get up," her mother says. She fusses around the bed, fluffing pillows, smoothing the comforter around Katie.

"Even if it didn't come out right, Mom, thank you. I'm going to pay more attention from now on."

"For the record," Dana says, grinning from her side of the bed, "I think we all agreed that you have to pay *less* attention to everything around you. Isn't that right, Mother?"

"Really, Dana," her mother says, hands on hips, "I don't understand your need to make a joke out of everything today."

But it was Dana who'd whisked Katie out of the courtroom, one arm securely around her waist, her face tight with concern. *Get the hell out of the way!* she'd screamed at a group of reporters outside who hadn't even noticed their approach.

They all turn at the sound of Katie's father pounding his way up the stairs.

"Everyone decent in there?" he bellows outside the door.

"Yes, Jimmy, and we don't all wear hearing aids either."

"Listen, Grace," her father yells from the hallway. "There's a guy downstairs looking for Katie. Ben something. Says he's a friend, but he looks a little suspicious to me. Possibly a reporter or a private detective."

Loud enough for the entire neighborhood to hear.

Her mother stares at the doorway. "God bless him," she says, wagging her head.

•

Her mother has stationed Katie on the sofa with her favorite blue plaid blanket over her legs, like Katie has just returned home from surgery. A slice of sunlight cuts through the bay window and across her knees, and Katie flutters her fingers in it as she waits for Ben to settle his lanky frame into the chair her mother placed beside the sofa.

"It's good to see you again, Ben."

His gray hair is thinner now, his face pale and flaccid. It's startling seeing him this close, but not just because he has aged so much in the past year; Katie is shocked by how much he looks like Sarah. *He has his mother's eyes,* Arthur said once, and he was right. They are the same deep blue as hers, curving up at the sides.

"Are you sick?" Ben asks her.

"No, I'm fine. I fainted today," Katie says. "In court."

His face grows pensive. "I should come back, Katie. Another day. I do not want to intrude, dear."

Inside the kitchen there is only silence: her family sitting at the table, eavesdropping.

"No, it's fine, Ben."

Ben nods his head thoughtfully. "I thought—and maybe I'm wrong, so if I am please excuse me—but I've been reading about the trial. In the paper. I thought your head would be filled with grief. I hoped I could take some of it away, if that is not too arrogant. My parents wanted that."

Katie nods, looks at her hands folded on top of the blanket. "I miss them, Ben."

"Me, too," he says quietly.

The sound of two short squeaks interrupts their shared sadness—a chair inching forward inside the kitchen. Probably her mother, so she can hear their conversation better.

"You're sure I'm not disturbing you?" Ben's face wrinkles up with worry, another reminder of Sarah.

"No, but there's something I have to tell you, too."

"Okay," he says with a smile. "Ladies first."

He listens to her story with a calm expression on his face, takes it better than she expected, her admission that she is still having trouble with his parents' documentary. He only nods when Katie tells him how much she watched Sarah and Arthur, how seeing them together, and listening to them, should have taught her something about her own marriage, but she wasn't willing, or able, to understand until recently. Katie only hints at the specifics, too embarrassed to tell Ben about her relationship with Nick—the passion, the physical connection that they shared almost until he left. How seeing Sarah and Arthur, who learned how to communicate and love each other so deeply without even touching or seeing each other, made her feel restless at times. *There is not only one way to show that you love someone,* Arthur had said once. A lesson, apparently, that Katie had refused to understand.

"That day you met my parents, Katie. At the restaurant?"

"They told you about that?"

Katie's face grows hot, wondering what Arthur and Sarah said to him. She imagines Arthur telling his son about her behavior, his big eyes even wider with disbelief. *This woman, she walks up to our table and stares at us for a full minute! I thought she wanted one of your mother's french fries!*

"They saw your unhappiness that day," Ben says. "My parents, they always said that you found them for a reason. That they could not let you down."

Her chin trembles, and she reaches up to cover it with one hand. Very soon Katie will have to tell Ben the truth, that *she* is the one who will let *them* down, because she doesn't think she can finish their documentary after all.

"You talked to them about your husband?" Ben prods gently. "Your marriage?"

"A little. They asked questions."

"They listened," Ben says. "And they watched you back, dear. They saw."

Those doubtful looks that Katie missed until recently, the questions about Nick and their marriage—not just light chatter to pass the time, but a lead-up to the real business of their meetings.

"Arthur was sick, wasn't he?" Katie says.

"All the coughing? Yes. But it was nothing serious," Ben says. "It was my mother who was becoming very ill."

"Sarah?"

"The doctors said she had Alzheimer's. Not a bad case yet, but she was starting to forget things. And she was starting to have trouble sorting out the present with her memories. Her thoughts were getting jumbled up quite a bit."

Katie recalls Sarah's looks of confusion, her blank stares, her frequent disorientation. Arthur's gentle nudges for her to focus, or to answer Katie's questions. And in the last reel Katie watched, the odd, girlish tone of Sarah's voice when she described the first rape. A dozen different things that should have alerted Katie that something was wrong with her—but again, she missed what was right in front of her.

"That's why they took their lives?" Katie says.

"They didn't want to experience it again, to live in the past. They wanted to move on. But before that, they both wanted to leave something behind."

Katie looks down. "I don't think I can finish the documentary, Ben. I'm so sorry."

He leans forward, places his hand on hers. Smiles. "They didn't care if you finished, dear."

"They didn't?"

"I told you once, on the phone, but I don't think you understood," he says. "It was their gift to *you*."

"I don't understand."

"That is what they wanted you to have. To leave behind. The peace they found. They wanted you to see. All the interviews, the stories, they were for you."

Ben dips his head down respectfully to give Katie a moment to herself, but the generosity of their gift only makes her feel their absence more painfully.

"And now they're gone, Ben."

"They are home now, with God. Some people think it was selfish, but it was the right thing to do, Katie. When my mother started to relive the rapes, we were surprised. For years she had the proof in front of her, every day, but suddenly it was too much. For my father, too."

"Proof? Of what?"

Ben opens his arms, smiles that mischievous smile that recalls Sarah in an instant.

"You?"

"My parents wanted many children. They talked about this on your films? My father wanted them all to have my mother's eyes, but they did tests on him in the camp. Experiments that lasted over a month. When it was over, he was sterile."

During the last taping, when Katie had met Ben, she remembers thinking how different he was from Arthur—so tall, soft-spoken. And she remembers Sarah's description of the new general. *He was a young man. Tall and quiet . . .*

"Do you mean the general—You aren't Arthur's real son—"

Ben meets her stunned gaze with a quiet smile: not Arthur's biological son, this look says, and yet—*still*—Arthur's son just the same.

"My father was proud of me, and he told me this every day," Ben says. "I was real to him in every way that mattered."

•

Before he leaves, he hands her an envelope. "When you are ready, dear," Ben says.

She waits until her family is gone, until she is in bed with Jack snuggled up close. She opens the envelope, pulls out a letter. It's only a short paragraph, filled with crowded, uneven sentences that slant across the page.

Dear Katie,

We are afraid, Sarah and I, that you will be angry with us, but we have prayed and we have our answer. It is our time to go home, and we do this willingly. The film, it is for you. We leave before it is done, but what does this word mean, "done"? It is a short time, here on this earth, yes? We finish, we complete our tasks, when it is time. My Sarah, it is her time, and so it is mine. And now, maybe it is yours? Not the same thing, but important. That is what we wanted you to know. We asked Ben to give you this letter when he thought you were ready. And so now we say this to you, our dear friend, Katie: Do not wait for this life to come to you, to see it all from behind a camera. With both hands, you must grab it.

Excuse me for this bluntness, but a man's touch—it is not all that life will give you. Happiness is something we must first find for ourselves, yes?

This makes sense, Katie? Yes? I am not sure. But I believe that it will. Eventually.

Your friend,
Arthur Cohen

7

There are rules, too many. Katie remembers only three: no sharp objects, no gifts, no touching. That's the most important one—no touching.

We don't want to give them any reason to ask you to leave, Patricia said to her, *so talk to him that way you do. He'll feel that.*

Okay.

Let him see how happy you are to be there.

Yes.

She's in a small room that smells like urine and burned meat—stagnant, nursing-home air. The walls and floor are scuffed and dirty, the only furniture a long wooden table with a thin layer of grime on it and two fold-down metal chairs. A two-way mirror takes up most of the wall on her right—just like the one at the Warwick Center, where observers could watch Nick working with his clients in the adjoining room. Where Katie saw Jerry for the first time, where she filmed the interviews.

On the thin strip of wall next to the window, someone has painted over an angry, scrawled message that is still legible: EAT ME, YOU FUCK-ING SPIES!

The door opens, and Katie jumps to her feet. A tall guard with a shaved head and dark, bushy eyebrows that make him look angry motions for her to sit down. Katie drops back into her chair. The guard turns and pulls a shuffling Jerry into the room, another guard trailing behind them.

"Kay-tee!"

The second guard is shorter, with a kind expression on his youthful face; he nods at Katie, his hand resting lightly on Jerry's broad back.

"Hey, Jerry," she says.

Jerry's face shines with excitement, despite all the chains—attached to a clamp around his neck, trailing down the middle of his orange jumper, attached to more wide clamps that circle his wrists and ankles. His left eye is swollen almost shut, the corners of his lips cracked and clotted with dried blood. The inflammation on one side of his face makes his grin crooked, painful-looking.

Smile at him. Try not to react to the way he looks.

I won't.

"I missed you, buddy," Katie says.

Jerry's grin stretches, and fresh blood seeps from the corner of his lips. He tries to rush forward, and the first guard pushes him back roughly with his forearm. Jerry teeters backward, the chains clanging, and the younger guard has to use both hands to steady him.

"Hold up, pal," the younger guard says, shooting his partner an annoyed look.

If Jerry weren't staring at her like that, Katie would fall apart right then and there from the tenderness in this guard's voice—Jerry has had a friend here. She thanks God for that.

"I was waiting," Jerry says.

"I know. I'm sorry it took so long."

His swollen, happy face says he doesn't mind, everything is okay now that Katie is here.

Don't stray from the questions we've practiced. They'll help Jerry lead up to it naturally. They'll see and hear everything between the two of you, so it's vital you don't digress, that you keep Jerry on track. Do you need to go over the questions again?

Maybe one more time.

They settle Jerry into the chair, the younger guard patting him on the chest.

"You need to stay put," the first guard tells Jerry, pointing at him. "You understand?"

"Kay-tee, I go home now?"

He tries to raise his chained hands, and Katie automatically raises her own until she sees the first guard watching her.

"Jerry," she says, "it's important that you sit in the chair, okay? If you try to get up, they'll ask me to leave."

His swollen face goes slack. "You leave?"

The younger guard squeezes his shoulders, leans down to his ear. "Just sit in the chair and your friend can stay." He pushes Jerry's hands down. "Stay put. Okay, guy?"

Jerry's eyes never leave Katie. "Okay, Mike."

"We'll be right outside," the first guard says. He points at the two-way mirror. "Try to speak up."

They'll record the entire interview, and depending on the outcome, decide if there will be a new trial.

I know that Richard is angry about the mistrial. It was my fault—

That isn't important now, Katie. Only Jerry.

The door closes behind the guards, and Katie smiles at Jerry. "How do you feel?" she asks. It's a stupid question, not on Patricia's list, but she wants to know this more than anything.

"I scared sometimes." He leans into the table with his chest, the chains banging.

"You have to sit back, Jerry. I'm sorry. There are rules."

His face darkens. "Lots of rules here, Kay-tee."

"I know."

"I drawed pictures for you," he says. "Dey say I can give dem to you, but now dey don't let me."

"You'll save them for me?"

Jerry's face brightens. "Course, Kay-tee."

He's been heavily medicated since the arrest, a necessity for obvious reasons, but it's made him sullen. They need to see who he really is, so before you start with the questions, find a way to make them see.

How?

Have you forgotten him completely, Katie?

"Do you remember that time," Katie begins, "that the wind blew all those leaves into the front yard?"

"We make a pile."

"We made a huge pile," she says.

She draws a house with her finger onto the table. The sweat on her finger mixes with the thin layer of grime on the table, but the outline is barely visible. Yet it's enough for Jerry, who knows this picture better than anyone.

He tracks the lines with his good eye, with the crescent of his other one. She makes a box in the middle of the house.

"Do you know what this is?" she says, tapping it.

"Window?"

"Your window, Jer."

"*My* room?"

"Do you remember your room? Can you see it?"

"Um—"

"Close your eyes, buddy."

He obeys her instantly, tilts his head back. "What I see?"

"Look beside the bed. On the bookstand."

Underneath his lids his eyes track back and forth, looking around his room. "Books. My pencils."

"What else?"

"Milk," he says, and opens his eyes. "Only don't leave it dere, 'cuz it cuddles."

"Curdles?"

A small giggle, perfect for the spectators in the other room. "Yeah," he says, "It stink. *Yuck.*"

"What else is in your room?"

Eyelids closing again, then a secret smile on his face. "Oh, no! My Bugs Bunny pillow, Kay-tee! You *forgot?*"

"No way, I love that pillow."

"Me, too," Jerry says, and his smile is so sweet that she wants to gather him up, whisper her apology in his ear, beg for him to forgive her. Knowing he would, that even if he could understand how she has betrayed him, he would forgive her instantly, completely, before she could finish asking.

I have to tell him I'm sorry.

He wouldn't understand, Katie. It would just confuse him.

I know, but—

It's important that you stick to the questions. Let's go over them again . . .

If the people in the adjoining room can see Jerry's face right now—if

Richard and the DA can see the dreaminess on it—it must be enough. This enormous man enraptured by the memory of his stuffed pillow. But just in case:

"Poor, poor Coyote," Katie says sadly. "He didn't stand a chance."

"He all burned up!" Jerry says. *"Bee-beep!"*

Jerry throws his head back and laughs. His whole body shakes, the chains rattling as water pools in the corner of his mouth. A long line of saliva escapes, and his tongue snakes out to capture it back.

"I drool," he says proudly.

"Gross."

More giggles, his one good eye filled with happiness.

Katie scans the window quickly, imagines Patricia and Donna Treadmont nodding in approval. She takes in a deep breath.

"I have to ask you some questions, Jerry. About Nick."

"Nick is died."

"I know. I want to talk about the day you shot him, okay?" She uses the relaxed tone of voice she practiced with Patricia. Folds her hands on the table, leaves a small, encouraging smile on her face—just as Patricia instructed.

"Okay, Kay-tee," he says, straightening in the chair. "I ready."

"Do you remember the group session you had that morning?"

Jerry lowers his head, eyes scanning the table. His mouth moving.

"Jerry? Do you remember?"

"We talk. We talk about love. About being married."

"Did you talk about anything else that morning?" she asks lightly.

Jerry stares at her. *"Sex,"* he whispers.

"That must have made you very upset."

"It bad."

"Did talking about sex make you mad, Jerry?"

Jerry looks down again, talking to himself. "No, Kay-tee. I . . . I . . . *scared.*"

When he tells you he was scared, wait a few seconds and make him say it again.

"You weren't mad at Nick?"

Jerry's lips move, practicing first. "Scared, Kay-tee."

"Why were you scared, Jerry?"

"For Nick."

"Why? Why were you scared for Nick?"

"He tell us," Jerry blurts out. "In group."

Not on the list, but she has to ask. "What did he tell you?"

"Nick tell us he not go home anymore!"

It's like knives plunging into her body in a hundred different places. Nick told his clients that he was leaving Katie for good, before he even talked to her? How could he do that to her? But wait—only Jerry now.

"Are you okay?"

Jerry tilts his head at her, confused. "Okay?"

"Jerry," she says quickly, remembering the correct wording again. "Why were you scared for Nick?"

He rehearses the words first, eyes on the table. "You . . . you not have a baby, Katie. Nick have sex. With someone else. He have a baby with someone else."

She gasps, asks it before she can catch herself: "Nick said he was going to have a baby with someone else?"

"He say someday he might. At lunch he say maybe."

It takes a few seconds for her to remember the next question.

"Jerry, can you tell me where Nick is now?"

"He gone."

Make him answer each question. If he doesn't answer, ask it again.

"Can you tell me where Nick is now?"

He says the words to himself first, then, "Nick in heaven now."

"Why is he there?"

"I . . . I . . ."

He practices the words, eyes moving back and forth, almost as if he can see them.

"I save him dere."

"You saved Nick?"

"Before he do it."

"Before he did what?"

"Nick go to heaven *before*."

"Okay," she says. "Before he did what?"

"What my fadder do. Make sin."

"You thought Nick was going to make sin?"

"My dad make me, and God got mad. He send him to hell."

When he starts talking about his father, help him. Redirect him to Nick.

"You thought Nick would go to hell?"

"Nick say someday he might meet a new lady. Not you. *You* his wife. He might have a baby with a new lady, and *you know*."

"God would be mad?"

Jerry nods, turns his head to try to wipe his nose on his shoulder, fails.

"Jerry? Why would God be mad about that?"

She watches his eyes tracking back and forth over the table—like he knows what he's trying to say, he can see the words right in front of him, but he can't understand them.

Katie stares, feels a tingle of recognition—the look on his face vaguely familiar, but she can't quite place it. And then, as she watches him struggling, she suddenly remembers: that first time he slept over, when he tried to repeat his mother's Scripture. Or when . . . or when . . . that time in the cafeteria . . .

It finally hits Katie, slams into her chest. That exact expression on Jerry's face, his mumbling lips.

"God punish him," Jerry says. "I not want him—I not want him to go to hell, Kay-tee. I . . . I send him to heaven. Time to go, *before*. Not like my fadder. Nick go to heaven *before*."

Katie turns to the two-way mirror, imagines Patricia's satisfied smile.

You did it, she thinks, and turns back to Jerry's hopeful look for understanding.

•

Patricia waits for Katie right outside the room. Next to the door of the adjoining room, Richard consults quietly with the DA and Donna Treadmont.

"You coached him," Katie whispers fiercely to Patricia. "You told him to say those things."

Patricia frowns, looks at the group only a few feet away. Richard's eyes lock with Patricia's, and then Patricia is signaling for Katie to walk with her. They move to the end of the corridor.

"Like when we first met in the cafeteria," Katie says, turning to her. "Word for word. You told him what to say."

Patricia crosses her arms. "I did what I had to do. For Jerry. I wasn't sure if seeing his mother in the courtroom would be enough."

"For what?"

"His reaction, a mistrial. Even if it worked, I wasn't sure what would come next. We might've been right back at the starting line."

"But was any of it true? What he said in there?"

"Parts of it, I think."

"What parts—what parts were true?"

Patricia checks on the group, lowers her voice. "You had a conversation with your sister, before Nick left. At your parents' house. Do you remember what you said?"

"We went over there all the time. I said lots of things—"

"The one Jerry overheard? About Nick having an affair? Jerry told us about that. He could repeat *that,* word for word, himself."

Sitting with Dana outside, talking about Nick. Telling her how they hadn't had sex in two months. *Sometimes I can actually see him with another woman . . . I couldn't handle it if he decided to be with someone else, if he wanted to start a family with another woman.*

"I should have talked to Jerry about that—"

"Yes, you should have. But at the time you were busy." Her glance leaves no room for doubt: busy stalking Nick.

"So then it's true? What he said in there?"

"You're underestimating the complexity of this situation, of who Jerry is and what he's been through. I don't know if we'll ever know the entire truth," she says. "And I think it's better if we leave well enough alone."

"I can't do that, I just can't. I wish I could."

Patricia scowls at her. "I don't think you want to hear this."

"Please," Katie says. "I have to know."

Patricia sighs through her nose. "Fine," she says. "We aren't sure of everything, how it all adds up. But do you remember telling your sister that if Nick left you to be with another woman, you'd die?"

Katie scans her memory. "No, I don't think so. Maybe not in those words."

Even if there's the off chance he is *seeing someone else . . . you would still live your life,* Dana had said to her.

No, Katie had replied. *No, I wouldn't. I wouldn't want to.*

"You were his 'best,' Katie," Patricia says. "Right from the start. Jerry didn't want to lose you."

"Why would he?"

"You said if Nick was with another woman . . ." she begins. She sighs loudly, impatiently. "Well, Jerry interpreted your words that day literally. If Nick was with someone else, you wouldn't want to live. He couldn't let that happen."

"Oh, God," she says, placing her hand against the wall.

"I'm sorry to tell you so bluntly, but we think there's a good chance it factored into his decision. You were like a mother to him, Katie." Patricia's gaunt face fills with accusation. "His mother, and probably more, now that he's finally opened up to me."

It's like Katie has stood up too quickly, her head filled with small pinpoints of light as she stares at Patricia. "What—"

"Months, Katie. For months I've tried to persuade Jerry to talk to me. I knew something was missing in this equation. Imagine my surprise just last week when it all came together. When I finally coaxed it out of him."

"I don't know—" she begins, but Patricia's look silences her.

"Why didn't you tell us about the shoes, Katie? Didn't you find that behavior disturbing? Or at least relevant?"

"Dana—my sister, Dana, said he didn't feel sexual toward *me*. They helped him relax. It wasn't hurting anyone."

"Surely," Patricia says, "you can understand the danger of encouraging a situation that complex? Surely you're not that naive?"

"I wanted to say something, I did. I knew it was complicated, but he trusted me."

"Yes," Patricia says, "he did. He trusted you with his life."

•

She's in the parking lot just outside the prison, her family gathered around her. The tears have finally come, guilty and crushing, as she repeats Patricia's words—though she is careful, even in her frenzied state, to keep the last disclosure to herself. Her father snuggles her against his body, her mother stroking her hair slowly while she tries to make sense of Katie's confession. Dana stands close, her hand in Katie's.

"We'll never know the whole thing," Katie chokes out at last, "but don't you see? It was *me,* too. Not just Jerry."

Her father pulls her closer, his face pale.

"Let's get you home, hon," her mother says. "Let's talk about it there, okay?" The look on her mother's face—the tenderness and shock combined there—makes Katie's body suddenly go limp.

"Let's go *now,*" Dana says, helping their mother and father half carry her to the car.

And then Katie turns, sees why her sister's tone is so urgent: Richard is striding out of the building, heading right toward them.

Dana is the first to move. She steps in front of Katie, holds both hands up before Richard gets close.

"You've done enough, Richard," she calls to him. "Walk away."

Katie sees the anger radiating off him, and suddenly she is wrestling away from her parents. There's this at least—the comfort of her own anger.

"You used me," she says, swiping her face. "The whole time. You—"

"Why the tears, Katie? You got your way, didn't you?" he demands. "And when this guy hurts someone else, when he—"

"Listen here," her father barks, taking a step forward. "I suggest you take my daughter's advice and move on."

"No, Dad, no," Katie says, pushing away the hands that reach for her.

"Kate," her mother says. "It's time to go home." Her eyes boring into Richard's as she says this.

"I want to know, I have a right," Katie says.

"You," Richard says to Katie, "I owe you nothing. He belongs in prison. Through all this shit, and all your"—he stops, shakes his head derisively—"your obsession with your husband, your lack of professional merit—I could have worked around it. You wouldn't be the first woman to lose herself in a man."

"Sir," her father says, "you are about to cross a line here. Do you understand that?"

"With all due respect, she wants to know." He turns to Katie. "You want to know when I realized you were a lost cause?"

"Stop this. Stop this now," Dana says, her arms circling Katie's trembling body.

"She told me," Richard says. "She was there for the final footage, this woman. *Patricia*. And she pulled me aside. Do you know what she told me, Katie? Can you imagine?"

It's like her whole family is holding her breath with her. "I get it," Katie says, because she hasn't told her family this part—they can't know *this* part.

"Do you? Really?" he says. "Patricia certainly knew. 'New information,' she called it. She didn't even tell Donna. Thought she might screw it up, or if it came out, Jerry would appear even more dangerous or twisted. Patricia was willing to sacrifice you—this woman you just worked with to help Jerry served you up on a platter to me. And you should get this, too: If this played out differently? I would have found a way. I would have made sure you took your share of the blame. Maybe not legally," he says, "but everyone would have known what you did. I would have made sure of that."

Katie bends her head.

"What is he talking about, Kate?" her mother says. And then to Richard, "You don't understand my daughter—she didn't want Jerry to overhear that conversation. She didn't know how he would interpret it—"

"I'll let *you* finish the story," Richard says, ignoring her mother. He lowers his head, stamps away.

"Katie," Dana says. "What's he talking about?"

They all stare at her now, three confused-worried faces, waiting.

"That day," Katie whispers to Dana. "That day—on your porch?"

Dana becomes thoughtful, her mind searching. "What day?"

"Jerry," Katie says. "On your porch."

Dana's eyes fill with understanding. "But, you told them, right? Back then? They already knew. Nick and—"

She stops when she sees Katie's look, the slow shaking of her head.

"What?" her mother asks, head turning back and forth between Katie and Dana.

"Later, Mom," Dana says, watching Katie. "At home. We need to go home now."

Epilogue

Summer has come to New England in full force. Just a few weeks of cold rain, and then the humidity and blazing sun have appeared each day, wilting newly planted gardens, causing tempers to flare and wavering mirages to hover over the hot asphalt of I-95 as Rhode Islanders make their desperate escape to the South County beaches.

Right now, Katie thinks as she drives, Scarborough Beach and Matunuck and Misquamicut must be jam-packed, blanket to blanket, the air filled with laughter and suntan lotion and blaring radios.

Katie wonders again how long it will take—how long until the world will stop offering Nick back to her so often, like this: As she makes the left onto Oakland Beach Avenue and heads to the seawall, she sees him again, standing on the rocks near Iggy's. His face raised slightly into the sun. Scanning the glimmering ocean, watching passing sailboats and Jet Skiers, munching causally on a doughboy. All the time in the world to stare and wonder at the beauty in this world.

It will happen, they've all assured her, and Katie believes them, even if she can't feel it yet. Although there have been moments already—fleeting, gone before she can sink into them—when he has turned back into one of the mirages she sees just up ahead in the road, his outline wavering, face blurring. The same way she used to see him in her dreams when they were still together.

She hesitates for a moment at the booth before she pays the three-dollar fee to park by the seawall; her plan was to sit inside her car facing the ocean, the air conditioner blasting, and let her mind silently

wander across the water for a few minutes before she drove to the address printed on the invitation—knowing that it would require some
fortitude not to feel envious, to experience one of those bottomless "this
could have been me" moments that had a way of lingering inside the
body for days, even weeks. But the parking lot is almost full, crammed
with cars and motorcycles and big SUVs, and with people who wander
and socialize or sit on their hoods, tipping back beers and munching
on greasy burgers and fries. The small picnic area is crawling with
people, too—families tending to smoking grills and coolers and racing
children who need to be reeled back in. Even the seawall is overrun
with men holding buckets and fishing poles, and children clambering
up and down the huge rocks to collect stones and shells to skip into the
ocean. Somewhere amid the happy noise and laughter is the deep call
of a father to *get out of the parking lot* and the slow, persistent bass of a
radio pulsing into the sticky air.

"Drivin' through or parking?" the boy at the booth prompts Katie,
tipping his baseball cap back and swiping his arm across his forehead.

Katie nods to herself, offers him a five. Tells him to keep the change.

"Youse guys should be at the *real* beach," he says moodily. "Crazy
people." He pockets the bill without thanking her, shakes his head.

Katie pulls between a Hummer and a motorcycle. For a few minutes, she tries to concentrate on the diamond light that flashes from
the tops of whitecaps, but then a young couple moves into view on the
rocks—about thirty feet off, slowly making their way to the long jetty.
The girl leads, jumping first onto a flat rock and somehow managing to
keep her hand intertwined with her lagging boyfriend's. The girl hops
again, her arm stretched back behind her, a look of studious concentration on her face as she searches for the next smooth rock. Her boyfriend
loyally follows, his eyes just as studiously tracking her ass. After two
more hops, the girl turns back suddenly, poised to say something to the
boy, but stops: she sees where his attention is focused. She turns all the
way around, smiles. Pulls the fist that their hands make together up to
her chest. Katie feels a choking moment building inside her throat, so
she pops open the door, gets out. She moves to the back of her car, jin-
gling her keys in one hand, and leans against the trunk. Keeps her eyes
on the cracked shells that are ground into the pavement by her feet.

The heat descends quickly onto her bare skin—within minutes she can feel the sweat pooling under her arms and then slowly trickling down inside her dress. The sounds of happiness are amplified now without the protection of the car—all around her is the noise of stubborn people stubbornly enjoying the crushing humidity. She finally looks up, crosses her arms—the picnic area is a blur of moving bodies at first, but then she allows herself a slow inspection: A father hauling his daughter up and onto his shoulders, the little girl's joyful-scared scream as her hands clutch underneath his chin. A man passing a heaping paper plate to a woman sitting cross-legged on a blanket—the way she offers him her thanks with only her eyes. Two little girls, knee to knee, wordlessly passing little clothes back and forth, dressing their Barbie dolls. A group of teenagers playing Hacky Sack, kicking the small ball with the sides of their sneakers, the tips of their bare toes. They ignore a lonely old man who walks by them slowly, leaning heavily on his cane, and Katie watches as the ball suddenly flies off course and in this man's direction—but then the cane is tipping up expertly, and the ball is shooting in an arc back to the teenagers. A roar of surprised happiness rises from the group, and Katie watches as they stop and stare, as one of boys moves forward to offer the old man his palm for a high five. A few seconds more and the teenagers are scooping their hands at the man, inviting him into their circle.

She's suddenly thirsty—more than thirsty; her throat feels like it's coated with shell dust. She should get something to drink, something tart and icy, but Iggy's, up the hill and to the left, has an endless chain of people waiting in the takeout line. For a moment Katie just stares at the odd movement around them until she realizes that most of them are fanning their faces with their hands.

And then she has an urge to walk to the picnic area, to offer a dollar to one of the families for a drink from their cooler. She thinks how bold this would be, wonders at the reaction she would get. Would they offer her one? Smile and say, *No charge*? Or would they stare wordlessly at her? Their eyes traveling up and down her body as they made hasty assumptions? (*Step away from the crazy lady, Susie!*) She has her keys, she could jiggle them a little: not a lunatic wandering around and begging, not a well-dressed homeless person, but a thirsty woman who owns a car and doesn't want to wait in a long line with all the hand-fanning people just up the hill.

Katie can't tell from watching any of them—if they'd smile or shake her hand, maybe even ask her name, or if they'd simply step back, send her away with a guarded look. She checks her watch—almost time to go—and then a silver minivan pulls right up into her line of vision, blocking her view of the picnic area. The window on the passenger side slides down, and, inside, Katie sees a woman in the passenger seat turned all the way around, the top half her body leaning into the backseat. Katie sees the sullen little boy back there, too—sitting beside a sleeping child in a car seat, his face being scrubbed with a limp tissue by his mother. He sees Katie watching, glares, and pushes his mother's hand away.

"Are you going?"

Katie looks past the mother, who has turned around to stare at her, to the person speaking: the man behind the wheel, younger than Katie but almost bald, with a weary, harassed-looking face. For a second she has the crazy idea that he has read her thoughts: *Are you going to get that drink or what?*

"Lady?" he says, pointing at her hand.

She holds up the keys, looks at them. "Yes," she tells him. "I was just leaving."

•

She checks the directions again: the last right off Oakland Beach Avenue onto Prior, and then a quick left onto Chelmsford Avenue. She sees the big house up ahead—an enormous gray Victorian with pink and blue balloons tied to the mailbox out front. The wide driveway is full, and cars are lined up on both sides of the street, so Katie has to park almost a block away. She hauls the plastic-wrapped basket off the backseat, opens the door, and steps into the humid air.

A tall woman who looks like an older version of Sandy greets her at the front door.

"How adorable!" she says, propping her hip against the door and taking the baby basket out of Katie's arms. "My Lord, you look like you're about to melt. Come in, come in!" She shakes the basket, the tiny silver rattle inside twinkling. "This is just precious!"

Katie introduces herself, enters the noisy, cavernous living room: women everywhere, chatting in groups and holding small china plates bearing finger sandwiches, some holding babies, a couple of them almost as pregnant as Sandy.

"You must be Sandy's mother," Katie says.

"Guilty as charged," the woman says, smiling. "Please, make yourself at home, Katie. I think Sandy might be out on the veranda—No, wait, there she is."

Sandy spies her from across the room, and with her eyes still on Katie says something to the woman next to her; she waddles over, one hand on her huge belly.

"You made it!" Sandy says, leaning in for a hug.

They try to embrace with Sandy's stomach between them, then give up, laughing; they lean in, press their cheeks together.

"Jeez, I'm a *whale,*" Sandy says, pulling back and grinning at Katie. She turns to the room.

"Everyone, this is Katie. My good friend Katie Burrelli," she says, her arm on Katie's shoulder.

Sandy points, introducing everyone. "Well, you've met my mom, of course, and then there's Kelley over there, almost as pregnant as me, and there's Lynn with sweet little Kim-Lee on her hip, and my cousin Susan . . ."

It isn't as bad as Katie feared, mostly because she finds herself pouring coffee and lemonade and collecting plates, and then helping Sandy's mother and one of her friends in the kitchen, even during the opening of presents.

"Why don't you go on now, enjoy yourself," Sandy's mother urges her at one point. "We can do this."

Katie peeks into the living room. A line of tiny clothes is making the rounds, the women cooing and smiling, and sharing their own stories about babies and husbands who are home watching the kids.

Sandy's mother peeks in, too, then regards Katie for a moment. "You know what?" she says. "We actually need someone to make a fresh pot of coffee, and if it's okay, maybe you could help me find those extra napkins?"

Later they are standing side by side at the counter, wrapping food, making leftover plates for some of the women, when Sandy wobbles in.

"Still at it?" Sandy says to Katie, then stretches up to kiss her mother on the cheek. "It was perfect, Mom. Thanks for everything."

"She's right, you've done enough," Sandy's mother says to Katie, then eyes Sandy's belly. "You, too, Sandy," she says, and they all laugh.

Sandy and Katie sneak away to the veranda, plant themselves on an iron bench facing a huge garden that is spilling over with flowers and creeping vines; tiny hummingbirds flutter above it, their wings almost invisible as they sip from enormous orange and red canna lilies.

"Well, you know I'm going to ask, girl," Sandy says. "How was it?"

"It was fun. You have so many friends—"

"No, no, not the shower," Sandy interrupts, "I mean yesterday and last week. How was it?"

"Weird," Katie admits.

"But you like this woman?"

Katie considers this a moment. "She's very patient."

"Well, *that's* a good thing," Sandy teases, and Katie smiles.

After months of Dana's gentle hints, and her mother's blatant badgering, Katie has finally given in, is trying to give therapy a chance. She doesn't know how long she'll last, because it's so unsettling and foreign to her—offering her feelings to a stranger, when she's spent a lifetime keeping most of them from the people she loves and knows best. But this woman, an old colleague of Dana's and in her fifties, is not only patient, she's also surprising insightful after only two meetings. *You can't stake all your happiness on another person, Katie. You can't hide behind them, or hope they'll eventually offer you something that will make you feel complete.*

For a while Katie and Sandy talk about the shower, and about Jill, whom Sandy is getting to know slowly.

"She broke up with *another* guy?" Sandy asks.

"What else is new?"

"That girl," Sandy says, shaking her head and laughing.

Katie laughs, too, thinks of Jill and how much their relationship has changed since their conversation last winter.

—I'm going to try to be better, Katie had said. —To be a good friend.

—You *are* a good friend, you idiot, Jill said. —And I wasn't sad about Amy at that lunch, Katie, I was sad about *us*. You barely tell me anything, but I thought that would change, with Nick, and the trial.

—I try.

—Do you? *Really?* Jill had said. —Do you have any idea how much work it is to be around you sometimes?

And there it was again, that impatient edge in her friend's voice.

—Do you have any idea how hard it is to keep the conversation going sometimes, to keep everything happy and upbeat, so I don't feel like it's just me, complaining all the time?

—I trust you, Katie had replied simply, knowing that was what Jill needed to hear. —I respect you.

—I know. I know you do, Jill said, sighing. —But sometimes it's hard to believe, you know? (Katie realizing suddenly that she wasn't so different from Richard after all: acting her way through life at times, putting on different faces for her family, her friends.)

But Jill has stuck by her, has even offered to go to therapy if Katie likes.

—I think for now I can handle it, Katie told her last week.

—I didn't mean for you, Jill joked. —I have a couple of issues with men I need to work out myself!

"Another baby," Sandy says now, shaking her head, her hands coming up to rest on her stomach. "I must be insane!"

Katie smiles, and then they become quiet. Inside, they hear Sandy's mother talking with her friend, the whir of the dishwasher starting.

"Sometimes I think I'll never have this," Katie says, spreading her hands at the garden, but Sandy understands.

"You'll fall in love again," she says. "You'll get your family, too."

Katie shakes her head—impossible to think of love again, of coming home to happy voices and the kind of chaos Sandy lives in. She doesn't even know if she *wants* children, or even another man by her side anymore, but that, apparently, is a good thing. *Not knowing means you're thinking about what you really want,* the therapist said. *And when you're ready, love will compliment your life, not define it.*

One of the last party stragglers steps outside with her son, and Katie helps Sandy off the bench so she can say her good-byes. Hanging back on this woman's leg is a little boy Katie had glimpsed during the shower—a chubby, shy little four-year-old with light blue eyes that remind her of Jerry's, and she thinks of him again, of who he would have been if his mother were a different person. Of who he would be today, if *Katie* had been a different person, too.

Sometimes, in quiet moments like this, she wonders what Jerry is doing, if he is drawing pictures of new families—if he is placing himself firmly in the middle of the new frame of his life. They've stopped mentioning him in the paper, and the last thing they reported, back in the spring, was that there wouldn't be a new trial—the DA deciding against it due to "mitigating circumstances."

Every once in a while now, Dana will reveal something to Katie—she used to work with a psychiatrist who's at the Institute of Mental Health—and Katie holds her breath as her sister talks. *He's making progress. His appetite has come back. There's a counselor there, a woman who has become really attached to him.* Katie isn't allowed to visit him, and she tells herself it's for the best—still not knowing, really, *who* it's best for: her, or Jerry. But sometimes she listens to Dana's updates and she puts herself inside those walls that have become his home now—sees Jerry in his room, the bookshelf beside his bed, filled with his pads and pencils. Pictures him sleeping, his arms wrapped around the Bugs Bunny pillow they let her send, his face peaceful. Even when the picture changes—Jerry waking, his eyes pulsing open in panic—she sees a woman walk into the frame, her arms wrapping around him, comforting him. And Jerry, trusting her more each day, letting his head drop to her shoulder. The tears leaving as this new person keeps him safe from the dark.

Katie doesn't know what the future holds for him, if he will ever be allowed to leave, if she will ever be allowed to see him again. But if it happens, if by some miracle they decide that Katie can be in his life again—his room has been put back into its proper order, waiting. A long shot, yes, virtually impossible. But the pictures are taped back onto his wall, the beluga whale propped back up on the mahogany dresser. Just in case.

"Katie?"

Sandy walks slowly to the bench, lowers herself back onto it.

"Sorry, what?"

"I said you look a million miles away," Sandy says. "What are you thinking about?"

"Jerry," Katie says simply.

"Okay," Sandy says, nodding. She pats her leg. "Spill it."

"It's nothing—"

"*Katie.*"

Katie sneaks a look at her friend. "I guess I was just wondering," she says, and then she turns her body around, until she is facing Sandy. "What do you think he's doing? Right now?"

•

The car has been packed since early this morning. She's getting ready to leave for a cookout at her parents' house, a little party to send her off on her trip tomorrow. Jack dances in circles around her legs, not helping one bit.

"Where's your leash, Jack?"

He runs to his wicker toy basket, noses around, pulls out a big rawhide. Wags his tail at Katie, supremely proud of himself.

"Nice try."

Her mother will give her a hassle about taking Jack along again, but Katie doesn't mind. Just last week she caught her mother sneaking a piece of chicken to him, as he sat underneath the picnic table, waiting hopefully.

"What?" her mother said when Katie smiled at her. "It was just a piece of skin."

If Katie decides to move, and it seems inevitable that she will once Nick's insurance money runs out, it appears that not only will Jerry's belongings go with her, Jack will make the move, too. *Keep him, girl. It's obvious he loves you to death,* Sandy said last December, over coffee. *And it's going to be even crazier around here soon enough.* Her hands covering the slight bump under her shirt.

Before long, Katie will have to find a job, go house hunting, but not before this trip.

She finds the leash hanging off the deck outside, turns when Jack sprints outside for one last pee before they go.

"Good boy, Jack."

He sniffs around the lawn, lush now thanks to her father's attentions. As soon as the rain stopped, he showed up every morning, spreading fertilizer and laying down new seed where the leaves had suffocated the grass over the winter. And watering like crazy, until her backyard was flooded in a dozen different places. Her mother wagging her head, eyeing the puddles from the deck. "Moderation," she had said to Katie. "A term your father does *not* comprehend."

Beside the shed, underneath the shade from the oak trees above, bright green sprouts of baby grass have pushed their way to the surface.

"I could get up on the shed," her father said last week, "cut down some of those branches and let more light in."

"Don't you dare, Jimmy," her mother replied. "You'll break your neck."

"You're the boss, Grace," he said to his wife. He turned to Katie, winked. "Hey, sweetie, did your mother tell you about those hoodlums we ran into outside the Blue Grotto a few days ago?"

"There was nothing wrong with those men, Jimmy. One of them had a *walker,* for God's sake."

After her mother shook her head and retreated to the air-conditioned house, her father bumped her arm, gave her another wink. "It drives her crazy," he said, completely unrepentant.

"Then why do you do it, Dad?"

He coiled the hose around his arm, walked to the side of the house. "I used to talk about all these dangerous men to take her mind off the cancer," he said. "To occupy her mind with something else. And now it just drives her nuts. A win-win situation." He grinned at Katie.

"Dad," Katie said, incredulous. *"I can't believe you!"*

"What?" he asked innocently, and turned to the big bag of fertilizer leaning against the house.

Outside in the baking car, Katie settles herself in as Jack pants and scratches at the window. She rolls it down, cranks the air conditioner.

She'll stop at Korb's Bakery for a loaf of Italian bread, maybe make a quick trip to the Green Thumb for flowers for her mother. *Suck-up,* Dana will say, without a hint of malice. Understanding that the tenderness and peace between Katie and her mother won't last forever, that at some point very soon there will be too many questions, too many looks that might still hint at her mother's opinion of her. But for now, while the fragile harmony lasts, Katie will take full advantage of it.

She casts one last look at the house—did she remember to turn the A/C down, shut off the dryer?—and Nick comes back to her again.

Part of trying to let him go in the past seven months has included looking around her house, trying to see it as a real home without him in it. But another part—more important than the first—has been her struggle to let go of all the questions she has about Nick, and for Nick—this need to continue waiting for answers from him, from Jerry. Attempting to forgive herself for her part in Nick's death, even if she'll never know the entire truth or how much of the blame is hers. But knowing, nonetheless: he may not have come back to her, but if it weren't for Katie he'd still be here. Not in her life, not the center of her world anymore. But still here, somewhere in the world.

She adjusts the rearview mirror, catches the expression on her face. It's all there, especially in her eyes. The guilt, the futility of forgiveness.

She knows that she will spend a lifetime wrestling with these guilty, tormented feelings—knows that they might ease, they might fade over time, but they will be a part of her life, always. She will carry them through the years, she will take them with her into new relationships, into a new home and a new job—they will always be as natural to her as breathing. And she knows she *deserves* this burden—for Nick and the life that was taken too soon; for Jerry and the love that saved him, and then almost destroyed him. Her burden such a small price to pay compared to theirs.

She puts the car in drive.

"Ready, Jack?" He turns to Katie, his paws slipping on the ledge of the window. "Here we go."

•

She reaches the Topsail Island exit in North Carolina just after midnight. Her original plan was to drive seven or eight hours a day so she would be rested and get to the house in daylight, but somewhere between the Delaware Gap and the heavy traffic in Washington, D.C., she decided to keep driving until she reached the house. The weariness of waking at 5:00 A.M., of what lay ahead of her, suddenly replaced by this determination to *keep going*.

The house is in darkness, no surprise. She should drive to a hotel, but instead she sits in front of the house and peers into the blackness. In the passenger seat, Jack whines in his sleep, legs kicking.

In the morning Katie will ask the new owners for Mr. Barber's phone number, or maybe his address, though she understands that even if they have this information and are willing to share it, Mr. Barber might refuse to meet with her. That he still might be "twitchy."

But if he does agree to meet, what then?

She rolls down her window, turns off the car. The warm air rushes in, and she closes her eyes, breathes in the scent of ocean and oleander.

•

In the dream she is clinking glasses with Dana, and then she is hammering a nail into one of the shelves where she stores her canisters of film, the sound growing in volume, until she realizes that the tapping is happening in real time, outside her dream.

"Ma'am?"

Katie blinks into the gray morning light. Not the police, thank God, because what would she tell them? *My husband left me and he wanted to buy this house and now he's dead and I'm sleeping in my car because I drove all night and fell asleep wondering why I'm here in the first place . . .*

The man tapping her windshield is anywhere between fifty-five and seventy—balding and heavy and deeply tanned, with a youthful, stubby nose that looks misplaced on his wrinkled face. His robe is tied tightly over his enormous belly, and he has a paper tucked underneath his arm. An empty coffee cup dangles out of one hand.

"You all right in there, ma'am?" he asks in a deep southern drawl.

Katie pats her hair into place, runs a hand across her face, her skin already sticky from the humid air. "I'm sorry, I fell asleep."

"Car broke down?"

"No, I drove all night—" Jack scurries onto her lap, and Katie pats him, too. She points to the house. "Do you live here?"

The man turns, surveys the house. Over the swell of the lawn, the ocean is just visible. "Going on forty years," he says.

"Are you Mr. Barber?"

He eyes her curiously. "Have we met?"

"I'm Katie Burrelli," she says. "I'm Nick Burrelli's wife. Or I *was* Nick's wife."

Mr. Barber nods, slowly. He watches her for a moment, nods again. "Suppose a cup of coffee might do you some good?"

. . .

"I lied to you, Mr. Barber," Katie says, wrapping her hands around the coffee mug.

Mr. Barber nods, keeps his eyes steady on the ocean. They're sitting in white rocking chairs in the gazebo, watching the sun peek over the horizon. A boat full of men trolls past them in the distance, their fishing rods pointing high into the sky. The wind carries their laughter across the water, and Mr. Barber throws up a hand in greeting. The men wave back, and Mr. Barber smiles. Jack lies at their feet, dozing softly.

"I couldn't go through with it," Mr. Barber says, talking more to himself than to Katie. "Selling this house. Tried a couple of times but there's too many memories here, I guess. Good and bad, but too many to give away."

They sit in companionable silence for a moment, taking in the water that is just beginning to sparkle under the sun's early rays.

"I didn't lie to *you*, exactly," Katie says. "I told Mr. Minsky that Nick and I wanted to see the house again. But Nick was already gone."

Mr. Barber turns to her, raises an eyebrow.

"He died last spring, shortly after you met him. He came here the week after he left me," Katie says. "And now I'm here, and I have no idea why."

Out of the corner of her eye, she can see Mr. Barber nod, turn back to the ocean. They watch a string of pelicans fly past, their wings resting on the air. Earlier, while Katie waited in the dining room for Mr. Barber to change and then pour them coffee, she tried to think of at least one good question for him. A reason that she has intruded into this man's life. She listened to his happy whistling in the kitchen, hoping the wistful melody would work its way into her body and make some sense of this trip that had seemed so important just yesterday.

Mr. Barber points to a fish cresting the water. "Most likely a blue," he says, rocking in his chair.

"Do you fish often?"

"Used to," he says, watching the water.

"I'm sorry for imposing on you like this," Katie says. "Thank you for the coffee."

She's about to rise when Mr. Barber places a hand on the arm of her chair, his eyes still on the ocean.

"Back when my wife was alive, I used to call her Old Busybody. There was always someone up there in the house with her, talking away, and my wife'd just sit there and soak it all up. I never understood it," he says, shaking his head.

He tilts his mug back, drinks the last of his coffee.

"I asked her once why she did it, and she said something that didn't make sense right then. She said when people tell their troubles to someone else, it's like they're handing over some of the weight of those burdens. Taking the things that make their shoulders bend and giving them over to someone who can hold on to them for a while. Said that's the greatest thing we can do for another person, carry around that weight until they're strong enough to take it back."

"Did you believe her?"

"Hell no!" Mr. Barber says, facing Katie and grinning for the first time. "I thought she just liked listening to their tales. Old Busybody, that's what I called her." His face grows serious, eyes tracking the water again as he looks into the past. "But then she got sick and was gone before I could even think about what being alone was all about. And I had me a neighbor here, right next door, been dead going on about a year now. Charlie. And one night me and old Charlie, we drank us some whiskey and it all came spilling out of me. I couldn't have stopped myself if I tried. All the good and the bad and the ugly and the sweet. And you know what? The trip back home that night was like walking an inch above the ground. I been grateful to him ever since. Always will be."

Another boat appears in the distance, a nest of seagulls chasing above it.

"When did you know you were ready to take it back?" Katie asks quietly.

"Don't know if I have yet," Mr. Barber says. "But I'm trying." He turns to Katie, raises his empty mug at her. An invitation.

At first she stumbles, trying to tell him about Nick, their life together. But Mr. Barber keeps his eyes on the water, calmly nodding his encouragement, and before she knows it, she's talking about Jerry, her family, the trial. How she'll never know exactly what part she played in Nick's death, but how she knows the feelings of guilt will never leave her all the way. She tells him about the Cohens, too, about what they offered her, what she refused to take. And how she always felt she was an outsider in her own life, always on the outside looking in, watching and waiting for other people to give her answers. Mr. Barber keeps nodding like he understands, his eyes squinting at the ocean as he rocks in his chair.

"I think it was the opposite for me, Mr. Barber. I wanted to hear their stories so I could understand myself. What my life was, or was supposed to be," Katie says. "Who I *should* be."

Mr. Barber stops his slow rocking. "And now?"

"I guess I'm ready for my own story."

Mr. Barber looks at her, smiles. "That sounds about right."

"But I've decided to finish the Cohens' documentary after all. I'm about halfway through. Their son, Ben, is helping me. He's narrating their life together."

Mr. Barber pats the arm of her chair. "They'd be real proud of you, your friends."

They rock side by side for a long time, quiet as the sun continues its journey upward, as the ocean fills with more boats and a few Jet Skiers. Mr. Barber finally stirs beside her, looks her in the eye.

"Nick didn't mention a wife," he says. "Just said he needed a break, to breathe a little bit easier and all."

"I know."

"But I sure got the feeling he was running from something."

"Me."

"Not exactly, no," Mr. Barber says. "Not a person, I'd say. Something bigger than that. But then I guess we all have our ghosts, don't we?"

"I guess so."

After a few minutes, Mr. Barber stretches his arms out in front of him, like he's trying to frame the entire ocean inside them. "Nice, isn't it? Watching the day wake up like this? Makes you feel like you could do anything, don't it?"

Not yet, Katie thinks.

But someday. Eventually.

Yes.

Acknowledgments

I am so very thankful to Kendra Harpster at Viking for all her hard work and insightful feedback, and for making this experience so rewarding every step of the way. It has been such a gift to work with her. Many thanks also go to Geri Thoma and Julia Kenny and everyone at the Markson Thoma Literary Agency. I'm deeply grateful to Maureen Sugden, too, for her careful read and great suggestions.

This book would not be possible without my amazingly supportive and loving family: my dad, who offers help in every possible way, without ever being asked and always with kind words and a smile; my sister Robin, whose friendship and faith in me has helped me endure and whose diagnostic expertise proved invaluable from beginning to end; my sister Kelley, whose friendship and love is tireless and sustaining—she always listens and keeps me sane; my big brother Joe, who has inspired me since we were kids and shared our special language—he is the best person I know, and he still draws the most beautiful pictures I've ever seen; and my brother-in-law, John, who gives such great advice, both now and through the years, and who keeps me on track—I'm so happy to have another big brother in my life.

A very special thank you to Evan Kuhlman for his thoughtful criticism and lasting friendship. He read this book from beginning to end more times than I can count and always with good cheer. I don't know what I'd do without him.

Judi Kolenda graciously read more than once, and is a supportive and encouraging friend and writer in my life. Her passion for storytelling always inspires me, and I would be truly lost without her. Kirsten Bischoff is a fearless friend and reader—I'm so grateful for her honesty, comments, and kicking me in the butt when I needed it.

Many, many thanks to my friends in the creative writing department at the University of North Carolina Wilmington, especially Philip Gerard, Rebecca Lee, Karen Bender, and Robert Siegel. A very warm thank you goes to Clyde Edgerton for his patient counsel and continuing guidance; I am so lucky to have such a kind mentor and friend.

Geoff Kantoris shared his legal expertise and then proofread the final copy. Jeanne Mullins, MA, CCC-SLP, provided detailed information about speech pathology and working with a challenged population. Dave Monahan from the film studies department at the University of North Carolina Wilmington gave me great advice about filmmaking, past and present. Nina de Gramont read two drafts and was so generous with her time after the book was completed. Matthew Hall and Jonathan Smiley read closely and helped with the finishing touches. My warmest thanks to all of them.

It's nearly impossible to put into words how grateful I am to Christopher Gould from the University of North Carolina Wilmington, who had faith in me and gave me the opportunity to do what I love. Special thanks also go to Jane Bullock, Donna Carlton, and Emily Matzke for all their support over the years. And to my students who made teaching such a fulfilling experience: I've learned so much from all of you.

I want to thank my first readers and friends, Shana Deets, Renee Dixon, Terri Meadowcroft, Rebecca Petruck, Andrea Quarracino, Lorrie Smith, Neil Smith, and Kate Tully for all their encouragement and invaluable criticism.

I'm also deeply appreciative of all my brother's friends at the Trudeau Center for letting me visit, for their enthusiasm and laughter, and for allowing me to tag along and help out once in a while at the Special Olympics.

And finally, above all, to my beautiful mother, G. Carol Boyajian, my greatest champion, for her true and unconditional love, her wisdom, her humor, and her unwavering belief in me in all things. She was the greatest and most inspirational woman in the world, and I miss her every day.